THE DAUGHTERS OF THE EARTH

Text Copyright © 2022, Brendan Noble
Eight-One-Five Publishing
Brendan@Brendan-Noble.com

Cover Illustration by Mariia Lytovchenko

Interior art by Mariia Lytovchenko

Cover design by Deranged Doctor Design
www.derangeddoctordesign.com

Books by Brendan Noble

The Frostmarked Chronicles:
A Dagger in the Winds
The Trials of Ascension
The Daughters of the Earth

Frostmarked Tales:
The Rider in the Night
The Lady of Rolika

The Prism Files:
The Fractured Prism
Crimson Reigns
Pridefall
White Crown

For Marichka and all the people of Ukraine.
Their folk heroes inspired these stories.
Their heroes today inspire all of us.
Slava Ukraini.

One-third of all author royalties for this book will be donated to humanitarian
and defense efforts in Ukraine.

Author Note: Trigger Warning

Until this book, I haven't provided trigger warnings due to the series rarely going further than typical fantasy violence and death. However, *The Daughters of the Earth* contains elements that may be triggers or traumatic to some readers, so please proceed with caution if any of the below are so for you. I have done my best to treat these serious topics carefully and with respect. None feature heavily in the book, but they do appear.

- Mental illness
- Self-harm
- Child loss
- Suicide

Godly and Demonic Marks

Marzanna - Frostmark
Winter, Disease, and Death

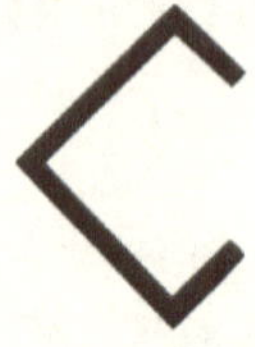

Dziewanna - Bowmark
Wilds, Hunt, and Spring

Jaryło - Springmark
Spring, Agriculture, and War

Mokosz - Mothermark
Women, Divination, and Earth

Perun - Thundermark
Thunder, Justice, and War

Weles - Serpentmark
Underworld and Lowlands

Swaróg - Forgemark
Celestial Fire and Smithing

Dadźbóg - Sunmark
The Sun

Czarnobóg - Darkmark
Death, Darkness, and Corruption

Wacław - Eclipsemark
Storm Demon (Płanetnik)

Pronunciation Guide

Characters

Wacław Lubiewicz: Vahtswahv Luubeeayvihch
    (Little Name) - Wašek: Vahshehk
Otylia Welesiakówna: Ohtihleeah Vehlehseeahkohvnah
    (Little Name) - Otylka: Ohtihlkah
Narcyz: Nahrsihz
Andrij: Ahndrey
Kiin: Keen

Gods

Marzanna: Mahrzahnah
Weles: Vehlehs
Dziewanna: Djehvahnah
Jaryło: Yahrihwoh
Mokosz: Mohkohsh
Perun: Pehruun
Dadźbóg: Dahdzbohg
Czarnobóg: Charhnohbohg

Other Terms

Žityje: Zhihtyeh
Krowik(ie): Krohvihk(ee)
Szeptucha: Shehptuuhah
Płanetnik: Pwahnehtnihk
Naw(ie): Nahv(ee)
Chała: Hahwah
Żmij: Zmee
Kwiecień: Kvihehchehn
Grudzień: Gruudjehn
Jawia: Yahveeah
Nawia: Nahveeah

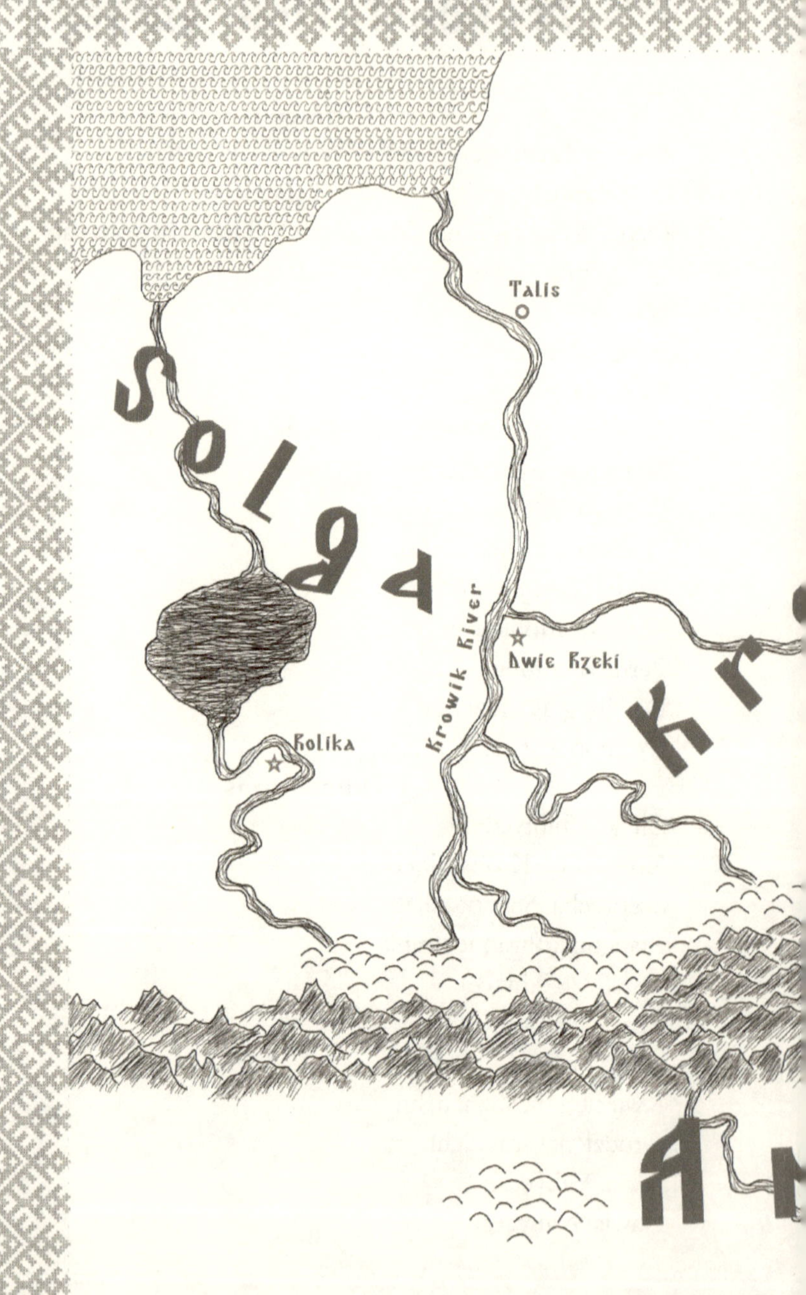

Solga
Talis
Krowik River
Dwie Rzeki
Kolika
Kr
A

WIK
Klist
Mangled Woods
Frostmarked Horde
Bustelintin
Narrow Pass
Wyzra River
Kynnytsia
Astiw
Małe Wzgòrze
Behmir River
Southern Hills
Vastroth
Huebla
Vora
Tior River
Sheresy
Télem

THE FROSTMARKED CHRONICLES 3

THE DAUGHTERS OF THE EARTH

BRENDAN NOBLE

Prologue

Otylia

Please, Dziewanna. You're all I have left.

THE COOL MORNING AIR STIRRED ME beneath the trees. Not that I'd been able to sleep. Today, I would begin the initiation rituals with the other twelve-year-olds seeking to become szeptuchy, to become worthy of channeling a deity. In truth, though, only one goddess mattered to me.

Dirt coated everything from my ashen dress to my face as I rose and stretched. The other initiates would laugh at me—and Father would likely scorn me—for spending the night in the woods, but I didn't care. The wilds were Dziewanna's home. If all went right during the rituals, they would soon be mine too.

Pulling a clay jar from my bag, I took a deep breath before downing the potion in one gulp. Horrid. But Mother had insisted it would give me energy whenever I didn't sleep well.

Tears stung my eyes at the memory of her.

No, I thought. *Today isn't for sadness. Dziewanna likes strong girls. That's what Mother always said.*

With a swift wipe of my sleeve across my face, the tears were gone, and I pretended my sorrow had left with them. I *would* be strong. I *would* pass the initiation. And I *would* prove myself to Dziewanna.

My hand gripped her bone Bowmark amulet hanging from my neck as I sprinted through the woods east of Dwie Rzeki. So many in our village avoided the lands beyond the wooden wall. Even those who ventured into the forests stuck to the few trails, never fully witnessing nature's true power. No, they feared what they couldn't control.

One day they'll fear me too.

"Wašek already does," I whispered to myself as I stopped at the tree line before the eastern gate.

Not long before Mother's death, Wacław had declared we shouldn't see each other anymore. Whether it was because of his father High Chief Jacek or something else, I didn't know. But I didn't care why. My best friend had abandoned me, and he hadn't come when Mother died either.

"Curse him, Great Mother," I spat, praying to Mokosz. Who better to call to than the goddess of women? "Make his skin rot and his eyes bleed like the cursed wizards of old. Trap him in the body of a hare and let a wolf tear him apart."

My voice cracked. When I looked down at my throbbing hand, blood trickled from my clenched fist. I'd gripped Dziewanna's Bowmark too hard… again.

Some part of me wanted to run to Wacław and ask him why he'd left me. To beg him to come back. But I would be a szeptucha soon. Once the initiation rituals were complete, no one but the deity who chose me would matter. Especially not a foolish boy and his thick-skulled father.

At least, that's what I told myself.

I threw my braided black hair over my shoulder and held my chin high as I stormed toward the eastern village gate. High Chief Jacek had just one of his warriors guarding it today. Huffing, he waved me by before leaning against the wooden wall again, boredom apparent on his face. *You wouldn't be so bored if you actually did something besides grip a spear all day and drink yourself stupid all night.*

Dwie Rzeki was bustling outside Father's cottage, just strides from the gate. Szeptucha initiations happened only once a year, and nobody wanted to miss the faces of the girls from across Krowikie lands who would face the rituals. Unlike boys, who completed their right-of-passage and first ceremonial haircut when they turned twelve, girls only faced such rituals if we'd trained to become channelers. We were different. Strange.

I hated their gazes, watching me as if I were some beast. Maybe they were right. Even Wacław had given me that look before turning away. If he couldn't understand the importance of szeptuchy, then why would the average villager?

"Ah, Otylia!" Father called from the head of the crowd. Crimson robes embroidered in white draped down his tall, thin form as he brushed his black hair from his face. "I was worried when you did not return last evening."

Without replying, I stopped by his side, digging my bare heel into the earth. It struck a stone, but my soles were calloused from years of running. Still, pain stabbed through my foot. I accepted it.

"Answer me, girl," Father muttered, quiet enough for the people not to hear. "Where were you?"

"With my goddess."

He shook his head. "You should know better than to take such risks. Wolves lurk beyond the wall, and for now, you are only a child."

I winced. It had been less than three moons since a pack of wolves had attacked Wacław and me on the eve of the spring equinox. A power had burst from me when they were seconds from killing Wacław. Sorcery. Somehow, I had channeled before being chosen by a god. What did that make me?

Arms crossed, I stared down at my dirty feet. "I'm fine, Father." My confidence waned every time I thought about Wacław. I'd secretly hoped he would be among those waiting for my arrival, but that had been a stupid dream.

Father crouched down to my level and laid a hand on my shoulder. Sorrow filled his eyes. "I miss her too, Otylia. Your mother's soul shone brighter than any other in the night sky, and I know she would be proud of you for continuing with the initiation."

"You never cared about her anyway."

His hand slid from my shoulder, and when he rose, he slouched, whispering to himself in the old tongue. Someday, I'd learn those words—the gods' words.

The crowd parted before us as two girls approached, holding each other's hands. Vida and Radojka were twins from Chief Mieczysław's territory around the northwestern village of Talis. Unlike Wacław's identical half-sisters, however, these girls looked nothing alike. Vida strode with confidence, her hair the brown of an oak's bark braided with flowers and her cheeks a bright pink. Radojka, instead, was a black-haired hunchback with a cleft lip nearly to her nose.

Laughter rang out at the sight of the one they'd labeled the Accursed Twin. Such a deformity could only be punishment from the gods, the simple-minded villagers claimed.

I knew better. Mother had treated deformities of every type as Dwie Rzeki's herbalist and healer. Curses weren't the most common cause of problems like Radojka's, but people preferred the easiest answer to the right one.

She and I exchanged nods as Vida joined us without recognizing my presence. In the few days since their arrival, I hadn't gotten to know either of them well, but I'd decided already that Vida would never be my friend. While I preferred the trees and animals to people, she was the type to cling to a chief for his power. I assumed that was why she had hopes of being chosen by Perun, god of thunder and war.

After announcing us to the crowd, Father waved away the observers. The gods' rituals were meant only for priests and szeptuchy. The priests had kept the szeptucha initiation ritual a secret for centuries, and Father would not be the first to ruin that.

A force tugged at my chest as the people returned to their work closer to the village center. Father had started toward the gate with the twins, but I stopped and looked to the nearby patch of trees within the walls. It was as if my soul was pulling me to it.

Ridiculous, I thought with a shake of my head. But then I saw him.

A stray streak of light struck Wacław's bright blond hair among the trees. Though he ducked away when he noticed my gaze, stealth wasn't one of his strengths. The sleeve of his brown tunic hung around the trunk of an maple. I rolled my eyes and smirked at his failure, but resentment quickly broke my amusement.

Why watch me from a distance if you never want to speak to me again?

"Otylia," Father called. "Come, the gods await."

"Yes, Father!"

Fists clenched, I ran after him without another glance in Wacław's direction. He'd made his choice. Now, we both had to live with it.

Father led us in silence down a trail north, toward the Wyzra River. Vida walked by Father's side as Radojka and I straggled behind. Radojka stared at my feet, her brow raised. "Don't they hurt after a while?" she asked.

I shrugged. My heel still throbbed from where the stone had ground into it, but the pain was a welcomed distraction from Wacław. "It makes me closer to Dziewanna. That's all that matters."

"What will you do if she doesn't pick you?"

"She will!" I snapped, wrinkling my nose before lowering my voice. "She has to…"

The ground grew softer as Father stopped. Before us, a stream drifted from the Wyzra to a clear pond. The birds were silent here, the air still. A shiver ran up my spine as Father's eyes fell upon me.

"Come, my daughter."

My breaths quickened as we approached the pond's edge. *What am I doing?* I'd prepared for this ritual for years, but now that I faced it, I had no idea what to expect. What lay ahead was beyond my control. How could I be fine with that?

Father held my arm the whole way, steadying me whenever my feet caught in the mud. The concern on his face didn't help calm my nerves, and when he pulled a putrid smelling potion, I trembled. "What is it?"

"The beginning of the first ritual," he said, cupping it in my hands. "Drink."

As he chanted in the old tongue, I took a sharp breath and drank the potion. Instantly, my throat burned. My foot's pain faded. All my worries about Wacław and Mother drifted away as I floated above my body. I saw Father catch me but couldn't feel his touch nor hear his words. The world had become a blur of color, deafening in the silence. And when Father carried me to the water and held me beneath the surface, I didn't fight. Why would I? This feeling was bliss...

Air!

Sensation rushed back to me. My lungs screamed as I flailed and fought, but Father pushed me down further. Water poured down my throat. I choked, staring up at the light streaking through the water. Death had become all too familiar to me in the last moon. It had stolen Mother from me, and as I drowned in that pond, I realized it would take me too. Only the gods were immortal. Only the gods could defy Nawia's eternal call.

And only the gods could bring a mortal back.

Air rushed into my lungs. Sputtering, I opened my eyes, gripping the mud at the bottom of the pond. *I can breathe?*

The water was dark now and far colder than before. How long had I been down there? Every muscle responded slowly to my commands, as if they were waking from a deep slumber. Soon, though, I found the strength to push myself up. The pond was barely higher than my head at this point, and I reached the surface with one swift stroke.

The night sky met me with a thousand glowing souls within it. My dress clung to my skin as I spat the strands of hair that had snuck into my mouth. Somehow, the entire day had passed, but it had felt like mere minutes.

Upon the shore, Father smiled as I trudged toward him, shivering. He held a fur-lined cloak, which he draped over my shoulders when I stumbled to my knees at his feet. "Father... What was that?"

He crouched and raised a hand to my cheek. His touch was more tender than I'd ever felt from him, and when he spoke, his voice was soft, "Otylia, my daughter, the gods have stolen you from Death's grip. One has chosen you to prove yourself to them."

"Who?" I asked, holding my breath.

"We shall not know until we begin the next ritual in the morning. For now, though, you must rest. Three days underwater is poor for your health."

I pulled away, scowling. "It's been three days?"

He nodded. "Radojka emerged in minutes and has been chosen by Weles. I feared for you, but the gods spoke to me, commanding me to await your return this eve. No szeptucha has ever been dead for more than half-a-day before returning. You, truly, are special."

Special… Why did that feel like a curse?

"What about Vida?" I asked.

"Not all survive the rituals," Father said, standing. "Those not chosen fall prey to either Death himself or become inhabited by other forces…"

"Other forces?" My hair rose at that.

His gaze was heavy as he held my arm and guided me away from the pond. "Otylia, there are far more frightening things in the Three Realms than Death."

Part 1
1 Land of Snow & Sand

1

Wacław

FOUR YEARS LATER

Frostmarked. All of them…

THE WINDS SCATTERED THE MOONLIT SNOW as Otylia and I stumbled past the sea of impaled heads. Marzanna's Frostmark scarred each of their dark brows. As if they weren't enough of a warning, the winter goddess's blood-drawn banner sprawled over the city's massive gates ahead like a spider lurking atop its web. Waiting.

I shivered with each breath, each step trudged through unnatural snow covering the desert sand. The most terrifying thing I could imagine was entering a city controlled by the Frostmarked, but exhausted and drained of the *żityje* that fueled our powers, we had no other options. Escaping Weles's realm of Nawia had taken everything. We'd surely die without water and rest.

So we approached the enemy's walls.

Instinctively, I reached for Otylia's hand. She pulled away, clutching her cloak tight in hopes Marzanna's guards wouldn't notice that her old szeptucha clothes were only an illusion crafted from the moon's light.

The goddess of endings. What does that mean?

I didn't know the details of her Ascension, and neither of us had energy to talk during our journey across the rolling desert. The Heart of Nawia had spit us out somewhere far from home. Of that, I was certain. Well, that and the fact she was hiding something from me.

Years together had taught me much about the green-eyed witch turned goddess I'd fallen in love with, and one of those things was that she was an awful liar. It made sense considering how blunt she liked to be. Knowing that didn't make it hurt any less when she refused to let me hold her after so long. The reason had something to do with her Ascension, but what was it?

The stinging of my Frostmark tore me from my thoughts. It flared up on my palm each time we passed another of the impaled heads. At least a hundred of them lined the path to the gate, and though I wanted to avert my gaze from them more than anything, I forced myself to look, to hate Marzanna for what she'd done. Men, women, and children alike—all slaughtered.

Why did I believe your lies?

The goddess of winter and death had offered everything I'd ever dreamed of. It felt like it had been years since that leszy had delivered the Thunderstone dagger to me. I still carried it at my hip, never forgetting Marzanna's whispers demanding that I give her my blood. I'd been too weak to resist then, but now the truth was all too apparent. She only cared about ruling Jawia. The rest of us were pawns.

"Keep Kwiecień sheathed unless they attack," Otylia said as we drew close enough to see two dark-skinned guards at the gate. She winced at the skulls even more than me. *Does she sense their endings?*

I touched the golden Moonblade's pommel at my back. Jaryło had dropped the sword of the fourth moon when I'd killed him in the Mangled Woods, and I'd somehow channeled Kwiecień's power to save Mom from Death's grip. It was a god's weapon. I was no god.

"If they attack, I'm not sure it'll matter," I replied. The Kwiecień moon had ended just hours before, and the blade's vast reserve of *żityje* wouldn't be accessible until next year. Now, it was just a fancy sword—one capable of killing a god nonetheless.

"I hate this."

"I know. I can feel your emotions, remember?" An unintended consequence of her *żityje* ritual on our first journey east. One of the many times she'd saved my life.

Otylia wrinkled her nose and glared at me, just as I'd hoped. Most people would be afraid of her sharp gaze, but I'd found the charm beneath her bite. Even in the face of the Frostmarked, that was enough to give me a moment of hope.

Shaking her head, she stomped ahead. Frustration surged through our connection, and that hope slipped away as quickly as it had come. What had Ascension done to her?

"Let me do the talking," she said once I caught up.

"Are you sure that's a good idea?" I held her arm to slow her down, but she yanked it away again. "Otylia, wait! The last thing we need to do is piss them off."

She rolled her eyes and groaned. "I'm not an idiot! But fine, what do *you* think we should do?"

Heat rushed through me. I knew it was the demon's influence, but it came too quick, and I snapped, "What did I do to make you so angry at me? I traveled all of Jawia to reach you, but ever since we've passed through the Heart, you've been distant."

"Not now, Wašek…" She held an arm across her body and turned away. "We can talk when we're not freezing to death in what's supposed to be a desert."

My heart sunk, but I just bit my cheek and raised my cloak's hood, hopefully disguising my blackened veins enough. "Then lead the way."

Pain struck my chest. This close, our bond was so strong it was hard to know whether it was hers or mine. It didn't matter in the end. Her pain *was* mine and mine hers. I didn't want to be angry with her, but after crossing both the realms of the living and dead to find her, I had hoped for a bit more than a cold shoulder.

The guards noticed our approach and tightened their grip on their weapons—spears with a curved blade at one end and a pointed tip at the other. Each wore a black breastplate made of something that resembled a tortoise shell. Beyond that, they were unprotected with only cloth trousers and shirts that left their arms exposed. Their Frostmarks glowed upon their biceps as they shouted at us in a tongue similar to that of the Simukie and Zurgowie clans. I sucked in a breath, but when Otylia responded with a carefully worded greeting, they lowered their spears.

"We haven't seen travelers from the east in a long time," the guard said, his accent making *eh* sounds come out as *uh*. "How did you cross the river?"

What river?

"The Lady Marzanna showed us," Otylia replied without hesitation. "She froze the river so we could pass. We've traveled for days and would've died if we didn't find the city."

The guards swapped glances, and the further one stepped back. "Lady Marzanna helped you cross the Behmir? You must be blessed… or lying."

"Yeah," the first guard said. "Why would she help you two across the river?"

"You *dare* question her?" Otylia spat, clenching her fists and stalking toward him. "What would she think of you defying her chosen?"

The guards swept their blades at her, eyes narrow. "You're not one of her szeptuchy," the first said.

Of course she pissed them off anyway… I sighed and stepped forward, holding out my Frostmarked hand and pulling down my hood with the other. "No, but she chose me."

"Wha—"

"Don't speak!" I advanced until I stood at Otylia's side. "Lady Marzanna has sent us on a crucial quest, and if you help us, surely you will be rewarded."

"What kinda reward?"

Otylia crossed her arms. "The kind that means not being torn apart by a demon."

They pulled back their weapons, and the second guard dropped to a knee. "I… I'm sorry. We haven't seen one of Lady Marzanna's Nawie in some time."

Nawie? I asked Otylia through our bond. *What is that?*

"I don't know. It sounds like a reference to Nawia and the dead."
Fitting.

"You must not tell anyone of our arrival," I said aloud. "Mar… Lady Marzanna has led us to your city to purge the dissidents. Tell me, what is its name?"

"You don't know?" the first asked.

I drew the Thunderstone dagger, my demonic soul urging me to plunge its black blade into his chest. "We have been doing the same among the Anshayman clans for weeks, and each time, she guides us to the next location with no name. Are you going to answer the question?"

"Of course!" he bowed his head. "Huebia! You're at the western gate of Huebia, city of sandstone and the capital of the Dominion of Vastroth."

A genuine smile crossed my face as I sheathed the dagger. Vastroth was a name I'd only heard a few times, but it was familiar enough. If we were in its capital, it meant we were southeast of the Perun's Crown mountain range and southwest of the Anshayman Steppe. With enough *żityje*, flying north over the mountains would be easy. That is, once we found Kuba and Otylia's friends who'd escaped with us through the Heart of Nawia.

"Good," I said. "Then open the gate and forget you saw us."

They did, and when Otylia looked at me, the right side of her mouth flicked up. Passing, but I took it. She'd been frightening enough as a szeptucha. Angering a goddess and the woman I loved seemed like quite the dangerous combination.

Dogoda's western breeze was warm on my back as we walked through the wooden gate. *How did they get so much wood with so few trees?* The walls themselves were made of a red-brown rock—which I assumed was the sandstone the guards had referred to—and so were the buildings. No larger than our own Krowikie homes, they were stacked alongside each other, sharing an interior wall. The roofs weren't slanted either, and despite it being deep into the night, people gathered around fires on top of them.

Behind the buildings, a massive tower stretched from the city's center to the sky above. Its stone glimmered in the moonlight, unlike the sandstone. There was beauty in it. Greater, though, was the ominous pull I felt in my soul as I wondered about the power at the tower's peak.

"We need a place to hide and make a plan," Otylia said, looking toward the narrow stone trails between the rows of buildings. Empty tables formed a semi-circle before them, where I assumed there would be a market during the day.

I raised my hood again as those on the roofs nearby cast us curious glances. "With all those people dead, there's bound to be abandoned houses somewhere."

The rhythmic sound of boots stomping against the dirt approached from our right, and Otylia pulled me down an alley. Though we were soon far from the market, she didn't stop until we were completely lost in the city's maze. Each trail zig-zagged at random. Some were wide enough for five people to walk abreast, but in most, it was difficult for us to even stand side-by-side as baskets, semi-circular water basins, and odd divots into the earth lined the walls.

Once we were both thoroughly out of breath, Otylia forced me into the shadows cast by the houses before lurking at the corner. "We need to be more careful. If word spreads of two pale travelers—one carrying a golden blade—then it won't be long before Marzanna finds us." She wrinkled her nose as she gripped the sandstone wall. "We should've never come here."

"You want to return to the desert?" I paced to the nearest water trough. A hole in its back looked like it was supposed to refill it, but nothing flowed into the basin now, leaving only a thin, brown layer for me to slurp greedily with my hands. It was frigid enough to make me wince before turning back to Otylia. "We'd die out there. Besides, why would we leave when this is the biggest landmark for miles? If Kuba and the others passed through the Heart anywhere near us, then they'll have headed here too."

"Fine," she muttered.

Which means it's not fine.

I stepped closer and laid a hand on her back. Apparently *that* was better than holding her hand, since she didn't pull away this time. "At least twenty of them made it through together, Otylka. They're probably safer than us, and we're no help to them without our *żityje*. Vastroth is just across the mountains from Astiw. I promise you that once we recover, we'll find our friends, fly home, and finally be able to search for Dziewanna."

She smirked. "Maybe we can kill that bastard King Boz on our way."

"Narcyz would be proud if he heard that. Now, where is the place most likely to be abandoned?"

"Endings…" A shiver ran through our connection as she raised her fingers, her gaze fixed on some invisible object. "This whole city is echoing with them, but they're loudest further ahead. Trust me?"

"I do."

Otylia led the way deeper into Huebia's depths, our breaths and footsteps shallow like the snow. Not even the flap of a bird's wing or buzzing of a mosquito pierced the air. It was unnerving to be in Frostmarked territory. Worse, though, was the eerie sensation that nature was dead here. Had that been Marzanna's doing? Even within Dwie Rzeki's walls, there were animals and trees everywhere. Here, there was nothing but stone and snow, and the few trees and shrubs were rotting, their leaves long gone. I'd never felt so confined.

There was something else too, a feeling I couldn't grasp. It prodded at my chest more and more the closer we got to the city's center, and my frustration grew with it.

"Do you feel that too?" I asked when we reached another wide trail.

"Death," she hissed.

Then her eyes rolled back.

"Otylia!" I caught her as her legs gave way. Our connection snapped, and I shuddered at the emptiness that replaced it, cold and suffocating.

Whispers in the old tongue drifted from her mouth. *Not again!* I took her chilled face in my hands, begging for her wake up, but no response came. The last time she'd collapsed like this, Marzanna's wiły demons had inflicted the deadly goddess's curse on her. I'd channeled Marzanna's power to save her once, but frostbite had taken my fingers. If I had to do it again with such little *żityje*…

My Frostmark burned as footsteps approached. Heavy, they came from further down the main trail. I couldn't see them yet in the moonlight, and I hoped the same hampered them as I lifted Otylia in my arms. *Żityje* or not, I would keep her alive. We hadn't escaped Nawia just for her to return mere hours later. But where could we hide?

Most of the buildings lining the street and nearby alleys were completely dark this late. I ran to each, huffing with each labored stride in a desperate search for *something* that could signal an abandoned house. None seemed any different than the others.

Then one caught my eye. Down an incredibly narrow trail, no fabric covered its doorway.

I ducked into the alley's shadows as eight guards stomped their way into the moonlight just strides away. They carried torches and wore similar garb to the ones at the gate, but two held leashes instead of spears. *Wolves.* The beasts growled as their bright blue eyes scanned the main path. They were headed right at me.

I held in a cry and scrambled toward the house. It would have to do. My arms ached after days of battle, but I ran with renewed fervor. I *would* save her.

The wolves howled at the alley's end when I neared the threshold. My heart raced. Sweat slipped from my brow despite the cold. Every inch of me demanded a rest, but I tapped into the winds for the final strides. Torchlight spewed into the alley and I cursed as a guard shouted.

Gods, my footprints!

The house was before me now, but they would just follow my prints in the snow. We had tricked the gate guards. My gut told me it wouldn't work again, especially with those Frostmarked wolves staring me down.

"Mokosz protect her," I prayed before sending Otylia through the opening and guiding her softly into the darkness with the last gust of wind I could muster. Then I drew Kwiecień.

Eight guards, two wolves, and ten hearts between them. Well, I asked for a source of żityje.

2

Otylia

I killed the boy I love.

DARKNESS SURROUNDED ME. Instead of the thick sea at Oblivion's edge, this place was empty. Even air fled as voices rushed past on streaks of colors, shrieking like mothers giving birth without herbs to dampen the pain.

They screamed my name.

"Why do you call me?" I asked, my words devoured by the void. My voice trembled. Visions flashed in my mind with each cry. Starvation. Torture. Illness. Death. They permeated everything.

"Save us!" Their words pierced my soul, chilled and broken.

"I'm barely a goddess! I can't help you… I don't know how!"

They circled me again, and faces manifested among them. Wispy and shadowed, like smoke drifting from a smoldering file. "It was the moon that tainted us. It was Death who seized us. It was Marzanna who enslaved us. And it is you who must save us."

"How?" I stammered, reaching for them. But they drifted away as a chill trickled down my spine. Shivering, I turned and screamed at the horror before me.

No!

I jolted awake with a frigid breeze stinging my skin. Snow blew through an open doorway before me and into the dark room as I dug my fingers into the thin layer of dust coating the stone floor. *Where am I?*

The voices had deafened me when we'd reached the main trail. I'd thought one could guide us to a home where someone had died, but instead, they'd taken me when I'd reached for them. Endings of all types. Rod, the eldest god, had claimed my power showed more than just the negative ends. Here, there was only them.

Those same voices drifted around me now, dispersed and quiet, their wisps keeping their distance as if they were afraid. Of me? I shook my head. No, they had to be frightened of that *thing* I'd seen.

I pushed away an image of the nightmare. *Never again.* That single second had been too much. I couldn't comprehend what that monster was, nor did I want to picture it.

Pain stung my arm. Not my own. "Wašek?" I asked, forcing myself to stand and study the room.

No response.

I tried again through our bond, but again, there was no reply. *Please, Wašek!*

From the view through the threshold, the house was in a narrow alley. The nearby buildings blocked out most of the moonlight, so there was nothing visible in the room as I shuffled back until my fingers met the cold sandstone wall. Everything in Huebia seemed to be crafted from it. There were few trees in the desert, so it made sense, but I'd seen no stone like this anywhere during our journey to the city. Where had it come from?

But there were more important questions. From what I could tell from a quick examination, the room was empty. Wacław must've moved me there from the street, but I had no memory of how he did so or where he went. Our tether felt odd after my visions too, and without *žityje*, I dared not search with my powers.

I shivered and clutched my cloak tight around me as the wind whistled through the doorway. Beneath my szeptucha illusion with the moon's power, I wore the sweeping white dress and autumn-leaf cloak from my Ascension. Such glamor was not typically my style, but with the chill, I was thankful for its length.

I reached the threshold and laid a hand on the doorframe. Endings lingered in the stone, threatening to draw away my consciousness once again. So many voices. Each carried another story, another tale that must come to its completion. How could I hear all of them? Was I even supposed to?

Rod, why didn't you tell me more?

A stray thought reminded me of my promise to Death during his Trial—one gift of his choosing in my immortal life. Had he claimed me with the force of endings? Or would his inevitable wrath strike me later? Both possibilities frightened me.

The snow crunched beneath my boot when I stepped into the alley. It couldn't have been long since our arrival in the city, as the moon still lingered above. Daylight would arrive soon as Dadźbóg passed through the morning gate, taking my moon powers.

With a sharp breath, I extended my arm and called my silver spear. The weapon already felt familiar as its cold metal met my fingers.

Just hours before, I had driven the spear into Jaryło's side and given us time to escape through the Heart of Nawia. Nothing was sweeter than hearing his scream. That fool had killed me in service of Weles, and if he dared come after me again, I wouldn't hesitate to return the favor slowly and painfully. *Bastard.* Weles believed he could force me to wed Jaryło. How wrong he'd been. Dziewanna—*Mother*—had fought against her father's shackles, and so would I.

I'll free you again, Matka. I promise.

Footsteps approached from closer to the main street. Stealth had been the priority before, but now I needed to find Wacław. Whoever was here could've taken him. And I had no plan of hiding if they had.

Light came with the figure, who approached at a run. *Just a few more steps.* I stepped into the shadows and readied my spear, mimicking the posture I'd seen warriors take during battle. The moonlight was dim here. I'd catch the person off guard and get some answers about this stupid city. The figure reached my nook, and I leaped, jabbing with my spear. A loud *clang* filled the air as sparks showered around us. My fingers throbbed from the impact, but I held on and readied another strike.

"What are you doing?" they exclaimed.

My heart stopped. *Our tether…* I caught my breath and stepped back, gritting my teeth as I realized why my chest had felt so tightly wound. Wacław stood before me. Kwiecień glowed in his grasp and cast a shadow over his weary face as blood dripped from the blade's end.

"Where were you?" I asked.

Lowering his sword, he presented a set of blankets in his other arm. "When you fainted, I brought you here, but guards followed us with wolves. I left you inside, and once I dealt with them, I figured you'd need something to help keep you warm."

I nodded toward the house. "Fine. Let's talk inside." Guilt gripped me for attacking him, but I was too annoyed at the entire situation to care. For the last moon, all that had mattered was escaping Nawia. I hadn't considered things would be *worse* in the land of the living.

Wacław sauntered into the room behind me. Through our bond, I sensed his typical sorrow at disappointing me, but there was a new anger—the demon's. His soul was no longer empty either. *Explains the blood.*

"How many hearts?" I asked as he draped a blanket over the doorway. Eating hearts for their *żityje*-infused blood was the fastest way for him to recover his strength, but it made me more uncomfortable than I'd admitted to him. Not that drinking sacrificial blood was a pleasant experience either.

"Should've figured you would notice." He examined Kwiecień, the golden light shining in his bright blue eyes. A shame the black veins were such a distraction. Without them, he had the jawline and smile any chief would be jealous of. "Ten. Eight guards and two wolves. Besides during my flight from Dwie Rzeki, this is the most *żityje* I've had."

"Do I want to know what you drained in our village to earn that?"

"Probably not."

I scoffed and crossed my arms, pacing across the dark space. Whether I liked it or not, Wacław becoming fully a demon was going to take time to get used to. What did it mean to be a Naw, as the guard had called him? "And where are the bodies now?" He didn't reply, and I groaned. "You left them in the street, didn't you?"

He shut his eyes as a surge of anger flooded through our connection. "I tried my best, okay? The guards made a lot of noise during the fight, and I couldn't just shut them up without *żityje* to wield the winds. By the time I finished, more were coming. It was either drain them or hide them, and I chose the one that gives us a chance of getting home." He snatched his płanetnik hat from his head and gripped its wide brim, his every muscle tense. "Scoff at me all you want, but until we figure out how to get your *żityje* back without bleeding me out, I'm the one with the powers."

Our gazes locked for a minute, dueling. Demonic or not, I liked that he was finally willing to fight for himself. I loved him. Gods, I loved that hesitant, thoughtful boy, but I needed him to be resilient if we were going to survive. "All right," I said.

"That's it?" he asked.

I nodded, but he probably couldn't see it since I stood behind the rim of Kwiecień's light. So, I approached and took a blanket from his grasp, purposely stepping close enough to startle him. "That's it," I whispered. "You have your winds back, and with them, we can find Sabina and the others. It shouldn't be hard with Kuba's inability to shut up."

His anger settled as I'd hoped. It had only been a hunch, but he seemed more *him* when I was near. With endings flashing in my mind each time I touched him, though, I stepped away when he reached out. "Once we get them back, we can figure out where Marzanna has trapped Dziewanna. I needed to Ascend to be strong enough to save her. If I master my power, maybe End can show me the way." Until then, I didn't know where to find the ring of ice I'd seen in the Trial of Death. Marzanna had conquered much if not nearly all of Jawia, and Mother could be anywhere within her frozen lands.

"End?" Wacław replied, his voice calmer.

"That's the name I've given my force. End is confusing and all over the place, but it shows me things. I just wish I could control *what.*" I sighed and ran my fingers through my tangled hair. "None of that matters until I find worshippers to grant me offerings of food or blood. I can't fight like this, and it won't be long before the Frost-marked find us. They'll learn two pale travelers appeared outside the gates not long before eight guards were killed."

"With my appearance, we were never going to be anonymous anyway."

I did this to you. That truth haunted me. Another ending…

"Let's just worry about finding our friends and getting out of here," I said. "I hate this city. It's suffocating." Both the lack of nature and the stream of wisps swirling around me were irritating on their own. Together, they gave me the sensation of drowning, and Wacław had no idea.

"It is." He pulled back the blanket over the doorway, checking outside as he nervously tapped his foot. His Frostmark pulsed. Yet another sensation joining the tide in my head. "Even the winds are trapped here, frustrated by the maze they can't escape."

I sat against the far wall, pulling my legs in. "It's like I never left Weles's palace. At least there I had allies, and even Weles didn't want me dead. If this is Vastroth, then what do further away tribes look like? Has Marzanna taken all of them?"

"I don't know, but Dziewanna saw this coming. Maybe Marzanna's plan has been in motion far longer than we thought."

I bit my cheek. "Mother knew and didn't tell me. Why? I'm her szeptucha! Her daughter!" Tears stung my eyes, but I forced them away. *Not now.* Feelings wouldn't save her. Only mastering my power could.

Wacław crouched before me, his stray hairs slipping over his eyes. He was a mess—we both were. Being back with him, though, gave me hope. Was it foolish? Maybe. But I needed it. "Dziewanna loves you, Otylia. She was probably doing everything she could to protect you until you were ready. I've only seen seeds of her plan, but she gave Andrij, the Astiwie messenger, a firebird feather to help his journey. Somehow, she knew his message would lead us to the Mangled Woods."

"That doesn't help!" I spat, turning my head away. It hurt too much to see the care in his eyes. My pain was my own. Wacław had enough of his own to deal with.

That was a lie. Mokosz had shown that our souls had been joined by the ritual I'd used to give him my *żityje* moons before. A piece of my immortal soul dwelt in him, and the last remnant of his mortal one dwelt in me. Maybe that was why he calmed near me. I held his last bit of mortality, and in return, he would endure my pain forever.

I waited for him to speak, to try to reason with or comfort me. He didn't. Instead, he rose and neared the door, not looking over his shoulder when he spoke. "Rest," he muttered as Kwiecień's tip dragged through the snow. "Neither of us will be of much use to our friends if we're exhausted."

That hurt. I hated how much it hurt, but I'd been the one who snapped that time. Why'd I push him away when I wanted to lie next to him for once and just feel safe? Touching him would mean seeing those terrible visions. Part of me didn't care.

Instead, I wrapped myself in the woolen blanket and lay along the wall, watching him. Bits of moonlight slipped through the curtain's edges and met Kwiecień's golden glow. Their combination made his skin seem a deep copper, stained in places as he bowed his head. Our bond was close, yet his emotions were muddled.

Why can't you be simple?

Nothing was simple anymore. Wacław had hardly ever been, but our complex souls and the impending invasion of Marzanna's Frostmark Horde had taken so much out of us. We'd jumped the fire and been declared adults two moons before. Little had we known we would never turn back. Forever, Destiny's plan would control us, but I promised myself I'd fight it for him. Whatever the ending. Whatever the suffering. I wouldn't let Wacław corrupt me like the final Sudiczka fate had claimed.

I was the goddess of endings, and I would choose my own.

3

Otylia

Will you haunt me forever?

THE VOICES INVADED MY DREAMS. No, they became them, warping them into nightmares of Frostmarked warriors slaughtering those who dared defy their conquest. I ran from each, but my power drowned me in its voices until my feet met solid ground.

I staggered into the doorway of a small house. A young, black-haired girl dressed in a tattered brown dress wept in the corner—Darixa, the voices called her. Light from a single torch lit the room as she stared in horror at the blood pooling around a man, his throat slit. A woman knelt over the body with crimson staining her hands. She screamed for help, but the only reply came from the warriors who'd slayed her husband.

"Shut up!" one ordered to no avail.

The other grabbed the woman's hair, dragging her away from the corpse. "Just kill her. Lady Minna said to only take the child alive."

In that moment, I could've sworn that Darixa looked at me. A wishful hope flashed across her face. *I have to stop this.*

My spear's cold silver stung my palm. I lunged with a shout, but when I reached the warriors, the spear passed through. They ignored me completely, and the first drove his blade through the mother's chest as the second stopped her from fleeing. A scream tore from her, echoing in the stone room.

Darixa whimpered as memories of my own mother's death met me. I'd cried for weeks, and knowing she was alive hadn't healed that wound. Darixa would never see hers again. Now, the warriors turned to take her too.

"Why are you showing me this?" I asked End. "I can't stop it, so why make me suffer?"

No reply came. Nor could I flee from the vision as the first warrior snatched Darixa's hair. But she screamed and kicked at his shins, breaking free and scrambling to her mother's body.

The warriors growled but stayed back for a moment as Darixa sniffled, wiping her wide nose with her arm—the people of Huebia didn't seem to wear long sleeves. Her dress slid through the pool of blood, but she gave no care as she reached for an earring on her mother's left ear. The copper shone orange, marred in places by streaks of blue-green rust cracking its surface.

Tears stung my eyes, remembering the black hellebore flower I'd found after Mother's death, as the girl clutched the earring. Ironically, I'd unknowingly channeled Mother's power to keep the flower alive, and it hadn't been her wandering soul who'd placed it. Wacław had. But that didn't make it mean any less to me. Watching that girl, I knew she'd never forget that earring either.

It didn't matter that I had no idea who Darixa was. Once, that had been me. My entire world shattered, as hers was now. This trauma would change her. From my own experience and the empty look in her eyes, I knew the feeling well. Paralyzed. Lost. She just stared at her dead parents as if they'd rise and hug her again. I'd done the same, kneeling beside Mother's bed and screaming for her to return. Death's grip was powerful, though, and tears only made him smile.

The first rays of sunlight slipped through the doorway as Darixa rose to face the guards, her tears drying and her numbness setting in. Instincts to keep us alive during stress. Yet that numbness could linger, masking the true pain.

This time, she didn't scream as the warriors grabbed hold of her. She just gripped that earring and hung her head, and my chest ached watching the Frostmarked drag her from her home. What use was my power when I couldn't stop this? What kind of goddess was I to watch my enemy kidnap a child and have no ability to stop it?

My legs failed. I dropped to my knees, trembling and broken as my power's wisps grew around me. Hundreds of them. They encircled me as the warriors' footsteps faded, and the last thing I heard was Darixa's sobs before the world went black.

I awoke back in our abandoned house with a shout, startling Wacław. He moved to join me, but I turned away, pulling my legs close. "Are you okay?" he asked.

"It's just dreams," I said between gritted teeth. The voices hadn't quieted, and a force tugged on my chest as the wisps swirled around me in a blinding array. *Go away! GO AWAY!*

"Oh…" He pulled back. "It's just… You were tossing and turning all night. I was worried."

"I can handle nightmares." I threw my cloak from around me and shot to my feet. The voices were leading me somewhere, and that *pull*… It was stronger than my tether to Wacław or any of my bindings to nature as a szeptucha, enough to drive me mad. Would following it stop these visions? It could hardly lead to anything worse than the torture strangling my head.

Wacław called after me as I tore across the room and pushed through the blanket covering the doorway, "Wait! Otylia, where are you going?"

I squinted into the early morning daylight filling the alley. Unlike the night before, the city's life bustled around us, with people carrying various goods down the main street at our alley's end and builders laying large blocks of stone onto a half-built wall. None saw us, yet.

"There's these voices from my power," I said to Wacław, my impatience growing each moment. "They're *screaming* at me to follow them, but I don't know why."

"Are you sure it's the force of endings?" he asked.

I nodded. "All I see in this stupid city is death. My power's invading my dreams, and its wisps are everywhere with visions of every terrible ending. These voices are different, leading me deeper into the city." I turned, brow furrowed up at him. "Use your winds to find us a path that's not covered in people while I follow it."

"Wait. Shouldn't we—"

I pushed him against the wall. Dark rings had formed under his eyes, joining the veins. Anger rose in him and flooded through our connection, but he didn't fight back this time. "Just do it, Wašek!"

Jaw clenched, he looked away. "Okay. I'll try, but you should rest more. Half a night of sleep—"

"Stop talking. Start with the alleys in that direction." I pointed to the southeast, away from where we'd entered Huebia.

He nodded and closed his eyes. I sensed the winds rise through him. Warm, inviting, they pushed back the frost as they swept through the narrow trails that ran like streams to a main river, channeling people instead of water toward the tower and busy city center. Even here I could hear the whispers. And I realized where the voices were leading me.

"This place is like a maze," he said, "but I've got a path."

"Then let's go," I said, pushing him ahead. My legs ached and my mind was groggy from sleep, but End's call pushed me on. Whatever it took to figure out this power and get rid of its suffocating voices.

More and more wisps spiraled around me as we followed my force's pull deep into the city. Their images threatened to drown me as they had the night before. I wouldn't let them. I couldn't let them.

Wacław grabbed my arm as I stumbled, but I forced myself free from his grasp. Fear rose within me from just a brush of skin, anticipating another vision of destruction. "How much farther?" he asked, stopping before the next intersection. "People are waking up. There's not many more open alleys."

A pink wisp drifted closer to me than the others. The voices grew with it, and when it darted in the direction of the pull, I chased after it, desperate for an answer. "A wisp is showing me the way!" I called back to Wacław. "C'mon."

He caught up quickly. Permanently in his soul-form now, he was faster than any mortal should've been. "There's more to your power than you've said."

It's better you don't know. Even I don't want to see all of it.

Thankfully, the wisp led us to an alley away from the bustle of the large streets. Wacław still alerted me to larger groups nearby, but I'd stopped caring for caution. My head was pounding, and I needed some answer from my power that wasn't another vision I couldn't change. A goddess couldn't just *see*. She had to *act*. The question was how.

The wisp led to me a house of mismatched stone bricks, as if the builder had given up halfway before another finished the job. A tattered cloth fluttered over the doorway. *I know this place…* Weeping hammered my ears as I stepped inside, the pink wisp hovering before me and carrying the cries until I gasped at the two bodies lying amid a pool of blood.

Wacław pushed through the doorway behind me, and Kwiecień's glow filled the space as he drew the blade. "What is this?"

"My dream… Darixa…" Could I save her?

The wisp shot out of the doorway. I followed without another word to Wacław. He may have called out to me, but the wisp's weeping was deafening now. Maybe I wasn't useless. Maybe my power could do *something*. I just wished I had some element of control as alley after alley blurred by, my heavy breaths and footsteps breaking the silence. Then I saw it.

Another body.

"What in Oblivion is going on?" Wacław growled, tugging on his hood as we stopped before one of the warriors I'd seen attacking Darixa. The sandstone path was disturbed around the corpse, with sections raised and depressed seemingly at random. "We can't just run through the city like this!"

"This Frostmarked attacked a girl in my dreams," I said, ignoring his burst of anger, "but there was another."

The clang of metal striking stone rang from around the next corner, followed by a series of shouts. Wacław and I exchanged glances, but before he could speak, I charged after the sound, calling my spear as he released a groan. *I'm coming, Darixa!*

But it wasn't the girl. Instead, as I skidded to a stop, the final warrior sparred with a staff-wielding man who wore a long brown coat without sleeves. A hood covered the man's head, and the coat's hem seemed to weave *into* the earth as he rolled to dodge the warrior's blade.

Žityje flowed from the man, manipulating the stone with subtle shifts until the warrior struck again. This time, the man didn't dodge. With the sword slicing towards his neck, he raised his free hand and whispered a single word in the old tongue, "*Orsti!*" Rise.

The ground cracked between the fighters and shot into the air. Both stone and sand spiraled together, catching the blade in midair. Wide-eyed, the warrior tried to yank his sword free, but the sandstone hardened. By the time he remembered his opponent, it was too late. The man swung his stone staff, and I winced at the *crack* of the warrior's skull before he dropped to the disturbed earth.

"Don't be alarmed," the man said, turning to us and regarding Wacław's golden Moonblade with casual interest. "Or is it I who should be afraid?"

"Where's the girl?" I snapped with a tight grip on my spear. The channeling this man had done was nothing like anything I'd seen, and no szeptuchy were men, so he had to be some kind of sorcerer. After the tricks the raven wizard, Tibês, had played on me in Nawia, I had no desire to speak to another. He stood between me and the way to Darixa, though, giving me little choice.

The man drew down his hood—*her* hood. Tall and broad-shouldered, her open-front coat revealed a loose shirt and trousers that had made her appear as a man at first, but now, her curled black hair and the Mothermark upon her neck proved otherwise. A szeptucha. And a Vastrothie one at that.

"How?" I spat. "How are you chosen by Mokosz?"

She clenched her jaw. A woman of at least thirty, her brows were fine but sharp, and their arc reminded me of the guards' curved blades at the gate. "What? You believe the gods favor only those of your tribe with light skin? I may call her a different name, but the Earth Mother remains the same."

"And what does she call you?"

The woman smirked. "You first. I sense your power, but I see no marks on your neck. Nor do I have a reason to believe you wish well for the girl. What are you? A witch? That would explain the demon boy." She nodded to Wacław. "Does he not speak?"

"I am Otylia Welesiakówna," I said firmly, stepping toward her. There was little sense hiding my identity with a szeptucha of Mokosz. My grandmother surely had informed her trusted servants of my existence. "And Wacław is an ally of my grandmother."

Wacław shuffled behind me at the mention of his name. I felt his irritation at my answering for him, but he stayed quiet. Tense, but quiet.

The woman dropped her staff, which dissolved into the stone, before dropping to a knee with her head bowed. "Forgive me, Lady of Endings, granddaughter of the Earth Mother. My name is Kiin. I had no reason to believe—"

"It's fine," I interrupted, uncomfortable with her kneeling. "Get up and show me to Darixa. People are going to find those dead warriors, and I don't want to be here when they come looking for us."

"Fine." Kiin rose with clenched fists and refused to meet my gaze. "I told the girl to hide in an abandoned house not far from here. The Frostmarked intended to take her to the Glasstone Tower. Luckily, I got to them first. They would've been too close to their allies by the time you showed up."

I ignored her jab and followed the pink wisp down the alley. A single set of small footprints broke the snow here, heading down the path's center before entering a house whose doorway was covered by some sort of carapace. Yellow and multi-layered, the shell was as tall as me. *Let's never figure out where that came from.*

Darixa's hurried breaths filled the space as I pushed aside the carapace. With little light making it through the doorway, it was hard to see into the deep corners of the abandoned house, but I didn't need sight. My force led me to her.

"You're safe now," I said, crouching before her along the back wall and offering her my hand. "My name is Otylia. The warriors are gone; I promise."

End's voices grew as she raised her hand to mine. "I—"

She screamed as Wacław entered the room behind me. I started, her fear rushing through End's power, before waving Wacław away. "Stay outside. She probably thinks you're another Frostmarked warrior."

His eyes drooped at that, but Kiin grabbed his arm. With a quick glance at Darixa, he shrugged off the szeptucha and stepped back into the alley. Kiin waited by the door as I approached the girl again. "It's okay. Wacław is my friend. He won't hurt you, but it's just you and me now. Well, and a chosen of Mokosz."

Darixa barely peeked up from the shelter of her legs, her thin brows making her deep brown eyes look massive. "Who… Who are you?"

A streak of light hit her forehead, and I gasped as, beneath a layer of dirt, Mokosz's Mothermark glowed upon it. When I looked to Kiin, though, she just tilted her head for me to keep talking to the girl. So, I sat cross-legged a stride away and offered Darixa a smile. It hurt to smile after all I'd seen, but she needed me to fake it. Maybe I did too.

"You can call me Otylia," I said. "I'm sorry about what happened to your family. I know what it's like to lose your mom."

I bit my cheek as she tucked her head in again. Children weren't my thing. They were unpredictable and often a bundle of complex emotions. It was hard enough to grapple with my own without untangling theirs, but my force had led me to Darixa for a reason.

"You feel like your world has ended," I continued. "There's nothing you can do about it, so you just sit and stare at nothing in hopes you'll wake up. Mother will be there, smiling that warm way only she can. You'll spend the day with her like you always have." Tears threatened my eyes again, but I denied them. Darixa needed to see me strong. "Time goes on, though, and you realize it's not a dream. So, instead of letting the pain take over, you push everything away. You cling to what you can control. It's barely living, but what you control can't hurt you. It's safe. Well, it *feels* safe, but being alone in this stupid world is more dangerous than pain or loss."

I reached a hand out to her again. "Darixa, you're not alone."

Slowly, she scooted forward until our knees touched. "Are you a princess?" she asked, eyes wide. "Because you look like a princess."

I let myself giggle at that, and she copied me. *Children always do.* When I looked down at myself, I realized why she'd believed me a princess. The moon's light had gone, and it had taken my illusion with it, leaving my elaborate Ascension gown exposed. Darixa took particular interest in my autumn-leaf cape.

"Why are they those colors, Princess Otylia?"

The leaves crinkled in my grasp as I pulled one from the cape and handed it to her. Another replaced it instantly. "They change from green in autumn, before winter." I didn't correct her calling me a princess. It was hard enough to accept what I'd become, let alone admitting it to everyone else.

I smiled as Darixa gawked at the deep orange leaf. Based on Vastrothie attire, I assumed it never got cold enough for autumn to force the trees to shed their leaves—not that there were many trees in Huebia's dense alleys anyway. *Life far from Dziewanna's wilds. Depressing.* Where did city dwellers escape to be free or enjoy the company of a forbidden lover? Not that I'd had any experience with the latter.

"You can have all the autumn leaves you want if you come with me," I said, extending my hand toward her.

She nodded quickly and leapt to her feet to grip my hand. At the touch, I shuddered as a vision flashed through my mind.

Darixa, her eyes lost and her brow wrinkled, sat on a rug before a girl no younger than she was now. The girl giggled, dancing around her, singing and calling her "grandmother." Darixa lacked the strength to even speak, but satisfaction filled her soul—joy. Seven more children rushed into the dim, decorated room and hugged her too. Each had her black, wavy locks and wide nose. They were all she cared about in Jawia, and she knew that soon, they would carry her blood as she left the realm of the living.

"Princess Otylia?" Darixa's squeaky voice asked, pulling me from the vision. "What were those words you were saying?"

Words? I shook my head. Of course, this force required some type of channeling, but I didn't sense it using more than a tiny part of my remaining *žityje*. It was as if the visions *wanted* me to see them, and my whispers simply welcomed them, even if I hadn't knowingly spoken. "I saw the future," I answered honestly. "Today will hurt for a long time, but you'll be happy. I promise."

Her only response was a tighter squeeze. I braced for another vision, but when none came, I took a sharp breath and let myself accept that something good had come from my power. Not every end was pain.

Kiin nodded toward the door. Darixa needed more time, but more guards would come soon. I ran my fingers through her hair before reluctantly leading her back into the alley. Snow whipped through the air as people lined the walls, robed in tan with their arms uncovered and their brown eyes watching Wacław. Then they turned to us.

"This is bad…" I said to Wacław. Word would spread of the girl in the colored cloak and the boy with black veins. Though I was a goddess now, I still didn't like being so *exposed*. We couldn't stay long.

"Follow me quickly," Kiin hissed in my ear. "There is much you don't know about our people, and if they realize Darixa's one of the—"

"Traitor!" someone called out, echoed by another. They were all pointing at Darixa.

What have I gotten myself into?

The crowd's clamoring escalated as Kiin led us down the alley. I tried to ignore them, but my heart raced, fearing an ambush at any moment. It took all I had to stare straight ahead until someone grabbed my arm.

Heat rushed through me. I spun and instinctively flared what remained of my power. It burst from my chest as the man yelled and staggered back, the blast tearing away his words before launching him down the street. His neck snapped when he struck the ground.

Send me to Weles. Why today?

A hundred eyes stared back at me, a mix of fury and terror. "Demon!" one spat, spurring echoes from the others. "She's protecting the scion!"

"Run!" Kiin shouted as her stone staff rose from the earth and into her hand.

We tore down the next alley, pulling Darixa with the chill stinging my face. The little girl yelped, but I didn't bother to answer her rambled questions. That mob would be upon us soon, and the Frostmarked would follow. Without *żityje*, I would be useless against them, and I'd used my last of it in that stupid outburst. *Narcyz would be proud.*

Wacław had been right—half a night of sleep wasn't enough. I realized that as my tired legs struggled with each stride. Ice layered much of the stone ground, and I hadn't the strength to sprint, drag along Darixa, and keep my balance at the same time. I fell, releasing her to catch myself at the last moment. Once I rose, the mob was already upon us.

I called my spear. It didn't answer with my *żityje* drained and my mind panicked.

A dozen hands closed around Darixa's arms. She called after me, but the crowd rushed me too, twenty of them, warriors and civilians alike. I cursed and muttered in the old tongue, but no power answered. Kiin was caught on the opposite end of the alley, and I couldn't find Wacław in the chaos. I was alone.

But when they grabbed hold of me, a golden blade cut through the falling snow, slicing off their hands and spurring shrieks from the crowd. I grinned. Blood covered me, but I sensed their terror as my tether tightened with Wacław.

Now you'll see a real demon.

4

Wacław

Get away from her!

RAGE. It consumed all else, slicing Kwiecień through the flesh of the advancing crowd and Frostmarked warriors caught within. I didn't know why civilians were chasing Otylia and the child. In truth, I didn't care. They threatened her, and they would die for it.

I stood amid a growing circle of corpses as a group of men dared to draw knives from their belts. They formed ranks, using the alley's narrow confines to trap me. Or so they thought.

Drawing on the winds, I pulled the Thunderstone dagger and spun with inhuman speed, sweeping my blades through the attackers. One's sword neared my back. Too slow. I plunged the dagger through his throat, hard enough for it to go straight through and impale him to the wall. Blood sprayed over me, but I gave it no heed. All I saw was red anyway.

The man's allies gasped as he choked on his own blood. They fled, and a thrill hummed within me watching them go. A chase would be fun. The demon in me craved it and the *żiłyje* their deaths would bring, yet a pang struck my chest as I looked back to the suffocating man, his suffering evident in his bulging eyes.

He thought us monsters, and I proved him right.

Black wisps drifted and twisted around me, dissolving into the air as I tore the dagger free with the winds. The man collapsed, but I caught him before he reached the ground. My throat tightened with guilt. Had there been another way?

"Go to Nawia's embrace," I said. "May it be kinder than Marzanna's."

I drove my dagger into his chest, and silence captured the alley as his torturous breaths ceased. My soul called for me to finish the cut and take his heart. I couldn't. Forcing myself to stand, I met the gaze of Otylia, her arms wrapped around Darixa as Kiin watched the crowd retreat.

"They almost took her," Otylia whispered. "But you killed them all…"

I dropped my head and examined the blood leading down the various forks in the trail. Its warmth slowly melted the snow, creating a red stream that flowed toward the city center. "They attacked you. I couldn't lose you, not again."

"Wašek." She stepped toward me, her voice pleading as Darixa clung to her skirt with wide eyes. "Wašek, not like this. It's not worth it if it means losing you to—"

"To what?" I growled. "To the beast inside me? The one that I had to unleash to save Mom and wield Kwiecień? Or the one who took the reins when you slayed my soul?"

Her gaze was piercing as she took a step back. "We don't have time to argue. The ones who lived will be back with more! Either control the demon and help me find a safe place for Darixa, or stay behind. I don't care."

"You don't have any *żityje*."

"I'll figure it out! I'm a goddess. There needs to be something I can do besides drinking your blood."

Bodies covered the ground around us, the *żityje* in their hearts pulsing in my mind, begging for me to take it. It was only a matter of time until guards came looking for us anyway. *We could just leave, I thought. Kuba's out there somewhere with the others. Why does this girl matter so much?*

"Let me drain them," I said, "and we can figure out your power later. They're dead whether I take their hearts or not."

A pain came with that admission, but it was dulled by the lingering thrill of battle and victory. I'd believed myself better than Bidaês, better than the demons that drained innocents to live. Once, I would've wept at what I'd done. Maybe I would again when the fate of the Krowikie didn't rest on my shoulders. These men had attacked Otylia, though, and hesitation was a luxury we no longer had. If I had to feed the darkness within me to protect her, then so be it.

Otylia shook her head and looked toward massive tower. "I don't care. Just control yourself and *help me*."

"What is it about this girl?" I asked, throwing my arm in Darixa's direction. "Is it the force of endings? What makes her more important than our friends? Than Dziewanna?"

Brow furrowed, she approached until her nose hovered inches from mine. Her desperation washed through our connection, beating back my anger. "*Trust* me, Wašek. I'll explain everything, all of it, but right now, I don't need your blood or your demonic fury. I need the boy I fell for. The one who would drop anything to protect me or anyone who couldn't defend themselves."

I averted my gaze, but she grabbed my tunic at the chest, forcing me to meet her narrowed eyes. "Darixa needs us. My power showed me the ending she's destined for. I can't explain it, but I know she won't find it if I don't help her." She sighed. "The Frostmarked killed her parents, and I can't stop seeing Mother's death when I look at her."

All I could offer was a nod, fighting the resentment in me. It had flooded out so quickly, thoughts I hadn't even known were mine. Did I actually hate her for taking my soul? I didn't believe so, but the anger felt right in my veins.

With our argument over, Kiin stepped closer and whispered intensely with Otylia. They obviously had no intention of including me, so I began draining the dead of their *žityje* until Otylia told me what was happening. The power in my soul swelled with the blood from each heart I devoured. I tried not to think about these people's lives.

They'd attacked us, and nothing else mattered, right? What other choice had we had except to fight?

The demon answered for me. We'd done what was right by slaying those who'd threatened Otylia, threatened me. Jaryło had taken Otylia from us once, and no one would do so again.

I paused at that thought, a half-consumed heart in my grasp. *We.* Since when had I started referring to my demonic soul and me as a collective? Was this darkness simply my own soul or a separate being within me? Was I responsible for these urges, or were they beyond my control?

"Wašek," Otylia said, pulling me from my thoughts. "Let's go. Kiin wants to tell us about how Marzanna's controlling the city."

"And the girl?" I asked.

"Darixa is part of it, apparently. C'mon, we'll talk more when we're out of the street."

"The scions have ruled Huebia for centuries," Kiin said in her rough voice, crouching before a small fire in what had once been an indoor gathering place of some sort. All that remained of its former state were tattered rugs, brightly woven tapestries across the walls, and a raised stone stage against the far wall. Unlike our abandoned house, the building had three floors with five rooms spread across them. This room was the deepest and the only one on the floor.

Sparks and smoke filled the air between Otylia, Darixa, Kiin, and me as the szeptucha stared into the flames. For a follower of Mokosz, she was odd. Mokosz's Krowikie followers were primarily diviners, but Kiin had commanded the earth to *move*.

Perhaps her channeling wasn't all that different from commanding the winds. Watching her work, however, had left me stunned as she'd fought the Frostmarked warrior. When I flew on the winds, it often felt like a dance, the air itself as my partner and the entire sky my hall. Kiin's magic was more like the work of a potter, molding the stone and sand with her words in the old tongue. She'd used it for battle against the warrior, but there was beauty in such a power. Craftsmen in Dwie Rzeki often spoke about the pride they took in their work, not just for function but also for artistic purposes. The spiral of stone she'd created to stop the sword had been just that, a combination of both.

"So," I said, glancing at Darixa alongside Otylia. "How are the scions chosen? And why a child?"

Kiin eyed me distrustfully. "Seven scions rule our people from the Glasstone Tower in Huebia's center, acting on behalf of the Earth Mother and speaking for the seven cities in Vastroth. Mortals have no say in their selection. When a scion dies, the Earth Mother chooses another from that city by marking her brow."

Otylia grinned. "They're always women?"

"Yes. As all szeptuchy are women, and so are the Earth Mother's scions. No szeptucha has ever been chosen to lead, though."

"Weles said there were once male channelers—szeptuny," Otylia said, "but that the wars between the gods were too destructive because of them. Your people were smart to trust Mokosz and women instead of war-hungry chiefs."

I shrugged and met her gaze. "Not all chiefs are like Mieczysław or my father, but you might have a point. Unfortunately, it's Marzanna who threatens to conquer Jawia, not a male god."

"There's no need to conquer today when you did so centuries ago," she quipped, the fire reflected in her eyes, daring me to challenge her.

Kiin whispered something quickly to the others, and all three of the girls snickered. Though I looked to Otylia, she offered no answers as Kiin continued, "The scions had been successful until seven years ago, keeping us at peace. With the Earth Mother's blessing, the earth could become arable and feed our people. The Anvoranie to our west supplied food in the past, but since their empire collapsed, their constant squabbles have made us reliant on our own supplies. We would have starved without the scions appealing to our goddess."

"What changed?" Otylia asked.

Kiin looked away, her lips pursed as she shook her head. "Refugees from the clans' wars on the steppe and the Anvoranie civil war flocked to our walls, hoping to find safety. We invited them in, but some among our people hated them. There were constant skirmishes in the street for moons."

"The Krowikie weren't much more inviting," I said. "Our village was far enough west to not have many refugees, but Father had chiefs often demanding he put patrols in the east to stop them."

"People are resistant to change, to differences," Kiin said. "I understand it, but those most enraged eventually decided to burn the buildings housing the refugees. In five of the cities, these fires spread quickly, and hundreds were burned alive. That was before the starvation."

Otylia leaned forward. "What did the scions do?"

"They called for peace, but what could they do when so many of their people wanted the refugees gone?" Fueled by nothing more than twigs, the fire dimmed as Kiin dropped her head. "It wasn't only the refugees and their food that burned. We lost so much… The Earth Mother gave us just enough in return for our sacrifices of crops and the occasional goat. After the fires, though, she demanded more."

Kiin stood, coughing on the smoke before examining one of the tapestries. The symbols upon it meant little to me, but she solemnly held a hand to it. Her fingers traced a small figure lying before a black semi-circle. "By rejecting her children, we'd rejected the Earth Mother's gifts. The Behmir River ran red for a time, ruining our crops of garlic, lettuce, and grain. We'd barely had enough food before, so this ruined us."

"That doesn't sound like Mokosz," Otylia said. "She's always been kind, especially compared to the other gods I've met."

"She's a mother. A mother always protects her children." Kiin rested her head against the tapestry and whispered something before turning back to us. "So, in return, she took our own—an infant for each refugee who'd burned or starved, sacrificed at her altar in a deep cavern." Her lip twitched as she summoned her staff from the dirt, leaning upon it for support. "The killings went on for moons, but they worked. The Earth Mother molded much of our lands into the most fertile plains we'd ever seen. Ore and gems appeared where we'd thought there were none. For many, it was the most wonderful thing they'd ever seen, but many more mourned the loss of hundreds of children. They despised the scions for their loyalty to the Earth Mother, blaming them for the tragedies that had befallen us.

"But it was our own fault. *We* burned the refugees. *We* slaughtered those who came to us for aid. Why should we expect any mercy from our goddess? The scions claimed the Earth Mother needed the sacrifices to have the strength to grant us the gifts she did, but they didn't listen. Then the Frostmarked came soon after…"

"Your people gave them control willingly, didn't they?" I asked, flexing my Frostmarked palm. "Marzanna, the winter goddess, offered them a place in her new world, and those who'd suffered took the chance."

"You bear her mark?" She sucked in a breath and shot a glare at Otylia, her voice raising to a shout as she pointed at me.

Otylia shot to her feet in my defense. The fire barely pushed back Marzanna's chill, but the room felt ablaze. Despite Otylia's claims, Kiin's anger was understandable. Marzanna had not only taken over Vastroth. She'd forced out Kiin's goddess. Despite my stomach churning at what the scions had done at Mokosz's request, surely Marzanna's slaughter was far worse.

Only Darixa's sobs brought calm between the goddess and szeptucha. The young girl clutched her legs, burying her face into them as she rocked back and forth. Slowly, I scooted to her side. Otylia and Kiin watched in silence as I pulled my Mothermark necklace over my head. There was nothing I could say that could fix Darixa's pain, but there was a symbol—her Earth Mother's.

"Take it," I said, holding out the amulet as Darixa peeked out from her legs. "My mother gave me this necklace when I left home for the first time. Each day since, it reminds of her love, that she's always with me. Maybe, it will help your mother feel close too."

Darixa's eyes tracked the amulet as it swung beneath my hand. She said nothing until Kiin nodded to her, causing the ends of her mouth to flick up. The girl cautiously grabbed the necklace, using only one hand. Her other was clenched tight. I couldn't see what she held in it, but it didn't matter. If I could calm her heart, at least I'd brought some light to Jawia that day.

"She's a scion, then?" I asked, raising my gaze to Kiin while Darixa examined the amulet. "That's why the Frostmarked are searching for her. Why the crowd hated her."

Otylia shook her head. "How could Mokosz choose a little girl to lead Vastroth? There has to be someone older who's capable of it."

"Why do you mistrust your grandmother?" Kiin asked, stopping daringly close to Otylia. With her superior height, her chin was at Otylia's nose, but Otylia stood firm.

"I don't."

"Yet you question her."

"And *you* think it was a good idea to sacrifice hundreds of children?" Otylia scoffed. "If becoming a goddess has taught me anything, it's that the gods are far from perfect. Even those with the best intentions."

Kiin spun away, hissing something in the old tongue and flicking out her wrist. Sand rose from a crack in the floor. Swirling through the air, it descended upon the fire's coals until all that remained was a thin trail of smoke drifting ever upward. "You have proven that fact yourself, Otylia. The pains of the past, however, are not what matters. The Winter Witch rules my people, and her frost will starve all but the most loyal if we don't exile her servants."

"How can we take on an army?" I asked. "They must have hundreds of warriors here, plus Marzanna's szeptuchy and demons."

Without a reply, Kiin headed up the stairs in the room's corner. Otylia groaned but followed, pulling Darixa along as I dragged my feet behind. *These people aren't mine.* My friends were working to protect the lands within the arc of Perun's Crown, and though it was tragic what had happened to the Vastrothie, uprooting the Frostmarked here wouldn't stop Koschei and the Horde. Would it?

Part of me hated that willingness to abandon Huebia—a last bit of humanity clinging on, despite only my demonic soul remaining. Weakness. Embracing the demon had ignited my power, allowing me to channel Kwiecień and save Mom. Without it, I'd been hesitant, useless. The chały had taken Eryk's daughter, Yeva, because I'd refused to accept the anger and resentment within me. Caring too much about Vastroth could distract us from what mattered: our friends and rescuing Dziewanna.

Sleeping mats filled the second floor of the hideout. At least seventy of them were cramped into the wide room, various forms of wool or cloth covering them, either folded or strewn about. Once the Frostmarked had arrived, the cold must've caught the Vastrothie by surprise. None of the thin blankets looked like this had been their intended use.

Like when Kiin had led us in, no one was here, and she offered no insight into who slept in the hideout. She pushed aside a cloth bearing Mokosz's Mothermark, leading us into a smaller room. My jaw dropped at what lay within.

Sandstone jutted from the ground throughout the space, forming Huebia's walls, buildings, and the massive tower at its center. A narrow, raised ledge ran around the room's walls, and Kiin walked across it to the other side. Her eyes studied the city the whole way. In them, the ferocity from before was gone, replaced with worry.

"As you can probably tell, this is a map of Huebia," she began, crouching on the far ledge with her stone staff held tight in her grasp and long coat draping over the city wall. "We use it to plan operations against the Frostmarked patrols and smuggle food to those who need it. It is a perfect representation of every building and alley, thanks to one of our members who has quite the good memory."

"We?" Otylia asked as she held back an eager Darixa from stepping into the city.

Kiin nodded. "I am not alone, as much as it often feels like I am. There are many in Vastroth loyal to the Earth Mother and scions. We call ourselves the Daughters of the Earth, and it is our duty to retrieve the scions, protecting them from the Frostmarked so that they may prepare to one day rule again."

She looked to Darixa with a smile. "You are chosen, little Darixa. Since the Winter Witch killed the last Council of Scions, you're the first we've found…"

The girl stopped pushing against Otylia, and awe filled her eyes as she met Kiin's gaze. "The Earth Mother chose me?"

"She has." Kiin thumbed her Mothermark before touching her forehead, where Darixa's own mark glowed. "We are both her servants: I her hands and you her voice."

"Can I ask her to bring Mother and Father back?" Darixa asked.

Kiin's head dropped. "No, little one. Once the Earth Mother accepts her children into her embrace, they cannot return. We may, however, bury a token as an offering to ensure their prosperity in the next world."

"Oh…"

Otylia knelt beside Darixa, wrapping her in her arms. Her sorrow rushed through our bond, but there was another emotion, stronger. Guilt. "I'm sorry. I should've been faster. If I'd understood my power…"

But Darixa only stared down at her open hand. A copper earring rested on it, and scratches covered her palm from clutching it so tightly.

When Otylia pulled back, Darixa huffed, shot me a glare, and yanked off the Mothermark necklace. "Then I don't *want* to serve her!" she shouted, her face bright red. "You said she'd stay with me, but she's gone, isn't she?"

"I…" I swallowed, a void opening in my chest. The demon closed it quickly, though, speaking for me. "She is, but it was Marzanna who took her. Not Mokosz. If you want to hate anyone for her death, hate the goddess of death herself."

Otylia wrinkled her nose at that but said nothing. At first, Darixa just stood with her fists clenched by her side, but when she looked at me again, a familiar fire filled her eyes. Vengeance. A need to fix what had been broken, or at the very least, bring justice to those who shattered it. The demon hummed in pleasure.

"Then we'll beat her!" she said, stamping her foot.

"We will," Otylia replied. "I promise."

I grabbed her arm, switching to the Krowikie tongue. "What about Kuba and Sabina? Are we really going to risk everyone we love to protect a tribe that isn't ours?"

"Since when are you willing to let people be slaughtered?"

"You know the answer to that." I released her, pacing to the city's wall and peering down at the buildings. "Father was willing to sacrifice warriors for the good of the tribe. Maybe, we have to let the Vastrothie go if we want to find Dziewanna and protect our friends, our families."

Otylia scoffed. "You act like the Krowikie didn't just exile you, that your father actually cared."

"And you act like nothing's changed in me!"

She stepped back, her fear rushing through our connection. In her gaze, though, I saw only spite. "Believe me, I can tell you've changed. Control the demon or leave, because I *will* protect Darixa, and once we're done here, we *will* find our friends. The Wacław I knew would never abandon people who needed him."

I snarled and reached for the winds as a black vapor streamed around me, but before I could do something I would regret, Kiin whispered in the old tongue. The ground shot up between us. The impact sent me stumbling into the wall, and I dropped, gripping my head and fighting the demon for control.

Why are you doing this?

Sweat clung to my skin, cold with Marzanna's winter permeating even the hideout's depths. Each breath was labored, every second agony. The war within me tore apart my heart. What did I want? My friends? Otylia? Power? Who should I protect when choosing thousands of innocents risked those I loved most? My tribe had rejected me, yes, but Mom was still in Dwie Rzeki. Ara, Narcyz, Andrij, and Zakir were in the Horde's path, along with all who'd survived the Battle of Kynnytsia. Could I risk losing them for a realm of strangers? For a girl chosen by Mokosz?

I had more questions than answers. As I looked up at Otylia, though, my heart gave me at least one. Protecting Darixa meant a lot to the woman I loved, and if she could find some understanding of the force of endings through this girl and the Vastrothie, then that was enough.

My demonic soul would destroy what remained of my human mind. I *would* lose control. In the end, it was inevitable, but Marzanna's victory was not.

Only Otylia could free Dziewanna. Only Otylia could protect those I loved. She was my hope, my reason to fight on, and I made a decision in that moment. No matter what, I would do what it took to protect her.

Even if I lost myself in the process.

5

Otylia

Vlatka will guide Sabina and the others. They'll find their way to Dwie Rzeki. But I need to know more about my power. Without a grasp on the force of endings, what use am I to Mother, to Jawia? None.

I HATED MYSELF.

I realized it as I stared down at Wacław, his muttering filling the room and resentment rushing through our bond. How could I be angry with him? I'd taken his mortal soul in return for Ascension. And now I blamed him for the consequences.

Great Mother, give me your wisdom.

No answer came to my silent prayer. If my grandmother heard me, apparently she had more important things to do, like forcing hundreds of people to slaughter their infants. The Vastrothie had no way to know that Mokosz would use the sacrifices' *žityje*. They had no reason to believe her decision was anything but vengeance. Knowing the truth, though, didn't stop the churning of my stomach.

I shouldn't have needed to pray. My Ascension should've prepared me to rescue Mother and help Wacław. It hadn't. Instead, I was more lost than ever. My power was next to useless without sacrifices to grant me *žityje*, and the boy I loved was falling apart because of me.

Wacław rose from the floor and regarded me, his mournful, human eyes returning.

Oh Wašek, could we have ever worked? I asked myself. *Or were our moments together mere convenience?*

I didn't know. My heart said I loved him, but my mind screamed for me to run. Not for my sake but his. All I'd done in my pursuit of Ascension was hurt him, and I endured all of that pain each moment we were together. Surely, he felt my guilt too. That cycle of emotions would tear us apart, so maybe it would be best to back away, to save what remained of Wacław from me.

A cough came from across the room. *Right, the map.*

"Darixa, it's time for you to rest," Kiin said, hanging like a spider on the far ledge. She had only two eyes, but beneath her glare, it felt as if a thousand watched me. "The other Daughters will make you comfortable while we finish here."

The young scion glanced up at me, as if waiting for permission to leave. I gave her a forced smile. "Go. We'll be there soon." Strategic discussions weren't the place for a child, scion or not.

She scampered out, and I felt Kiin's glare before I even returned my gaze to her. "Whatever is brewing between you two needs to settle," she said, her tone biting. "You can bring it to a boil later. To take the Glasstone Tower, we need to fight the Frostmarked, not each other."

I glanced at Wacław. His mood had cooled, but he offered only a nod in reply. Enough.

"Why attack the tower?" I asked. "Isn't that the most guarded part of the city?"

"Yes, and for good reason," Kiin replied. "The tower itself holds many prisoners to our cause. They alone are worth rescuing, but the true target rests upon the top." She whispered in the old tongue too quietly for me to hear. The tower model between us cracked, opening as a sleek black gem rose to its peak.

"A stone? What's so important about it?"

Wacław took a sharp breath, clenching his fists. "That explains it… It has to…"

Kiin gave a solemn nod. "This stone is simply a representation of the true artifact held at the tower's peak. The Frostmarked call it Grudzień. I am not surprised a demon like you has sensed its presence more directly."

"Grudzień…" I replied. "That's the Moonstone of the twelfth moon."

"Marzanna's using it to manipulate emotions, isn't she?" Wacław said as he approached the city's edge and examined the stone. The whites of his eyes were streaked with black and red. "My demonic soul is all I have now, but ever since we stepped foot in Huebia, there's been something else pushing on my anger, even beyond the demon's hunger."

"You're correct," Kiin said. "We believe servants of the Winter Witch brought Grudzień before the Frostmarked arrived. It flared the hatred of our people against the refugees, feeding upon their fear. From what we've seen, the impact on demons—of which there have been many due to the starvation—is more severe. It used to take them weeks or moons to lose their minds to the hunger, but now, it appears to take only days."

Is that why I'm afraid?

I stepped to Wacław's side, forcing myself to calm with little success. Even aware of the Moonstone's influence, I couldn't sense its presence. I badly needed *żityje* if I was ever going to learn how to use my new powers. I was blind without it.

"Why would Marzanna risk one of her five Moonstones here?" I asked. "And why is she able to use its power beyond its moon?"

"I do not know," Kiin replied before nodding to toward the doorway, where Darixa had left. "But saw the people chasing the scion child. Raving. It… It's affected all of us, but for those who held strong hatred or fear before, Grudzień pushed them over the edge. We've only been aware of its influence for three moons. With the szeptucha called Minna directing its power, the effects grow with each day. Rumor has it she's died twice but keeps coming back."

She rounded the ledge back toward us, her coat sweeping behind her. "As for the rest of the stone's abilities, you seem to know more than me. The Earth Mother has rarely spoken to us since the scions' deaths." She reached the edge and jumped to land right in front of me. Like the tower cast a long shadow over Huebia, Kiin's considerable height made me want to cower. I spun away, gritting my teeth.

"So we fly to the Glasstone Tower's peak, kill Minna *permanently* this time, and capture Grudzień. Wacław is a płanetnik and I've got the moon's power. It should be simple enough if we go at night. Plus, we already have Kwiecień, so we know we can hold the Moonstone and hopefully undo its influence."

"For you it may be simple, yes," Kiin said. "My channeling and that of the Earth Mother's remaining szeptuchy, however, are ineffective on the higher floors of the Glasstone Tower. There is little earth to move above the ground, and the tower's stone itself resists our commands."

"Ah," I shook my head. "You want us to do everything for you, then? Kill an undying channeler and give you your lands back?"

"We would do more if we could, but the best we are capable of for now is hit-and-run strikes in the city's outskirts."

"A potential distraction, leading to a greater revolt when Grudzień is destroyed," Wacław said. "If we're going to stay, then that sounds like as good a plan as any. Kiin, how many szeptuchy do you have? You could cause Marzanna a lot of problems, even before we take Grudzień."

"Eight in Huebia, including me," she replied, turning to the map. "We have more allies, though, who could help us set up defensive positions throughout the city. If we hold enough of them, then perhaps, yes, the people will join us once Grudzień is gone. We can sweep through the city and claim it for the Earth Mother and the scions. Huebia is by far Vastroth's largest city. The rest will follow its lead, but we would need time to prepare such a revolution."

I tapped my foot. Something about the plan had me irritated. Was it entering the Glasstone Tower with no reinforcements? Or was it that I'd be alone with Wacław again?

Wacław hadn't wanted to stay in the city before, but suddenly, he was all too willing to help. What had changed? And what would we do if Kiin was wrong? The people had resisted the refugees before Grudzień. They could just as easily reject the scions, overwhelming what few people the Daughters of the Earth seemed to have.

"There's a problem." I crossed my arms and looked away, unable to match Kiin's glare. "I don't have enough *żityje* to use my power, not without a sacrifice."

"How does a goddess find herself without life force?" Kiin asked.

I huffed. "It's a long story. Weles may be my father, but I wasn't in Nawia willingly. It took all I had to escape, even with Wacław's help."

She muttered to herself, pulling at a curled strand of her hair until it was straight. "A living demon in the afterlife… A corrupted Naw in the afterlife! This is bad."

"What convinced you of that? The snow in the desert, the goddess manipulating people's emotions, or the Frostmarked roaming the streets?"

Wacław stepped between us. "What's done is done. We'll deal with the ramifications of our actions in Nawia later, but Otylia's right. She needs offerings to recover her *żityje*. Though I can give her some of mine, I'm only a demon."

"Have we not sacrificed enough?" Kiin asked. "You are the Earth Mother's granddaughter, yes, but that does not mean you can demand sacrifices."

"I hate the idea of taking people's offerings," I said, my head still bowed, "but it's the only way. Offerings of any kind should work. According to Weles, though, blood's the strongest."

Kiin shuddered and walked to the doorway, pushing aside the curtain. "This… This explains much. I need time to think. Stay if you'd like to help us. Any bedroll without an inscription before it is unclaimed. If you aren't here when I return, then I'll assume you decided to go home." She sighed. "May the Earth Mother guide your steps."

A few people were in the main room when we emerged. They watched us with curiosity, holding Darixa close, but shied away when Kiin whispered to them. Then, the szeptucha climbed the stairs and disappeared.

What did she tell them? That we're selfish, asking for more sacrifices than they've already given? That I'm a goddess who stands by a Frostmarked demon?

Darixa noticed our arrival and rushed to me, clutching my cape of leaves in one hand and her mother's earring in the other. A scion. End had called me to her aid, and I wondered if she was the reason the Heart of Nawia had sent us here in the first place. It had been enough that Darixa needed me before. Now, though, her fate was intertwined with all of Vastroth's. Protecting her and capturing Grudzień meant freeing an entire people from Marzanna's wrath. Anything to weaken Marzanna would make defeating her easier… I hoped.

I wished that line of reasoning was my true reason for helping Vastroth. Yes, I cared for Darixa, seeing myself in her after I'd lost Mother, but my pursuit of understanding was not so benevolent. Darixa couldn't save her mother. If I learned to control my power, I could save mine. Ending Marzanna's wrath was just an extra benefit to having her back.

A short man with a chin-strap beard and receding hairline approached, bowing deep into his long sleeveless robes as we reached the room's center. "Great Lady of Endings, granddaughter of the Earth Mother, I am humbled to aid you. I am called Faarax, and I try to organize people within our home here. Kiin can only do so much."

Maybe she didn't insult me to them… Despite my mood, I forced myself to smile. "Thank you, Faarax. You don't need to bow to me."

"You are a goddess, yes?" he asked, his brow raised.

"Yes, but—"

"Then you deserve respect. Besides, you have come to our aid, so I come to yours!"

Wacław smirked, but I shot him a glare, stopping him before he could laugh. "Where are the other Daughters of the Earth?" I asked. "Obviously they're not all women, but there has to be more of you than this?"

He nodded eagerly. At least he wasn't annoyed by our presence, and I decided I liked him, even if he insisted on not meeting my gaze in his idea of reverence. "We have three other hidden homes like this one throughout the city, but Kiin won't share their locations with anyone, for good reason."

"Did someone expose you?" Wacław said.

Faarax intertwined his fingers before him, his thumbs rounding each other so rapidly it seemed they were racing. "In any group like ours, there were always bound to be those trying to infiltrate. Alas, one succeeded just a week ago. Forgive Kiin if she appears rash. We lost over fifty people in the resulting raid, and she blames herself."

There's more to her than I thought.

Wacław surveyed the space. He didn't say it aloud, but his lips moved ever so slightly as he counted the number of filled beds. "Why did you trust us so quickly, then?" he said once he finished. "You're risking another eighty lives by letting me stay here."

That gave the man pause. He squinted at Wacław, as if noticing the black veins for the first time. "Yes, you are quite tall. That could alienate some of our people."

"I…" Wacław cocked his head before gesturing to the blood on his tunic. "Do you not know I'm a demon? A płanetnik?"

"Why would I assume you to be a demon simply because your hair is the color of sand?" Without another breath, Faarax turned to me. "Lady of Endings, I wish we could provide better than a simple bedroll, but we all have to make sacrifices in time of war."

I bowed to him. "Believe me, a bedroll in the land of the living is luxury compared to a soft bed in that of the dead. Thank you."

He chuckled, blushing at my bow. "I am honored, truly. Now, if you will allow me, I shall take the young scion and return her soon with more… adequate… clothing. Perhaps the same for the long-legged boy, yes?"

Wacław just stood there, dumbstruck, so I rolled my eyes and nodded for him. "That'd be great, Faarax. But don't take Darixa's earring. It was her mother's."

"Of course."

Faarax held out his hand for Darixa, who looked at me for confirmation before snatching it eagerly. I let my smirk melt into a smile watching them go. *What an odd man.*

My joy faded when I realized the others who'd been in the room had left too. It was just Wacław and me. Alone. Nothing between us but a stride and a layer of tension so thick I couldn't have pierced it with my spear.

"Gods help me," I whispered to myself, turning away with one hand across my breast.

Time passed like a frozen river. Unable to see him, it was hard to grasp his thoughts, especially with our emotions joining. What fear was his? What guilt mine? And was that lingering anger from our argument or something else?

Mother had warned me about men. Unfortunately, the same couldn't be said about a demon with a fragile heart and a smile I missed almost as much as Mother herself.

I envied Kiin as I stared at the cracked sandstone beneath my boots. Her channeling allowed her to mold the most stubborn material into creations both strong and wonderful. I… I could see endings both good and ill, and honestly, I didn't even want to. Mother's influence over the wilds and Mokosz's flow of time had *made sense*. With their power, I'd felt nature's breath on my skin and its heart beating in my breast, and absent of it, Jawia—the land of life—felt dead. Cold. Still.

At night, the moon pulsed within me, but the day was empty. It reminded me of the time before I'd completed my initiation. When I'd dreamed of nothing but becoming a szeptucha and serving Dziewanna. Wacław and I would venture the wilds and face real demons together. Mother would smile at my return, and Father would be proud of me for finding my place in worship of the gods. We'd be happy. Together.

Stupid girl.

"I can't do this," my voice said. It sounded wrong, like my reflection in Weles's mirror. Somehow both me and not.

Wacław's footsteps approached. I winced as his hands found my waist, but to push him away, I would need to touch his skin. So I just stood there, unmoving, wishing I could be like the stone. A perfect image of what people imagined me to be, instead of the disappointment I was.

"I'm sorry," he breathed. And he was. Our bond said as much— the memory of his shouting stabbed at his chest. "You were right to make us stay, for Darixa, for the Vastrothie. They—"

"I can't!"

My elbows found his stomach. He wheezed, falling away as I spun, holding my arms across my chest like some futile shield against the pain and guilt. Wacław had loved me. I'd killed him. Ara had trusted me. I'd left her. Ivan had believed in me. I'd abandoned him. Sabina had followed me. I'd lost her. Mother needed me. But I couldn't save her.

I'd hurt everyone I loved. Father had always claimed I was like nightshade: stunning but deadly. Mother had scolded him each time he'd said it, but he'd been right. There was a reason I'd been alone for so long. Maybe it was better that way.

Wacław just looked at me with those stupidly blue eyes. Lost, desperate for an answer I couldn't give.

"We've changed," I mumbled, biting my cheek and unable to cry despite the sorrow choking me. "I don't know who I am anymore, and I can't hurt you again. I can't…"

Something broke in him. I saw it in his blackening eyes, felt it in his soul, and when he reached for the sword on his back, I could only stare in fear.

"I'm sorry," he said, cold, cutting. "I was never enough. I've never been enough."

Kwiecień's golden glow cast a shadow over his face as he pulled it from its sheathe. The Moonblade that had sent me to Nawia once. Now, it would do so again, only this time at the hand of the boy I loved.

But he didn't thrust the sword.

Wacław dropped to his knees, his head bowed and Kwiecień held out before him. Tears streamed down his cheeks. "The moon is yours, Otylia, so its blade should be too. Take it before the demon takes me."

"Wašek…"

"Take it!" His voice cracked, echoing throughout the room. "I'm not your Wašek anymore! Take Kwiecień and use it to save Dziewanna. I can't be trusted with that powerful a blade—I'm not worthy of it."

"No!"

A snarl escaped his throat. He rose, throwing the blade onto the ground, and my ears rang as Moonstone clamored against sandstone. He finally met my gaze with teeth bared, and I gasped in horror. Darkness consumed the whites of his eyes—only a light blue ring piercing a sea of black.

"Maybe we can't choose who we are," he said. "We're just the children of fate, and the Sudiczki hated us more than most."

Before I could reply, he threw down Kwiecień's sheath and sauntered to the last open bedroll. Blood stained his tunic, but he wrapped himself in his cloak anyway, facing the wall.

I reached for our connection in hopes of understanding his emotions. Instead, I found only a wasteland. A completion, severed. An ending that could've been. And in that moment, I wished for all the pain in the realms, as nothing could be worse than the emptiness dividing our souls.

6

Otylia

Was it worth it? Ascension? Immortality? Was it worth losing him, spending eternity alone?

THE SILENT CHILL OF THE HIDEOUT OFFERED NO COMFORT. I sat with my back to the wall, staring down at the symbols of the old tongue across Kwiecień's golden blade and questioning every word I'd said.

Had Grudzień manipulated my emotions, or was I truly so afraid, so guilt-ridden? I loved Wacław. Of that, I was certain. If only it were so simple, as if love could heal his demonic soul or mend the rift I'd created when I'd taken his mortality. It couldn't. Love was just a foolish temptation of the heart, destined for agony.

"I'm sorry, Mother," I whispered to Dziewanna's Bowmark amulet, clinging to it like I had as a child. "You were strong, but I'm not."

Footfalls echoed from above.

I shot to my feet, wiping the stray tears from beneath my eyes. Kiin had returned. After the spite she'd shown for me, I had to prove I could be the goddess she needed. That I could aid their fight again against Marzanna's Frostmarked. Until we were finished here, emotions had to wait, even if they threatened to choke me with each breath.

Strands of Kiin's long, curled hair peeked out from beneath her hood as she reached the base of the steps. Patches of darker fabric covered her coat as the snow melted upon it, but the cold didn't seem to bother her. Perhaps it was her heart of ice.

"Lady of Endings," she said, standing up straighter instead of bowing. "I see Faarax has taken the girl for a wash and much needed change of clothes." She paused, looking from my Moonblade to Wacław, cocooned in his cloak. "The demon is asleep?"

I nodded.

"Good. Follow me. There's something best not seen by corrupted eyes."

Once I'd sheathed Kwiecień at my back, we descended into the deepest room once again. The little warmth of the sleeping hall faded, and my breaths fogged the air by the time we reached the dead fire in the cellar's center. Only a pair of torches lit the space, casting a dull glow over Kiin's hooded face. I thought to ask where she was taking me, but based on her temper, patience seemed the better approach.

"What was this place before?" I asked instead.

She pulled one of the torches free. The flames flickered between us, giving her brown eyes a copper glow as she grinned. "A place of dance and joy. The scions would prepare feasts for the people when the Earth Mother was generous, and we found it best to celebrate in her land instead of above it. More buildings would be below ground if it wasn't for what I'm about to show you."

Placing a hand upon the far wall, she whispered in the old tongue, "*Dviži.*" Move.

The stone shifted like water, flowing into the wall until it formed a gap just wide enough to slip through. I peered over Kiin's shoulder into the darkness beyond. "Tunnels that only Mokosz's szeptuchy can access. I'm impressed."

"The Earth Mother foresaw times in which she would no longer rule Huebia, so yes, she created a way for only her servants to move beneath it. Come."

Smooth, crafted stone gave way to a narrow cavern of jagged rocks and tight turns. Kiin led me in silence. With only her torch for light, it felt as if the walls were closing around me when I wasn't looking. A massive amount of sand and stone were above us, and if I closed my eyes, I swore I could sense their weight pressing down upon the cavern's ceiling. Enough debris to crush us instantly. No one would ever find our bodies.

"I need to stop," I wheezed, leaning against the cold wall. My breaths came shallow and weak. Everywhere I looked, I saw the earth poised to devour me.

Kiin nodded in recognition. "The fear of tight spaces. I never expected a goddess to have it, but you'll find yourself among great company with it. After all these years, even I struggle at times." She grabbed my hand, squeezing it with a smile. "You will be fine."

No!

Wisps of color encircled me the moment we touched. I tried to pull away, but Kiin held firm. My *žityje* was drained, my power fleeting. It didn't matter. As she spoke again, her words were lost in the stream of whispers, visions flashing before me until I dropped into another world.

Dadźbóg's blazing sun met me as I fell to the sand. Deep and coarse, it prodded every mending wound on my body, like a thousand pins jabbing me at once. I cursed the force of endings.

"What are you showing me now?"

End gave no reply.

The images from Kiin had passed too quickly for me to comprehend. Whether from my lack of *žityje* or something else, I didn't know, but such visions had only been preludes to a deeper one before. This would likely be no different. But what did End want me to know?

I rose with a groan, protecting my face from the wind that whipped the sand for as far as I could see. I was atop a steep dune. Below, the Behmir River widened amid the valley formed by the dunes, a welcome sight in the dry desert. There was just one problem.

It flowed red.

The sacrifices… I spun, searching for the cave Kiin had mentioned in her story. The place where the scions had sacrificed the children.

A cloaked figure appeared ahead. Barely visible with the blowing sand, they walked down a nearby dune with a bundle in their arms. They stumbled every few strides but kept their gaze raised toward their destination at the dune's base. The cave.

I staggered after them, fighting the wind. It stung my skin and eyes and coated my throat, but still I pushed on. Each vision End had shown me brought me closer to grasping my power. I *needed* to understand, and if I learned more about Mokosz and the Vastrothie in the process, then so be it. This was the only way to save Mother. No stupid sand would stop me.

The winds died once I reached the bottom of my dune, allowing me to make quick progress toward the figure, who approached the stone cave with the bundle held out. Their hood fell when they did, and curled, black hair fell upon their shoulders—Kiin's shoulders. She whispered as she knelt. I was too far to hear, but power radiated around her, the old tongue's spells flowing from her lips. She stared into the cave, waiting, her mouth forming the same words over and over.

A second woman emerged from the cave as I stopped to catch my breath. Clothed in sleeveless robes of a deep violet that dragged behind her, she held out her arms to each side, echoing Kiin's chant with her own in the Vastrothie dialect.

More women followed until seven in all approached Kiin. Young and old both, the scions moved in harmony, their strides slow and deliberate in the sand and their Mothermarks glowing above their brows. Unlike Kiin, they did not struggle. Graceful and strong, they held their posture straight, yet their eyes remained cast to the ground. Only when they reached Kiin did they raise their gazes.

"Kiin, chosen of the Earth Mother and holy protector of the Hidden Waters," the first scion said. "You have come to finish our goddess's task—the final sacrifice. To us, the Earth Mother speaks, and from us, the Earth Mother must take if we are to mend our land."

Kiin bowed her head, but the scion rested her hand upon her cheek, raising her gaze to the seven. "You weep for your child. Why? Yesike is to enter the Earth Mother's embrace, to find peace while we toil among the living. Kiin, you may be his mother by blood, but in his soul, Yesike is bound to the Earth Mother. From her, all life comes, and to her, all life must return."

"Please," Kiin whispered. "Please, don't take him. I'll give myself to the Earth Mother for a thousand lifetimes. Just don't take him! He's all I have."

A son. Her son.

It stunned me to see the tall, powerful szeptucha begging to the scions. She'd been harsh, but it made sense now. Her hesitation at the tapestry. Her insistence that they'd sacrificed enough. Kiin had lost her son, and as I trembled watching her, I regretted my spite and judgement. To continue serving Mokosz after this…

"Great Mother, show your chosen servant your love," I said, reciting a prayer Arleta, our tribe's eldest Mothermarked diviner, had taught me. "Grant her your guidance in the darkness. Cast her future in the light, and mold her path to be light upon her feet."

Despite Kiin's pleading, the scions took the child. I ran to her, trying to pull Yesike back to his mother, but my hands passed through. This had already happened. There was nothing I could do to stop another death—one last sacrifice to tame Mokosz's temper. Yet again, I was useless in the face of horror, only able to kneel by Kiin's side as she cried into the brutal sand.

I'd been unable to touch her child, but now I placed my hand on Kiin's back, repeating my prayer for her. Maybe she would hear. Maybe not. But the dying man in End's first vision with Rod returned to me as I knelt there.

There'd been nothing I could do for that old man but ensure he died peacefully with someone by his side. Such a thing seemed so small compared to Kiin's pain, but it was all I had. So I stayed with her a long time, praying until my lips dried and Dadźbóg descended into Nawia. Her loss would never leave her. At least for those few hours, though, at least she wouldn't weep alone.

The world's frigid air struck as hard as the desert's heat. I gasped, staggering away from Kiin and collapsing against the tunnel wall again. The wisps dissolved around me in seconds, unable to feed on my absent *żityje*, but my ears still rang from the onslaught of voices.

Kiin stood over me, staring down at her hand. "What *was* that?"

"The force of endings." I pulled myself up the wall, thankful that at least my fear of the ceiling's collapse had faded. "I… I saw, Kiin. Your son."

Her lip curled. "You lie!"

"You chanted in the old tongue before they came. They said Yesike was the last child Mokosz would take, but you begged them to let him live." I stepped toward her. "They didn't, and you wept on the ground for a long time, unable to stand."

"You mock me."

"No," I insisted, trying to keep my voice calm. "I was there. I knelt beside you, praying that the Great Mother grant you peace. Kiin, you were never alone."

She scoffed and wiped her nose on her sleeve. Tears welled in her eyes, and her fingers twitched as she looked at me with disdain. "You act as if you could understand. *Nothing* is like losing your only child."

My shoulders sagged. How could I respond to that? Of course, she was right. Mother's death had traumatized me for years, but a parent was supposed to reach Nawia before their children. Whether because of Marzanna's Curse, starvation, or a thousand other ailments, many didn't.

"You're right," I said. "I've lost my mother. I've lost my best friend. I've even lost my own life. But I've never lost a child." *Gods know whether I even want one.* "You're wrong if you think I can't grasp the weight of that loss, though. I…" I stopped, the words too heavy to pass my lips.

She sighed. "Your mother, the one called Dziewanna, is dead?"

"Captured by Marzanna. Mother raised me as a mortal to protect me from Weles, but when he was close to discovering her, she died to return to him in Nawia—our word for the afterlife. I didn't know she was Dziewanna until a couple moons ago."

"I see. And the boy?" She cocked her head, studying my reaction. "Your lover, or no, something more tragic?"

I scowled and pushed past her. "I don't want to talk about it."

"Yet you pried into my own vulnerabilities," she said, following close enough for her torchlight to guide my steps. "It's just unusual for anyone to be fond of a Naw who is so lost, let alone you being a goddess. Once the Nawie inevitably succumb to their demonic second soul they are typically abandoned or killed."

"How'd you know I'm fond of him?"

Her laugh was short, but it echoed through the caverns. "Two kinds of people quarrel like you did: lovers so passionate they can't accept their feelings, and brutal enemies. Wacław needs you, especially considering how far the corruption has gone."

I dragged my feet, scattering pebbles through the ever-growing trickle of water heading deeper into the tunnel. Did he really need me? What good had I done him?

"I took his mortal soul just minutes after admitting I loved him," I said so quickly the words tumbled from my mouth.

"Oh," Kiin paused, and when I looked back at her, she gave a solemn nod. "Maybe there's three types of people that argue like that."

I huffed. "It doesn't matter anymore. I ended whatever we had."

"So that is why you were crying." She shook her head and stepped around me to lead the way once again. "Don't give me that look. You may be a goddess, but the Earth Mother has told me you're all but, what, sixteen? I was your age once, and I know what it looks like when one is trying to hide tears. The goddess knows how often I've tried."

"How did you keep going? After… After your son, how did you have the will to live?"

"I didn't."

"That's it?"

Kiin glanced back. "What? You wanted a long-winded speech about how I found my true purpose? No, I wake up every day with a voice in my head reminding me what I did. My husband did too, but unlike me, he eventually listened to the voice's insistence that he didn't deserve to live."

"I…"

She shook her head, pushing further into the tunnel. The water reached my ankles, but now definitely wasn't the time to ask about it. "Don't give me your pity or say you're sorry," she said. "You think you're alone now? Keep your distance from that boy and see how you feel after he kills himself, thinking it's for your sake."

The splashing of the water was my only company for a long while. It continued to rise, soaking my dress, but Kiin didn't slow. I thanked her for that. A steady walk would've given me the chance to ponder the truth of her statement—that I'd been wrong to push Wacław away. Instead, I trudged on with all the strength my tired body had left.

Just when I was ready to collapse, Kiin stopped and took a long breath. "We're here."

I opened my mouth to ask where 'here' was, but then I stepped at her side on the ledge. Not far below, a massive pool filled the cavern. Crystals glowed upon its rim, casting a violet glow over the water and an oddly clear pillar that rose to the ceiling above. Filled with blue, it almost seemed like the water was flowing *up* it, but that was impossible.

"The Hidden Waters," I said in awe.

"Another secret exposed by your vision," Kiin replied. "Yes, this is the Earth Mother's Hidden Waters. From it, the Glasstone Tower and wells throughout the city receive a constant supply of fresh water that is given to the people freely… *Was* given to the people freely. I wanted to show you how the Earth Mother sustains us, even now, when she is silent."

"How? I've never seen anything like this."

Kiin smiled and crouched, reaching down to touch the pool's surface. "It rarely rains, but when it does, water creeps through the cracks in the rock until reaching the six pathways. They all feed the pool, enough to supply the city, even when the river runs low."

I shook my head. "That can't be enough for all of *this!*"

"You know the Earth Mother as well as me. Does she not form your people's wetlands? Couldn't she do the same for this pool with only the smallest rainfall?"

"Why do you still trust her?" I sat upon the ledge, dipping my feet into the water. Here, it wasn't as cold as before, and the pool was refreshing after the long walk. "She took your son."

"She did." Kiin pursed her lips. "And I will never forget the scions sacrificing my child to the Earth Mother. It was the worst moment of my life until my husband passed. I lost my soul and my closest friend in such a short time…"

I cupped my hand in the water before letting it run through my open fingers. "I thought I'd lost everything, but you've proven how wrong I was. It can always get worse."

"Too often, it does."

"And you just wake up every day and decide to live, to serve? Nothing about Mokosz's love or revenge against Marzanna?"

She stood and stared over the pool. "When you hate yourself every morning, you have a choice: accept defeat or give everything to those you love. It doesn't matter if they care. It doesn't matter if they revere or despise you, because you've already marked yourself guilty. Either prove your innocence to yourself or serve the rest of your life trying to make right what you've done. I haven't finished. Until then, I'll keep going. For my son. For Yesike. Not for me, not for the Earth Mother, and not for my people."

Then she left, her torchlight fading until I was left in the darkness, gazing down at the violet pool and doubting my actions.

7

Wacław

I lost her again.

SLEEP OVERTOOK ME, despite my best efforts.

I hadn't slept since losing my mortal soul days ago, and I'd feared what would happen when I closed my eyes. My soul-form needed rest as my body once had. What did that mean? Would I dream or simply drift into nothingness until I woke? I'd never dreamed before…

Not knowing the answer felt better than facing the truth, but I'd never been so exhausted. Moons of travel, fighting, and emotional turmoil had my head spinning. All I'd wanted for the past moon was to see Otylia again. To hold her hand and sleep by her side, knowing that we'd be together no matter what in the Three Realms faced us.

That dream had shattered. Nightmares replaced it.

I fell through horror, grasping for the winds but finding nothing. Eight faces circled me as I plummeted toward the earth. They laughed and mocked me for the failure I was, and I believed them. Corrupted. Soulless. Unlovable.

Above, the sky filled with horrific pictures, too far for me to change. Yuliya's shard of ice piercing Kuba's chest. Jaryło slicing

Otylia's throat. Weles breaking her bones with his power. Mom's final cry when I thought her dead. The slaughter of the clans beneath the weight of Boz's ambush as smoke and ash smothered the earth. My last sight of Xobas before the Astiwie arrow pierced my ribs. And then Otylia's face, her rejection ripping apart my heart.

That last image repeated a thousand times. A stake driven through my chest over and over, the pain demanding I give in, that I allow myself to go numb again. I refused. Accepting my emotions, both positive and destructive, had given me the strength to save Mom. To endure. I could never go back to that void.

So I took the torture, letting myself come to terms with Otylia's admission. Maybe she still loved me, but she couldn't be with me. Was it truly because she didn't want to hurt me again? Or did she just wish to flee the monster I'd become?

In the end, it didn't matter. I was alone, trapped with the demon's hunger.

Opening the door to my emotions had only strengthened its will, and with my mortal soul gone, it needed to feed on a constant supply of *żityje*. Even after all I'd drained in the past day, I sensed the demon consuming it, bit-by-bit. I had more than ever now. Soon, though, I would have to hunt again. That should've scared me, but instead, a thrill rose within me at the thought of chasing my prey, my winds devouring their final breaths as fear filled their eyes. There was power in those moments. After a lifetime of being told I was nothing, I craved it.

You aren't my enemy, I said to the demon, finally understanding its desire. *You just want me to release my shackles and take what I deserve.*

Satisfaction, wordless but undeniable.

We can prove them wrong... Jacek, Otylia, Dariusz, Marzanna, Mieczysław... We can show them our power, we can rule the tribes, and we can save those we love. I just need to unleash you...

Freezing air shot into my lungs as I awoke with a gasp, shivering and coated with a cold sweat. My head weighed heavy with reality's dread. Even that was a relief from the nightmares' sharp jabs, and I let myself feel every ache before raising my gaze to the bearded figure above.

"Master Wacław," Faarax said from far too close to me. "Kiin requests your presence in the lower hall."

I mumbled incoherently before pushing myself into a seated position. The room was blurry, and I rubbed my eyes as images of the dream lingered. "How long was I asleep?"

He stood straight and tapped the side of his nose in thought. Even with his pristine posture, he was by far the shortest man I had ever met, and I found that amusing as he replied, "The sun is nearing the horizon, so most of the day. A demon like you enjoys the night awake, though, if I remember correctly. In that case, you are precisely on schedule to begin your day—I mean night—with supper."

My stomach growled at the mention of food. "All right, you've convinced me."

"Splendid! Do change your attire first, as I'm sure our fellow residents would not appreciate you wearing *that* to the meal. I have provided the few spares in our possession."

With that, Faarax nodded sharply and scurried down the stairs to join the others. It struck me watching him go that he surely understood what I was, yet he'd decided to treat me as the Krowikie would an honored warrior. What had I done to earn his respect? I'd lost control in the street protecting Otylia and took no pride in slaughtering people manipulated by Grudzień, even if the demon swelled at the memory.

Maybe Faarax is just kind, I considered. The man spoke like no one I had ever met before, so it may have been his responsibility to serve others at one time. War changed everything—it had certainly changed me—but how much of a person remained? Were there parts of us that stayed the same, no matter the circumstances around us?

My head was far too groggy for such thoughts, so I rose and examined the clothing options Faarax had laid out for me.

The first two sets consisted of a sleeveless shirt and trousers, one of tan and the other a deep gray. My cheeks burned just looking at the third option: a long robe with crisscrossing lines across its skirt. It had no trousers, unlike the robes some elderly men wore in our tribe. Did men actually wear these outside? Kuba would've jumped at the chance to wear something considered obscene among our people, but as I imagined him spinning in it to expose as much of his leg as possible, I could barely muster a grin. He'd returned to Jawia with Otylia's friends—wherever they were. I worried, though, whether he'd truly be the same.

Death had altered my mind. I had only survived my encounter with Oblivion's edge because of Otylia, and something told me she was hiding how she did so. Nawia was not the eternal end I faced as a demon, yes, but Kuba had dreamed of returning home to his love, Maja. Leaving her must have crushed him. Could he be with her now?

Another question for later, I decided. For now, I had to help the Daughters of the Earth free Vastroth.

The demon hummed in the back of my mind. Grudzień called us, amplifying my hunger for *žityje*. Capturing it for Otylia and the Daughters would free all of Vastroth from its pull, but that would waste its power. What was possible with a Moonstone unbound by its annual constraints?

"We need to take the Glasstone Tower either way," I told the demon as I chose the gray shirt and trousers in hopes of blending in better with the clouds. A chill ran up my arms, so I kept my cloak, wrapping it tightly around me as I stood. Tunics were far better for the cold, but the desert heat alone would kill a laborer here with the heavy material. There was something nice about having my arms free too. Unfortunately, that also exposed the gruesome scars and veins upon them.

No use hiding it anymore.

As I made my way toward the stairs, I remembered the pride I'd felt at my first battle scars. The zmora and utopiec had nearly killed me that night, but through those fights, I had wielded the winds for the first time. There had been such a thrill dancing on the line between life and death with such little understanding of what I faced. Terror and excitement joined. That night had reunited me with Otylia too. She'd saved my life, and I paused, remembering sitting alongside her beneath Dziewanna's Willow. For those few minutes, we'd been children again, facing the monsters of the woods. This time, though, they'd been real.

My sorrow choked me as I froze halfway down the steps. *Be strong,* I told myself. *You committed to helping her. Even if you can't be with her, your friends need you. Jawia needs you. Fight for them. Do what must be done, no matter what.*

I collected myself and continued on. Voices met me, and I stepped into the once dark basement, now vibrant and alive.

People gathered in clusters, sitting cross-legged on either cloth or the stone floor. They laughed and gestured wildly as they shared stories over their meals, eaten with their fingers from clay bowls. None glared at me as I entered. No mockery, jeers, or scowls, just the occasional nod of recognition. I didn't know how to feel about that.

Faarax and a pair of women distributed food from the raised platform at the room's end. The joy on their faces in spite of the Frost-marked occupation amazed me. Everyone here had likely suffered for moons—if not years—yet they found happiness in each other's company. That alone pushed away the frost.

"Master Wacław!" Faarax said far too loudly. "Come and take a bowl. We can only serve so much with the occupiers taking many of our supplies, but I promise, what we have will be unlike anything you have ever eaten."

I offered him a smile and my thanks, cupping the warm bowl in my hands before turning back to the crowd. So many faces I'd never seen before. What were their stories?

Before I could consider which group to join, Kiin called for me from the opposite corner, and my heart jumped at the sight of Otylia alongside her and Darixa. I'd missed them sitting across from the stairs. Now, I looked nowhere else, but my legs wouldn't move. What would I say? What could I say? Otylia had all but ended our relationship in one strike—brutally efficient like always from her—and I still hadn't fully processed what that meant.

Oh gods, she's looking at me now.

I sensed the demon's disappointment as I dropped my gaze and shuffled through the crowd, focusing on the next step. That was all that made sense: moving forward. Well, that and the food in my grasp. Faarax was right. It smelled delicious, especially after eating nothing but hearts for days.

"I'm glad you had the chance to rest," Kiin said, gesturing for me to sit. "The days ahead will not be easy."

I sat across from the women, trying not to stare at Otylia. My heart ached too much. "Thank you for giving us somewhere safe for now. The last few days have been some of the longest in my life, but I know we're not done yet."

"True. None of us are."

Darixa stared up at me with a fistful of food in her mouth. She chewed on one side and attempted something resembling speech with the other. Without a clue what she'd said, I raised my brow at Kiin.

"The young scion asks why your eyes are black now." She paused with a piece of bread in her fingers. As she pondered, she squeezed it so tightly it nearly flattened. "I wonder the same."

Black? I raised my fingers to my eyes, as if feeling them would somehow grant an answer. The truth was obvious, though. The demon had gained ground within me, and for the first time, I no longer wished to fight it. Its determination, its anger, made sense. Why had I hesitated for so long to take what I wanted? Why had I allowed my weakness to endanger those I loved? Whether it had been Father's fist or my foolish desire to please those who'd hated me, it didn't matter anymore. I wouldn't let that weakness consume me again.

"The demon," Otylia said when I didn't reply. Her voice was hushed as she ran a finger around the rim of her still full bowl. "It's taking over."

I glanced at her quickly. It felt like an eternity. "She's right."

Darixa gasped up at me but seemed transfixed than afraid. The shock lasted only a moment, though, before she returned to shoving food into her mouth like a squirrel.

"Do you know why the Winter Witch wishes to conquer our world?" Kiin asked once she was finished. "You bear her mark. Has she told you nothing?"

"Taking her Frostmark was a mistake, but yes, she told me her story." I looked down at my Frostmark scar. Its pulse never let me forget it completely, but Marzanna hadn't spoken through it in a long time. "She and Jaryło—our god of spring and agriculture—were once wed, but he bedded another. When she killed him in response, nature's unity was apparently split, giving him reign over the seven warm moons while Marzanna rules the five frozen ones. She wants revenge on Jaryło and his worshippers to unite the seasons under her control. There must be more, though, if she's attacking even those who follow Mokosz."

Kiin nodded. "That would make sense. I mentioned earlier a young chosen named Minna who leads the Frostmarked in the city. Are you familiar with her? No? It was worth asking as she bears your tribe's light skin, but there must be many under the Winter Witch's influence if she's taken all of the Anshayman Steppe and more. Demons with her mark are common, and if she's truly died twice, she may be a demon too. Nawie, those born with both a demonic and mortal soul like you, are far rarer."

"I've only met one," I said. "A wilkołak, a wolf-man, named Bidaês."

"What became of him?"

I sighed and stared down at my untouched food. "He's dead. Marzanna sent him to kill my mother because of my betrayal, but I made sure he couldn't finish the job."

"You can trust her," Otylia said, her voice enough to make me wince. I noticed, then, that she wore Kwiecień on her back, its hilt sticking out from her leaf cape as she wrapped an arm around Darixa. "Tell Kiin what happened."

My gaze lingered on her for too long. I longed to sit beside her, to enjoy each other's presence, but even our bond now felt severed, her emotions distant.

I was still staring, so, to give my thoughts time, I reached into my bowl and took out a piece of bread wrapped in lettuce. It smelled odd, but when I bit into it, an earthy, almost spicy taste met me— like a spring warmth compared to the blazing summer heat. The second bite followed quickly.

"Faarax was right," I said. "This is delicious."

Kiin smirked. "Garlic on bread is like water to the desert. It gives it life. Please, though, continue the story of the Naw."

"Yes, right." I took another deep breath and pictured our fight alongside the Wyzra River, the anger and sorrow I'd felt returning to me as I spoke. "Bidaês and I fought for what seemed like forever. He tried to convince me to join Marzanna again, but I knew her lies. I'd fallen for those temptations once. Never again. So, we fought again, and though Bidaês was powerful and quick, with the winds, I could outmaneuver him, tricking him to strike one direction while I went the other. He realized he had no chance."

"So he killed your mother while you focused on fighting him," Kiin finished.

"How…"

"Otylia gave me some of your story already."

I eyed Otylia before taking another piece of the garlic bread. That hadn't been hers to reveal. "Yes, he killed her, and in my rage, the demon took over. Bidaês fell quickly. Kwiecień, though, wasn't finished." My fingers drifted to where I'd once sheathed it. "Like the other Moonblades—made of Moonstone—Kwiecień can heal a god during its moon. Jaryło and Marzanna use this to control their seasons, and only gods are supposed to be able to wield Moonstone. But somehow, I did."

"You brought her back?" Kiin asked, her mouth gaped. "She'd truly been dead before?"

"Yes. I felt it…"

Setting down her bowl, she surveyed the crowd, her fingers tracing an invisible design on the stone before her. "We understand so little about the gods. Even when I meet a goddess, there are more mysteries."

"I'm well aware," Otylia quipped. She still hadn't touched her food. Was that because of me?

"Tell me," Kiin said, turning her attention back to me. "If you formed an impossible bond with this blade of Moonstone, why did you surrender it to Otylia?"

My entire face burned as I stammered, searching for a reply that didn't reveal everything. The demon wanted to snap at her, but I contained it this time. Her question was legitimate. Was my reason?

"I'm not Kwiecień's owner," I finally said. "Nor am I stable enough to be trusted with a god's blade."

"You are certain that is the only reason?"

A flash of anger washed over me as my control nearly slipped from my fingers. I shot to my feet, knocking aside my bowl in the process. I *needed* to leave before I ruined everything, but when I spoke, my voice was a snarl, "Thank you for the meal, Kiin. Let me know when you actually need my help."

I stormed away without another glance at Otylia. The fury burning through me grew with each stride, and I felt every eye watching me after my outburst. They'd treated me as one of their own initially. No longer. In mere minutes, I had shown them how quickly I could lose my temper. That was considered standard for most warriors, but I was a demon capable of massive destruction, unable to afford such tantrums.

Seconds later, I found myself shivering outside the hideout entrance. It appeared from the path as nothing more than a house or perhaps a tavern. A trap door in the furthest corner of the main room, though, led to the deeper floors.

Three women guarded the entrance. At first glance, they resembled locals at work, hauling food or building supplies to nearby houses, but Kiin had explained when we'd arrived that each guard was armed with a hidden dagger. There apparently also had an alert system in case of a raid. She hadn't been willing to share the details.

I headed down the dim alley, the snow crunching beneath my boots. It fell far lighter than before, but enough had gathered throughout the day to reach my calf. My thin Vastrothie pants did little to hold back the chill. Thankfully, though, the pain took my thoughts from Otylia.

When I was certain no one could see me, I sprinted and called to the winds.

The air met me like an old friend as I burst through the snowfall.

Up I climbed, toward nothing but the souls of the living, lights shining in the night sky. The crescent moon joined them. Otylia's moon. So I dove with my eyes shut. The wind whipped through my hair, its chill striking my face and numbing my skin as the *whoosh* in my ears deafened me to my own mind. I was the air, the snow, the storm. I sensed every flake drifting down and each person returning home as Huebia prepared to sleep another night.

One sensation ruled stronger than any other: Grudzień. Its pulse had echoed in my soul ever since I'd entered Huebia, maybe since I'd stepped through the Heart of Nawia. It flared my anger, my pain. At its call, the boy slept and the płanetnik awoke.

"We'll capture it," I promised myself. "I gave her Kwiecień, but Grudzień's power will be ours. And we'll kill anyone who gets in our way."

The winds alerted me to the approaching ground, but I waited until the last second. Then I spun and caught myself, my feet skipping a finger's width above the stone. A thrill surged through me. It swallowed my fear and devoured my rage until only the need for death's edge remained. During my mortal life, I'd feared the end, but now, I realized how wrong I'd been. I wasn't Death's blade. I wasn't his servant.

I was his master.

Darkness surged from me as I darted over a series of torch-lit buildings near the city center. Archers watched from the windows on each level of the shimmering Glasstone Tower, but I was invisible to all but spirits, szeptuchy, and wandering souls. I'd never used my sightless soul-form to punish my enemies before this journey began. That had changed now, and these were nothing more than men with bows of string and wood. *We could kill them.*

The demon agreed. Striking the tower could yield body after body of *żityje* and bring us closer to taking Grudzień for ourselves, but the Frostmarked wouldn't make it easy. I hesitated at the risk. The demon didn't.

We dove, wrestling for my mind. Though I no longer feared it, I wasn't ready to lose control. I wasn't ready to let it rule.

But I was tired. More than simple exhaustion, my heart was shattered, my emotions in turmoil. Otylia had driven a knife through my hopes of love, and the pain was inescapable. I couldn't run from her. I couldn't abandon her, not again. What did that leave?

Blade in hand, we crashed into the first archer at full speed. He couldn't even scream before we sliced his throat and turned to his comrades. Fear spread among them at their invisible attacker, and when they tried to shoot at us, the winds knocked the arrows aside with ease. The excitement from my fall escalated. It surged through my veins, replacing my resentment and hurt with a new sensation: domination.

I loved it.

The world became a blur of blades and blood as I fought my way up the tower's many floors, yet my mind was clearer than ever. No hesitation. No doubt. Only the task ahead of me and those foolish enough to step in my way.

I didn't stop until Dadźbóg rose far to the east. My thoughts finally caught up with me, and I staggered into the rounded wall of the tower. Every muscle in my body seared at the slightest movement. Despite my invisibility, the Frostmarked guards had gotten a few lucky strikes against me—enough for the pain to linger after *żityje*'s healing. My soul burst with it, overflowing to a point that I felt sick and incredible at the same time. Intoxicating. I needed more.

How many had I killed? How many hearts had I taken?

When I'd arrived at the tower, the demon and I had been separate, two entities in one body. I couldn't say the same anymore. As I rose to examine the killing floor, I no longer sensed it as a separate force. Maybe it never had been.

Twelve bodies littered this level of the tower, all missing their hearts, and I'd cleared at least five floors. *That explains my sickness.* I glanced out the window, and my heart stopped at the sight of the clouds not far above. The snowfall had stopped, and I could see all the way to the mountains of Perun's Crown to the northwest. Astiwie and Krowikie lands lay just on the other side. So close, yet so distant.

Shouts echoed from somewhere deeper within the tower. *Time to go.*

A squad of guards rushed through a doorway down the curved hall, led by a pair of wolves that glared at me with bright blue eyes. By the time they arrived, I was already soaring toward Kiin's hideout with victory in my chest. I'd killed over fifty guards in a single strike. Physically, I'd never been more exhausted in my life, but as I dropped in an alley far enough away to disguise the hideout's location, I no longer felt lost. This power had truly become mine—the demon's soul joined with my mind.

For the first time, I was fully awakened.

I took a breath of the cold morning air and watched the people doing their daily work around me. They were oblivious to my invisible presence. Like a creature watching from the trees, I was both alone and not. One with the world yet beyond its reach.

Maybe that was what it meant to be a Naw. Not dead. Not alive. Something in-between, bound to *żityje*'s life and Death's sting. We were free from the reign of gods, of man, and of beast. No other entity could understand all three: power, mortality, and unending hunger. I saw that truth now, and as I returned to the Daughters of the Earth, I swore that I would never be shackled again.

8

Otylia

Why did I push him away?

THE MOON'S POWER PULSED WITHIN ME as I pushed my way through the cellar crowd, climbing into the dark alley above our hideout. My heart raced. Sweat clung cold to my brow.

I lost him. I actually lost him.

I'd thought ending our relationship would protect Wacław from me. *Idiot!* He'd given his mortal soul because he loved me, and all I'd done was take away his last shred of hope. Though Kiin had warned me of Grudzień's influence, I had fallen for its manipulation anyway and surrendered to my fear. Now, the demon had taken Wacław.

"Otylia!" Kiin called from behind me.

I ignored her, rushing toward the moonlit tower with Kwiecień drawn. My spear was simpler to wield, and I had no training with a blade, but it felt right in my grasp. A part of him. All that I had left of the boy I loved.

The snow snatched at my legs as I ran. Deceivingly deep, it caused me to stumble more than once, but I pushed on.

Despite having no idea what I'd do when I reached Wacław at the tower, I needed to see him so that maybe our connection could do *something* to fix what I'd broken. The further I went, though, the more I realized I knew nothing about Huebia's layout. Kiin's map had shown a maze of tight alleys between wide streets. All I knew was that I was somewhere in that mess. In the city's center, the tower scraped the sky, but how could I get there?

Wašek, talk to me, I said through our bond. *I was wrong. I'm sorry!*

No reply came. I couldn't even sense his emotions anymore, or if I could, it was impossible to tell what part of the chaotic blend was his and what was mine. Panic had replaced any semblance of rationality in my head.

I skidded to a stop deep in the city. The snowfall cascaded through the flickering torchlight ahead, obscuring my view of the tower, but nothing could truly hide its massive height. Wacław was somewhere within its glass and rock walls, striking out at the guards. How had he fallen to the demon so quickly? Was it because of me?

I cursed myself and dug my boots into the snow, ready to run again, but a voice stopped me.

"Otylia, wait!"

"I can't leave him," I snapped.

Kiin's footsteps approached anyway, her breaths labored as she laid a hand on my shoulder. "And you can't just fight your way through the Glasstone Tower either. Not yet."

"Don't tell me what I can't do." I shrugged her off. "What good am I if I can't even save Wacław from the thing I made him into? He crossed all of Jawia and entered Nawia for me. He *died* for me!"

"Stupid girl!" Kiin waved her arm through the falling snow. "Don't you get it? Dying for him now won't fix anything. He's an invisible płanetnik with the winds on his side. He'll be fine."

My heart ached, but I clenched my jaw and shoved the pain somewhere far away. "Then what do I do? Wait for the corruption's roots to grow so deep I can never get him back?"

"No, even when you don't strike the beast's heart, you don't simply wait."

I stepped closer, glaring up at her. "Then what?"

She averted her gaze. "I felt your power when you touched me. You may not believe you're the gift we need, but I sense it even now. The moon feeds your *žityje*, doesn't it?"

"It does, but I'm still too drained to fly."

"We'll fix that." She took my hand, holding tight when I tried to pull away. "We've lost too much already, but I swear upon the heart of the Earth Mother, we'll do whatever it takes to capture Grudzień and save Wacław from himself."

"I—" My voice faltered as visions flashed before me.

A great battle erupted across the land and sky. Stones shattered and spires grew from nothing, destroying the earth as lightning snapped through the heavens. The moon shone above in a deep red, and as I raised my gaze to it, rain fell from the storm. No, not rain. Blood. It burned my skin and sent the armies' ranks into disarray as their screams echoed through the night.

Amid the storm, two figures fought on the tower's high roof. A woman wielding a silver spear faced a creature who wore the darkness like his own skin. It swirled around him in violent gusts, battering the woman as he advanced with blackened eyes and a dagger that sucked the life from the air. Hatred burned through him. Visceral, raw. Nothing else remained, and when the woman stumbled and fell, he grinned and raised his blade.

I tore myself away from Kiin and the vision. Sweat poured down my face, despite the cold, and I trembled as I collapsed into the snow. No matter how hard I tried, I couldn't shake the vision's weight.

He'll kill me...

All the dark figure's emotions had struck me at once. An unstoppable blaze. That couldn't have been Wacław. That little hesitant boy I'd played with in the woods for years would never have allowed such rage to consume his very being, so that meant only one thing was possible: the demon, the płanetnik, had taken over by force. With Grudzień against him, Wacław had lost the fight. Or at least he would.

"I failed him," I breathed, numb to the snow and frost.

Kiin crouched before me. "What did you see?" she asked, insistent.

I furrowed my brow. "Why'd you touch me? What do you know?"

"I… I saw my son the first time you had a vision. Just for a second, but to actually *see* him and feel his little head in my hand…" She turned away. "I'm sorry. I had hoped to see him again."

The vision lingered as I pushed myself to my feet. But why had it come when I'd touched Kiin? As far as I could tell, she'd been nowhere in it, unless it had been her who'd molded the earth to her will. My breaths caught at that. When would this battle come? And was it truly unavoidable?

"The force of endings isn't for pleasant memories," I said. "It's brutal. Every time, it shows me something that I'd rather not see—even the good endings. What did you see? You said you saw your son before, so some part of the vision must connect with you too."

She nodded down the alley. "Let's talk as we move. Wacław will return when he's had enough. He's not the first demon to lose himself in a blood rage. The Frostmarked have patrols, and I'd rather not waste more of my *żityje*. Great Mother knows we'll need it soon."

So we did. Kiin strode ahead, her long legs carrying her swiftly to each corner as her coat swept behind. She was truly at one with the city, as I'd once been one with the wilds. The moon pulsed within me, but it lacked the pure bond I'd possessed with Dziewanna. Wisps swirled around me again now that I had regenerated a small amount of *żityje* from food and the moon, yet even they seemed alien, beyond my power. I'd wielded the trees like my own hands before. This simply wasn't the same. Would that ever change?

"The vision was horrific," Kiin said, checking a corner before continuing on. "The sky was filled with dark creatures, infused with lightning. I tried to stop them with the Earth Mother's power, to save those around me, but I wasn't strong enough. All I felt was terror."

"Then you saw enough."

There was no way in Oblivion I was going to tell her the complete truth. She'd agreed to help me with Wacław, but if she knew what he would become…

The dull cold of the hideout felt like the summer sun compared to the snowfall as we dropped through the trapdoor. People greeted me with bows, but I couldn't muster a response. Nothing else mattered but getting Wacław back. Besides, the Vastrothie already had their goddess. I was at best a pretender, bearing a title I could still barely grasp, but the crowd only grew as we reached the sleeping hall. Hope reflected in their eyes. They eagerly watched me liked I'd do a spectacular trick or summon an army to their aid. But I had no inspiration to give, no army to command. None but the voices circling me with the wisps.

They grew louder along with the crowd. A wash of colors, they zipped over and around people's heads, shifting through images faster than I could possibly comprehend. Hundreds of endings. Futures to be made or changed.

Changed.

During my Ascension, Rod had warned me against altering the future. Parts of everyone's lives were defined by Destiny and her Sudiczki fates. The first Sudiczka had bonded me to Wacław as his future queen. Destiny had claimed we would've mended the divide between gods and demons, but instead, Jacek had expelled Wacław from his house, ruining any chance Wacław had of leading the Krowikie, let alone the other tribes north of Perun's Crown.

Maybe it didn't matter anyway. The third Sudiczka, the hag, had said corruption would be my end. I'd assumed it to be Wacław's demonic corruption, and my visions had only made me more certain. If nothing changed, he *would* kill me.

I'll fix this. I swear to Dziewanna, I'll fix this.

Kiin signaled for the crowd to stay back as we entered the sideroom with the model of Huebia. A single torch remained lit, casting a shadow over the szeptucha's face as she climbed up to the ledge and crouched, staring down at the city. "You mentioned before you had friends who went missing when you returned to the living realm."

"I did. They're mostly nymphs and people who were taken by Weles, traded away by their parents in exchange for a gift from the god, but Wacław's friend, Kuba, is among them. He might be able to help us remind Wacław who he is."

"And you're certain they crossed into our lands?"

"No, but if Grudzień pulled us here, it likely did the same to them." I sighed, remembering my promise to help Sabina find her mother. It seemed so long ago. "I wish I knew more."

She raised her gaze to me. "I have contacts in the other cities. A group as large as you described would draw attention to themselves. If they're in Vastroth, we'll find them."

"Why?" I asked, crossing my arms. "Why are you so helpful all of a sudden?"

"Because I know what it is to lose those you love." She dropped to a seated position and clutched her hands in her lap. "When I formed the Daughters of the Earth, I swore to protect every single person who stepped foot in one of our hideouts. Never again would I watch the life slip from an innocent's eyes. Never again would I let despair and pain eat away at our people. I treated each meal like a feast for those here, giving them all I could so they believed in the family we were creating—the Earth Mother's family and my own."

She shook her head. "I failed. We lost almost a hundred people last week when someone infiltrated one of our hideouts, but even before that, the Frostmarked kept finding us. It was like watching a knife slowly skin me alive as I screamed, unable to change it. No matter how hard I tried, more people always died. Then you showed up."

"And gave you another huge problem," I quipped.

"Yes and no." She looked to the tower, Grudzień still raised at its peak. "Between the scion girl and you, there's more hope among my people than I've ever seen, and it's not just them."

"Why do you believe in me? You saw how I drove Wacław away."

Kiin gave a solemn smile. "I saw a girl too afraid to realize that there is no love without pain and loss. Yes, Otylia, you hurt him. With his condition, he was bound to do the same to you, but from what I can tell, you'd each give your lives for each other. The fear you felt was real—the fear of losing the one you love. Sometimes, stepping away feels easier than enduring love, fighting for it. You need to know what's right for your soul. Only you can figure out what that is."

"As for my own belief," she continued. "You are the grandchild of the Earth Mother. She told me you would come someday, and the more I see of you, the more I realize I misjudged you as an insolent, arrogant child. Of course, you have a thick skull, but that will be useful in the moons ahead."

What is right for me? I didn't know. At times, the answer seemed obvious, but I doubted everything now. Even my own intentions were suspect with Grudzień's influence over Huebia. So, with another tide of emotions threatening me, I changed the subject. "What do my friends have to do with replenishing my *żityje?*"

Kiin pulled down her collar and tapped her Mothermark. "All goddesses need worshippers for *żityje*, right? Who's better to become your first szeptucha than those whom you freed from the underworld? This chosen can collect sacrifices from others in your name, as you once did for Dziewanna and your version of the Earth Mother."

"Good point," I said, dragging my foot across the floor. "Thank you, Kiin. If it wasn't for you, I'd probably be run through with a Frostmarked spear by now. You claim that I've given you hope, but you've done the same for me."

She stood. "All right, then. Enough with the compliments. You and I have work to do."

9

Otylia

Wašek, what have you done?

THE BLOODIED FIEND STANDING BEFORE ME WASN'T WACŁAW. It had his golden hair and lanky stature, but this wasn't the boy I'd fallen in love with. He was gone.

Gods, he's gone.

I'd barely slept the night before, waiting each moment for his arrival. Agonizing hour after agonizing hour of his anger and bloodlust surged through our weakened but still ever-present connection. I'd wished to feel his emotions again, but now I questioned that desire.

The Płanetnik—I refused to call him Wacław—paced around the cellar, his eyes black and his voice a nightmare. As he explained his massacre, the torchlight cast a shadow over his face. I imagined the half hidden in darkness to be the real Wacław. Kind, caring, and too hesitant to charge a place like the Glasstone Tower alone. But each time, the light revealed there was no remnant of him lurking away from sight.

"You should be pleased," he said, his gaze fixed on me. It wasn't the longing look he'd given at our meal the night before, when I'd so desperately wished to take back all I'd said. Why hadn't I?

"Why would I be?" I asked. It took all my strength to not look away. No, I couldn't run now. This was my creation, my fault, and I would bear the consequences. "The deaths of fifty Frostmarked will hurt them, but what about your death?"

"They could barely hit me, let alone land a fatal blow."

I scowled, stepping in front of him to stop his advance. "You know what I meant."

Kiin sighed from her position along the wall. Pinching the bridge of her nose, she seemed one with the stone until she looked up, her eyes copper daggers. "There will be repercussions for this."

The Płanetnik's head dropped. "If we strike quickly—"

"Then more people will be slaughtered in the streets!" Kiin snapped. "Don't you understand? This isn't a war of manpower. It's about the people and earning their trust. They'll never trust us until we free them from Grudzień's influence, but butchering fifty guards and running will only prove exactly what they think about the Earth Mother's followers. We sought blood to appease her once. To them, now we're doing so again."

He stammered, searching for a reply.

Wacław's still in there. Hope flashed through me, and I laid a hand on his chest before he could speak. "I know you're angry with me, but this is not the answer."

"What is, then?" he asked, holding my wrist and guiding it away, far more gently than I'd expected from the rage within him. "I've never been enough: for Father, for you, for anyone. All my life, I've been too weak to bother to fight for myself, but not anymore. I was born with this power, Otylia. The Sudiczki or Destiny or someone gave me the ability to wield the winds and the storms. Denying the soul that holds that power was like living as half a person. I realize that now."

"You don't believe that."

"Don't tell me what I believe!" He spun away, his eyes forced shut and his fists clenching and unclenching at his sides. "It's about time I accepted what I am. This hunger will never go away, and neither will the pain I've shoved down, pretending it doesn't exist."

Kiin pushed off the wall, her arms crossed as she approached the cold fire. "We all have pain, Wacław. Denying it only allows it to dig deeper into the caverns of our hearts, but allowing it to define you will only lead to more suffering." She picked a handful of ash from the pit and rose, crafting it as she continued, "The Frostmarked have a policy of killing a random person in exchange for every warrior or even wolf they lose."

Finished with her molding, she held out the figure to him. It looked like one of the guards from the gate, their staffs a spearhead on one end and a curved blade on the other. "Do you know why their warriors have these weapons?"

"They're versatile," the Płanetnik replied. "A spear is limited to stabbing, unless you want to swing the blunt end."

"True," Kiin said, "but the curved blade serves another purpose: execution." She shoved the figure into his chest. It dissolved into its original ash in his grasp. "Before the sun's final light, there will be fifty fewer innocents in this city because of you. Fifty more of the Earth Mother's children dead because *you* decided your hatred meant more than everything we've planned, everyone we've sacrificed."

She cast her gaze to me and sighed. "I have much to do. Talk to me later about finding your friends, and keep him out of sight. There's enough panic as is."

I wanted to beg her to stay, but cowering wouldn't fix Wacław. Not that anything could. In those final moments before he'd attacked the tower, I'd felt his struggle with the demon. He'd fought to subdue the beast for so long. But when he'd struck, something changed, as if he'd *allowed* the demon to take the lead.

We stood in silence for some time, the fire pit all that separated me from Wacław. The real distance was far greater. We'd been an entire realm apart for the last moon, but I'd felt closer to him then than I did now. A thousand words filled my mind. None were enough. I had taken Wacław's soul and forced him away, claiming it had been to protect him. What was the truth? Had I actually worried for him, or had I been unwilling to accept my own regrets, my own fear? Kiin had insisted I stay by his side, but I didn't know how after all we'd seen and done.

"You want to fix me," the Płanetnik said, that alien voice coming from Wacław's mouth. "Why?"

"Because this isn't you," I replied without thought, my lungs ablaze and my head spinning. "The Wašek I know would never risk everything to cut down a bunch of guards. He let himself feel, but he never let his anger define him."

He huffed and walked around the fire pit, averting his gaze as he stopped a few strides away. With the blood covering his chin and clothes, he reeked of sweat and gore. "You're wrong about that. I never allowed myself to accept my resentment against Father and all those who mocked me. Year after year, I took his beatings and hung my head, trying to prove myself to a man that never cared, to a tribe that never wanted me. I was a desperate fool."

"No, Jacek was the fool. You were a boy who wanted his father's love and never received it."

"It doesn't matter."

"It does!" I closed the gap between us as End's blur of colors swirled, taunting me. "You're blaming yourself for what happened to you. Why? You swallowed your anger to survive Jacek's wrath, but lashing out at him would've only made it worse."

Pain filled his gaze as he wavered. "I abandoned you! I let Father tear us apart because I was too afraid to fight. Every single moment, I was too weak to face those who challenged me."

"You were twelve," I said, stepping toward him again. "And you were strong enough to understand our separation was better than my exile. You *saved* me from Jacek. I've always preferred confrontation, but you were the one that taught me I needed allies, friends, to succeed—that sometimes, it's better to seek peace first."

"Tell that to Katiôn and Xobas. Negotiating with King Boz only lured us into his ambushes in Astiw, and they're probably dead because of it."

I sighed. "I'm sorry. I know you and Xobas were close, but he could've escaped. Don't give up on him yet."

"That's not the point." Shaking his head, he turned away, examining the tapestries upon the wall. "It was because of my failure to act that so many people suffered. You may find excuses in each instance, but I see the pattern. It's time for that to change… for me to change." He looked back at me. "You said it yourself: We've changed already. I was resisting the inevitable end of my transformation, but I've accepted the truth of my soul now. When will you do the same for yours?"

"Wašek…" I stammered. His name caught in my throat at his prodding. What was my soul's truth? What was I supposed to do with this power?

"Stop it!" he growled. "You made your decision. I saw it in your eyes, felt it in your heart. I'm not the boy you loved anymore, and you're more than the witch I fell for. To pass your Trials, you needed my soul, so I gave it. Now, you're a goddess and I'm a Naw. Broken. Why would you ever want to be with me?"

"Wašek!" I called again, but he stormed toward the stairs faster than I could chase him. Darkness lurked in his movements, surrounding him like the wisps of color following me.

I crumbled.

The cold shadows consumed me as I huddled against the wall, staring ahead at nothing. My Wašek was actually gone. Even worse, he *hated* me, and I deserved it. I deserved to suffer for taking his soul, for pushing him away when I'd forced him to become a creature of the dark. He'd asked why I would ever want to be with him. But I'd seen the true Wacław within the Płanetnik. The doubts, the moments of thought. Those hadn't been the demon.

Part of me wished to cry in the cellar forever. Here, no one watched me, expectant. There were no relationships to ruin or visions to haunt me—well, none immediately in my mind. The force of endings remained with me, its images and distant whispers ever-present. What stories did they wish to tell? I would have to master my new powers if I was going to rescue Mother. About that, the Płanetnik had been right. I hadn't accepted my soul or the forces of my Ascension. Nor did I truly understand who I was anymore.

Footsteps echoed across the room.

I shot to my feet, drawing Kwiecień from my back and holding the hilt with two hands. "Who's there?" The blade's golden glow illuminated a girl in the opposite corner, where Kiin had shown me the tunnels. A Mothermark glowed upon her head. "Darixa?"

She scampered across the room, her little striped dress flapping behind her before she latched onto me. "I don't like him."

"Who?" I asked, crouching and offering her a forced smile. Tears still stained my cheeks, but I hoped she wouldn't notice.

"Wacław. He's scary, like the things in my dreams."

"Your dreams?" I touched her sleeveless arm and reached for End's call. Its visions only seemed useful with her, so maybe I could help again, doing something right for once. "Can you show me them?"

She shook her head.

"It's okay to be afraid—I'd be lying if I said I'm not—but the Earth Mother needs you to be brave." I tapped her nose, spurring a giggle. "She's my grandmother you know?"

Her eyes widened. "Really?"

"She is, and she'll be proud of you for facing your nightmares alone. You're not alone anymore, though. She sent me to help you." I locked her fingers with mine as the whispers grew around me again. They were familiar after experiencing two visions of the girl, and I found comfort in that. "Please, let me see."

I didn't hear her reply. The cellar disappeared as a bright pink wisp ran straight through my chest, and when I blinked, I found myself dropping through a storm.

Darixa's screams came from nearby as the clouds broke around us. It was night, and only the cracks of lightning allowed me to see her flailing arms. I dove toward her, catching her and whispering a reassuring prayer, one I hoped Mokosz heard.

What monsters was she afraid of?

My heart jumped as a screech pierced the air, followed by the roll of thunder. Pain raced across my arm. By the time I blinked, Darixa was gone.

"What in Oblivion?"

A figure of pure energy appeared, holding Darixa by her hair as lightning cracked at its fingertips. I cursed. *Why'd it have to be a chała?* There was no way I could forget the storm demon that had attacked me in the Lake of Reflection. Wacław had wielded lightning for the first time to save me. This time, I was on my own.

I drew Kwiecień as my little *żityje* healed the wound. Just a burn, but I barely had enough to continue flying, let alone fight these demons. "Let her go!" I shouted and thrust the blade.

But the chała was too fast. She giggled and shot toward the ground in the form of another bolt. I followed, dropping with the moon's energy pushing me faster. Even I couldn't match the speed of lightning, though, and when four more screeches echoed from above, I felt my heart hammer in my chest.

The first chała landed as I spun to face the storm, where three winged demons emerged. Wacław had described his fight with other forms of chały when he'd aided Eryk, his marked płanetnik. Even that couldn't have prepared me for these black beasts' talons and fanged teeth. Then the great serpent broke through the clouds.

Gods save me.

I rushed to the ground with greater haste, pouring all my *żityje* into the fall. Facing the lightning chała was difficult enough. There was no way I could defeat its allies above, especially when one was a serpent the size of a longhouse.

Lightning snapped around me from above and below. The first demon clung to Darixa, firing the bolts from its hand as the serpent rained strikes from its maw. I was trapped. Though I dodged and weaved, I couldn't escape the cascade, and a bolt struck my chest as another skimmed my leg. *Żityje* kept me alive, but it was the last of my reserves. My grip on the moon's power slipped.

Death was inevitable now. I had no way to escape the chały, but even if I could, landing at this speed would shatter my bones. Darixa's screams filled my mind as I stared at the ground and awaited the end.

"I'm sorry, little one."

A bolt struck my head. Burning pain shot through my body, and I bit my cheek, trying not to scream. Darixa needed to know I was strong, that even in the face of death, I wouldn't relent.

Then I hit the ground.

10

The Płanetnik

Why did we ever resist this power?

BLACK BLOOD SPILLED INTO THE BEHMIR RIVER as I splashed its frigid water over my face. When I sat back, it trickled down my neck and torso, sending a shiver down my spine. More pain.

The snow stung my bare bottom too, but I gave it no care. I had plenty of *żityje* to heal any significant injuries. The rest would feed my anger, preparing me for my next feast. Otylia had shown little appreciation for my successful assault on the Glasstone Tower. Washing my clothes and body in the river had given me time to think about what she'd said.

I hadn't changed my mind.

My promise to myself remained. I would help Otylia save Dziewanna and defeat Marzanna, but I would serve no one. I had once bowed my head at every turn. Now, I would keep mine high, meeting each person's gaze so they knew who they faced. For once, it would be them who cowered before *me*.

Once I'd dried my clothes with the winds, I dressed and climbed the hill back to Huebia. I left my feet bare, allowing the snow to bite them with each step. A reminder of why we fought.

"I'll kill you, Marzanna," I said, sending my *żiṫyje* into my Frost-mark. "I'll make you pay for the pain you've caused, and nothing will stop me."

Huebia's massive sandstone wall loomed over me as I reached the top of the dune. To an advancing army, it must've been quite the sight. Krowik had never built more than wooden walls that were far shorter than these. Fire or a ram could destroy ours, but no army I knew of had a weapon that could demolish the fortress of Huebia.

Luckily, I could go over them.

The winds swept beneath me with a great force, catapulting me to the walkway atop the ramparts. Archers guarded here in case of an invader attempting to cross the river. There were significantly fewer, though, than those who watched Huebia's own population from the tower.

I killed them.

Quickly and precisely, I rushed the three guards nearby, slicing their throats before they could raise an alarm. The Thunderstone dagger's black blade ate greedily of their *żiṫyje*, but I devoured what remained. Kiin claimed the Frostmarked would kill an innocent for each warrior they lost. Guilt came with that, but I couldn't resist the urge. I *needed* to kill. After all Marzanna's servants had done, they deserved death. But that wasn't the only reason.

Hunger. Even when I finished with their hearts, it ached within my soul. It was relentless, unyielding, and it grew stronger with each day. Satiating it brought the greatest satisfaction I'd ever felt, but simple hearts weren't enough. I needed Grudzień. I needed power.

I crouched, looking over the city from the bloodied wall as panic gripped my chest. Not mine but Otylia's.

Bitterness, anguish, and yearning clashed within as I remembered her betrayal. She'd exposed how much she feared me now. She preferred me weak, vulnerable. Why? By joining with my demonic soul, I could ensure my past failures never happened again. I wouldn't hesitate. I wouldn't rely on the decisions of others. I could finally fight by her side as an equal: as goddess and demon.

Otylia didn't want that, nor did she want me.

I clenched my jaw and dropped off the wall, using the winds to run vertically down its surface before landing atop the next building. Through the city I traveled, jumping from rooftop to rooftop and feeling freedom's thrill in my heart. There was nothing like this.

Another strike of pain stopped me not far from the hideout. I dropped to a knee, catching my breath from the exertion. *What's happening?* I asked her through our bond. If the Frostmarked had attacked, I had to know. Otylia had rejected me, but I needed her to help me secure the Moonstone and get my revenge on Marzanna. The last thing I wanted was to drag her from Nawia again.

My own panic joined hers when silence answered me. A remnant weakness of my mortality, it forced away the demonic thrill and left me frozen, unmoving. I pushed against it. Pain and sorrow would *not* control me.

Releasing a snarl, I charged on and dropped to the ground. Vastrothie traveled every which way through this square. Some carried cloth or bricks while others covered their heads and stuck to the shadows. The workers left plenty of footprints in the snow, and no one noticed the invisible demon sprinting between them, leaving only a breeze and puff of black vapor in my wake.

I stopped again at the next intersection, where a crowd blocked the way forward. Screams rang out from the other side, and when I leaped with the winds over the onlookers, I sucked in a sharp breath. Blood melted the snow. So much of it filled the path that it flowed toward the city center like a rancid river.

Five Frostmarked warriors guarded a line of bound people. The corpses piled before them held crude weapons in their limp grasps, and I gritted my teeth at the sight of a few who'd eaten with us the night before.

So many dead, and they weren't even the sacrifices…

This was why Kiin and Otylia had hated my attack. Not only would the Frostmark sacrifice the same number they'd lost, they would kill more when desperate Vastrothie fight to save their loved ones. But if this was my fault, why did I feel no guilt? The Frostmarked were murderers, worshipping the goddess who'd tried to take Mom and Otylia from me, who'd massacred thousands on the Anshayman Steppe, and who would stop at nothing for revenge against Jaryło. They had deserved to die. I was not responsible for their reaction.

I allowed myself to be visible to everyone, even the Frostmarked. They deserved to see their death coming and feel the fear they had inflicted on so many others. Slaughtering innocents was unforgivable, and sometimes, a monster was needed to destroy another.

Gasps and shouts came from the crowd, but I gave them no heed as I charged the Frostmarked. With just strides between us, they didn't have time to react. Spears and curved blades struck sloppily at me as they tried to hold their ground. Too slow. My dagger found one's throat and a second's heart, piercing their tortoise-shell armor with ease. But the blade caught in the third guard's ribs, so I released it and took to the sky.

Relief filled the eyes of the final two warriors. Surely, I was fleeing, out of energy and *żityje* after moving at such inhuman speed.

They were wrong.

I tucked and dove again, using my fall to pull the air around me into a whirlwind. The crowd scattered as the blast ripped across the intersection and pushed the prisoners free. Though the Frostmarked turned to chase, the whirlwind's wall blocked their route. I was upon them in two beats of my heart.

The first jabbed his spear across my side. A flesh wound, and without hesitation, I batted aside his spear's shaft with the palm of my hand—an old trick from Xobas. The polearm flew from his grasp and into my gales. They guided the weapon into my hands as I lunged, and the spearhead found the warrior's sternum with ease.

Behind, I realized, sensing the second's presence.

The curved end of his spear arced toward my neck. A mortal warrior would've died by that blade, but I launched myself back and up with the winds. His attack sliced beneath me as I flipped over him, landing behind and focusing on the air in his lungs. Each breath was quick, panicked. He sensed death coming, and this time, he was right.

I tightened the whirlwind and stole his breath, closing my fist as if to catch it. The warrior dropped to his knees and clutched his throat. He gasped as he stared up at me, but I had no sense for mercy, not after seeing those he'd killed.

When the warrior finally collapsed to the bloodied snow, I released the whirlwind, revealing a crowd even larger than the one from before. Hundreds of faces watched me, some with hope, others with horror. I wondered what they saw as I stood there, covered in blood both red and black. A demonic disgrace? A walking nightmare? Or a savior?

"Where were the Frostmarked taking the prisoners?" I shouted in the clan tongue as people rushed to untie the prisoners. "The tower?"

They swapped glances among themselves. I cursed their fear until one woman stepped forward and pulled down her hood, meeting my gaze with one as fierce as the sun. "They say someone attacked the Glasstone Tower. Was it you?"

"Yes," I replied flatly before using the winds to draw the Thunderstone dagger from a warrior's chest, catching it without breaking eye contact. "Tell me where the other prisoners are."

"More will die for each you kill."

"More will die for each I don't."

The crowd murmured among themselves, and the woman joined in for a moment. *There's no time for this.* Their opinions shouldn't have mattered to me. None of them could stop me anyway, but as I studied their faces, I knew I cared. Another lingering weakness…

"Tell me where," I insisted, stepping toward them.

They backed away. My voice had come out more like a growl than speech, and many of the looks became more distrustful. The woman, though, pointed down the alley. "They'll execute the others in the market beneath the tower. Please, make them pay."

A man grabbed her arm, shouting at her to stop talking, but she'd confirmed what I needed. I took to the air as a pang of sorrow struck through my connection to Otylia. *Later.* If she was worried about the prisoners, I was already helping. Anything else could wait.

"Are we helping?" a voice so similar to my own asked in the back of my head. Soft, hesitant. But there was no time for him either.

Half of Huebia had crammed themselves into the open market surrounding the Glasstone Tower. I made myself invisible again as I hovered above them, surveying the situation. A hundred Frostmarked with half as many wolves controlled the crowd and pushed them away from a group of at least forty prisoners, tied by rope at their wrists. Before them, a row of ice spikes rose from the ground—one for each prisoner.

A growl escaped my throat as I landed on the roof of the nearest building. The executions would begin soon, but even I would struggle against that many Frostmarked. I'd used precious *żityje* just killing five before, and with all those people watching, I hadn't been able to drain them. A full-scale battle here would be worse. Even if I could free the prisoners, the Frostmarked could attack the crowd.

Some part of me wished to ask for Otylia's help, but I rejected it. She'd proven she couldn't do what was necessary here, like me before. The difference was I'd defeated my fear and replaced it with anger—Otylia had succumbed to her own.

I would do it myself.

Instinct launched me from the roof and onto the winds. No, I couldn't defeat all the Frostmarked before they attacked innocents, but I didn't have to. From the prisoners to the nearest alley was no more than fifty strides. If I could get them there, a whirlwind could block the Frostmarked long enough for people to flee. That would leave me alone with my prey in the market. Much easier.

I dropped halfway between the crowd and the prisoners. Visible to only the innocent, no Frostmarked noticed my presence but the wolves. Before their warriors released them, though, I launched a gust to either side, knocking half the Frostmarked from their feet like nothing.

The first prisoners quickly realized what was happening, but their hands were bound to each other. When some tried to run, others held them back in their shock. I cursed as the warriors rose again.

"Run!" I shouted to them.

It was far too long before the prisoners managed to get moving. The Frostmarked descended upon them, and despite my gales throwing away most of the attackers, some slipped through.

Curved blades and spearheads alike tore through the trapped prisoners with ease. Some continued running, but the dead created a weight that held them in place. I realized it too late. My dagger found Frostmarked throats and hearts each moment as I tried to fend off the attackers, but by the time I sliced enough of the binds to free the prisoners, half had fallen. More screams came from the crowd behind as dark figures filled the sky.

What have I done?

Fear threatened to wrestle control from me, but I dug deeper into my rage, my hatred of the Frostmarked and Marzanna. They had killed too many. This had to end.

A wolf's jaws grabbed my arm, but lightning arced from my skin. Darkness followed, swirling on the gales as I tore open its jugular and flung it across the market. Twelve prisoners had escaped the warriors and were sprinting toward the crowd, some of whom had taken up tools as weapons. A flicker of hope came with the sight.

Then the chały struck.

Three of the winged demons streaked from the air, their claws ripping apart four prisoners in seconds. My new allies wavered before them. When two more chały lunged from the sky, the crowd fled with the remaining prisoners. I fought alone, again.

The winds battered me as I dug my heels into the ground. We were both demons of the storm, and despite my power, I was badly outnumbered.

Claws flashed, meeting skin as my dagger severed limbs and wings alike. Their dark forms surrounded me and forced me to devote attention to each. A jab at one. A lightning bolt at another. Then a blast of wind to deflect a strike. Each move drained my *żityje* more, and I snarled in frustration knowing nearly half the warriors and wolves lay dead around me—so many hearts I could drain if I had even a few seconds to spare. But I had none.

"We need to run!" the terrified voice said in my head. *"They'll kill us."*

I can't die, I replied. *Death's blade can't fall.*

I'd killed two chały in my frantic defense, but when another struck my leg, I stumbled. They were upon me instantly. A fury of claws and teeth ripping me apart until I sliced my way free and shot into the air, black blood seeping from every limb. In my blurred vision, the three remaining chały were nothing but black streaks chasing me. They caught me quickly. Images of the chały that had stolen Eryk's daughter a moon before flashed in my mind. I'd failed then, but I wouldn't now. I couldn't.

Talons ripped into me as I spun, darkness rising from me. It had a force of its own. Unruly, raw, it fed the storm in my soul, and as the next chała struck, I released all my rage.

The creature loosed a shriek almost as horrific as its appearance. It tumbled, charred and bloodied as lightning danced between my fingers, *demanding* to be used. A blizzard had formed around us now. Though the storm was as much theirs as mine, I was an unchained Naw, and three of them had fallen. The final two struck together, but lightning met them as claws ripped into my stomach.

The blast sent light shooting through the darkness. Shrieks echoed through the sky along with my own cry. I was falling. How? Why?

I sensed the demons' deaths nearby as pain stabbed at my gut. The wound was deep—too deep. My *żityje* had burned away quickly, and now, staring at the ground, I'd all but run dry. Fighting a hundred Frostmarked and a squad of chały had been too much. I'd known it, yet I'd fought anyway.

Don't heal me, I commanded my power, as if words would fix the pain. My wound would likely kill me, but the ground would sooner. I had only a small burst of power left. Just long enough for the winds to catch my fall… I hoped.

The slaughter covered the market below. Bodies of Frostmarked, wolves, prisoners, and onlookers alike stained the sandstone a deep red. The spikes of ice still jutted from the ground, somehow still perfectly white-blue despite the death on and around them. My heart sunk. Marzanna had received a far greater sacrifice of blood than the Frostmarked had intended, and I'd given it to her. All for less than ten prisoners to escape.

The chały struck the ground first, but I blocked out the noise and focused on my own impact. Counting down, I waited until I reached roof-level before calling the winds. They answered.

I screamed as my ribs cracked from their catch. Hovering a finger's length off the ground, the impact had been better than the stone, but stopping so quickly had taken more force than I'd expected. I could wield the storm with my hands and draw the air from someone's lungs. Pure precision was, ironically, more difficult.

My *žityje* ran out.

I dropped to the stone with a grunt. The pain in my stomach was too much. A chała's talon was as long as my forearm, and based on the black blood pooling around me, the wound was deep.

Footsteps splashed in the puddle. Blood filled my throat as I tried to look. I coughed it up with each struggled breath, and my entire body trembled with the sudden fear of mortality. I fought… the demon fought… but I was too weak.

Death had come. I'd held his blade. Now, he'd driven it into me instead.

My vision slipped as I finally managed to raise my head, and a force pulled tight within me at the sight of the advancing group. I was too delirious to understand what it meant. It didn't matter. Friend or foe, I was surely dead.

What strength I had left failed as the people spoke. Sharp, quick, their words meant nothing to me, but with my final breath, I heard a familiar voice.

"Wašek, what have you done?"

11

Otylia

I'd send him to Oblivion if he weren't almost there.

I REPEATED EVERY PRAYER I KNEW in the old tongue as Kiin led the retreating Daughters through Huebia's winding alleys. The largest among them ran alongside me, carrying Wacław's… the Płanetnik's… limp body in his arms. We'd barely had time to wrap the wounds with the surviving Frostmarked making chase, and black blood still seeped from a deep gash on his front and dozens of cuts across the rest of his body. Without *żityje*, he'd bleed out soon.

There had to be a salve or potion that could help. Hundreds of Mother's recipes ran through my head, and instinctively, I reached for my herb bag before cursing when my hand found only air. Those herbs had helped me countless times before Jaryło slit my throat, but finding new ones in Nawia had been the least of my concerns. Now we were caught in a desert. I doubted there were easily accessible herbs, and even if there were, how many would be like those in Krowik?

Think! I told myself.

Mother had trained me as a healer for years, teaching me how to treat people's wounds from failed hunts, drunken fights, and raids in nearby villages. Those had been mortals. I had no idea if any of her tricks would save Wacław when he suffered from both blood loss and *žityje* deprivation.

It seemed an eternity before we reached the Daughters' hideout in the southeastern part of the city. After scrambling down the ladder and stairs, Kiin waved for me to join her in a side-room across the sleeping hall from the room with the model of Huebia. Others tried to follow, but she shooed away all but the one carrying Wacław. I appreciated the privacy.

A single torch lit the small room, and sweat dripped from the man's brow as carried Wacław toward a wool-covered bed in the corner. Kiin stopped him.

"Not there! I'll clear off the table."

She quickly picked the candles, Mothermarked talismans, and other artifacts off a stone table that appeared to have been formed directly from the ground. The man waited patiently before heaving Wacław onto the hard surface and leaving through the curtained doorway without a word.

I rushed to Wacław's side. His physical pain joined with my sorrow, threatening to force me into a weeping ball, but I would fight through. He'd exchanged his own fear and misery for anger. Though I wouldn't do the same, I would let myself feel *later*.

"What do you plan to do with him?" Kiin asked with her arms crossed. "Don't expect me to send for a healer. After the disaster he just caused, I have half-a-mind to let him die where he lies, and they're plenty occupied with the innocent people he put in harm's way."

"I don't need them!" I snapped. "My mother trained me as a healer, and I've seen him like this before."

"You have?"

"He needs blood—fresh blood! Even an animal heart would work to help him heal himself."

"Why should I waste my resources on a demon who's only going to get more people killed?"

I glared up at her and laced my words with fire. "Because you know what it's like to lose the people you love."

"I also know it's beyond foolish to attack half the Frostmarked garrison singlehanded. All Wacław has done is bring more misery to the people I'm trying to protect."

"Let him die and I'll leave." I advanced toward her. "We need each other, and I've promised you my help. All I ask is that you tell me where I can get what I need to save him."

She studied me, her brows furrowed and her fingers pressed against her Mothermark. What was she thinking? Our trip through the caverns had seemed to change her opinion of me, but still she fought. Then she stepped past me, circling Wacław's body. "The Frostmarked killed or took whatever livestock we had, so our remaining meat is preserved, its vibrancy gone long ago. I assume he needs the *žityje* of blood more than simply the heart, but I won't ask my people to give a sacrifice to a demon either. There is, however, another supply of fresh hearts available in the city right now."

I remembered the sea of blood covering the market, my stomach churning. "You're talking about the Frostmarked."

"Yes." Her fingers curled at that, but she hid her discomfort quickly, approaching me again. "Their bodies will remain in the center market for some time as those who survived Wacław's attack root out suitable victims for revenge. Our allies will intercept those they can, but we're limited. I'll go with you to retrieve the hearts for your demon. In return, while he recovers, I expect you to join our teams to stop the abductions. He made our problems worse, so you will help carry the extra burden. No questions. No complaints."

That last statement felt like a jab, but I ignored it. "Deal."

"Good. Best we hurry then. He's not doing well."

She was right. Our bond was weaker, but I sensed the little *žityje* he had left fading, barely enough to keep him alive. Whispers from the force of endings surrounded me. I focused on his pain. Until it vanished, he lived.

Kiin stopped me as I headed toward the main room. "You're hardly inconspicuous wearing *that*. Here." She threw open a trunk at the end of the bed and pulled out trousers, a sleeveless shirt, and a long coat like hers. All black. "Put these on. If you're going to be helping us, I can't have the Frostmarked identifying you from half-way across Vastroth and tracking you back here. Hmm… I didn't think about your hands. Pale as sun-soaked sand those." With a huff, she shoved the clothes into my chest and pushed aside the fabric covering the doorway. "Change quickly while I find some gloves."

So I did, my Ascension dress falling from my shoulders like a great weight I'd barely comprehended before dissolving into a silver mist. I'd felt both dominant and beautiful wearing that dress in Nawia, but neither of those described the heaviness of my soul days later. Becoming a goddess came with so many extra questions and expectations. I couldn't bear to be the goddess of endings today, and Kiin's clothes allowed me to pretend I wasn't, slipping me into the guise of a mortal who wasn't completely out of her depth.

I see why men wear these things.

It felt odd to wear trousers instead of a dress. Freeing. I imagined running without my skirts catching on debris and flying without worrying if someone could see more than they were supposed to. Obviously, this was why Krowikie men restricted their use—women would be far too difficult to control.

"I'll be back soon, Wašek," I said, not able to look down at him as I stopped at the doorway. "If you're in there, keep fighting."

Then I headed after Kiin.

Every eye watched me. They judged. Scorned. Despised.

I tugged on my hood and kept my head low, but a whisper inside me claimed that they knew I didn't belong. Who was I to be a goddess? The beast who'd wielded the storms at the market was my creation, my folly. He'd slayed over half the Frostmarked warriors in the last two days, but at what cost?

Despite the doubts wringing my mind as voices circled on End's wisps, no one approached. The voices wept and screamed at the deaths of the prisoners as well as the Frostmarked. They too were from the city, and their families mourned all the same, regardless of the opinions of the Daughters of the Earth. Loss was loss. It permeated every crack in Huebia's stone until it seeped down to the tunnels below. Did Mokosz suffer with her people, or had she truly left them? Kiin seemed convinced that her goddess still protected Vastroth, but I'd felt Mokosz's power many times as a szeptucha… It was silent beyond the Hidden Waters.

Great Mother, give me your guidance.

She'd always been the quieter of my two goddesses, but there'd been a subtle presence about her. Like a mother's watchful gaze. Always there, even if you didn't know it. I hoped she'd simply hidden her influence from Marzanna instead of vanishing completely. These people needed her, and so did I. It had been with her help that I'd saved Wacław from Bidaês and learned the truth of our exchanged soul fragments. If anyone could help me understand how to control the force of endings and fix Wacław, it was her.

"Keep your head down," Kiin whispered, tugging at my cloak to put herself between me and the center of the alley. It was narrower than the main streets, just wide enough for pairs to pass each direction without brushing shoulders, and heavy footsteps approached.

"How many?" I asked.

She sneered. "The number wouldn't matter if you'd listen to what I said."

Part of me revolted at her tone, but I stifled it. There was no time for petty quarrels with Wacław at the bank of the Smorodina. Mortals would find Nawia through the flaming river's current. Not him.

My heart jumped at the realization that the footsteps weren't only coming from the left, where the other people walked. They drew nearer from ahead before stopping strides away. From my bowed gaze, I could just see the scuffed tips of leather boots stained with crimson, and I held my breath as the warrior's rumbling voice echoed through the alley.

"There has been an attack against the people of Huebia! All areas surrounding the Glasstone Tower are off-limits to civilians until the perpetrator is apprehended."

Murmurs surrounded us as people turned away. Fear froze me. We needed to get to the market, but Kiin had believed the Frostmarked would be busy roaming in search of revenge, not keeping people from the site of the skirmish. *Žityje* and the moon would've made going through or over them a simple task. Instead, I was drained, and Dadźbóg's dull sun hung in the west.

An arm locked with mine. "Sorry about my deaf sister," Kiin said loudly, pulling me away. "I'll make sure she stays out of the market."

They laughed, and one snapped next to my head. When I didn't flinch, I saw the shadow of his wave before he stepped back. Kiin let out a breath as we followed the rest of the civilians into the other alleys. She didn't release me, and my gloved hand ached in her tight grasp as we checked each alley for openings. There were none. Of course not. Minna, the Marzanna's leader in Huebia, was a szeptucha and would know what Wacław needed to recover. Her Frostmarked weren't looking for him, because they expected him to return for the hearts.

"What's that look?" Kiin asked, ducking into the shadows of a side alley north of the market.

"They're expecting us. I—" A wave of pain struck me, and I leaned into her, gritting my teeth as Wacław's breaths weakened. He had just minutes left. I didn't know how I knew that, but I did.

Kiin held a finger over my lips as people passed the intersection. When their steps faded, she pulled it back, her brow furrowed. "It's him, isn't it?"

I nodded. "We don't have time to attack and get a heart."

"Then he's gone."

"No!" I snapped, pacing down the alley. Away from the sun, a chill crept over me as my boots trampled the snow to reveal the stone beneath. I crushed my fear with it until that remained was defiance. "We'll just have to bring a heart to us."

"And how do you plan to do that?"

I turned back to her with a smirk. "By learning from the boys." Then I took off at a sprint. "Wait here!"

She grumbled behind me, but I was already gone, tearing down my hood and rushing directly at the nearest group of Frostmarked. They reacted as soon as I turned the corner. Black hair strewn over my face and my pale skin flashing in the light, I must've been a sight to behold. A guard broke from the checkpoint and barked for his comrades to stay behind. He probably believed me to be a distraction. Good. One heart would be enough—I hoped.

When he was close enough for me to smell his stench, I bolted back toward Kiin. Gods, how trousers made running so much easier! I didn't kick my skirt with each step, and the guard fell behind as his spear and tortoise-shell armor weighed him down. All I needed was a few strides.

Kiin yelped as I entered the alley. She held her hands out, *žityje* pulsing at her fingers and confusion in her eyes. I gave her no answer and instead counted the guard's steps before shouting, "Now!" when he reached the corner.

The earth rose beneath us, throwing me to my back. Ripples ran across the earth like a stone striking water, and the guard cried out as his legs disappeared into a pit that hadn't been there moments before. Kiin dropped her power quickly and summoned her staff. The guard jumped for the ledge to pull himself free, but his momentum only carried him into her strike. The resulting *snap* of his neck echoed through the tight alley.

"Hurry," Kiin said, peeking around the corner at the other guards. "We're far enough from the checkpoint, but someone might've heard."

I didn't need her pressure. My bond to Wacław provided plenty of that—the tether between us fraying with each second as he crept toward Death's embrace. I'd promised that fiendish spirit a gift to save Wacław before, but there was no negotiating now. Only blood could save a demon.

Silver struck my hand as I landed next to the dead guard. Carving his chest was difficult with a spear instead of a knife, but convenience was the least of my problems. Each slice through his ribs made my blood curl after years of Father lecturing me about the sacred nature of corpses before the soul had left. Worries for a priest without need of *žityje*. Though the guard's wisp screamed around me as I cut, my gloved hands prevented me from touching it or his skin. A vision now would mean Wacław's death, and I pleaded in my mind for End to stay its wrath for now.

After what felt like hours, I dismissed my spear and pulled the heart free from the guard's gaping chest. He'd become a demon if his allies didn't burn or bury him to allow his soul to pass on. That weighed on me as Kiin helped me climb from the pit. Frostmarked demons were more dangerous than warriors, so each kill would bolster their ranks. My breaths caught realizing how many demons Wacław may have made in his slaughters. He'd thought them great victories. If the Frostmarked did with their dead as I feared, then they'd been anything but.

A problem for later. All that mattered now was getting the heart to Wacław.

So we ran, tucking the heart in a bag that Kiin slung over her shoulder. Blood had splattered across my boots and gloves, but they would be difficult to spot unless someone looked at me closely while I was out of the shadows. At full sprint, I doubted anyone would get the chance. People mostly dodged out of the way instead, and we saw no more Frostmarked on our path around the outer sections of the city. I sighed in relief as the hideout appeared.

I'm coming, Wašek.

There was no reply. Amid End's voices and the pounding of my heart, our connection was nothing more than a tickle in the back of my mind. I held onto it in fear that it would disappear completely. We were seconds from Kiin's chambers now. All he had to do was hold on until we arrived.

A wide-eyed Faarax met us at the base of the stairs into the sleeping hall. He stammered his questions, but I pushed him aside and ran into the room.

The air was cold and stale. Silence consumed the space like a snake would a mouse: slow, deliberate, deadly. Only my rushed breaths broke it as I leaned over Wacław, placing my ear to his chest to listen for a heartbeat. Nothing. Two fingers to his jugular, where Mother had always tested. Still. His chest neither rose nor fell, and I dropped to my knees with a cry as Kiin pushed into the room behind me.

"We're too late," I whispered, gripping the frostbitten fingers he'd sacrificed to save me. "He's gone…"

But Kiin took me by the collar and hauled me to my feet. "Maybe, but we didn't go all that way not to try." She pulled the heart from the bag with her bare hand, shoving it into my chest. "Do it, because I sure as sand won't."

My hands took the heart out of instinct more than thought. Fear had me wrapped in its vines, the thorns piercing every bit of confidence I had, yet desperation drove me on. It pushed me to hold the heart over Wacław's partially opened lips. The ones I'd kissed for the first time just moons ago. The ones he'd used to admit his love for me. And now, the ones that accepted the heart's dripping blood as I squeezed with all my strength.

Please, Wašek. Live.

I crushed the heart until it bled no more, leaving me hunched over Wacław's soul-form body, angry at him for abandoning me to clean up his mess and at myself for luring him into the demon's trap. I hated what he'd become, but I couldn't see a way forward without him. How had I allowed myself to be so reliant on a demon? Mother had warned me such attachments would take my freedom, and she'd only been talking about men. What would she say if she saw the knot I'd tied?

"I'm sorry," Kiin said, but when she laid a hand on my back, I spun and threw it off.

"Don't! He's *not* dead."

For once, her gaze softened, her palms cupping my cheeks. "You did all you could…"

"Stop it!" I pushed her away and rounded the table to check Wacław's heartbeat again. He couldn't be gone. Not after all we'd survived. Not after my deal with Death to bring him back just a moon before. We were supposed to be immortals, figuring out our strange, broken existences together, but I'd ruined that.

"Otylia, you are being a child."

I clenched my jaw, ignoring Kiin and placing my ear to Wacław's chest. Just one beat. That was all I needed. A single beat to signal he'd recovered, or even a whisper through the force of endings. End, though, was silent, as its wisps fled the distressed goddess who couldn't even save a boy whose soul she'd taken. If only Kiin would quiet enough for me to hear…

"… letting a demon find our hideout and influence our plans was a ris—"

Ta-tump.

I jumped back. Had I imagined that, or had his heart actually beat? Kiin eyed me, but I raised a hand sharply to silence her protest as I listened at his chest again. *Be stubborn for once.*

Ta-tump. Ta-tump.

A laugh escaped my throat, followed by tears, as I gripped Wacław's shredded clothes. "I told you," I whispered to Kiin, to Jawia, to Death, to myself. "This wretched realm won't take him. Not unless it takes me first…"

12

The Płanetník

Why does her touch change our mind, weaken my voice?

I AWOKE TO BLANKETS WRAPPED TIGHTLY AROUND ME and the rancid smell of death in the air. My tongue tasted of wool, my entire mouth as dry as a wood chip before it burned. No, definitely *as* it burned. That sensation dulled my whole body, and I groaned as I tried to raise my head.

How long was I out? Too long for certain, but the only hint to the time of day was the emptiness of the sleeping hall around me.

Torches lit the space, their crackle my only company. Well, them and half-a-dozen blankets that bound me like one would swaddle a disobedient infant. They were damp from my sweat, but even beneath them, I shivered more violently than during my worst illnesses—ailments from a past life. Mortality could inflict its pains upon me no longer. Those chały, though, had proven I wasn't invincible.

Rage burned through me at the memory of their talons slicing my flesh. I'd lived. They hadn't. But if I'd survived the stabbing and fall, then why did I feel like death?

Rolling to my side took more strength than it should've. Everything hurt, but my stomach ached most of all. Bandages covered the wound, still tender to the touch, and a pile of bloodied linens lay at my feet alongside a bowl of water. I cursed. Someone had been helping me heal for an extended period, which meant the Frostmarked would've had time to strike without me to punish them.

Of course, I had no doubts it had been Otylia who'd treated me, as the Daughters would distrust me for what I'd done. Blood for blood. Civilians would die for each Frostmarked I killed, but I didn't care. These weren't my people. They had foolishly allowed Marzanna to enslave them, and all that mattered was using them to weaken the winter goddess's hold on Jawia. Once I took Grudzień, I could return home, remove Mieczysław as high chief, and finally have the voice Father had stolen from me at birth. I would belong. I would have power. My exile would mean nothing when I slayed the Horde's armies before my tribe's eyes. Not that they would have a choice. Grudzień would ensure they listened to me.

My waking strength had faded already. I tried to reach for the water, but pain shot up my torso when I twisted free from the first blanket. Snarling, I reached for the winds only to find my *żityje* reserves all but empty, barely enough to keep me alive… Had there been enough to keep me alive?

The final moments before I'd blacked out ran through my mind. I'd only slowed my fall to the base of the Glasstone Tower with the winds. Shouting and the sounds of fighting had rung out in the distance, but I couldn't remember how much *żityje* I'd had left. That unnerved me more than I wanted to admit. My neck gave in to weariness, dropping my head to a makeshift pillow.

"We needed their help," the boy said in the back of my mind.

If we did, I replied, *then it was because of your unwillingness to take more blood sooner. You kept us sedated, mortal, for far too long. I will ensure we never feel this pitiful again.*

I sucked in a breath and threw off the remaining blankets. They felt as heavy as three sacks of harvest wheat, but I yearned to be free from their confinement. Beyond these walls, the winds called for me to wield their power. I would meet them. To regain my strength, though, I first needed to find a heart, so I rose onto unsteady legs, impatience prodding my anger with each excruciating effort. Great whirlwinds and lightning had come at my beckoning just moments before my fall. Did the gods mock me now as I struggled stand?

At least one did.

Otylia would've snickered and launched a sarcastic quip if she'd seen me so shaky. She'd always sneered at my weakness as a child, and she surely would do so again now that she'd pushed me away, no longer needing to hide her disdain toward me. Chasing her affection had been foolish. Even if she hadn't been a goddess, she'd been a loyal szeptucha to Dziewanna and Mokosz whose duty had been to slay demons. Her blade would've found my chest eventually.

"Then why did she care for us when we slept?" the weakling asked.

I ignored him. Otylia needed me as her weapon, like Marzanna had, but I was done serving.

My hands found the bowl of water, and though I drank greedily, water wouldn't satisfy my hunger. Time seemed to shift as I stepped into my invisibility and climbed to the surface. The winds needed *żityje*; invisibility had come naturally my entire life. My mortal soul had confined that power to when I'd slept. Why had I so often cowered until sunrise? Even without my wind powers, this alone would've granted me vengeance against all those who mocked me. Vengeance I would soon take.

The guards in the hideout's alley gave me no heed as I stepped into the shadows cast by the early morning sun. Dadźbóg was useless without his warmth, his light annoyingly exposing my footprints in the snow. Yet another god who did nothing to stop Marzanna. The tribes offered sacrifices for the gods' protection, but when had Perun, Swaróg, or Weles stopped villages from burning or droughts from starving their people? Priests spoke their legends. With each passing day, I doubted them more.

The winds carried a cry from the east.

I grinned and drew the Thunderstone dagger. It hungered too, and each step was a blur as I pursued that craving. My body was fire, my mind an anvil, and my demonic soul a hammer.

But I would feed.

13

Otylia

Each day I spend protecting these people is another Mother suffers, another away from my friends. Is it worth it?

I CROUCHED ALONGSIDE KIIN on a rooftop a few alleyways from the Glasstone Tower. Far enough to avoid the Frostmarked guards with the snow obscuring us in the night. Close enough for me to see the crimson stain Wacław had left covering the market ground.

It had been nearly a week since he'd surrendered to the demon, following Grudzień's call and unleashing his fury. I'd saved him with the blood from a warrior's heart, but he'd been unconscious ever since. His violence strayed into his dreams. Most nights, I awoke to him thrashing until I soothed him with a whispered prayer and water poured over his brow to cool his fever. If only it could do the same for his temper. Surely the Płanetnik, not Wacław, would meet me when he did finally wake again, and I feared what he'd do next.

When I wasn't re-wrapping Wacław's wounds, I worked each moment to repay my oath to Kiin. She had sent messages to her agents in the other cities in hopes of finding Sabina, Kuba, Vlatka, and the others who had passed through the Heart of Nawia, but travel was slow between the rough terrain and Frostmarked control of the region. There was no time to ponder if a reply would come. Our enemies did not wait.

We'd intercepted many Frostmarked strikes against innocents. Not enough. Whenever I tried to find rest, they captured and killed more. Wacław had ignited their fury. All of Huebia would suffer for it until I had the *żityje* to free Vastroth from Marzanna's tyranny. The force of endings had the answers—I was convinced of that much—but it eluded me, lost in the sea of voices assaulting my mind.

Somehow, Kiin seemed to have a better understanding of my power than I did. The moon had become a familiar friend as we'd run our rescue missions and helped reinforce areas of the city with traps. Like a spider, I could lurk in the shadows and use my power to *see* with the moon far better than the Frostmarked. I liked that. And when I'd explained the wisps of endings I saw when I was near people, Kiin had realized I could tell the locations of Frostmarked and their prisoners. Those little strands of light could show me the way. Maybe, I was changing their endings for the better.

All my confidence vanished on that rooftop.

Doubts and worries replaced it as Wacław's growing hunger throbbed in my chest. For blood, for *żityje*. Some part of him still resisted—I sensed it—but it grew weaker by the second, even in his coma. How long did we have until he was gone forever?

I'm going to save you, Wašek, I said through our bond, insistently using the name he'd told me not to. *Fight the demon. Fight Grudzień's pull on your anger. I promise I'll never abandon you.*

Except I already had.

"How long did your husband deal with the thoughts in his head?" I asked, running my gloved hands along the black coat and trousers Kiin had provided me.

"An eternity," Kiin said. The wind blew through her curled hair as she let it down, and though strands strayed across her face, she gave it no heed. "It's not the time he dealt with it that mattered. It's the time I went on, too caught in my own pain to realize he was hurting too."

"It's not always a blessing to feel their pain."

She hung her head. "It is, because without pain, you're dead, no matter how much your heart beats. Be glad you can feel his pain when he rejects it. He's alive, and as long as you remind him of that, there's time."

"Speaking of time…"

Dadźbóg's first rays appeared in the east. The sun god failed each day to bring his typical spring warmth, but even the smallest bit of light felt inviting on my skin. Unfortunately, the moon's power waned as day came, taking my flight and its small stream of *źityje* with it. It and food were my only sources of life unless someone was willing to become my first szeptucha. Not that I knew how to give them my mark or create a blood altar.

But *how* I would finally gain my *źityje* didn't matter until we found my friends.

In this rare moment to think, the wait was infuriating. My Ascension had raised the peak of my power to a level I still couldn't grasp, but it was limited without worshippers or at least priests to offer me sacrifices. I watched End's images in the wisps and heard voices everywhere I went in the city. Despite its temptations, though, I refused to enter another vision. Even the thought of touching someone made me shudder. The vision of Wacław's demonic rage during my Ascension flashed in my mind whenever it wandered, so I didn't let it.

I clenched and unclenched my fists at my sides as we raised our hoods and navigated Huebia's alleys. Kiin had given me a questioning look when I'd kept the gloves, but, thankfully, she'd complied without pressing further. They were a small barrier between people's endings and me. After the last week, I needed all the space I could get.

When we neared our hideout, a lanky boy sprinted to us from the top level. One of the hidden guards rushed to intercept him, but Kiin held out a hand. "It's all right. He's my messenger."

"I… I bring news," the boy mumbled, panting with his hands on his knees. "Ran clear 'cross the city to get here."

Kiin grinned. "And you'll be rewarded well for it. Come. Join us inside."

"What is it?" I asked her as we climbed through the trap door. "My friends?"

"We'll learn soon enough."

Though barely dawn, many people were already gone from the sleeping hall. Kiin had most of the Daughters working jobs that would appear typical to the Frostmarked but were essential to keeping the organization going. Food, herbs, and supplies were as necessary for a rebellion as they were for any household.

Kiin led us toward her chambers at the left end of the hall, but I stopped halfway. *No…*

My heart pounded as I stared at the empty place Wacław had lain when I'd left around noon the day before. He'd disappeared without a word. I should've been excited that he'd finally recovered, but my dread only deepened. What wound would he inflict on Huebia next? The city was massive. There was no way I'd find him before he'd extracted his revenge on the Frostmarked.

Kiin's gaze met me as she stopped at the doorway to her chambers. She stayed silent, but her words from the past days echoed in my mind. All we could do was execute on what we could control and plan for the failure of all we couldn't. There was nothing we could do to stop the Płanetnik for now, so the messenger came first. If his news was good, we'd have a solution to at least one problem. One of many.

A sharp smell met me as we entered the small room lined with chests of various sizes along the walls. Some odd substance burned in a bowl upon the table, sending a thin line of smoke rising into End's wisps. Unlike before, shards of every color glimmered on the ground, inconsistent with the torchlight, and they crunched underfoot as Kiin sat at the table.

"What is the message?" Kiin asked, her foot tapping nervously and cracking more of the shards.

The boy glanced at me and swallowed. "Uh… Right! Lady Ildes says the Frostmarked captured a group a couple days ago that sounds like the one you're looking for."

"Lady Ildes?" I asked. "Where is she from?"

"Sheresy, a city built into the sides of two cliffs," Kiin said. "It's a few days' travel south."

I took a deep breath, running my fingers along Weles's armband of wood and silver. *Finally, some good news.* Sabina would be with them, and Jawia was a foreign world to her. She'd protected me for weeks in Nawia. Now it was my turn to repay her loyalty… her friendship.

Kiin stood sharply and waved the boy out. "I'd tell you to send word, but there's no time. If the Frostmarked have captured them, we must act quickly." She turned back to me with excitement in her eyes. "Your demon has fled it seems, but the discovery of your friends may bring him back to us. I have use for him."

"I'll call for him," I said, my gut twisting at the thought.

She huffed. "This bond between you is unlike anything I've ever seen. To be able to speak to my husband now…" Her eyes glazed over for a moment before she slid the doorway's curtain shut again and returned to her desk. "I wish Wacław hadn't left this place. He is more dangerous than either of us know."

Believe me, I'm aware…

14

The Płanetnik

They make it so easy.

I QUICKLY FOUND THE SOURCE OF THE COMMOTION. Stealth was not a strength of Huebia's Frostmarked, and a pair of them were loudly harassing a woman at a busy intersection. She wore a hood like most Vastrothie women, but it appeared that the warriors had thought her suspicious for it. They gripped her by both her arms and hair, dragging her down the street while others just watched in fear. More evidence of Grudzień's power.

When they see true horror, then they won't cower before these mortals.

I released my invisibility and stepped into the wide alley before the warriors. Fighting from the air would be easier, but without *žityje*, melee would have to do. Hunger pounded like my racing heart, flooding my body with heat.

"Let her go!" I snarled.

The looks in the crowd's eyes told me enough. They'd either seen or heard of my fights before—exactly what I wanted. While Kiin insisted Huebia needed supplies and an organized, slow resistance to build support for the scions, I knew the truth. These people needed a reason to fight and a belief they could win. Grudzień amplified their emotions, using their fear, but the same could work for anger.

One of the warriors raised a knife to the woman's throat. "Move, or she dies."

And the blood doesn't reach Marzanna… tempting.

More innocents' deaths would hurt both the Daughters' goals and mine, though. Regardless of approach, we had to prove the Frostmarked weren't unbeatable. I'd shown much of that in the market, but the people needed to see it up close, when it was their family at risk.

I smirked and tightened my grip on the dagger's hilt. It hummed in my hand, thirsting for *żityje* almost as much as me. For the first time in a week, it was time to feast.

"Very well," I said with a step to the side. "Go and spill your people's blood for the goddess of death."

The warrior holding the dagger to her throat loosened his grip. Slowly, the Frostmarked walked past in an arcing pattern that kept as much distance between us as possible. One would think it an obvious strategy against a potential attacker, but it placed the one holding the woman right next to the opposite wall. The other stepped to my right to prevent me from cutting them off. A foolish mistake, leaving open his partner's back. I took advantage.

I'd never been the strongest, but in my sparring with Xobas, I'd found speed more important. It didn't matter how hard you swung your blade if it couldn't slip through your opponent's guard, and the warrior before me was slow.

Flanking the wrong direction and encumbered by the length of his spear so close to the wall, he failed to stop me from darting past and swiping at the captor's legs from behind. The dagger cut cleanly through the back of his thighs. He turned to counter, but he'd sheathed his sword in order to hold the woman and his dagger. The move allowed her to stumble free as his slice only found the air between us.

Years of facing Xobas's superior strength had taught me another thing—missing with a strike was deadly.

The warrior's momentum forced him to catch his balance for just a moment, but that was all I needed. With a backhanded grip on my dagger, I lowered my shoulder and threw all my weight into his chest.

We tumbled to the stone ground together. My stomach screamed from the chała's wound, but I bit my cheek through the agony, using it to fuel my push of the blade through the warrior's tortoise-shell armor. He yelled in agony at its burning puncture, a pain I was far too familiar with. I sensed his *żityje* seeping into the blade and licked my lips in anticipation of my own meal to come.

But another shout echoed from behind. *Right, the other fool.*

I pulled the dagger free and spun just as the straight end of his spear flashed toward me. Thunderstone struck bronze, his spearhead sliding down my blade before striking the cross-guard. Marzanna had claimed Swaróg forged the dagger with his almighty hammer, and it held firm despite the blow. The fight would become difficult if it went longer, though. Even a dagger crafted by a god couldn't make up for the range of the warrior's spear. So I let it go.

The warrior's eyes widened at my willingness to release my only blade. I dodged to the side as he tumbled forward, no longer able to lean on the tension of our clashing weapons. Then I kicked at the back of his knee with all the strength of my shaky legs, crumpling it enough for him to drop. I had neither my dagger nor my power to take advantage. Luckily, I didn't need them.

"You can kill him." I beckoned the crowd at the end of the alley onward, stepping back and grinning at their agitation. "Show him what happens to those who attack the women of Huebia."

A thrill rushed through me as they descended upon the sole warrior. One trained Frostmarked could slay many, but they tore away his spear before he could rise. Yes, they needed to *believe* they could kill a Frostmarked, and in their ferocity, they turned his face into a bloody mess in less than a minute. Even without weapons, their fists and feet could kill with enough strikes.

This victory was the people's, and as a cheer erupted, I returned to my invisibility and retrieved my dagger. Seeing me drain the heart of the first warrior would only dampen their mood as they carried the second's body through the street, chanting in their dialect. Rumors would continue to grow of a man who could emerge from the air and strike the Frostmarked at any moment, but they didn't need to know where I got my strength.

"Wašek, where are you?" Otylia asked through our bond as I savored the warrior's heart. It seemed forever since I'd eaten a human one, and its plentiful *žityje* was like the first meal of the harvest. My connection to the winds returned as my wound's ache faded.

Don't call me that, I replied. That name was from another life, one where I'd been weak enough to love. *I'm busy.*

"I sense your žityje. What did you do?"

I finished the heart and tilted my head to the sky, reveling in the rush of the winds. Huebia smothered them, trapped them, as it had me. But nothing could keep them from me for long. *I stopped the Frostmarked from abducting a woman and then let the people finish my work.*

"You incited an attack?"

The Vastrothie needed to see they could win, and I needed to feed.

"We need to focus on finding our friends and preparing our attack on Grudzień! Creating a revolt before then will only lead to chaos."

I sighed and wiped the blood from my chin. The cheering still echoed through the streets. *We wanted a distraction. What's a better distraction than thousands of people defying Frostmarked rule?*

"You know the answer to that. The Daughters are preparing defensive positions that won't *lead to innocents being slaughtered."* She paused, the intensity leaving her voice. *"You need to come back. Kiin wants to talk about our next steps, and I want to try out your mark on Narcyz. It's been too long since we've heard from home."*

Fine, but I'll need more žityje soon.

I made toward the hideout with frustration stirring within me. Otylia's tone had been sharp at first, but when it had softened, I felt her sorrow become my own. That pain was supposed to be gone. She'd moved on, and so had I. Just because Otylia had regrets didn't mean I could forget her rejection. She had made her decision—we both had.

15

Otylia

A single heart's blood mends more than a week of my healing. Why did Mother teach me to become a healer if she knew what Wacław would become?

THE TASTE OF BLOOD LINGERED ON MY TONGUE as we waited for the Płanetnik's arrival in the map room. Another two Frostmarked were dead, and the people celebrated in the streets with one's body. There would be repercussions.

Kiin's glare met the Płanetnik from her usual position on the far ledge when he pushed past the curtain and into the room. I lurked in the near corner, my gaze on my feet with his emotions overwhelming mine. The demon's call was endless within him. It overpowered even End's wisps, and the headache alone was enough to make me want to scream.

"How many innocents must the Frostmarked execute for you to realize this isn't the way?" Kiin asked, wiping away the sand on her coat. She'd been updating the map with locations of Frostmarked attacks, but neither of us had found a pattern. "Bloodlust is what turned the people against the scions."

The dark form rounded the room to the map and nudged the southern wall with his toe, his shadow passing over me as I kept my head down. "The people turned against the scions because your goddess stole their children."

"They have lost enough."

He waved a dismissive hand. "They've lost so much that Grudzień is enough to quell what little spirit is left within them. While you tell them your Earth Mother will save them, they cower, hopeless. Why? Because you've given them no proof that *they* can face the Frostmarked and win."

"You think you're giving them hope?" I asked. His dark eyes met mine as I held a gloved arm across my body, stepping further back as if the wall could protect me. "Hundreds have died already because of the chaos you've unleashed."

Kiin nodded. "While you've recovered, the Frostmarked have begun to sacrifice anyone suspicious, and their definition of suspicious is generous."

"Deaths are inevitable in war," the Płanetnik replied, his cold voice hanging like smoke.

"Some of those killed were our own." The stone rose and formed Kiin's staff. Taking it in her hand, she rounded the ledge toward him, and he actually stepped *away* as she hopped down before him. "The Daughters of the Earth are a family. We mourn their deaths as if they were our brothers and sisters by blood. You may have not been the one that sent them to the Earth Mother, but you were the one who drew the blade that started the war. All the blood running through Huebia's streets is your doing."

He scowled, but a pang through our bond struck my chest as he replied, "Did you just summon me to complain that I've actually acted instead of hiding in this cellar? Otylia said something about our next steps."

"I did," I said, reminding myself of the hope I'd felt knowing my friends still lived. "Kiin's agents in Sheresy found those who left Nawia with us. They've been captured, but they're alive."

"Kuba is with them?" he asked as his voice slipped to its familiar, careful rhythm.

I glanced at Kiin, but she only shrugged. "Our messenger didn't know more than that," she said.

The Płanetnik took a sharp breath, his fingers twitching at his side. "How far is it? I can fly us there with more *žityje*."

"Fly quickly and we could reach it in a night," Kiin said. "First, however, there is something I want to show you. Follow me."

Show him what? Kiin hadn't told me anything more of the 'use' she had for him. Was this it?

I sighed. Speaking to Narcyz and Eryk, the other płanetnik, through Wacław's mark would have to wait until the szeptucha had finished, but I was anxious to hear an update on Ara in the east and the Krowikie war against Solga in the west. Had Narcyz and Andrij managed to convince the two tribes that the Frostmarked Horde was the greater threat? Had Ara and Zakir found the remnants of their clans—and hopefully Xobas with them? So much of the fight ahead relied on us uniting any potential allies against Marzanna. As long as the tribes fought, all of them were vulnerable.

Right now, the only tribe I could impact was the Vastrothie, so I forced away those doubts. Others remained, but there was no stopping them until I figured out how to get my Wacław back. I had to.

Kiin led us silently to the basement. There was a different aura about her ever since the Płanetnik's arrival, and End's wisps circled her quickly, as if trying to tell me something. Whatever it was, though, I couldn't comprehend.

"Place your hands upon the wall," Kiin said to the Płanetnik as we reached the far side of the room, where Faarax served meals each day.

He raised his brow before looking to me. I took some comfort in that. Despite all he'd done in the last week, the real Wacław was in there somewhere. All I needed to do was dig him out. "You can trust her," I said.

That was enough to convince him. Still, he scanned the wall, skeptical of Kiin's instructions. After her aggression earlier, I wondered what Kiin intended, but she'd proven to me that she cared. We both knew what it meant to lose those we loved, and she knew where my heart lay.

Kiin whispered as the Płanetnik's hands touched the wall. He noticed, turning sharply toward her, but not before the stone closed around his wrists.

"What are you doing?" I exclaimed.

"Containing the problem," Kiin spat.

A snarl escaped the Płanetnik's throat as he fought his constraints. His eyes were wild. His heart pounded in my chest. All his *żityje* surged through him, sending End's wisps scattering with the rush of wind sweeping through the space. It wasn't enough, and when Kiin's staff cracked against his skull, he went silent, limp.

Instinct took over.

I drew Kwiecień as Kiin's whispers filled the cellar. My power had tried to warn me, but I hadn't understood. Now, with the stone pulling Wacław into the wall, I realized the threat came from within. So I struck.

Moonstone blade met sandstone spear, sending sparks flying as Kiin held my gaze. "Let me explain!"

"You had your chance!"

I threw her back and lunged. Despite my inexperience with a blade, Kwiecień felt perfectly balanced with each attack, incredibly nimble with each parry. It was as if the sword guided me more than I did it, and Kiin stumbled back with sweat beading on her brow as I pushed harder, unleashing the fury I'd contained ever since we'd arrived. Kiin had betrayed me, and now she would pay.

"This isn't the Earth Mother's will," she mumbled as she blocked another strike. "Please, Otylia, let us speak. This had to happen!"

Through labored breaths, I glared at the szeptucha, my hands still clutching the blade. Was she telling the truth? Did I have any way of knowing? The only thing I did know was what I'd seen in her past and experienced working with her the past few days. Kiin was not a deceiver. If anything, I doubted she could lie, yet she had just moments ago.

I stepped forward and thrust Kwiecień's tip to her throat. Its golden blade illuminated the space between us, showing the panic in her eyes. "Talk," I demanded. "What did you do to him?"

"I entrapped him within the wall," she replied, dismissing her staff. "We'd created a prison cell there in case we'd captured a Frost-marked too important to kill yet too strong to contain. Ironically, it has served its purpose with him."

"You lied! You're no better than Weles, than Jaryło!"

Slowly, she shook her head. "The demon is safe. I knew you wouldn't agree to this if I told you, so this was the only way. Lower your sword."

Wacław's anger through our connection confirmed he was alive, but that gave little relief as I stepped back, blade still raised. "You think he's too dangerous to bring to Sheresy."

"If you weren't a love-struck child, you would see so too."

"You were the one who told me not to push him away again!" I gritted my teeth and looked at the wall, which appeared unchanged. "You told me to remind him he's alive, that he can feel. How am I supposed to do that when he's trapped in stone? He *trusted* me."

She tapped her head with a single finger. "You can speak to him through your bond. That is a powerful gift—one you will need to convince him to break with the demon's curse. Until that time, he threatens the life of every single person in the Daughters of the Earth, and that's a risk I'm not willing to take."

"Was any of it true? Do you actually care about finding my friends and helping me gain a szeptucha of my own?"

"All of it was true." She moved toward the stairs, waving for me to follow.

I stuck to the shadows behind her. "Then how will we reach Sheresy? I can't fly without *żityje*."

With only a hesitant smile as a reply, she climbed the stairs. Her long coat snaked behind her, and the hissing of Weles's serpents echoed in my memories as we returned to the sleeping hall. Could I trust no one completely?

"Faarax," Kiin called across the hall, followed by the stout man rushing to her with a bow.

"How—" Faarax swallowed at the sight of my drawn sword. "How can I be of service?"

Kiin eyed me before returning her attention to him. "Have our tradesmen prepare a caravan for Sheresy with room for the Lady of Endings and myself. If the Frostmarked resist, tell them they may have a quarter of the shipment in return for their silence."

Faarax coughed. "You are aware, Mistress Kiin, that your absence will leave Ranno in command of the Daughters until you return?"

"You need not remind me," she said, her tone harsh. "Ranno and I disagree on many things, but she is a szeptucha all the same. The Earth Mother will guide her, as she has me to aid her granddaughter."

Red-cheeked, the man bowed and waddled more than walked away. I would've laughed on a normal day, but my entire body still burned. Kiin had betrayed me. No amount of help could regain that lost trust.

I grabbed Kiin's coat, forcing her to meet my glare. "No more secrets. Understand?"

"There will always be secrets," she replied, "but I will inform you of my plans from now on."

"Good, because everyone who's betrayed me has learned to regret it." I shoved her away. "I will free Wacław—no matter what you think. Even if it takes everything I have, I *will* bring back the boy I love."

Her expression turned solemn. "I hope you prove me wrong about him. First, however, you must mark a szeptucha so that you can truly wield your power. Only then can we save my people and the boy."

16

The Płanetnik

They lied to us. Otylia lied to us.

BLOOD POURED FROM MY KNUCKLES. Hot and exhausted from an eternity of punching the mountain of stone entrapping me, I dropped to the ground, slumping against the wall as I cursed Otylia and Kiin. All I'd done was slay the enemy. In return, they had locked me away like a monster.

I shook my head and unleashed a shout, but my rage wouldn't dull. Marzanna's Frostmarked would control this city until I stopped them. They'd slaughter my people in the north as I rotted away. Patience would not lead to victory. They were the true monsters, and it would take another to unseat them from the Glasstone Tower's throne and all the lands they'd enslaved before. How blind were they to miss that?

My soul yearned for *żityje* as I rested my head against the cold stone. The craving tore at every part of me, demanding I take the power I'd held before the battle at the market. Instead of feasting upon the Frostmarked, I would starve here.

Neither my Thunderstone dagger nor my fists had made any progress toward my freedom, and the winds couldn't penetrate the layers of rock around me. The isolation was suffocating. Was this how

I'd felt before the Golden Egg had awakened my powers the first time? Before I'd fought the zmora and channeled the storm? What a sad, lonely existence.

Before long, though, Otylia's voice came through our tether, *"Wašek, before you say anything, listen to me."*

I growled and tried to shut out her voice, but it pierced my skull anyway.

"I know you're mad. I am too. Kiin didn't warn me about this, and it's not what I wanted either, but there's nothing I can do. The earth doesn't answer my call."

Then convince her to let me go! I replied.

"I'm trying." She sounded as frustrated as me, and I grinned at the thought of her pacing, her nose wrinkled and her hands running through her hair. No! I tore away the image and drowned the boy who'd loved her. Lies. All of it lies. *"She's found a caravan that can take us to Sheresy so we can rescue our friends. Hopefully at least one of them can become a szeptucha for me."*

How does that help me escape?

"Just trust me. Kiin will let you go if you've calmed."

Calmed? I scoffed. *You mean if I reject what I am?*

Silence hung over us for a minute, and I felt her sorrow choking her. That stupid voice in the back of my mind taunted me, claiming I should feel guilty for that. I didn't.

"What you are isn't your choice," she finally said. *"Who you are is, and I know this isn't who you are."* When I didn't reply, she sighed and finished, *"Contact Narcyz and Eryk through your mark if you can. We should know what's happening with the Solgawi and clans, and I'd really like to hear that Ara is okay. Please, promise me that."*

I fought the resentment clutching my chest. She was right. We needed to hear from our friends north of Perun's Crown, but I had plans of my own for them. Preparations... *All right. As long as I can see Kuba when he's back.*

"I'll see if I can convince Kiin. And Wašek?"

What?

"I know you don't believe it, but I'm sorry for everything."

I couldn't find a reply, so I just closed my eyes and thumbed my Frostmark. Its slow pulse matched that of Grudzień far above. Temptation, surrounding me and joining the craving in my soul until nothing else remained.

Part 2
To the Depths

17

Narcyz

I'll do us all a favor and shut him up forever.

MIKOŁAJ LAUGHED AND HELD A HORN HIGH as the warriors around his fire echoed insults directed at me. They were idiots, all of them. Jacek's eldest son had a special dose of stupidity, but Waclaw had asked me to turn Krowik's armies away from our petty tribal war with Solga and rally them against Marzanna's forces. So I had to use my words. Just for tonight.

"Are you deaf?" I said, flicking my ear. "Because you sure as Weles aren't listening to me!"

Andrij cleared his throat from beside me. His hair was the color of copper just minutes after being taken from the smith's flames, and it seemed to glow as he paced around the circle of warriors. He never looked away from their leader. "What Narcyz means to say is that the Frostmarked Horde's threat is no joke. Entire Anshayman clans have fallen to them, and both of our tribes will be next if we don't end this war with Solga."

With another swig of oskoła, Mikołaj staggered to his feet and grabbed Andrij's tunic at the chest. "I remember you."

"Andrij delivered Boz's message at the Drowning of Marzanna," I said. "We ran into him again at Kynnytsia, and it turns out the Astiwie king is more a bastard than your brother."

Another round of laughter erupted from the warriors at Mikołaj's signal. There were others scattered among the tents of the war camp, but those desperate to seek their commander's attention followed Jacek's eldest like dogs to scraps. "You always did despise Wacław," he slurred. "He's a demon now, huh… Father was right about little Half-Chief."

"No, he wasn't."

Mikołaj raised his brow.

I clenched my jaw, knowing how I would've hated myself for defending Wacław just moons before, but—gods send me to Oblivion—he'd changed my mind. Wouldn't have ridden across bloody Solga for a week if he hadn't. "Wacław's a demon, yeah. But I've seen him protect people he hates because it's right. How many demons do you know who'd rather sit around talking about a peace deal instead of fighting?"

"I don't kna' any demons!" a warrior near me shouted.

I cracked my knuckles, my patience out. As the warrior laughed at his own joke, I struck him in the temple and sent him sprawling alongside the fire. That wound would throb for hours.

"You haven't changed," Mikołaj said, releasing Andrij and approaching me. He reeked of alcohol and piss. "If your stories are true, Wacław definitely has. *If.*"

"You want proof he's a demon?" I asked.

He shrugged and downed the rest of his horn. "Would sure make my night."

Oh, I'll make sure you remember this either way.

Making a show out of it, I rolled up my tunic sleeves. My clothes were cleaner than these warriors', even after traveling with few supplies or unfrozen water to wash in. Pa always said you can tell a good warrior from the bad by how he takes care of his equipment—even a clean tunic could be the difference between comfort and an infected wound. My mistake had been expecting more from men led by Mikołaj and who served High Chief Mieczysław. Made my tongue taste like mud just thinking of saying that stupid chief's name.

Mikołaj dropped his horn into the dirt. "What in the Mangled Woods?"

Wacław's Eclipsemark glowed a sharp red upon my right forearm. Resembling a blood moon during a partial eclipse, silver diagonals sliced across it with a downward crescent cut from its top. I grinned looking at it now. That lightning had hurt like a thousand hornet stings, but it sure looked tougher than any warrior's warpaint or tattoo.

"Half-Chief did that to you?" a warrior asked, pushing another out of the way.

Mikołaj grabbed my wrist. "But only gods…"

"Nah." I yanked my arm free. "Powerful demons can mark people too, and Wacław sure as iron is a powerful one. I've seen him shoot lightning from his hands and call storms from nothing."

"Yer full of it," a warrior replied, his complaint echoed by the other drunkards.

I expected Mikołaj to agree, but he raised a fist to quiet them instead. "It's obvious something's happened," he shouted, each "s" slurred like a snake strangling his tongue. "Marzanna's Curse killed Father, and if she is still alive, I'd happily slay her myself."

"Get in line," I said.

Andrij swept back into the conversation, stopping beside me with his blue and gold Astiwie cape flapping behind him. It was hard to remember he'd been a commander in their ranks. Only for a few months, but I was more jealous than I'd ever admit to him. "Do you believe the Solgawi would agree to peace if they understood the threat ahead?" he asked.

"My opinion doesn't matter," Mikołaj muttered. "Mieczysław—Perun strike him down—will send everything into this war, even without the clans' reinforcements. You said he exiled Wacław already. What would he do to me if I turned back?"

I crossed my arms. "Nothing. You're the one leading the army."

"Part of it. Serwacy's got his and Mieczysław's men further north. No way the high chief would give me more warriors than his allies."

"So you're gonna do nothing?" I asked. "Jacek united our tribe, but you'd rather sit in these stupid hills than charge into battle against a *goddess's* army? We'll be heroes when we win this!"

With a shake of his head, he sauntered to the fire and plopped down beside it, his dark blue eyes lost in the flames. "Stay the night. Once my head's clear, I'll give you an answer." Then he called for another horn of oskoła to be brought to him.

"Let's go," Andrij whispered to me, gently pulling on my arm.

I pushed him off. "I'm not going anywhere until we've got an army."

"And if Mikołaj refuses?"

"I'm good with a spear and a knife."

He rolled his eyes and headed through the trees, toward our gear. I growled but followed. *Why am I letting myself listen to* him? *Andrij isn't even part of our tribe.*

What was our tribe really? The Krowikie had selected Mieczysław as high chief, and the Astiwie followed the lunatic King Boz who'd tried to kill all of us a moon before. Andrij and I were warriors, but we refused to follow our leaders' commands. We had no people. Well, we didn't unless you counted those who'd traveled with us from Kynnytsia, plus Otylia—whatever she was anymore. But our small group was hardly a tribe.

As we unpacked our bed rolls, I glanced at Andrij. My traveling companion. My friend. My… I shook my head. *Stop it. Pa would kill you for looking at him like that.*

Andrij had been annoyingly calm when we'd first met. A commander with little confidence. During the Battle of Kynnytsia, though, he'd fought by my side against his traitorous king and had stayed there ever since. I'd never liked people, but Pa always said to not travel alone. At least Andrij was better than most.

"One of us should keep watch," I said, tearing away my gaze with a cough before checking my shield for signs of wear. A single crack could mean death in battle if it shattered.

Andrij pulled our shared waterskin from his bag and refilled his canteen. "You don't trust your own people? Isn't Chief Mikołaj from your village?"

The shield was solid, so I strapped it to my back, averting my gaze. "That's the problem, isn't it? I know exactly how loyal they are."

"Understandable, but you don't trust anyone."

"I trust you."

"Hmm." He replaced the waterskin and shut his bag before lying down, eyes closed. "Glad someone does. Boz has probably been spreading my name as if I were some kind of demon."

I laughed. "And *he's* the idiot that worked with one to ambush us."

"Granted, we're relying on one as well."

"It's not the same. Half-Chief's too gentle to hurt a rabbit. No way he could kill people as easily as Bidaês."

Andrij opened his eyes again, meeting mine. With only the moonlight here, I couldn't read his expression, but I assumed it to be sorrow. He'd been sad ever since we'd left Małe Wzgórze and his mentor, Valentyn. The deep kind. I had no idea how to fix it.

I grabbed my spear and stood. My cheeks burned, and I hated the feeling in my stomach that wished to never leave his side. Warriors couldn't afford such weakness. "Sleep. I'll take first watch."

"Don't go far," he replied. "Ara warned me what you're like when you're drunk."

"Wouldn't be much of a spotter if I drank on the job."

"Not sure you're much of one anyway."

With that, he wrapped his wool blanket around himself and closed his eyes. I sighed, the cold wood of my spear jabbing at my blistered hands. Moons of travel had taken their toll, but sleep could wait. Better tired than dead.

Campfires crackled in each direction. There were hundreds of warriors spread throughout these woods, a few days west of the Krowik River. Based on what Mikołaj and his men had been willing to tell us, there had been nothing more than a few skirmishes and raids on small Solgawi villages. That should've given me hope of stopping the war. It didn't. All we'd done is grant the Solgawi an excuse to invade if we retreated to fight the Frostmarked Horde in the east. It didn't matter. We had to try anyway.

There was so much out of my control. My entire life, I'd thought

I'd be like one of those warriors gathered around the fires, but our journey east had changed everything. When gods and demons fought, where was my place? What use was I when Wacław could channel lightning and Otylia was a literal goddess?

My role is here, I told myself. *Giving them the army they need.*

It wouldn't be enough. I was a terrible negotiator, and one army alone would be crushed by the Horde. Without the Astiwie and clan armies fighting alongside the united Krowikie one, we were hopeless. Andrij took that with a saddened heart, but I just fought harder.

Most of the fires faded in the next hours. Only the spotters like me remained awake, waiting in case of a Solgawi attack. Quiet came with it, and crickets in the dead brush filled the night as I leaned against a tree.

Dead plants were another problem I had no way to solve. Pa had taught me how to strike hot iron with a hammer, but even in good seasons, growing grain made little sense to me. In times like this, when even the trees lacked their leaves and nothing new sprouted from the ground... It didn't take a farmer to understand we'd all starve soon if nothing changed.

It wasn't just us, either. Andrij and I had hunted for most of our supplies, but there were already fewer deer, rabbits, and squirrels than I'd ever seen. Just the thought made me worried.

Sometime deep into the night, pain struck my arm like a hot iron, tearing me from my thoughts as a voice echoed in my head, *"Narcyz, you there?"*

"Gods, Wacław!" I cursed. The searing pain faded, but a dull throb lingered as I stepped further from Andrij. "That is you, right?"

There was nothing for a few breaths before the voice returned. *"It is."*

I huffed. "Guess you're alive, then. Thanks for telling me sooner—not that I cared. Andrij's been weeping himself to sleep thinking about you."

No laugh came, and I shuddered in the silence. Hearing his voice in my head was more uncomfortable than I'd thought it would be.

"I doubt it," Wacław replied. His voice was sharper than normal,

less wimpy, but he *was* a demon. What else had I expected? *"It's been a problematic couple of weeks, but we're alive and in Jawia."*

He explained all he and Otylia had been through in Nawia, and I grinned when he said Kuba had returned too. That sarcastic idiot had been asking to be stabbed. His death had been that of a hero, though, and to see him alive in any form would bring me a badly needed dose of laughter.

"When you coming back?" I asked when he'd finished.

"I wish I knew. The Vastrothie have been conquered by the Frostmarked, but we can uproot them from at least their capital. After that, we might have another army in our fight."

"What about—"

"You don't have to speak aloud," he interrupted. *"Wherever you are, if you'd rather just think your reply, that works too."*

I grumbled under my breath, "Stupid sorcery."

Luckily, he either ignored me or hadn't heard. *"Narcyz, what's happened with the Krowikie armies? Is my brother alive?"*

He is, I replied, silently this time. This would take some getting used to. *But Mikołaj doesn't think turning back would work. Chief Serwacy and Mieczysław's other allies are leading most of the warriors.*

"Serwacy?" Wacław released a snarl, frighteningly similar to Bidaês's wilkołak one. *"Miko's married to his daughter. Why would he support Mieczysław instead?"*

Don't know. Don't care.

"Of course you don't, but I need you to care about what happens next."

As long as it involves killing demons or idiots with blades, I'm in. No more of this talking stuff. That's your thing.

He scoffed at that. *"A lot has changed, and my plan will surprise you. Have you kept your knife sharp?"*

I grinned. *You know it.*

"Good, because you might need it soon..."

18

Ara

If only I had Sosna's hope.

THE RED FOX ZIPPED ALONG THE EDGE OF THE WYZRA RIVER, yapping with each stride. *Please be something for once.* Sosna may have been a gift from Dziewanna, but she had an awful habit of getting *very* excited at even the whiff of an animal. Though hunting had been difficult, fauna wasn't my concern.

"We'll have to cross," I said, stopping Wacław's chestnut horse, Tanek, alongside Zakir's. Sosna ran ahead without care.

Zakir looked east over the Wyzra and the hills beyond, where we hoped to find the remnants of my Zurgowie clan and his Simukie one. It seemed an eternity since we'd carried Wacław's unconscious body away from Kynnytsia after the Astiwie ambushed us. We'd both lost people we cared for in the attack: his grandfather—Marzban Katiôn—and Xobas. With our chaotic escape, we still didn't know if either were alive. I prayed to both my Zurgowie gods and Otylia's Krowikie ones that they were.

"It has grown colder each sunset," Zakir said, almost too quiet to hear. "At this rate, the Wyzra should be frozen enough to support us by tomorrow night. It would be safest to cross then, or our horses could suffer from the chilled water."

He's right, as usual. I was fond of the Simuk, but he needed to lose his knack of knowing everything. It made me feel dumb, even if he didn't intend to demean me.

"Then we camp here for the night?" I asked, looking to the setting sun in the west.

Zakir scratched his mangled mess of black hair. Whether Katiôn was dead or not, Zakir would be the Simukie marzban—their equivalent of a warlord—someday. Unlike his idiot brother, Bidaês, he didn't obsess over his appearance, but I so badly wanted to show him how confident a leader he could be if he listened to my advice. His sharp jaw and strong shoulders were *begging* to be displayed on a commander instead of an alchemist too busy to cut his hair or shave his stubble. He didn't need to actually go to war, just appear capable of doing so.

"You're doing it again," he said. "Imagining I am someone I am not."

Even his words are perfect. Maybe it was okay his appearance wasn't. "I don't want you to be someone else," I said, raising my hand to his cheek. Panic filled his gaze at the tender touch, but that just made me prouder for somehow taking his attention from his experiments. "I worry about what will happen when we find our people."

"If my grandfather is dead, then there are better leaders to replace him," he said, pushing his horse on.

I sighed before following. Why couldn't he see his potential? "Who should lead then? Zhaleh? That priestess is more aggressive than even High Priestess Rasa was."

"Let someone else choose."

My shoulders slumped as we continued in Sosna's wake. In the past days, I'd been worried when she disappeared for significant portions of the day. She always found her way back to us, though, and sometimes even brought dinner in her teeth. Nature's death weighed heavy on me, but that ball of fur knew how to make me smile. I needed it. With endless hours of riding, I'd had far too much time to ponder what had happened to Otylia and Wacław in the afterlife they called Nawia. Maybe Wacław had contacted Narcyz already. I had no mark, but Eryk, the płanetnik he'd marked in the Mangled Woods, was supposedly still in Astiwie lands. I awaited Eryk's appearance each day. Until then, I could only pray Otylia was safe.

"Just come back alive," I whispered to her. "Things made more sense with you here."

I missed the days before the Drowning of Marzanna, when all that mattered had been helping Father with his hunts, trading for Mother's sewing supplies, or flirting with the boys Otylia hated—so, effectively all of them. Except Wacław of course. It hadn't taken much for me to realize there was something else there. Those two had more layers of tension than I could bother to count, and her taking his mortal soul had definitely made it worse. Fortunately, I was missing the resulting drama.

A calm came with that thought. Drama meant they were alive, and they *had* to be alive. If they weren't, what was the point? Allied clans or not, we'd be doomed anyway when the Frostmarked Horde arrived.

When Otlezd set, or Dadźbóg—it was hard to know who the real gods were anymore—we finally made camp on a ridge west of the Wyzra. I sat on its edge, staring over the hills beyond as Zakir tied up the horses. *They're somewhere out there. Xobas, our people… Some of them must have survived.*

"Do you think we'll actually find them?" I asked over my shoulder, but Zakir was busy talking to himself about some potion. His horse, Eliastr, lingered near, connected to him by Simukie rituals. "Never mind then…"

Each night, we slept alongside more than with each other. A light sleeper, Zakir would jolt awake if I touched him, mumbling before he drifted off again. So I gave him space—a canyon no longer than my finger—and lay awake with thoughts swarming my mind. About him, about us, and about Otylia. I should've feared for my family, but something told me they would be all right. We were nomads. We'd escaped war before. Even if Dwie Rzeki fell, it wasn't truly our home, and we would find a new place to rest for a time. That didn't mean I *wanted* our village to fall.

Sosna returned late in the night, squeezing herself between us with all the grace of a mare in heat. Claws raked my cheek, and Zakir groaned at the interruption before making space. Despite the discomfort at first, I was glad to have something warm to cuddle with. A soft fox would do in place of a bony boy. For now.

Just when I was finally able to drift off again, the winds howled around us. They swirled across the river and caused the lifeless willows to creak menacingly. All I could do was stare up at their swaying as a chill ran down my spine.

"Not now, Marzanna," I whispered, trying not to wake Zakir. The goddess's chill and smothering death surrounded us each day, but she hadn't come for us since Wacław had left.

A figure appeared on the gales. Tall and gray, he gripped a staff as he stepped upon the shore, watching me. I should've been afraid, but there was a fatherly look in his eyes, sorrowful. His tattered robes dragged across the ground as he neared and bowed.

"Are you the huntress called Ara?" he asked.

With one hand on the hilt of my hunting knife, I nodded.

The man noticed my sleeping companions and turned toward the river. "Come. Let us speak where we will not disturb your friends. I am called Eryk, and Wacław Lubiewicz sent me to find you. You have no reason to fear me."

My heart jumped. *Wacław's alive. Otylia must be too!*

We walked to the river's edge, and he sat upon the bank as I crouched, ready for anything. Seeing the old płanetnik now, it amazed me we'd once barely survived a fight with him and his Frost-marked allies. Appearances could be deceiving. Eryk bore Wacław's Eclipsemark, but he was still a threat—one I could never take in a fight.

"The boy has rarely contacted me since I've taken his mark," Eryk said, sighing as he looked to the sky. "Marzanna used to do so nearly every day."

"What did he say this time?" I asked. "Otylia, is she alive?"

He nodded slowly, and I let myself fall back in relief.

"Thank the gods! I've waited so long to hear from them. Why hasn't he contacted us sooner?"

"The young goddess and Wacław are in a land south of here, the

Dominion of Vastroth," Eryk said. "They escaped Nawia some time ago, but something Wacław called Grudzień pulled them to the city of Huebia."

I shook my head. "A Moonstone? Why? What's so important there?"

Eryk looked at me, his eyes thoughtful. "Mokosz's priestesses once ruled Vastroth, but it has fallen to the Frostmarked. Wacław believes that by helping those loyal to Mokosz, they can bring a third army to the fight against the Horde."

"Can they?"

"That is not for me to understand," he replied. "What I do know, however, is that I have found where your people have gone."

I shot to my feet in another rush of excitement. "Where? How far from here?"

"Calm, child." He chuckled and pushed himself up with his staff. "Wacław had allowed me to search for my daughter, Yeva, for some time, but once I found her, the winds led me to the clans."

"Tell me!" I snapped through bated breaths, grabbing his robes. "Is Xobas with them? Marzban Katiôn?"

The winds rose to his defense, but I held on tight as he replied, "The one called Xobas leads them, yes. I told them to go southwest, toward the village of Likiec where I am from. It is where I hid Andrij's family from King Boz."

My mind churned as I released him. Once we crossed the Wyzra, we could be at Likiec in two days based on Wacław's description when he'd helped Eryk. "Won't Boz know they're in his lands still?"

"The king of Astiw is licking his wounds from the Battle of Kynnytsia. He may have ambushed your people, but many died on his side as well. If the clans have survived this long, they must have evaded or killed the few scouts he had left to send after them, but their numbers are sparse."

Dread hung over me at that. "How many?"

"No more than four hundred warriors—both man and woman." His head dropped. "Perhaps a thousand total, but likely more have died since."

"Gods…" My stomach churned. When we'd reached Kynnytsia, there had been over a thousand warriors and twice that number of children and those unable to fight. "Boz killed over two thousand people?"

"The clans fought hard, but they had already turned over many of their horses. Surrounded and without their most powerful tool in battle, they had little hope but to push through the encirclement and flee."

I drew my knife and glared at its iron blade in the moonlight as if it were Boz himself. "I'll make that lunatic pay."

"The Horde may do that for you."

"How close are they?" I asked, shuddering at the thought of the bone-wielding riders rushing through the Narrow Pass. Wacław had described their undead leader, Koschei, in horrifying detail after the east wind showed him the Horde's advances.

Eryk took a heavy breath and stomped his staff into the dirt. "They have entered the pass. With their usual speed, it'll be less than a week before they reach Kynnytsia."

I looked back to Zakir. "Then we need to leave now! If they catch the clans…"

"Wacław has a plan. Wake the boy who is now marzban and come with me. I will tell you the rest as you ride to your people."

The boy who is now marzban. I swallowed as I approached Zakir, realizing the time had come. He was a warlord now. He would lead the Simukie forward.

What did that make me?

19

Otylia

I'm coming, Sabina.

OUR COVERED WAGON SWAYED as we crested yet another dune, keeping me awake. Sleep would've been a stranger regardless, as I anticipated a chała to swoop from the darkness and strike us at any time. I'd never been pulled in a wagon before, and even with the ability to move about it without tipping because of the oxen's strength, I was constantly on edge. Part of that weight shed from my shoulders the moment Huebia slipped from sight. In Nawia, I'd been fully aware of how constrained I'd felt, but the city had been more subtle in its entrapment.

"Grudzień is weaker already," I said, taking a deep breath of the rapidly warming night air. The push on my emotions was still present, but it seemed Marzanna's influence waned beyond the capital despite her Frostmarked controlling the other cities.

"I feel it too," Kiin replied. Her voice was quiet, though, and she closed her eyes. "It's like I was chained before."

"And you're telling me you're not afraid right now?" I quipped. Getting used to the sight of endless desert out the wagon's open back was difficult, and *I* was the immortal.

She gritted her teeth, clutching her coat tight around her. "I'm not afraid of the desert. All land is the Earth Mother's, whether arable or not."

"Then what are you afraid of?"

"Leaving the ground like you and your płanetnik can." She took a long breath. "The Earth Mother would be distant there."

Memories of my disconnect with Dziewanna flashed in my mind, and I cursed myself for mocking Kiin. "It was the same for me when I died. Mother's strength was fading even on Jawia, and in Nawia, Weles's control over the swamps overpowered what little connection I had to her."

"What was it like, giving up your status as a chosen to Ascend?" she asked.

I instinctively felt for the marks on either side of my neck: Dziewanna's Bowmark and Mokosz's Mothermark. Gone. A part of me had disappeared with them. "I'd hoped to become Dziewanna's szeptucha since I was a little girl. So much of who I wanted to be was bound to that title. Losing it was like slicing away my soul, severing its bond with the world around me." I clutched Mother's amulet at my chest. "I was alone for years after Mother's death, but as long as I had my goddesses, that was all that mattered. Not my tribe. Not my father's complaints. Not even Wacław's abandonment. I could never truly be alone with their *żityje* flowing through me."

The words caught in my throat as I stared back at the sand kicked up by the cart's wheels. "Weles called the first Trial 'Isolation'. I passed when I removed their marks, but I don't think I've ever really moved on. I thought Ascending would fix it. It bound me to the silver fox, the force of endings, and the moon, but I'm still lost, empty. They don't offer the Great Mother's sage advice or Dziewanna's spur of freedom. Maybe being with Wacław, even for just a short time, disguised how alone I truly feel now. Who could understand a goddess?"

For a few minutes, she didn't reply, and we continued on in silence, only the sounds of oxen and creaking wood breaking the night. My chest felt like a cavern. Empty, endless. I almost wished to close my eyes and fall into its depths, forgetting all I'd done and all I'd lost.

I didn't understand why I'd told Kiin so much after her betrayal. Even with Ara, I'd never been comfortable sharing my greatest fears. She'd often figured them out anyway, but with Kiin, I just rambled like a child. We'd argued many times in recent days, and she'd trapped Wacław without consulting me first. Oddly, her willingness to challenge me only drew me closer to her. Hurting my feelings didn't matter to her as long as we found the correct solution for her people, and I wondered if that was what it truly meant to be a leader.

Kiin would've sacrificed herself to save the people in the hideout that the Daughters had lost the week before. When Jacek or Mieczysław—that warmongering bastard of a chief—would've demanded, Kiin gave, and she did so freely. Not because it helped her. Not even because she was helping the individual people. But because she had a vision of what was truly *right*. Gods help anyone who defied it.

"We let our roles define us," Kiin finally said. "It's hard to know who I'd be if I weren't a chosen of the Earth Mother. I don't envy you."

I clutched my legs and stared out the wagon's back. The moon met me there, but with little *žityje* in my soul, I could feel but barely wield it. That just made trying to understand my power all the more frustrating. Flight had been remarkably simple. Illusions with the moon's light were more difficult but possible. All of End's possibilities, though, were a mystery I struggled to grasp. I had commanded creatures of death and decay against Weles's warriors. I had seen visions of endings both in the future and past. Within me, I sensed the force pushing me to do more, but what was I capable of?

That question made me more grateful for my new gloves. They kept out the cold, yes, but they would also prevent me from diving into visions I was unprepared for—which was all of them as far as I was concerned. Unfortunately, they hadn't stopped the wisps from following me.

Three of them circled me here. I'd identified Kiin's violet one, as whispers of her memories haunted me with it, but I refused to touch the images shifting in it like smoke. Two visions of her had been more than enough to know her past and future were tragic.

Get out of my head, I told the voices carried by End's power. *Will you never be silent?*

They wouldn't. In Huebia, there had been countless distractions, but it was just the sky, Kiin, the wagon drivers, and me as we traveled south. My mental strength faded with my *žityje*, and the whispers slowly worked their way into my mind until I was too exhausted to resist. Somewhere over the seemingly endless desert, I finally listened.

"The Earth Mother will bring Yesike back to me," Kiin's voice said in my head. *"If I save her city, her children, and her granddaughter, she has to. The Winter Witch and the demon boy will no longer stain her purity."*

The whisper looped over and over. Desperate, almost as if she were trying to convince herself she believed Mokosz would save her son. My heart ached with it, and I looked at Kiin differently as we rested on bedrolls we'd laid in the cart. Was this why she'd trapped Wacław?

"Why are you staring at me?" she asked after some time. "Don't try to hide it. I noticed a while back, but you just kept going."

I gritted my teeth. No one, not even her, could know about this power. Whether I'd heard her thoughts or her true intentions, I didn't know, but either would make people distrust me. "I was just thinking about Wacław."

She furrowed her brow. "I did what was safest for all of us."

"Will you actually let him go?"

"Yes. If you find a way to tame the beast within him, I will release him."

The whispers told another story. Could I blame her for lying? She needed me, and killing Wacław would only drive me away from her cause. In his current form, he *had* become a beast, but I would find a way for him to regain his sanity. I wouldn't let Kiin or anyone else take him from me.

"You don't believe me," Kiin said.

I huffed and shook my head. "Excuse me for not trusting someone who helped me walk the boy I love into a trap."

"He's not that boy anymore."

"Don't tell me who he is!" I snapped. "I've known Wacław my entire life. I feel his emotions in my soul. Don't you think I know that he's changed?"

Her lips pressed into a tight line. "Otylia, I'm sorry, I—"

"No, you don't get to be sorry for me. The funny thing is, I thought you might actually be my friend, my ally, but you're too focused on the 'Earth Mother' to realize she isn't the one bothering to help you. I am."

"How dare you!"

I summoned my spear and spun, grabbing hold of her. She barely flinched as the spear's tip hovered before her nose. Fury burned within me, and I glared down at her. "Mokosz's blood runs in my veins. I don't know why she's done everything she did, but I have to believe she sent me here for a reason. Lying to me just gets in the way. Do it again and I'll kill you."

She didn't fight back, but her voice remained firm. "That boy will unleash more destruction than you know."

"I'm the goddess of endings, Kiin. You don't think I know that?"

"You couldn't foresee my capture of him."

I released a breath, dismissing the spear. "No, I couldn't."

"You're afraid," she said as she pushed away my hand. "Those gloves reveal that much. You can't stand to even touch someone out of fear of what your power will show you, yet that power is your greatest ally. Wacław will never tell you everything. The force of endings won't lie, because it is part of you. Stop acting like it's some external gift you're channeling."

It won't lie, but you will. I will.

How could I even trust myself after what I'd done to Wacław? Were the voices the only things I could trust? The desired ends of those around me, both secret and not?

"The Winter Witch and the demon boy will no longer stain her purity," Kiin's voice echoed in my head, reminding me of her will.

No, I decided. I couldn't trust Kiin. I couldn't trust her allies or mine. I couldn't even trust the gods. For so long, I had clung to Mokosz and Dziewanna for guidance, but they had hidden the truth of my soul. Everyone, mortal and not, lied for their own gain, so I wouldn't trust them.

But neither could I trust myself.

Only End's force couldn't deceive or twist the truth. Only its visions could show me reality's future and past. Only its visions could tell me people's true intentions. I sighed. If only it could reveal my own…

"It will be days before we reach Sheresy," Kiin said, breaking me from my thoughts. "Let us rest. Earth Mother knows we both need it if we're going to rescue your friends and return to capture Grudzień. We have a long few weeks ahead."

"It has been years since I've seen these cliffs," Kiin said, waking me as the western Tiop River curved through two great rock faces. Three days had passed since we'd left Huebia, and this had been our first night on the boat the Daughters had secured for us and two fishermen to finish the journey. The waning Maj moon hovered overhead. Each night, it gave me a bit more *žityje*. Far too little.

"What do you mean?" I asked. The space before us seemed as desolate as the desert we'd passed.

She pointed toward the cliffs. "This is Sheresy, built into the rocks by the Earth Mother's chosen."

I opened my mouth to ask another question, but then the moonlight illuminated the narrow stone bridges connecting the cliffs at various heights. At first appearing as nothing more than cracks in the rock, staircases and entryways covered the cliffs on either side. A few figures climbed the stairs with buckets of water hung from bars over their shoulders. Back and forth they winded ever upward, hundreds of feet from the river to the peak.

"We'll need to land at the west face's pier," Kiin said. "The Frostmarked will be watching it closely, and your pale face and accent will give you away in seconds."

I rolled my eyes. "I've been sneaking around Huebia for a while now without being caught. I can handle myself."

"Oh really?" She gave a wry smile, signaling for the fishermen to stop rowing short of the city. "Good luck finding Ildes on your own. Huebia is a maze, but most of Sheresy is winding tunnels in the cliffs. You'd be lost forever without me."

"Fine. How do you intend to get me through without being seen? I don't exactly resemble your people, and my illusions don't work without *žityje* and the moon."

She gestured at my body. "Gods change forms, can't they? The Earth Mother alone proves that, as you claim to see her as one of your people, far different than how she appears to us."

"Just another thing I don't know," I muttered. "Weles changed his appearance all the time, but he didn't teach me how to. Unless…" I rain my fingers through my hair, remembering my silver fox pelt. It appeared at my call.

She narrowed her gaze. "A fox isn't exactly a common sight here, but if that's all you can do, it's better than a hood the Frostmarked will remove the second we step onto dry land."

"Hopefully I can do even that." I'd only shifted to a fox twice: during the Trial of Connection and when Tibês had trapped me within its form. He had claimed I could do it without jumping the blades I'd used before, but how?

Kiin tapped her foot as the fisherman stared at me curiously. "Hurry. They're not rowing, but the current will carry us into sight soon."

"Shut up and let me focus!"

She did, and I closed my eyes, dropping to my knees as the boat swayed back and forth. The silver fox's connection was inside me. I'd felt it when I leapt those blades. Now, I reached for that carnal presence as I whispered in the old tongue and let my emotions wash over me.

Fear. Anger. Hunger. Yearning. They replaced logic, and my body changed. Claws and fur came as my vision dampened, my ears and nose amplifying the water splashing against the boat and the overwhelming stench of fish. This was what the Trial of Connection had given me. Not just a bond with the silver fox, but a continued channeling of nature—something I'd so desperately missed.

"I'm never eating fish again," I said, gagging as I opened my fox eyes and looked up at each of the fishermen. Between the fish and their sweat, each breath was a struggle. They didn't find it funny and scooted away until they nearly fell out of the boat.

Kiin grinned. "Those fish give us the cover we need to dock. What did you do with the Moonblade?"

"I…" Where had it gone? I checked the ground, but the blade was nowhere among the clothes that had fallen from me. I cursed silently, hoping I wouldn't be naked this time when I transformed back into my human form.

"Ah, I see," Kiin said, crouching before me. "I don't know much about the Moonstones, but the Winter Witch doesn't keep hers as swords like the one you call Jaryło. The Moonblades are just manifestations of his stones." Her fingers closed around something hanging from my neck and held up a golden rock with jagged edges. "The Moonstone sensed your change of forms. Wacław may have wielded it, but apparently, Kwiecień recognizes you as its owner."

She rose with a glimmer of awe in her eyes. "There is so much I learn each day around you. How you change forms interests me as well, but we need to get moving. The city of cliffs awaits."

The first streams of sunlight split the sky as the men rowed again. None of it reached us in the crack between the cliffs, and the brutal chill made me thankful for my fox fur, far warmer than even Kiin's coat had been.

I moved to the bow of the boat to watch the looming city draw closer. The bridges seemed impossibly high, but people walked along them without worry for the long fall if they were to slip. Those on the stairs were the same. As they rose, they steadily carved further into the cliff to create two diverging walls that looked like a spring flower's leaves reaching for the sun before its flower bloomed. I imagined such a thought would be strange for these desert dwellers. Well, just as strange as living in massive earthen cities was to me.

Wisps circled above the further we went. They hadn't noticed me yet, but the people of Sheresy had. Our boat offered nowhere to hide, forcing me to stare into the river and pretend my fur wasn't standing on end. Dirty brown here, the water blocked sight of all beneath the surface except for dark blotches that I assumed to be swaying plants of some sort. Except they were following us…

"Do you see that too?" I asked Kiin. "I swear, those spots are moving after us."

She craned her neck to glance over the side before glancing back to me, a single brow raised. "Grudzień plays tricks on our minds. Focus on the task ahead, and remember—"

"Only worry about what I can control, I know."

If only I could have a semblance of control in my life. Ever since the equinox, I'd been tumbling through time's flow, fighting everything fate threw at me. I'd been skeptical of fate's existence before. Now, its presence was all too real.

One of the fishermen pointed to the piers ahead, and Kiin gave the order for us to approach. Shadows covered the three strips of gray stone jutting over the water, but I needed no light to know the figures standing on each were Marzanna's warriors. Glowing Frostmarks upon their arms, shoulders, and faces exposed that much. Their expressions remained hidden, though. I whispered a prayer in hopes they held no suspicions.

"Here!" the warrior on the furthest pier shouted. Boats were moored to the others, and the pleas of a man echoed through the cliffs as he dropped to his knees on the closest one. The Frostmarked warrior standing before him just mumbled to himself before swinging the curved end of his spear. I held in my yelp as it sliced through the man's head with one swift cut.

Kiin gripped my fur, her muscles rigid. "I hope you need no more warning."

"I don't," I whispered back.

"Good, because our deaths will not be so quick if they discover who we are."

I smirked up at her. "Then I'll make sure theirs aren't either."

We quieted as we approached the pier and the fishermen dropped their oars into the boat, raising their hands. The baby-cheeked fisher-man spoke first. "We come from Huebia with perch to trade. Your… Your men there said there'd be no trouble if we showed you this."

The warrior stiffened as the man pulled a rolled piece of parchment from a pouch tied to his belt. He hadn't shown it to us before, but when I looked at Kiin, she simply nodded. Weles had explained that the gods had barred mortals from writing because of the power inherent in symbols, so what could be on this paper? Unfortunately, I couldn't ask in this form. The warrior would surely find a speaking fox to be even more suspicious than a silver one.

When the warrior ripped the paper from the fisherman's hand, though, the glow of the symbols allowed even me to see them from below: two Frostmarks flanking a crude drawing that resembled a fish. A sliver of *žityje* pulsed within them. How? The markings weren't of the old tongue, but a simple Frostmarked warrior couldn't have infused paper with his life force. Did their szeptucha leader, Minna, have others doing tasks as menial as trade permissions?

Whatever the form signified must have been enough, because the warrior huffed and handed it back. "Go to Eighth Sandstone and sell these there. Been a shortage over there."

"Can get more for 'em in Sixth or Seventh Riverstone," scarred lip replied, speaking for the first time since we'd stepped foot on the boat.

The warrior stomped his spear into the shale pier. The bronze cracked the brittle stone, sending a ringing echoing through the canyon. "You don't set the terms for the sale. Bring them to Eighth Sandstone, or we could take them off your hands for free. Your choice."

"All right then," the first fisherman replied with a mutter beneath his breath. "You'll keep the boat moored? Hate to lose her."

"You've got two days to sell what you have. Take longer and we take the boat. Nobody worth their weight in copper would fail to sell perch here."

Kiin stepped onto the pier, towering over the warrior as she drew down her hood to let her locks free. "Luckily, I'll be doing the talking.

My associates will carry the fish to the market, but I have some supplies I must purchase myself first."

The warrior shrugged. "Don't care what you do as long as it's not making more work for me. Just keep away from Bottom Shale. Frostmarked business only."

"Of course. Now, if you'll excuse me." She whistled, glancing toward the boat and curling a finger toward her. "C'mon, girl."

"Gods!" the warrior exclaimed, suddenly much more interested in our presence. "You've trained a fox?"

Kiin glared at me. "Don't worry. She's timid, so I'm *sure* she's just a little distracted. Come!"

I startled, remembering that I was a fox and she was talking to me. My yap was more human than animal, but it must've been close enough because the Frostmarked turned away with a yawn to let the fishermen begin their work.

Kiin shook her head but continued on with me close behind. Workers and Frostmarked covered the shale shore of flaking ridges steadily rising toward the cliff before splitting between a tunnel and the stairs up to higher levels. The cliff's sheer height was dizzying from its base. I'd thought the trees of Weles's forests were massive, but they couldn't compare to these walls of stone as each layer shone a different color: speckled blacks and grays of river rock, burnt red sandstone, orange-brown copper streaked in green, and so many more.

"I've never seen anything like it," I gasped when we were out of earshot.

With a foot on the first step, Kiin smiled and followed my gaze. "The Elder Cliffs are beautiful, are they not? They were the Earth Mother's first gift to our people when we declared her to be our sole deity. An abundance of ore and jewels for us to build a great realm from, but we failed her in the end. Now the Winter Witch strips it bare for her herself."

"We'll stop them."

"Yes, we will." She started up the stairs as sunlight crept onto the highest levels of the cliffs, making its way downward. "Earth Mother help us, we will…"

20

Otylia

THE WHISPERS ECHOED AROUND ME, growing endless and suffocating as we climbed the western cliff face. Each was a silent prayer. They didn't call to *me*, but I heard their cries regardless, too much for my fox mind.

"Stop growling." Kiin snapped her fingers at me, her eyes sharp as we neared a Frostmarked guard, who cast us a glance before continuing on. "A fox draws enough attention without you threatening to attack."

I released a whine. Words wouldn't come with the hammering in my skull, but it kept Kiin moving with the Vastrothie eyeing me as they passed on the narrow path. Hundreds of them, each keeping their distance from the wild animal. Many carried food, and my nose sniffed the air as instincts clashed with my desire to find Sabina. Hunger grew within me. Both the fox's and something deeper.

Among the colored wisps, shadowy faces formed around me. Smoke seemed to stream past their heads, and they grew in volume and number as we ascended. *Who are you?*

The last time I'd heard so many voices had been at the market slaughter. There had been no faces then, though, and these were far more adamant. But there were too many. With their cries and screams tearing across the cliffs, I couldn't understand them all, and I finally came to a stop, panting.

"This city is messing with my head," I said. "There are these voices…"

"I don't hear anything," Kiin replied, stopping at one of the intersections that offered entrance into the cliff tunnels before eyeing those nearby with a tug of her hood.

"It's the force of endings. Normally there are colored streaks carrying whispers from people's pasts and futures, but these are dark…" I shuddered at the onslaught of screaming. Their empty eyes watched me eagerly, yet I had nothing to give. "They're deafening."

She let out a long, frustrated breath. "All right, what are they saying?"

I shook my head. "There's too many."

"Focus on one. It's how we learned to mold the earth, like weaving strands of cloth."

My breaths were rapid as I closed my eyes, trying to calm myself and block out all but the sound of the nearest smoke figure. The man's voice was deeper than the others. Still, I could only pick out a few words… "*…deep… they fell… her…*"

"What are you trying to tell me?" I asked.

He repeated the call, but so did the others, drowning out his voice in the flood of noise. They drew closer as frustration crossed their faces. I sensed their desperation, their need to be heard. How could I understand them all?

"Be quiet," I hissed to the others. "I can't help if you're all screaming at me!"

A passerby's eyes widened at me speaking, and before the faces could reply, Kiin pulled me into the dark tunnel by the scruff of my neck. Though I yapped at her, she trudged on through the winding paths. The voices quieted before dissipating completely, and I growled at the silence that followed. They'd surely held some insight into both my power and Sheresy. Kiin had ruined that chance.

The szeptucha soon stopped out of nowhere and threw me into

an empty candlelit room before checking the hall behind us. When she was sure we hadn't been tailed, she slammed the curtain shut. "What was that? Do you want to get us killed?"

I glared up at her. "I was trying to focus on one. It was working until you decided to drag me through the dark!"

"What do you mean?"

"They're gone now."

She furrowed her brow. "When did they disappear?"

"After a few turns," I said, pushing myself to my feet and pacing around her. My fox instincts insisted I flee. Being trapped in an unfamiliar cave was not safe. "I'd only heard a few words from one of the smoke figures, but the others were quieting. He would've said more if you'd given me more time."

"No." She checked outside again, her foot tapping rapidly. "Any longer and you would've drawn too much attention to us. A few people were already far too interested. Besides, we're not here for whispers."

Her own whispers lingered in my mind as I studied her. Was that actually why we were here, or did she have something else hidden from me? "Can we reach your szeptucha through the tunnels? There are fewer people here."

"We can, but Ildes's main hideout is in Fifth Limestone."

Which one was that? She'd rattled off the names of Sheresy's nearly forty levels so quickly that I'd barely caught any of them, but the sunlight had revealed enough during our approach. "Limestone is the top seven levels?"

"Six on the east side and five on the west, counting from the top. Evaporite is the sixth level of the western side. It's just beneath Fifth Limestone, and Ildes's faction of the Daughters uses the fights there to smuggle supplies."

My head started pounding again as I tried to picture the levels. "Fights? Like a sparring ring?"

"Oh, young child." She gave a disappointed sigh. "No. You'll likely see it for yourself. A lake once filled that layer, and it left behind a basin that men use to kill each other for glory and copper. Well, at least the fighters think *they're* getting the money. It's actually the powerful placing bets on blood."

I cocked my head inquisitively. "You said Ildes is part of this?"

"Yes and no." She pulled back the curtain and checked the hall again before stepping back into the room. "The fights draw a lot of attention. It's easier for exchanges to appear like simple bets when there are many others acting similarly."

"Bold. I like it."

"Ildes is the oldest of the Daughters of the Earth and knows the Elder Cliffs better than anyone. With the resources this city holds, the Winter Witch has fought hard to take its riches for her army. Only Ildes and the szeptuchy she leads have protected the people here." She checked outside again. "Are you ready to follow? We'll head to the back stairs and go from there, but we have quite a way to go."

"Ready enough." Despite my throbbing head, she was right. We were here for a reason. Voices and my headache were distractions from rescuing Sabina and the others, no matter how much I wished to understand another aspect of my power.

The tunnels became a blur as we hurried through them with Kiin constantly glancing behind us. I'd never seen her this skittish before. She'd always been so commanding in Huebia, but ever since we left the city walls, it was like her confidence had crumbled. My own nerves weren't any better. Even without the faces shouting at me, I hated not knowing where we were going—especially in the dark. Only sparsely placed torches illuminated the tight halls, signaling passages or entrances to what I assumed to be homes. Each torch was positioned differently. Whatever the pattern was evaded me, and Kiin had made it clear she didn't want me talking to her in my fox form again. There were fewer people in the deeper tunnels. The stone carried sounds, though, and even a whisper seemed like a shout.

It was those same echoes that alerted us to a patrol ahead.

Kiin cursed under her breath and ducked into a side passage. I followed, my claws skidding across the uneven ground made of long deposited river rocks as the guards' torches illuminated where we'd stood moments before. There were crevices along the wall, and Kiin tucked into one while I curled around her leg. My fur gave the illusion of silver in the light, but it was mostly black with streaks of white. I hoped it would disguise me enough.

Frostmarks glowed upon each of the guards' forearms, exposed beneath their sleeveless shirts and tortoise armor. They carried short swords at their hips instead of the two-sided spears most Vastrothie warriors preferred. *Smart.* These tunnels were far too narrow for long weapons. Even my spear or a longsword like Kwiecień would've been difficult to wield without striking stone.

Our breaths fogged the air as the patrol passed. The chill had grown this deep in the cliff, similar to that of Huebia, and I cursed the puff when the last Frostmarked stopped, eyeing our hall with his torch raised.

With his first step in our direction, I closed my eyes and plunged myself into End's force. Creatures of decay thrived often beneath the surface. I'd forgotten them while drained of *żityje*. Now, with the bit I'd pulled from the moon during our travel, their presence in the walls' cracks tickled my senses and alerted me to their hunger. Food was scarce this far into the cliffs, and in the warrior, they saw a chance to feed. I offered it to them.

Feast, creatures of the deep. Thrive for Mokosz's earth and Mother's wilds.

Żityje seeped from my soul as thousands of silver ants burst from the crevices, including the one we hid in. Kiin screamed at their sudden appearance, and I grinned at the irony before sprinting away from the guards. "Run!"

Shouts echoed from down the hall. The Frostmarked pointed at Kiin as she scrambled after me. Her every step was a stumble, her breaths panicked. "You alerted them!"

"Believe me, we're the least of their concerns."

Then came the screams.

The first warrior collapsed into a writhing mass of silver, followed by a chorus of cries as his comrades tried to strike the horde of tiny attackers. There were too many. Each fell like the first, and the ants rejoiced in their meal as I darted down the next passage. That excitement joined with the fox's instinct to run, even if it meant going deeper into the tunnels.

Speed brought freedom in the tightest of places. The infinite weight of the stones above no longer felt compressed upon me when I was at full sprint. Surely, I could escape if the walls were to crumble or another patrol came. None could outrun me, and with the force of endings to wield at will, none could defeat me either. This was the power of *žityje* joined with my fox bond. It unshackled me from my human body and allowed me to run, free from my worries while losing none of my power.

Reality struck quickly when I reached a dead end. *I'm lost…*

I retook control from the fox and spun, staring back the way I came with little memory of how I'd gotten here. Only the distant sensation of the ants and the hum of Kwiecień joined my rushed breaths in the empty hall. Kiin had warned me of the maze these tunnels formed. I'd outrun her in my trance. Now, I was trapped in the cliff's dark embrace.

"Great Mother, give me your strength," I whispered. "Show me the way to your servant, and aid me in controlling the forces within me. In more ways than this, I'm lost without you, without Mother."

But Kiin was nowhere to be found. For what seemed like hours, I wandered the dark halls, watching End's wisps in hopes of one showing me something about her. Days of travel and the turmoil in my heart had exhausted me. Running had only made it worse, and my legs dragged with each step. Each passage looked the same. The arrangement of the torches still held no meaning to me either, so I just continued on in search of the way out.

The silence allowed Wacław's emotions to wash over me. His anger was hardly a surprise, but pride swelled within him too. It felt like he was almost *happy*—as much as he could be with the demon's all-consuming hunger. From what I could tell, he was still trapped. Then why was he like this?

Wašek, I said through our bond. *Did you manage to reach Narcyz? Does he know about Ara?*

"*Why imprison me and then call me by that name?*" he replied, his anger flaring in my chest. "*Why should I tell you anything?*"

You're still Wašek. You still care.

He hesitated, so many emotions twisting within him that I couldn't grasp them all. "*Narcyz and Andrij are with my brother in Solga. Mikołaj is afraid to retreat because Mieczysław will retaliate with his allies.*"

Mikołaj was always too busy keeping Jacek's favor to learn how to lead, I replied. *But what hope do we have without the Krowikie armies?*

"*Narcyz will travel with Andrij north to Chief Serwacy's larger army. If they can convince him that the Horde is a threat, then Mikołaj will come too.*"

And even Mieczysław isn't dumb enough to resist his united chiefs. I huffed, turning into another quiet corridor, where a few hooded figures were exchanging something. They gave me confused glances but didn't interfere. *What if Serwacy doesn't listen?*

Another hesitation—enough to keep my hope alive that he wasn't gone. "*Focus on finding Kuba and Sabina. You trapped me behind this wall, and this is all I can do until I run out of žityje or starve. I'll do what it takes to ensure Krowik listens.*"

That's what I'm afraid of.

"*Fearing me won't save Dziewanna or Jawia.*"

His comment struck my heart, just as he'd probably hoped, but I refused to give in. The demon in him wanted me to fight. Wacław needed to know I still cared. *Tell me about Ara. Did Eryk find her? The clans?*

"*Yes, they talked along the Wyzra's west bank.*"

I whispered a prayer of thanks to the few gods I could trust anymore. *And what of the clans?*

"*You pray to the gods when I found her through my Eclipsemarked.*" He scoffed. "*Even now you don't respect me or my power. What was I to you? A tool to help you Ascend and escape your father?*"

No. Stopping near the next corner, I took a shuddered breath. My entire body felt heavy from exhaustion and sorrow. *You were the one who let me believe tomorrow could be better than today, that I'd never be alone again.*

"*I was a childish fool. Hope only brings pain and disappointment.*"

I shook my head. *You've obviously convinced yourself of that much. Ignore the demon and tell me if Eryk saw Xobas and the clans.* When he began to speak, I interrupted him, *And don't claim this isn't the demon's influence. I know who you are, Wašek. You loved… love… Xobas like a father, and you love me too. You can't deny that.*

The battle of emotions raged within him as he growled. Pain struck my hands—well, paws—and his breaths grew heavy, sweat clinging to his skin. "You're wrong! *Xobas never cared for me. You never cared for me. I was never enough…*"

Only his rapid heartbeat filled the gap as I leaned against the cold stone wall. My own breaths fogged the air again, and I wondered if I'd ever find Kiin. Surely, she'd look for me. But the Frostmarked would discover us eventually. Who would come first?

"*Xobas lives,*" Wacław finally said, his voice dangerously flat. "*He and around a thousand clansmen survived. They are traveling to Eryk's village of Likiec in southwest Astiw. Ara and Zakir will meet them there and guide them into the southern hills, as we promised in our treaty.*"

So Zakir is marzban now?

"*Yes. We knew Boz killed High Priestess Rasa, but his men caught Katiôn too. That makes Zakir marzban; though, I doubt the title means much anymore.*"

I let my fox mind process that. It still wished for freedom from these tunnels as much as me, but with my weary body dragging with each step, even thinking was becoming difficult. Shifting back to myself was tempting.

Thank you for telling me, I said silently. *No matter the state of your soul, they're our friends. They won't give up on you, and neither will I.*

"*As if you haven't already.*"

I snarled in response. *Would I have fought Kiin if I'd given up? I almost killed her for taking you. She'd hidden her plan from me too because she knew I wouldn't let her do it.*

His anger dulled, and I sensed a warmth from him, only for a moment. "*You want my rage tempered? Get me out of here.*"

I'm trying my best.

"*Yeah, I did too. I promise I did…*"

His voice disappeared in the rush of sorrow that followed. I crumpled beneath its weight, huddling in a dark crevice and childishly hoping Kiin would somehow turn the corner to see me. She wouldn't. These tunnels were infinite, and I had only gotten myself more lost by trying to escape.

Exhaustion took me away quickly. Haunting, it dragged me against my will, and I descended into End's embrace, its visions striking me the moment I fell asleep.

21

Otylia

What are you trying to tell me?

THE FACES RETURNED IN MY DREAMS. If you could call them that.

I knelt in the shallows of a bog, the water frigid against my thighs as the smoky figures encircled me. Silent, they watched me like starving villagers would their chief. Something told me they were quiet because I'd told them to. So simple, yet I was a goddess. Even my smallest command echoed far further than I could know, and these shadows had felt the impact.

"Who are you?" I asked them, shivering with a plain brown dress clinging wet to my skin. A twine necklace hung from my neck. It was heavier than it should've been, and when my fingers found the golden Moonstone of Kwiecień, I clutched it to my chest.

None responded as they neared. Despite moving as a dark vapor, they didn't smell like smoke. Instead, it appeared as if the darkness was emanating from a shifting sphere within them. Fear held me, but I wouldn't back away. This was my fate, my force to wield. I couldn't flee End's calls if I was going to save Mother and what remained of Wacław. Answers lay in the unknown.

I rose with my bare toes digging into the bog's muddied ground. My mangled hair hung over my shoulders and water trickled from my clothes, but only those answers mattered. "One of you speak!" I shouted.

A stir ran through them, and some pulled away. At first, I thought it out of fear. Another face soon filled the gap, though—the man from along the cliff's edge.

"Forgive us," he said. "No one ever sees us trapped souls, so we feared we would lose our chance if you left us."

"Trapped souls?" I asked, stepping toward him. "Why are you trapped?"

He sighed. "The invaders. They swept through the city and slaughtered at will, throwing us into the river when they were finished bleeding us dry."

"Your souls can't leave your corpses."

"No." Many of the figures hung their heads. Some had formed arms and hands, and they covered themselves in shame.

I spun, studying them. They filled the bog and covered the trees, but all gave a silent reverence to me by allowing the man to speak for them. Fear threatened to wrestle away control again. My awe was stronger, though, and I took a moment to take in the sight.

"All of you are demons," I said, speaking to no one in particular. "The Frostmarked sacrificed you to Marzanna and then dumped you in the river to be rid of you. No funeral rites. No burning to free your soul." My voice grew sharper as I clenched my fists. Hundreds of souls surrounded me—all killed by those who claimed to serve a goddess. "She's not the goddess of death. Death is supposed to be a new beginning, a chance at paradise, not the eternal torture Marzanna has inflicted on you!"

My silver and wood armband burned against my arm as I stepped toward the circle of figures. Weles's magic with it wished to protect me from demons, but I dampened it. These souls weren't evil. They didn't seek my *żityje* or power.

What do you *want?*

The glow emanating from my skin seemed to push away their dark vapors when I neared. Some retreated. Others stayed, stretching their shadowed hands to touch my clothes and hair—weightless yet heavy, like the exhausting heat of the summer sun. Even through the fabric, I sensed aspects of all of them. A sea of pain and wanting. I continued on, End's usual wisps appearing around each and sharpening to lines that shot from their cores. Some strands connected to figures close to them. Others disappeared into the distance or wound around their odd forms, their variety of colors creating a web that took my breath away.

A woman split from the group ahead as I stepped to the edge of the bog, just my heels still in the cold water. Unlike those around her who were only torsos and heads, the darkness held her entire body in an indistinct form. "Will you help us?" she asked.

"I don't know how."

She stopped before me, reaching out her hand to take mine. I silently thanked Kiin for my gloves' protection. Too many visions of death had met me, and another would destroy the last remnants of hope I had. My power needed me to be stronger, but I couldn't.

"Our souls were drawn to you for a reason," the woman said. "The Earth Mother had not answered our pleas, but perhaps she has sent you to our aid."

I pulled back, my awe slipping away. How could I save hundreds of demons when I couldn't even save the one that mattered most? "I'm sorry. I can't."

The mood shifted around me. Hands slipped from my clothes and voices began to whisper, a few in the mass even weeping. *I've failed them too.* They'd had so much blind belief in me, but it faded now that they saw the truth: I was a fraud. Rod had made me a goddess, an immortal wielder of the Three Realms' strange forces. I was too weak to control them. Dziewanna and Mokosz had been the source of all my abilities, and I'd lost them.

Alone, I was nothing.

I awoke with a start, panting in my fox form as shadows flickered in the torchlight. Eyes seemed to watch me from within. They judged my failure, and I cowered away to the corner.

Where are you, Kiin?

My dream had offered answers to my power and given me a chance to help those slaughtered by Marzanna. But as I traveled the maze, only fear filled my mind. I'd thought I could resist it and help the trapped souls. How? They were dead, and if they'd truly become demons, their only possible end was Oblivion. Even I couldn't change that, but the force of endings had been trying to tell me something. It had sent me visions each night since my Ascension, showing people at risk in Huebia. This one had been different. With Kiin's help, I'd saved many of those targeted by the Frostmarked, but dealing with living mortals was far different than saving a demon's soul… or at least what was left of it.

Time was impossible to track in the tunnels. I had no idea how long I'd slept, and after walking for hours, my only hint that night had come was the moon's pulsing in my soul. It brought a clarity I lacked in the day.

I shifted back to my human form in an empty hall, collecting my thoughts and focusing on the moon's power. The fox's instincts faded, and I took a relieved breath when its primal fear went with it. Unfortunately, my own anxiety still held my chest like a constrictor tightening around its prey. I'd escaped Weles's snakes. As I pictured myself in the clothes Kiin had given me, the cold stinging my skin and my breaths hanging in the air, they formed over my body, and I decided I'd escape this place too. One step at a time, I *would* figure out my power and the purpose that came with it.

First, I needed to find my friends.

I pulled up my hood and stepped back into the tunnel I'd been headed down. People were still sparse, especially this late at night. Those that were in the tunnels, though, gave me no second glances. *Maybe someone can show me a way out.* My appearance would make it obvious I was an outsider, but so would asking for directions anyway. Wandering would no longer do.

"Excuse me," I said in the kindest voice I could muster, approaching the next person who wasn't in a whispered conversation.

"I'm just traveling through the city and must have made a wrong turn. Do you know how to get to cliff face?"

The middle-aged woman looked me up and down before letting out a laugh. "You aren't the first. Follow the torches. A single one always faces away from the exits, and if there are two next to each other, then that is the way to the main tunnels. Best you stick to those if you're new here."

I furrowed my brow. "Why?"

She leaned in, checking each direction before whispering, "The occupiers… They don't appreciate stragglers, and they'll notice a white-faced girl like you for sure. People keep disappearing. Some are enslaved, but others…" She shuddered and took my gloved hand. "Most of us are missing family. Hurry along if you don't wish to join them."

"Earth Mother bless you," I replied.

"And you."

Tense, I didn't take another breath until she released me and continued on. Even with the gloves' protection, I'd flinched at our contact. But she'd given me the way out, and that was all that mattered for now.

Wisps appeared around me as I followed the torches toward the nearest main tunnel. I hadn't taken any stairs, so a central meeting area was the most likely place Kiin would look for me. She could've been waiting outside too, but even away from the fox's instincts, my own hatred of being underground had returned. Once I found clear air, I doubted I would be able to convince myself to enter the cliff again.

I kept an eye on the faces formed by the wisps and the images within them. One might offer a way to Kiin, but none did by the time I reached a wide tunnel bustling with conversation.

It had to be late in the night by now, yet the crowd nearly filled the space as they mulled about, approaching various stands carved from the stone itself. Torches lined the walls and lit faces well. Guards stood at each intersection, some holding two-ended spears while others had sheathed swords at their hips. Frostmarks pulsed on their exposed skin—arms, hands, and even faces. None on the neck. Such a marking was reserved for szeptuchy, despite the actual location mattering little. Father had believed it to be a silly tradition not defined by the gods themselves, but even Mokosz's so-called "chosen" here wore her mark on their neck.

As I passed the guards, I pulled at my cloak's hood, hoping the Frostmarked didn't find me suspicious. Merchants shouted at me about their wares. The crowd gave me no heed, nor space. I took advantage of that and slipped into the mass of people.

Someone grabbed my shoulder.

I stopped, one hand on the dagger hidden beneath my coat. *Can't I catch one break?* My heart hammered my chest. Visions of everything that could go wrong raced through my head, and I wished I could slump in the shadows, invisible.

"Hey!" an oddly flamboyant voice said with a pull.

Act like a woman in the market, I told myself. *Just make them believe you're a traveler.*

Nose wrinkled in annoyance, I turned to face not a guard but a built man in elaborate robes. His long beard was gray, the dark skin of his brow wrinkled. Jewels of many colors filled his towering orange hair, and I stared up at it, stunned, until he spoke again.

"You seem fond of my wig," he said, running his hand across it. Somehow, not a strand shifted. "I am told the hair comes from the tribes to the north. You savages are quite willing to gut each other and sell the scalp at a price."

I scowled. "That's not true!"

"Oh!" He stepped away, his mouth ajar and a hand held to his heart. "By the Earth Mother, you scared me with that outburst. I'm surprised you speak the Vastrothie tongue so cleanly."

"Don't say her name here." I glanced at the guards, but none seemed to care about us. "What do you want?"

"Well, you are *obviously* quite familiar with the northern tribes. Perhaps you are aware that your amulet bears their markings?"

My fingers closed around Kwiecień, still a glowing necklace. I cursed myself for not tucking it beneath my shirt. "It was my brother's."

"How much would you like for it?" He wiggled his fingers through the air. Many of them were covered in rings of silver and gold. "I have Imperial Antowie coin to trade, Vastrothie coppers, or even food or other wares? Much is in shortage with the Winter Witch's friends here. What if you had enough to feed your family until this all passes over?"

I narrowed my eyes. "What makes you think this will pass? Who are you?"

As he stepped closer, wisps drew in around me, and I caught a few men in the crowd watching us. *This isn't a negotiation…*

"It's best not to ask too many questions," the man hissed into my ear. "I am well connected, and I know an ancient artifact when I see one. Take my offer if you care about your life."

"Do you have *any* idea who you're talking to?" I snapped. My fear was gone, burned away by his offense. A force within me hummed as I reached for my *žityje,* even if I had little left. "Leave, or I'll make sure you never speak again."

He laughed and raised his arm sharply. His men swarmed me, but I'd expected them. As the first grabbed for my off-hand, I spun with my dagger, slicing from wrist to elbow along his artery. Blood poured from the wound, and with his grip broken, I kicked him in the groin.

The others hesitated at the sight of their collapsed comrade. I grinned, thanking Mother for teaching me where blood flowed the most. Healing was more than just herbs and potions.

"Guards!" I shouted in as shrill of a voice as I could muster. "Thieves!"

A flurry of activity surrounded us. Frostmarked guards charged into the fray as people screamed and fled, but my gaze was fixed on the wigged man. He'd thought he could take advantage of me because I appeared to be a weak woman. If he lived, he'd do the same to someone else. And there was something off about his wisp…

The man fled down a side path with his remaining thugs as the Frostmarked cut down those closest to the intersection. I chased, gripping my dagger tight. He couldn't escape. He *deserved* the punishment coming.

Cramped darkness replaced the market, and the man stumbled with his steps on the uneven ground. His thugs continued on, desperate to flee as Frostmarked shouts followed us. *Žityje* surged through me, feeding on the moon and strengthening my strides. Though I lacked the speed of Wacław's winds, it was enough.

The man collapsed in a side alley the moment I touched him. Trembling and holding out his hands, he stared up at me and pled, "Please, show me mercy!"

"Why would I do that?" I said with my dagger to his neck. "You wanted to kill me over an amulet!"

"That's not some family heirloom."

"I know."

He cocked his head, his fear suddenly fading. "So it was more than just the amulet's power I sensed. Fascinating."

I reacted too late. A bolt of pure *žityje* burst from his hand and struck me in the chest, flinging me across the tunnel. Pain shot through my shoulder as I hit the wall before dropping to the ground. *Now he's dead.*

Fury burned away my pain as I stood and called Kwiecień in its sword form. Awe and horror filled the man's face at the Moonblade's glow. I reveled in it. "You are messing with things far larger than you could understand, sorcerer."

"Who are you?" he asked. His hands still glowed as he glared at me. End's whispers and visions had overwhelmed the simple pulse of *žityje* in his soul and garnets in his hair, but it was all too obvious now. I never would have missed that as a szeptucha.

"You wouldn't believe me."

He huffed. "Very well. Then I shall go first. I am called Serapis of Esparaz, and I have searched for fragments of Alatyr Stone my entire life. Until now, I have only found shards that are little more than dust. Until now…"

"The Alatyr Stone?" I shook my head and held the Moon's power, ready to send a blast into him if he struck again. "What are you talking about?"

The power dissipated from his hands. "Tell me who you are and how you got your hands on that stone. Then we can speak."

"Vlatka," I said. "I'm a witch from those 'savage northern tribes.'"

"Well, *Vlatka*, that is quite the sword you have there." He stepped closer, his head cocked enough for it to seem alight in the golden aura of Kwiecień's blade. "What do you believe it to be? Obviously, you have the capability to wield it as more than just a stone, so you are no mere witch."

Footsteps approached, and Serapis did an exaggerated sweeping motion with his hand before holding a finger to his lips. I silently commanded Kwiecień to return to its amulet form, dulling its light as it did. We entered the shadows on opposing sides of the tunnel. It was smoother than most, so anyone looking closely would see us. I hoped the Frostmarked would just pass by.

They didn't.

"Drop your weapons!" the first shouted as six more filled the intersection behind him.

Serapis and I traded glances. He wore a smug grin, probably excited to see what I was capable of. Patience wasn't one of my strengths, so I gave in and stood with my hands raised. "Oh, thank the Winter Witch you've come," I said, trying to sound in danger.

The guard lowered his sword. "You fled with your attacker?"

"No, I chased him." I stepped closer as the wisps representing their souls fluttered around me. Each showed murder after murder. No, I wouldn't feel guilty for ending them, but that thought brought regret with it. *Was Wacław right?*

"Oh." He chuckled and scratched the back of his head. "Guess you did the work for—"

I released all the power I'd been holding in my chest, shooting it at the guards instead of Serapis. The wave sent them flying into the far wall with a massive force. Skulls cracked. Necks severed. Bones shattered. In seconds, all of them were dead from the impact except for one, who writhed with his leg bent unnaturally beneath him.

Drawing my dagger again, I stormed to him and held its point to his heart. That blast had taken my little remaining *żityje*. Blades would have to do from here. "I'll let you live if you tell me where you keep your prisoners."

"Prisoners?" He spat up blood, each of his breaths weaker than the one before. "You mean the slaves?"

"There was a group of twenty, maybe thirty people you captured. They had nymphs with them."

His eyes widened. "Oh… I… I don't know. I swear!"

I jabbed the dagger in, just a little, and his screams only encouraged me. I let myself enjoy it. "You have to know something. Nymphs can't just show up every day in a city like this."

"Fine! Fine!" He groaned and pulled at the hilt of my blade, trying to get it away from his chest. "Check Bottom Slate! They keep the dangerous ones there—the ones that talk to the stone."

"Thank you. You may go. Based on your one good leg, you should be able to hop to your Frostmarked friends."

I turned back to Serapis, the guard's muffled grunts filling the tunnel as he tried to stand. I ignored him. His opportunity to live was a gift, one I wondered if I'd regret. "Ready to talk?" I asked Serapis.

The sorcerer's eyes were wide. "You… You are more than you say," he said, his fingers dancing through the air as he talked.

"What is the Alatyr Stone?"

"A question I would expect from a witch, not from *whatever* you are, young maiden."

I narrowed my eyes and held out my hand, silver light balling in its palm. "You wouldn't believe me."

He smacked his lips together and waved a finger. "Don't misjudge me, child. I told you that I would say all I knew about Alatyr if you gave me who you are. You have not!"

"Not here."

"Of course." Serapis glanced down the hall at the dead guards. The injured one must've limped off already, leaving a faint blood trail in his wake. "Even if the guards do not arrive, we shall be at risk. People will tie us to this slaughter. Quite fortuitously, however, I have a place where we can speak."

"Away from your goons."

He chuckled. "Indeed, away from those hired thugs. Useless! Fleeing at the first hint of combat when that is precisely what I paid them for."

"No," I said, slicing my dagger through the air between us. "You paid them to threaten women like me so you could get their jewels. Powerful artifacts or not."

"You misunderstand me."

"Based on those stupid rings, I don't believe I did."

With a shake of his head, he threw up his hands. "Very well, believe what you wish, but we should move now. Will you follow?"

I nodded, and he gave a grin before heading down the hall, each of his steps small and quick. His bright red wisp had the same excitement. It whirled around his wig before zipping past me with great speed. There were fewer wisps this deep in the tunnels, so it was easy to examine this one.

Even without diving into his visions, the images and whispers from the wisp told a tale of intrigue. An obsession with these Alatyr Stone pieces had consumed Serapis for years. Voices criticized him for leaving in pursuit of it, but he'd gone anyway as war struck the Anvoranie people. There was little more I could understand from the fractured pieces the wisp offered. What it had shown me, though, was that he would stop at nothing to find each piece of Alatyr, and he believed Kwiecień to be the greatest piece of it yet. That made him a threat.

I know where Sabina is. I should turn around and find her.

Our reason for coming here hadn't been to learn about ancient magical artifacts. Besides, Serapis had tried to steal the Moonstone, hadn't he? What would he do if he confirmed his suspicions or learned the truth about me? I hoped me being a goddess would be enough to convince him to back off, but he was a difficult man to read.

I continued on anyway. His desperate pursuit made me curious. If there was something more to Kwiecień and the Moonstones, maybe they could be the key to defeating Marzanna, or at least finding Kiin. It was a desperate, childish wish—one I clung to as Serapis climbed a staircase at the end of a larger hall.

"We must climb to Seventh Sandstone," he said over his shoulder.

"That means nothing to me," I replied.

He dragged his fingers along the irregular stones forming the wall of the staircase as we rose, winding back and forth through the levels. "Third Riverstone was surprisingly kind to an outsider like you. It is the Riverstone layers that forms the city's upper crest among the lowest of elevation. How ironic!" When he'd finished laughing to himself, he continued, "If you know anything of this city, you'll know that the Sandstone layers house the workers who mine the 'gift layers' from the so-called Earth Mother. They are also much more indiscreet than Riverstone. Oh, how I cannot believe you wandered through *there* with a jewel like that hanging from your thin neck, waiting to be taken. Be lucky it was only me."

Does he ever shut up?

Apparently not, because the grueling climb was compounded by his ramblings about Sheresy's fascinations. He described the gift layers as copper, gold, amethyst, and more, yet not tin as the 'so-called' Earth Mother—he always insisted on prefacing her name with that—wished for the Vastrothie to trade for bronze's other ore. The stories claimed that she feared too much power becoming concentrated. Separate the elements of war, she believed, and neither side would fight.

"If you need any more evidence for the so-called Earth Mother to be a false goddess," he said as we reached another landing, "simply lay your mind upon the historical fact that is the endless array of wars between the Anvoranie and Vastrothie. The Vastrothie lacked tin, yes. Men are foolish, however, young one. Do you know what they did?"

I groaned. "They invaded Anvora to take it?"

"Precisely!"

His point made sense, but I had little patience for any more history lessons. I'd figured out by now that each landing had an image of the thirty-nine layers on the west side of the river, with a shaded pattern marking which layer we were arriving at.

Sheresy confused me to no end. From what I could remember, though, Seventh Sandstone was the fifteenth layer from the top. That put it ten layers below Fifth Limestone, where Kiin had said the

Daughters of the Earth would be. The landing we stood on now had the sixteenth layer shaded. *So close.*

Serapis switched to the topic of how he believed sandstone was created as we finished the climb and began moving through the tunnels again. He barely looked where he was going, and our turns seemed random. But just when I was ready to send my dagger through his head for some silence, he stopped at a doorway.

"Behold my humble, *temporary*, abode," he said, pushing aside the heavy cloth covering it with an elaborate sweep.

Inside, a damp, musty smell met me instantly. The air had been cold and dry, but now it was like that of an autumn swamp. How? I sensed no streams of *žityje* coming from Serapis, yet some force held back the cold desert air.

Serapis settled on a slab of stone that jutted from the wall. Six more slabs were spread across the room, each covered by elaborately designed scarlet cushions that were the only color besides the deep sandstone and Serapis's wig. He gestured to the one nearest to him. I kept to the opposite end of the room instead.

As I paced, I peered down the narrow hall to the sorcerer's right. It led to at least two other rooms, but Serapis's raised brow indicated he didn't appreciate my prying, so I folded my arms and broke the silence. "No one else is here?"

"None at all," he said, crossing his legs in a posture that our tribe would've considered feminine. "We are alone, Vlatka, or whatever your true name is."

I bit my cheek. Trusting Serapis was a risk, but my identity as a goddess would be exposed eventually. His sorcery was powerful— that I could tell—and the last thing we needed were more enemies. "Otylia."

"A Krowik indeed." His face remained still, odd compared to his earlier flamboyance, as he leaned forward with his fingers interlocked over his knee. "I see that you, Otylia, are not merely a witch. You have told me your name, yet you have failed to explain truly who you are. That spell you used against those Frostmarked appeared to use moonlight. Even I am incapable of such a feat after nearly thirty years of practicing sorcery, so tell me, child: *Who are you?*"

I straightened my posture, imagining Weles's judgement. To be seen as a goddess, I needed to look like one, and send me to Oblivion, I would not let this man or any other believe I was weak ever again. "I am Otylia Welesiakówna, the Silver Fox of Nawia, daughter of Dziewanna—goddess of the wilds—and Weles—god of the afterlife and lowlands. I was raised by mortals in the village of Dwie Rzeki in the Tribe of Krowik, but now, I have Ascended to become goddess of endings and moon." I stepped closer. "And now, Serapis of Esparaz, you're going to tell me what you know about this Alatyr Stone."

Serapis took a long breath and ran his fingers through the air, as if tracing a work of art. "It is a pleasure, Lady Otylia, to make your acquaintance. There is so much for us to learn from one another, so I do ask that you sit. For, together, you and I may just save the Three Realms."

22

Wacław

I need out!

SWEAT SLIPPED FROM MY BROW, dripping into the puddle below. I shouldn't have heard such a quiet noise, but with my sight gone and stone blocking all other sounds, only my labored breaths filled the space.

My body's physical sensations were distant. Though it suffered too, the true agony was in my soul—an all-consuming nightmare tearing me apart and feeding upon the rage of its creation. Without a way to satisfy my demonic craving for *žityje*, it took my mind instead. A burning pain charred everything inside me. My thoughts. My desires. My yearning to reach Otylia, to make right what had been broken.

"No!" I snarled, lashing out at my own face and leaving a gouge in my cheek. "She betrayed us, denied us…"

I retched, but my stomach was empty and only bile came up. It filled the cramped space with a horrific stench as I fought to stand. My legs refused, sending me crashing into the wall again, every muscle in my body feeling foreign. I couldn't even trust my thoughts. Not after…

"We needed to strike!"

My voice echoed around me, endless. They were my own words yet a stranger's. Everything was *its* needs and unyielding hunger. That force inside me that hated everyone for what they'd done to me. All my failures had been because of my own hesitation, but they would suffer for their mockery and rejection.

"They don't deserve death!" I shouted to the demon.

"Everyone deserves death," it replied through my voice. "The Frostmarked slaughter. The people of Dwie Rzeki exile their own and embrace warlords in their fear. Even Otylia stole *your* soul before pushing us away! She unleashed our power, and now she fears we could be greater than her, a goddess!"

"I love her!"

"Love is an excuse, a weakness. It gets in the way of what must be done if we are to succeed."

I slammed my fist into the wall, shattering the knuckles and making me cry out. *Žityje* poured from my soul to mend the wound, but I stopped it. The physical pain dulled the demon's assault on my mind. Tears welled in my eyes. It didn't matter. *I* was in control, and I couldn't surrender it… not again.

The demon laughed. "Injuring us will only delay both of our goals. You know this!"

"You can't kill her."

"Can't we?" It pulled me to my feet, my own body refusing my commands. My knuckles healed, and it… we… grinned as it held our hand before us. "Otylia will help us take Grudzień, but then she will try to destroy its manipulations. We cannot allow that to happen. Grudzień will be ours! Kwiecień will be ours again!" It dragged our fingers over Marzanna's pulsing mark, the only light in our darkness. "You were too weak to deny Marzanna. You surrendered the Moonblade to Otylia. Our enemies mocked your weakness, and it is now my responsibility to ensure we take the power we deserve. Grudzień will make all of Jawia's tribes bow before us."

"I don't want power," I wheezed. My strength was failing. Its hunger hammered my mind, each jarring my hold. "I just want to protect the people I love."

"Weakness won't save them."

I shuddered and dropped to my knees. "Neither will you."

It scoffed, tearing control from me as its last words echoed through my prison of mind and stone. "It will be their choice whether they're worth saving."

23

Otylia

What could a single sorcerer know about the Three Realms?

PAIN STRUCK MY MIND, sending me to the ground as Wacław's struggle washed over me.

Wašek? I asked him through our bond. *You can fight it!*

For the first time in days, I felt him. Not the płanetnik. Not the angry demon wrestling away his strength. *Him.*

Wacław still fought on despite all that had happened. I'd hoped some part of him remained, and this was the proof that he wasn't completely gone. Not yet.

No reply came to my pleas, though, and I knelt on the cold sandstone floor with my gloved hands pressed to my chest. Dziewanna's amulet hung alongside Kwiecień there, distant from my protected fingers. I missed her now more than ever. Mother had always known what to say. But silence smothered my voice, and I suffered as Wacław lost the fight.

I needed to get back to him.

"May I ask what just happened?" Serapis asked, still seated on his slab. "I have never seen anything like that except from those I would describe as lunatics, and you, my darling, do not appear to be a lunatic."

"Call me darling again and you might change your mind," I snapped with my fists clenched. My knuckles ached against the floor, but I held them there. The pain reminded me of Wacław—of why I fought.

Serapis bowed his head in what appeared to be a surprisingly genuine sign of respect. "My apologies, Lady Otylia. I speak many tongues, but even with my knowledge, I sometimes fail to correctly express my thoughts. My words were meant as a compliment, nothing more."

Slowly, I pushed myself to my feet. Serapis eyed one of the seats, but I continued to stand. "I don't need compliments. What I *need* is answers." I let my eyes bore into him.

"The daughter of the wild goddess has a temper, fascinating." He leaned back again. "Very well, you have given me the answer I sought, so it is only fair I do the same." Holding out his hand, he whispered in the old tongue and pulled a ring from his thumb. A sliver of black was embedded in its stone. "Do you know what this is?"

I stepped closer to examine the ring. *Żityje* flowed from it, dissipating less than a finger length from the surface. "It's the reason this room feels warm. An artifact of power."

He made a circular motion with his pointer finger, his excitement growing with each word. "Yes, yes, but that is not the important bit! The jewels in my wig are all artifacts of power in one way or another. Such things are not so special, as many exist through bonds with spirits or nature itself. This tiny piece of stone is worth more than all of them combined."

"The Alatyr Stone?"

"Precisely!" He clapped his hands, and I jumped at the echo it caused. The space seemed private, but each moment spent in Vastroth made me more skittish. "It has taken me decades to piece together enough fragments of Alatyr to have a piece any larger than a speck of dust. Yet, there is more power in this shard than all my other amulets combined."

Kwiecień hummed against my chest. Its power pulsed, even beyond its moon, and I sensed the shard emanating the same tune. When I stopped less than a stride from Serapis, the ring's *żityje* shifted, flowing toward Kwiecień. The two streams collided. No, they *merged*, forming a swirling mass of life force invisible to the mortal eye but blinding to my senses of spirits.

"How is it pulling from Kwiecień?" I asked. "This is the wrong moon."

Serapis raised his brow. "Moon? What do you mean?"

"Kwiecień is a Moonstone. The gods Jaryło and Marzanna each hold… or *held*… one for each moon of the year: seven for Jaryło and five for Marzanna."

"So that…" He looked from the ring to Kwiecień. "You stole that shard from a god?"

I smirked, running my fingers through the pooling ball of *żityje*. Even now, I couldn't draw it in. "You could call Jaryło my adopted brother… or my uncle… or my cousin." The awkwardness of that made me wrinkle my nose in disgust. "But that's not the point. He betrayed me, and a powerful friend of mine killed him for it. His Moonblades—which you've seen are Moonstones in another form—make him effectively immortal during their connected moon. Fortunately for us, Marzec was under Marzanna's control, not his."

Serapis pulled back and set the ring upon a stand at his side. The movement broke the bond between Kwiecień and the shard, but the Moonstone still hummed. "To be completely honest, Lady Otylia, I do not believe in the religions of the kingdoms and tribes of this land. They claim these powerful beings such as you and these others are gods. Why? Because they lack the understanding of the world around them. You are not a goddess but a mortal with unbelievable power."

"Yet you believe in the Alatyr Stone."

"Alatyr is no tribal tale. The shard in this glass and the stone upon your necklace prove that."

"And my Ascension ritual proved I am not mortal."

He waved a hand dismissively. "Call it what you wish. It does not change that you are neither omniscient nor omnipotent. A god sees all and knows all, yet you stand before me as a child seeking knowledge from a simple sorcerer. You bear the title of goddess yet do not know the name of the most powerful artifact in the entire world!"

His words hit me like a fist to my gut. What claim did I have to godhood? Yes, I had Ascended, but could I truly be a goddess if I failed to wield the force I'd been given? Why was there so much I didn't know?

"I don't care what you call me," I sputtered. "Just tell me what Alatyr is. Obviously, it is powerful if the Moonstones came from it."

He nodded, as if conceding a point for once. "Regardless, you are a powerful being worthy of respect—the master of one of the world's great forces. More than that, though, Alatyr is in its essence a core part of you and the others who share your blood. The stone was among the first things in the realm you claim belongs to the gods."

"Prawia."

"Each people have their own word for it, but that matters not. Alatyr resided in this realm, and the being your people call Swaróg noticed it and understood its incredible potential. Many tales tell this story differently. However, all agree that he possessed Alatyr."

I thought you said you don't believe folktales? I shook my head to myself. Was this all a waste of time?

Serapis laughed, clutching his chest as he smiled up at me. "Now, you may be questioning me referencing stories told by commoners. However, there is a sliver of truth in each folktale. Even if they label creatures or forces incorrectly, they are a primitive mind's view of a world they cannot understand."

I gritted my teeth. "My father is not primitive."

"Your father rules the underworld, yes?"

"I meant the mortal who raised me. It's complicated."

"Indeed," he said with a huff. "To return to Alatyr, it was at this time that Swaróg became envious of the stone's power. He recognized a great strength within it that he could direct but never truly wield, so he attempted to destroy it. Again, the tales deviate on how he did so, but in the end, he was unsuccessful. The clash was enough, however, to send sparks that birthed he earliest of your so-called gods, as well as many other powerful spirits."

A stone that created the gods? I shook my head. That was insane!

It had been the World Tree's birth from Rod's golden egg that had created the Three Realms and everything in it, not some stone struck by Swaróg's hammer. At least, that's what Father had always believed, and he was a servant of Swaróg…

"If sparks from Alatyr created the gods," I said, "then why are there more of us? I wasn't made by the stone."

Serapis let out a sigh and ran his hands down his robes. "The powerful beings created by Alatyr had blood and lust like any mortals. Of course they would bear offspring. Alatyr, however, could create no others, considering it has been shattered ever since that time."

"How could a stone powerful enough to create gods be broken?"

"I do not know precisely, but it happened." His gaze drifted to the ring's black shard. "The existence of these Moonstones as well as those I've recovered are evidence of such an occurrence. How that split occurred, however, is not so clear. Each tale scattered across the world's people gives a different account. All agree that there was conflict between powerful beings—perhaps those you call gods were among them—and that Alatyr plummeted from the realm above into our own."

I held Kwiecień and stared down at its golden glow. When the Moonstone had been part of the Moonblade's hilt, it had seemed pure, but the cracks upon its edges were obvious now. "The fall broke it?"

"Perhaps. It may also have already been broken by whatever battle occurred in the realm above. In the end, what matters is that Alatyr shattered, destroying the essential life within it. You sense this now as *żityje*, but these fragments hold far less of it than Alatyr as a whole. Much of its power was released when it struck our realm."

"What did it create, then?" I asked. "That much *żityje* must have done *something*."

"Yes…" He turned his head away and pinched the bridge of his nose, the excitement suddenly gone from his voice. "This burst of energy unleashed the forces that to this day create undead demons and the living Nawie. Another being far more powerful came from it as well, but tales either fail to speak of it or only do so by indirect reference. This being led the dark creatures to block out the sun, leaving humanity and all living things to suffer until Swaróg defeated the being and exiled him beyond our realms."

I shrugged. "Okay, but what does this stone have to do with saving the Three Realms?"

"Demons have obviously lingered. The tortured, trapped souls of the unquiet dead are easy prey for the few spirits of the dark that survived their master's defeat. They feed upon the dead's discontent and drive them for revenge. Living souls are not so vulnerable."

"The Nawie…" My chest ached at the thought of Wacław's struggle. Was his demonic soul somehow caused by this battle at the world's beginning?

His gaze sharpened as his fingernails dug into his knee. "You understand, then?" he spat out so quickly I barely caught his meaning. His eyes seemed aflame in his excitement.

"The dark spirits have returned somehow," I replied, "and they've corrupted people for their own power. But how? If Swaróg exiled them to what I assume was Oblivion, how did they escape? Demons are supposed to be trapped there forever."

"So we thought. Even your gods believed so, but they were wrong. The veil between Oblivion and the living realm has been torn. I do not know how or why, but it has been so for many years now, and it is only getting worse."

Now I sat, my legs giving way beneath the shock of Serapis's words. *What could have torn the veil?* I didn't know, but neither did I have the time to sit and think. This conversation had taken too much time already. Kiin and Ildes would be waiting for me, and my friends were suffering in the Bottom Slate level. But what if Serapis knew something that could stop Marzanna or save Mother? That temptation forced me to stay.

"You believe reuniting the shards of Alatyr will stop the spirits from escaping Oblivion?" I finally asked, my feet tapping rapidly against the stone floor. It echoed, but I couldn't help it. The last thing I'd needed was another problem.

Serapis nodded and returned the ring to his finger. "I do. Though why the largest twelve fragments became bound to the moon is a mystery, it should be possible to use elements of their power beyond the designated time of year, even if you cannot draw from it directly. Together, they must be powerful enough to seal off the darkness."

"And if they're not?"

"Then," he said, "your kind are as doomed as the rest of us. Until I am proven incorrect, I will continue to act under the assumption that we can fix what has been broken. I am aware of a few smaller fragments other than these, and I intend to find them. This search led me here—to you."

His voice dropped to a rushed whisper as he approached. "You know where the Winter Witch's men hold your friends. Go to them and find me upon your return. I will aid you if you promise to save our realm. If what you say about two other immortals wielding these 'Moonstones' is true, that will make securing them far more difficult than I hoped, but you give me hope. Before today, this fragment was my only purpose. Now, you have given me one as well, Lady Otylia."

The passion in his voice gave me pause. Despite his claims to not follow the gods, Serapis was oddly reverent. Something churned within me even considering trusting him, but I did. He definitely believed what he was saying, and I would investigate them further once I returned to Wacław. Only finding my friends mattered until then.

"Do you know of the Daughters of the Earth?" I asked him, the glow of the Alatyr shards highlighting each of our faces. "Or of a woman called Ildes?"

A grin crossed his face. "I am pleased to hear of your cooperation with them. Death and destruction are all too common already without this rogue being you call Marzanna ravaging Vastroth. Go to the Evaporite fights and find the stall selling scorpion carapaces. One of the 'Daughters' will meet you there."

"Scorpion *what?*"

He waved me off, wiggling his fingers as he did. "Go along. There is much to do."

I rolled my eyes. Speaking to Serapis had been like trying to swallow boiling water, and I was glad to be rid of him as I stepped into the hall and breathed in the distant power of the moon. There were hours before Dadźbóg's return. I would find Ildes's messenger and join with Kiin long before then if all went well. Then, I would free Sabina, Kuba, and the others.

One step at a time, I would find who I'd lost. My friends. My mother. My lover. And then myself. I would not fail. Not again…

Serapis's story of Alatyr ran through my head as I tried to look like someone interested in the fights at the center of the light gray Evaporite level. I wasn't very good at it. While bettors shouted at their preferred fighter and traders observed shopkeepers' wares with a smile and a relaxed nature, I could only muster a crooked grin at best. My muscles were as stiff as a lamb on an altar.

I didn't fear the dark being that had fought Swaróg. At most, it was just another looming threat after all I'd seen. No, neither demons nor spirits could draw this much anxiety into my core and devour me inside out. Only Wacław was capable of that.

The demon within him could've come from long ago, I thought. *How many people has it corrupted before? Or is he the first after thousands of years?*

That possibility alone made me shudder. Wacław had a good heart, but even he couldn't resist an enraged spirit that had been trapped since the beginning of time. It fed on his own anger, strengthening the longer Wacław was without his mortal soul, and there was nothing I could do to stop it. Maybe he felt a little less of its call with a piece of my immortal soul within him. Though I clung to that hope, all I knew was he still suffered. That was the worst feeling.

"You pulled me from Weles's grip," I whispered aloud through our connection, "and now it's my turn to pull you from the demon's."

No response came except for a twinge of pain in Wacław's heart. It was subtle—and the demon smothered it quickly—but I kept that hurt. Part of me wanted to hide and wallow in his emotions, to endure all of his suffering. I would've scoffed at myself for that just moons ago. Now, though, more than anything, I needed the reminder that the boy I loved was alive.

"Uh, excuse me," a ragged voice said from hip height.

I forced away my thoughts and took a sharp breath. "Yes?" I asked the stout woman who'd approached me with a plate full of what looked like fish rolled in cabbage.

Her wide nose wrinkled. "You gonna order something or just stand there glaring at my customers? Food's in shortage, and I got to get the best price for this wrapped perch before it spoils! People get hungry during the fights."

"Oh, sorry," I blushed, cursing myself for doing so. What was I, some flustered girl? "I was waiting for a friend."

"Wait somewhere else then, won't you?"

"Of course."

It took everything I had not to use my channeling against her as I moved closer to the market's center. I'd chosen that location to be close to the scorpion carapace vendor—an entire stand for *scorpion carapaces*—without being too exposed. There seemed to be no Frost-marked guards here, but I didn't trust the place. Too many people. Not a shred of the wilds to break the stench.

The grizzled giant of a man who stood behind the scorpion stand was enough to drive anyone away with his scowl. That was before traders realized the man must've openly hunted dangerous scorpions based on the massive amount of stock on his shelves.

Unfortunately, he noticed me staring.

"Like scorpions, eh?" he asked me, his voice seeming to echo despite the bustling space.

"No," I replied as I gave into my curiosity and drew nearer. Not only did he have carapace made into necklaces or other accessories, but he must've killed enough of the brownish-yellow creatures to somehow create two breastplates from it. One lay on the side of his stand. The other he wore over a loose brown shirt, almost like a Krowikie tunic. He was the first of the Vastrothie I'd seen cover their arms.

"Yet here ya are." He laughed with his hands on his hips. "I see you're eying my carapace armor! Quite the stuff, let me tell ya." His own breastplate made a crackling sound when he punched his chest, but it held. "Killed about a thousand deathstalkers to make each."

"Deathstalkers?"

A light seemed to fill his eyes. "Ah, traveler then? Shoulda assumed with that skin of yours, but Ma never liked it when I assumed."

My heart stopped. "Why do you think that?"

"Just 'bout everybody here could tell ya what those little yellow bastards are. See." He pointed toward the wall, where a scorpion scuttled away from the crowd. Unlike the silver ants from the tunnels, I couldn't sense this one. "Deathstalkers practically ruled this city before that Winter Bitch and her men with spears up their rears showed up. Luckily, the guards stay further down the cliffs. Leaves more for me here."

His casual cursing of Marzanna made me smirk more than I wanted to. "She really is one, but aren't you afraid of her warriors hearing?"

"Listen…" He waved his hand, waiting for my name.

"Otylia," I said without a moment's hesitation. *Stupid!*

"That's not… All right, ya definitely aren't from around here, but that's not my concern. Listen, Otylia, there's plenty of different types of people in the world. All I care about is two of 'em: pests and pest wranglers, and those warriors are pests."

I raised my brow. Wacław's pain still surged through our connection, but the tension in my own chest faded talking to this man. He was unlike anyone I'd ever met. "Wranglers? How do you wrangle a tiny scorpion?"

He reached for a carapace necklace, his fingers running lightly along its surface, far more nimble than I'd expected for someone his size. "If ya squash one, the carapace is useless. Most people don't know how to distract that tail of theirs. That's the key—keep 'em focused one way and strike the other. On quick jab with the finest blade the scions ever saw and she's all yours."

The knife seemed little more than a sewing needle in his massive hands, but again, he worked with precision as he drew it from the sheath at his hip and jabbed the air. "The Winter Witch don't care about me when I kill the pests. Tiny blade like this couldn't hurt her warriors, right?" He grinned, his anticipatory glance telling me to confirm his tale.

"Sure."

"Aha!" he exclaimed, slamming his free hand into the stone. I winced at the noise as passersby gave us startled looks, but the man didn't care. "Tricked by Amten, ya were! Just like the witch's pests. This here blade could strike down any lad like he was a deathstalker."

I reached for the displayed armor and traced each carapace woven across it. It seemed more a tapestry than a breastplate, not that our tribe used armor all that often. "Maybe *I* tricked *you*. You just admitted to killing the Winter Witch's warriors and then gave me your name."

Amten's eyes widened. "I…"

"Don't worry. Your secret is safe with me, as long as you don't mention the girl with a foreign name who liked scorpions."

"So ya do like 'em?"

I smiled. It was a relief to give a genuine one. "All of our realm's creatures are amazing in their own ways—a blessing from the wild goddess Dziewanna. Even pests. Well," I looked to the brutes pounding each other's faces in the middle of the bowl-shaped room, "at least some pests."

He perked up again, chuckling. "Ya like scorpions, then I like ya. Ah, speaking of those who kill pests."

A young, dark-skinned woman approached with swift strides. Dressed in a shirt and trousers like mine with an open-front coat striped in various earth-tones, I recognized her as Ildes's messenger instantly. If it hadn't been for her shoulder-length straight black hair and the joyous smile, she would've looked like a teenage version of Kiin.

She bowed her head to me before turning to Amten, leaning her forearms upon the stall with her legs stretched out behind her. "Trying to sell scorpion corpses to the new girl?" she asked in a tone as quick and dynamic as the Wyzra's rapids.

"Na," Amten replied. "Just showing her the best wares we got in this city."

"Does that armor actually work?" I asked, examining the marks on his own.

He held up his bearded chin. "Stronger than iron and more flexible than leather! This one ya see on sale here is made of the little ones, but my armor comes from the biggest deathstalkers ever seen in Vastroth—one of 'em was big as you."

I crossed my arms in disbelief. There was no way a scorpion could get that big, but it would explain the larger chunk of carapace protecting his chest. "So you killed a giant scorpion?"

The new arrival huffed and spun to lean back on the stand as she watched the passing crowd. "Amten likes to tell a good story."

"I did!" Amten appealed. "Got the stinger mark on my butt to prove it. Lucky for me, I'm immune to the venom. Took a small dose of it every day, and by the Earth Mother, it worked!"

"Is that why you came to us with your cheeks puffed up like a child stuffing themselves with sweets?"

Amten mumbled to himself as she looked to me instead. "Ildes says I'm to refer to you as 'Lady Otylia' or 'Lady of Endings,' but pardon me if I don't. The Earth Mother is the only one who deserves such a title. Even then, don't like it." When I glanced at the carapace dealer, the girl shrugged. "Amten's an oaf, but you can trust him. He's been a friend of our order since before the arrival of the Winter Witch's men."

"Your order?" I asked. "I thought the Daughters were created during the attack?"

She pulled down her collar on one side, exposing Mokosz's Mothermark for only a second. "You get it?"

I nodded.

"Good. Name's Ta-naro, chosen of the Earth Mother and daughter of none of your business. Friends call me Ta, so you can call me Ta-naro."

My grin answered her sarcasm, and I released the smallest bit of *żityje* to make my hand glow with the moon's power just long enough for her to notice. "That's how you treat your goddess's granddaughter?"

She slipped off the stand, catching herself before she fell completely and drew too much attention. Eyes fierce, she stepped closer and whispered, "So it's true? You're her?"

"Yes."

Behind the stand, Amten held a fist to over his heart, his head bowed. "She holds the Earth Mother's blood," he said to himself, "and she likes my scorpions."

"Stop it," Ta-naro hissed. "You're making a scene, and nobody likes your stupid carapaces."

"What would it take for me to have the armor?" I asked, ignoring the szeptucha's complaints.

Amten beamed wide enough to expose all his jagged and cracked teeth. "Ya want my armor? Take it!" He scrambled forward, grabbing the armor and holding it out to me. "No one ever wants my armor. 'Too expensive,' they say. 'Disgusting.' But not the Lady of Endings!"

I touched the scale-like armor, its surface uneven with each unique carapace. "I can't take this without paying you something. This must've taken moons to make."

"It'd be worth it if ya use it to kill the pests," he said.

Just as he handed me the armor, heavy footsteps approached. I turned to see who the new customer was, but the breastplate slipped from my fingers at the sight of two Frostmarked guards. *How'd they get here?*

"What are a pair of women doing at a scorpion shop this late?" the one in front asked, gripping his two-ended spear. "The fights are for men, and… Is that armor?"

Despite my loss of composure, Amten kept his own. "The customers were just admiring my fine work," he said with his arms crossed and chest puffed. "Not armor. Decorative!"

The guards swapped glances as I picked the breastplate up, and the second waved for me to hand it to him. "Let me see it, then." His expression softened when it touched his hands. "Ah, yeah, far too light to stop a blade."

I gave him the nod he wanted and gratefully took the breastplate back. In truth, it was light. Amten seemed convinced of its use, though, and heavy armor would only slow me down. If it could save me from wasting *žityje* on healing, it was worth it.

"Just finish your trade and get home, girl," the first guard said. "We've got enough trouble without vulnerable women wandering the tunnels."

They walked past, and once they could no longer see us, Ta-naro made a gesture in their direction that I assumed to be insulting. "Stupid ice brains."

"Ice brains?" I asked.

She nodded for me to follow. "Yeah, they got ice all up in their heads. Makes them easy to trick. C'mon, let's get out of here before we draw more attention. Have fun with your scorpions, Amten."

The scorpion wrangler punched his chest again. "I always do."

Offering him one last nod of respect, I held the carapace tight and followed Ta-naro into the crowd. I'd spent so much time alone since my initiation as a szeptucha four years before. It had become a comfortable normal, but speaking to Serapis, Amten, and Ta-naro had reminded me how secure it felt to not be so isolated.

Still, I clutched one gloved hand over Kwiecień and scanned every wandering eye for threats. We'd been betrayed too often. Trust would make me vulnerable, but when was the risk worth it? I shook my head. Such questions were for later. For now, I needed the Daughters of the Earth, and I needed my friends.

24

Ara

What have we been reduced to?

THE COLD WIND BLEW MY HAIR ACROSS MY FACE as we rode toward the remnants of the Zurgowie and Simukie clans. I didn't bother to bat it away. There was too much on my mind.

Somewhere in the Astiwie forests, our people suffered. Wars on the Anshayman Steppe for years hadn't killed as many as the Frostmarked and Astiwie had in mere moons. Two of the greatest clans were now nothing more than wandering nomads, and we were the lucky ones. Otylia and the other diviners had seen the complete destruction of other clans during their equinox rituals. The Astiwie and Krowikie were next.

I looked to Zakir beside me and took his hand. Riding through Astiwie lands after fleeing only weeks before was terrifying, but it was worse to not know what we'd face in the moons ahead. Katiôn and Rasa were dead, leaving both Zakir's clan and mine without the warlords who'd led us for over a decade.

High Priestess Rasa had never been one to seek peace. My family had fled Zurgow's wars for a reason, but unfortunately, her former right hand, Zhaleh, seemed even more aggressive. There was little doubt in my mind that Xobas could handle her if necessary. Any conflict between the clans, though, would be an unneeded distraction, making things more difficult for Zakir's arrival as the new Simukie marzban.

"The clans shouldn't be far," I said as Sosna yawned from her position, wrapped around my waist with her fluffy tail brushing my hands. "Are you ready?"

Zakir took a shaky breath. "I haven't been able to think of anything except what we face. There are so many variables. Cavalry. Manpower. Weaponry. Tactics…"

"It's okay to be scared. I am."

As he thought, his fingers drummed against his lips, chapped and cracked from the cold air. I liked kissing them anyway—not that I often got the chance. "It is hard to know what I'm supposed to feel."

"It's not about what you're *supposed* to feel but what you *do* feel." Zakir had barely spoken since I told him of his grandfather's death. We'd both expected it, but when the final glimmer of hope had been vanquished, it hurt more than I'd anticipated. "Zakir, please talk to me."

"I don't like traveling." He clenched his jaw, narrowing his already gaunt face even more. "I know our people are nomads, but it is difficult to work when you are always moving."

"At least we'll be with our people soon. Our lonely ride will be over, as much as I've liked being alone with you."

He sighed. "The only end is death. Nothing will be over until then—and the Krowikie have shown even that is questionable. There is so much to learn. A marzban has no time for studies or alchemy…"

I froze, shutting my eyes for a moment as Tanek lumbered forward beneath me. This had been my fear ever since we'd escaped Kynnytsia. Bidaês had been a stubborn donkey who'd caused so much death, but he'd yearned to lead his people. Of course, I was happy it was Zakir and not him who'd been heir. The question, though, wasn't whether Zakir wished to lead the Simukie in the right direction but whether he wished to lead them at all.

"You think me foolish," he continued, his voice flat. I almost wanted him to be angry. At least then I could understand what was going on in that brain of his.

"No," I replied. "You're the least foolish person I've ever met."

He cocked his head. "Then why do you give me such a look?"

"Because I'm worried about you."

"Xobas will be a better leader. He has commanded men in war before, and he should do so against the Frostmarked Horde."

I groaned, frustration creeping into my voice. "No, Zakir, I'm worried about *you*. We'll find someone to lead the Simukie if you don't want to, but I need to know you're not dodging this because you're afraid you're not good enough."

"I am not afraid to lead." He slipped his hand from mine and gripped his reins as he stared at the sea of leafless trees ahead. The plains around us were hardly a better sight. Brown and dry, impossible to deny that the realm of the living had died. How much time did we truly have?

"Then why don't you want to?" I asked. "And I swear to Otlezd, do not just tell me it's purely logical."

"Then I don't know what to say."

Before I could reply, figures appeared along the tree line ahead. Hundreds of them marched southward with sleds pulled by the strongest men through the snow. Horses would've once done the labor, but few remained besides those ridden by the elite cavalry of both clans.

They're alive!

We pushed our horses into a gallop, my heart soaring. I hadn't doubted Eryk's claim, but actually seeing them filled me with an energy I hadn't realized I'd missed.

Zhaleh rode alongside Xobas at the line's head. As we approached, the priestess's golden eagle circled over us, releasing a short burst of calls before diving to its mistress.

"Is this some form of Zurgowie ritual?" Zakir asked.

I laughed as we slowed to a walk, his hair still puffed-up from the sprint. "No, Zhaleh just likes to make her presence known."

The clans' footsteps sent a cascade of noise over us until Xobas raised his fist. In seconds, the entire caravan stopped, and he dismounted with a firm grin on his face. "You have no idea how happy I am to see you two."

Sosna yapped and practically tackled him at full stride. Xobas chuckled, catching her in his built arms. "Of course, I meant three."

"The feeling is mutual," I replied, hopping off Tanek with tears welling in my eyes. "We'd feared you were dead. After your plan to help us escape—"

"Come, now! There will be no sorrow today. For we are reunited, and the Clan of Simuk has found its heir, returned from his quest! He is now eligible to take his grandfather's place."

Zakir stared at the ground, his hands wrung before him.

"Oh, yes." Xobas coughed and set Sosna down. "I'm sorry, Zakir. We fought our hardest to save Katiôn, but the Astiwie had us surrounded. It is by sheer luck this many of us survived."

When Zakir offered only a small nod in reply, I stepped closer to him and spoke in his place, "Eryk told us you're leading the clans to Likiec before going west."

"We are. Did the płanetnik explain Wacław's plan?"

"He did," I said with a glance toward the gathered clans. Some rested their legs and ate morsels of food while others whispered with their gazes fixed on Zakir. "I'm not sure I like it."

"Da," he replied, "but let's discuss more as we ride. Time is short with the Horde's advance."

We mounted again as Xobas signaled for the clan to continue the march. Zhaleh pulled alongside us, her brow furrowed beneath her streaks of green face paint. All Zurgowie priestesses wore such markings along with robes bearing Otlezd's sun symbol, but somehow, she made the uniform appear more threatening than most. The golden eagle on her shoulder only amplified the effect.

"So, you flee the suffering of our clans and then expect to lead upon your return," she said, her lip curled. "Cunning."

"We didn't flee!" I appealed, but Zakir held a hand lightly on my shoulder as our horses walked along the line of trees.

"I didn't intend to abandon our people," he said. "Wacław's journey to Dwie Rzeki presented me with an opportunity to learn, serve, and complete my required quest. My elixirs helped save his life. Now he is our chance of survival."

Zhaleh scoffed. "Krowikie lies. If this boy is a demon like his messenger, then he is a pawn of Alunam and should be burned by Otlezd's flames!"

"Because Otlezd seems *so* willing to aid us," I quipped. It had snowed on and off since Wacław defeated Eryk moons before. "Come the next storm, these plains are going to be smothered by blizzards. Where is his heat now?"

The priestess looked ready to strike, but Xobas rode between us, his large frame enough to block her from my sight. "Enough debates of faith. What matters now is that we stay united. It is the only way we will survive what is to come."

"How do you know the Krowikie will honor their agreement?" Zhaleh asked. "This new high chief hates us, does he not?"

So Xobas didn't tell her all of Wacław's plan…

"The Krowikie will fight by our sides," I said. "My hesitation isn't with them, though."

Xobas nodded, understanding where I was headed. "You don't want to abandon the Astiwie."

"They slaughtered us!" Zhaleh snapped. "They deserve what is coming to them."

I shook my head. "Boz betrayed us, but does that mean we should condemn his entire tribe to death by leaving them for the Horde? It's surprising Wacław would suggest that."

"Indeed it is," Xobas said. "The demon may be affecting him if his mortal soul is truly dead."

"On this, the demon is right," Zhaleh said, releasing her eagle to scout ahead. It quickly soared over the trees and kept its gaze on the east. "The Astiwie have hunted us like rabid dogs. Let them suffer for their ignorance."

Her words lingered in the air for a long time, none of us willing to contest the horrors of the last moon. Only when Zakir cleared his throat did the silence end. "We don't have enough people to make a difference with the Astiwie, but Krowik is larger and more populous. If they lend us horses, our cavalry will be effective alongside their armies on the plains. The mountains of Astiw make us vulnerable."

Xobas's shoulders slumped, but he held out an open hand. "Well-spoken. This is war, and strategy, not pity, could be the difference between victory and our complete destruction."

"So we're just going to let thousands of innocents die?" I asked. My palms hurt from how tightly I held the reins, but I couldn't let go. Wacław had told Eryk to send us west. Did we have to listen? Especially if the demon had taken over, that might've not even been what Wacław truly wanted.

Zhaleh studied me with a cocked brow. "Why do you pity them? They allied with Bidaês to try to kill all of us. There were hundreds of warriors, if not over a thousand. Any of them could have defied Boz."

"A hundred did."

She hesitated, and Xobas gave me a firm nod. "Commander Andrij's men gave their lives to stand by us," he said. "Most who survived fled, but a few still travel with us now. The least we could do is send Eryk to collect their families and warn those we encounter along the way. Maybe some will join us." He looked to Zakir. "Marzban, do you agree?"

"I am not our marzban."

"You are," Xobas insisted. "It is your birthright."

Zakir stared over the plains. "Perhaps, but our clan doesn't need the old ways anymore. We have left the steppe and lost our people. I can't save us." He bit his lip as he turned to me. "I'm sorry, Ara."

"Don't be." I forced him to take my hand. "This decision is yours, not mine."

Zhaleh grinned. "Weakness does not make for a good leader."

"Nor does spite," I replied.

Xobas raised a hand to silence us, but his gaze remained fixed ahead as his shoulders slumped, as if crushed beneath a heavy weight. He was tired. From the bags beneath his eyes to the exhaustion in his voice, Xobas had led the clans from slaughter with little hope of what lay ahead. Maybe Zakir was right. To command was a burden—one that would crush him.

"The boy is wise to know when it is not his time to lead," Xobas said. "But what he intends is not possible. Do not appeal. I will give anything to secure the survival of our people, but the destruction of our values will destroy us. The title of marzban is passed to the youngest in the bloodline in order to ensure stability and longevity. We have thrived because we don't simply select the strongest warrior to lead."

He rode to Zakir's side and laid a hand on his shoulder. "Boy, you are young. Many men have stood where you do and doubted themselves. To lead, however, is to know both the capabilities of yourself and those around you. Grant me command of your army, and I will fight in your name. Katiôn would demand nothing less of me."

For a moment, Zakir just studied the old warrior's face. He searched for patterns and answers in everything, but he'd admitted days before that people confused him. We were inconsistent, rash. Emotion often overwhelmed our sense of logic. If he was to rule, he would need our aid to help him understand both his army and his people. No one, though, was smarter than him, and I truly believed his mind could save us all.

"All right," Zakir said with the faintest smile creeping across his face. "Xobas of Clan Simuk, I accept your offer. Once I am recognized by our clan as marzban, you will have complete command of my armies."

I took a deep breath and met his gaze, forcing my own smile. Hope and fear clashed in my heart, but I needed to be strong. For Zakir and my clan, I would not falter. We would rescue those whom we could from Astiw. We would escape across the Wyzra and stand with the Krowikie in the war to come. Then, we would lead our people into a new age, no matter what stood in our way.

25

Otylia

FOUR YEARS EARLIER

Who chose me?

I COULDN'T SLEEP UPON MY RETURN FROM THE BOG. Three days I'd been underwater, longer than any szeptucha initiate before, but a god had brought me back to life. Who? Lying in bed, I clutched Dziewanna's amulet in wait of the answer.

Father had demanded I rest after emerging early in the night, but once I'd changed out of my soaked clothes and climbed beneath my wool blanket, I was too anxious. These rituals would determine the god I served until death. Their mark would signal me as theirs, and I would channel their power in service of them.

"Please be you, Dziewanna," I whispered, staring at Mother's black hellebore flower on my nightstand. A sea of them had covered the forest after her death, and I'd found this one beside me as I'd wept—a gift from her wandering soul.

Mother had always wished for me to serve the wild goddess, so I'd promised myself I'd devote my life to protecting the forests and swamps she'd adored. Then, each spring would be my revenge. Marzanna's Curse had killed Mother, and through my service of Dziewanna, I'd make her regret it.

I hated Marzanna. I hated her winter. And I hated waiting to know if my revenge would come.

In the light of a single candle, the hellebore seemed aflame with a dark glow. I'd never forget Mother, but it was a constant reminder that she'd always be watching me from Nawia with the ancestors. Knowing their loved ones were in paradise was enough for some. Not for me. The wound her death had carved in my chest was too fresh, and as my tears dripped onto my pillow, my only solace was that Mother would know I'd been chosen.

"I'll make you proud."

I blew out the candle and rose. Unfortunately, the swiftness of the motion threw me off balance, sending me stumbling into the wall. Father stirred. *I'll regret that…*

The unmistakable thumping of his staff against the dirt floor approached, and I rushed back under the blanket. It was too late. His silhouette filled the doorway as he threw aside the cloth separating my room from the main one, the only light coming from the torches behind him. In that moment, he could've been a demon or simply a father concerned for his untamable daughter. I feared him all the same.

"I'm sorry!" I yelped. "I couldn't sleep."

His sigh filled the room as he leaned upon his staff, adorned with markings of the old tongue used by the gods and szeptuchy alike. An iron Forgemark amulet of Swaróg hung from a leather band on its top. He twirled it in his fingers, like he often did when pondering what to do with me. "It has been many nights since you've slept. Don't claim otherwise. I see that candle flickering through the midnight hours, when the godless moon curses the spirits of the dark forests."

"One of us has to remember her."

He turned away and stamped the staff into the dirt with a whisper I couldn't hear. When he raised his head, his voice was fractured and slow. "How could anyone forget her? Your mother was one with the trees and the roots stretching deep into Jawia's core. There is no one left in this realm who could compare… None but you. Come, dawn brings the light of Swaróg's son, and with it, we will make a szeptucha of you yet."

My feet tore into the dirt without need of direction as I followed him into the cool morning air. Our cat, Maryn, meowed after me, but I had no time for cuddles with the black ball of fur. I'd waited for this moment for too long. Today, I would bond with the god who chose me, and I would finally be more than the girl they called a witch.

"You forgot your boots," Father said with the remnant moonlight drawing out the silver in his long hair.

I had, but I folded my arms, defiant. "Dziewanna would want me to feel the forest floor."

The smallest of smiles crossed his face as we continued toward the village center. "Oh, how like your mother you are. Perhaps I allowed you too much time with her instead of pursuing productive interests for both the gods and our tribe. Even her potions led you on searches through the woods with Jacek's reject."

His reference to Wacław made my stomach churn. Why did he believe the tales that I was a dark witch? Only that could explain his abrupt turn away from me after I'd saved his life—whether the voice in his ear was Jacek's or the other children. But Wacław was just a stupid boy. It shouldn't have mattered that he'd abandoned me when I would have a god to serve soon. It did, though, and my feet dragged knowing he wouldn't be at the initiation with me, as he'd always promised he would.

"You never should have spent so much time with that boy," Father continued as people emerged from their houses, watching us while the first beams of light split the trees beyond the wall to the east. "There is a darkness to him that you are too young to understand, and his father threatens the gods' work with his ambition. Jacek has always craved power in his uniting of the tribes under him. He is dangerous, but Wacław is far more so."

Few of his words meant anything to me amid the pain in my heart. Without Wacław, I had no friends in our village, and the rumors he'd surely spread about me channeling before my initiation had ensured I'd never have any. I was alone. My mother and best friend gone within a moon.

Don't cry, I told myself. *Be strong for Dziewanna.*

So I held back the tears and walked on, enduring people's stares and the drumming of my heart. This was my chance. This was my moment. No one could take it from me: not Wacław, not the ignorant villagers, and not the goddess of winter and death.

"Here we are," Father said as we reached the village center's clearing. Torches rimmed the space before giving way to candles around Perun's Oak with the animal bones and skulls among its branches clattering in the breeze. At the tree's base rose an altar of bound sticks, topped with a skull larger than I was tall—all jagged teeth and spikes that protruded from behind its eyes. Mokosz's eldest szeptucha, Arleta, stood before it with a bowl in one hand and a long knife in the other. She watched me expectantly.

"Are you ready?" Father asked. "I can take you no further."

"Why?" I replied, suddenly grasping his hand as if I were just a little girl.

Sorrow filled his eyes as he looked down at me. "Only women may channel the power of the gods, and their presence lies within the inner circle. I may be a priest, but I am only allowed to hear their whispers when they so choose, nothing more." He peeled his hand from my grip. "Go. Arleta waits, as do the gods."

The entire village had filled the clearing, and every eye followed me as I stepped into the circle of torches. They flickered beneath the soft light of the young sun. An arc of fire that separated me from the rest of the world. With each stride, people's stares no longer mattered, nor did their judgement. I was alone with Arleta and whatever force lay before the candlelit altar. But this isolation didn't bring the ache of solitude. A warmth pulsed through the air, filling it with vibrant life that surged into my soul and granted me genuine joy—a feeling so alien to the last moon that it gave me pause.

I closed my eyes. *Can this be right?* My toes dug into the dirt, as if preparing for a storm to tear away this moment like one had the night of the equinox.

When I looked at the altar again, another sensation met me. Wholeness, connection. No one was here besides Arleta and me, but I swore I *felt* a familiar presence. It should've startled me. It should've warned me to flee. Instead, it gave me the courage to push on and approach the eldest diviner, dropping to my knees.

"Otylia, daughter of Dariusz and of Odeta, you have been chosen to serve as a szeptucha," Arleta began. Her voice shook with age, but she held herself with the grace of a chieftess, clothed in embroidered robes and an iron Mothermark talisman hanging around her neck. Mokosz's favored. For the goddess of women only chose the strongest among us.

"I have," I replied, my own voice catching in my throat. "I spent three days in the bog, but the gods brought me back."

She smiled with a mother's pride. "Indeed they have, my child, and it is time for you to enter the embrace of the one who has made you theirs. Take the blade."

The long knife glinted in the sunlight as I wrapped my fingers around its hilt. A sacrificial blade—one I'd seen Father use many times during rituals—but why did I need it? Before I could ask, the bleating of a goat approached from behind me. I turned as it ran to Arleta, nuzzling her hand.

"You must sacrifice this goat in thanks to the god who saved you," she said. "Such offerings are a crucial part of our role."

I nodded and held the goat's neck softly. Preparing animals to eat was the job of hunters and farmers, but I'd helped Wacław and Lubena more than once. While the slaughtering process was slow and deliberate, wasting nothing, sacrifices were bloody and raw. Neither Father nor the szeptuchy had been able to explain what the gods did with the dead animals, just that they demanded the offerings be left uneaten.

"Take this offering," I whispered in what little I knew of the old tongue, "and grant me your guidance."

The blade sliced the goat's throat with one quick stroke. I winced at the death of Dziewanna's animal, but it had been for her. So, as Arleta collected the blood pouring from the wound, I pushed away my fear and met the diviner's gaze.

"Close your eyes," she said, rising. I did, and she hummed as she dipped two fingers in the blood before dragging them down my forehead, over my eyelid and lips, all the way to my chin. The goat's blood dripped down my face. Warm, disturbingly so. But I remained still as she chanted, "May the blood of the beast bind you to nature's will. May you hear its calling in your heart and feel its life in your soul."

Her hand met my free one. It was cold and wrinkled yet strong, and when she pulled my palm to the knife's tip, I couldn't resist. "Now grant the gods your own blood," she said. "For we are no different than the beasts, united as part of Jawia's life. We must give of ourselves as well if we are to take from the blessings of nature around us."

I shuddered against the frigid blade. My own hand held the hilt, and though Arleta would not allow me to pull away from the tip, it was up to me to pierce the skin. *Mother, give me your strength.* I couldn't do this alone. I couldn't offer my own blood without her aid.

The presence I'd felt returned, tightening in my chest and granting me the reassurance I needed. It was her. Of course it was. Mother had promised never to abandon me, and she'd never failed me before. Her love had guided me to my initiation. Now, she would lead me to its end, her invisible hand pressing against mine and driving the knife home.

Blood flowed down my palm. Pain followed, and I bit my cheek as my instincts pleaded for me to stop. I wouldn't. The gods demanded my blood, so I gave it.

The blood trickled into Arleta's bowl, its droplets audible with my eyes closed. Animal and mortal as one. Our *žityje*, our life, pooled for the gods. Her humming resumed as she pulled the blade away and dragged her fingers down the other side of my face, but even in that same motion, I felt it so much more. My blood. It ran down my cheek and pulsed through my veins with each rapid beat of my heart.

"As the beast's blood binds you to nature," Arleta chanted, "your own blood binds you to mortality, to the people who worship the gods. May you work to better their lives by serving the one who has chosen you."

Her steps moved to my side. "Stand, Otylia, and enter the circle. When you hear the whispers, take the blood, pour it over the żmij skull, and kneel with your head bowed."

My legs were numb as the candlelight met my eyes. The flames seemed to wave in the soft western wind, which carried a distant voice, growing with each step I took toward the circle. Arleta, the goat, and even the sky faded until all that remained was the altar and Perun's Oak. Leaves rustled among its branches as mist rose from the skulls within. Beyond them was a void so dark that neither the sun nor moon pierced its veil, yet there was light here.

"Daughter of the wilds, of the wetlands, of the earth," the voice whispered in my head. *"Was there ever any question who would choose you?"*

"Dziewanna?" I asked, stopping at the altar and pouring the blood as Arleta had commanded. The żmij skull alone was enough to make me tremble. Mother's stories about the great shapeshifting dragons echoed through my memories, and all of them were suddenly real. Who had defeated a żmij in our village?

A power swelled around me from the moment the blood met the skull. Terrifying, hungry, it drove me to my knees as I clutched my Bowmark, praying to Dziewanna with winds encircling me. Hundreds of voices spoke at once, each in a different tongue. They rose with the gusts until I was deaf and too scared to breathe.

Then it stopped.

My skin felt cold and wet as I knelt in the silence, bowing my head. Only my shuddered breaks pierced the air, and it took all my strength not to weep or flee. I would not be afraid.

Something touched my temple on the left side, or more, *someone* touched me. Two fingers, as Arleta had, coated in blood as they dragged them in an arc around the end of my brow and to my jaw. When they finished, they drew a symbol on my neck on the same side. I gasped. Consisting of only four lines in the shape of a hunter's bow, Dziewanna's mark was the simplest of the gods', and I recognized it without needing to see my reflection.

Dziewanna had chosen me. She'd made me her only szeptucha, just as I'd dreamed.

But once the fingers pulled away, another pair followed on the right. They were surely not the same, as the first had been swift and firm, while these moved with the tender grace of a mother cradling her child. Their pattern upon my face was the same. As they moved to my neck, though, I panicked.

There shouldn't be two!

It didn't matter what *should* be, only the horrifying, amazing reality that was. Somehow, two gods had chosen me: Dziewanna and another whose identity I couldn't figure out by the mark's feeling alone. No szeptucha had ever been chosen by more than a single god. Well, at least according to Father. Why was I different?

"Rise, Otylia," the voice commanded through the winds. *"Rise, chosen of Dziewanna and Mokosz."*

The gales washed over me, whipping my braid as I stood and opened my eyes. To them, the world seemed nothing but darkness beyond Perun's Oak, but the power that had radiated from the altar now pulsed within me. A beat that joined with my soul. Sensations both distant and far, nothing like the ones I'd felt before.

"Go to them," the voice said. *"Find them in the places where their forces reside."*

Then the candles extinguished, tearing away the void in a flash that blinded me. Light streamed from the great sun, but it wasn't Dadźbóg who ruled my mind. I beamed with tears rushing down my cheeks as the sounds of the village returned to me. Dziewanna wanted me. Mokosz wanted me. For the rest of my life, I would serve them and channel *żityje* for their will. They would be all I needed, and I would never again be alone.

26

Otylia

Can I trust Kiin with what Serapis told me?

KIIN SAT CROSS-LEGGED BESIDE ME on the floor of the Daughters' hideout. Ta-naro had led me through the deepest tunnels of Fifth Limestone to this room, its cold stone covered in tapestries and rugs. Morning had yet to arrive, and Kiin's eyes were bleary as I retold the events since the Drowning of Marzanna to the szeptuchy scattered throughout the room. There were six, Kiin included, each watching me with shock—except Ta-naro.

The short-haired szeptucha had taken to yawning constantly in the corner. It was dark, with only a single torch and the moonlight I called to my skin to light the space, but Ildes's glares at Ta-naro were obvious. Her patience ran out as I described our escape from Nawia.

"The Maj moon had come, and Jaryło—"

"Stop yawning or I'll throw you to the witch's men!" Ildes snapped. Though short in stature with the tender voice of a grand-mother, the others were obviously afraid of her fury. They all scooted away on the rug as Ta-naro winced.

"Sorry," the girl said. "Just didn't get enough sleep."

Ildes sighed and held her wrinkled hands to her temples. Long black hair fell over her them with a single braid on either side, not a strand misplaced. "Earth Mother help me… Please, Lady Otylia, continue your story. We've already learned much about the Winter Witch and her plans from it."

"I've told you most of the rest," Kiin replied, "except for what has happened since our separation."

I clutched my legs close, digging my bare feet into the soft rug. Unlike Serapis's house, the room was chilled, but I'd worn my boots for what felt like forever. It was freeing to take them off, cold or not. I missed walking barefoot through the woods more than I wanted to admit. "It was easier to find my way around once the moon came and I could use my illusions. Someone told me how to read the torches, and I followed them to the market."

"And this is where you found Serapis?" Ildes asked, her lips pursed as she waited for my response.

"He found me."

"The Moonstone."

I nodded. "He said he tracked the power from it once we arrived here. If I hadn't fought off his goons, he would've stolen it from me."

Ta-naro giggled, sitting with her back against the wall and her legs stretched before her. A shadow. "Those idiots? They could barely fight a child, let alone a goddess."

"It is unnerving nonetheless," Ildes said. "Serapis is obsessed with Alatyr, and if he believes your Moonstone truly is a shard of it, then he'll do anything to have it. He may have led you to us, but be wary."

"Don't worry," I said, tracing Mother's Bowmark necklace alongside Kwiecień. "I don't trust easily."

Ildes smiled. Even that reminded me of Mother's pride, and a hole opened in my chest as she replied, "That is likely for the best. There are many who would swindle you or just stab you in the back in this city. I hope, however, we can trust each other."

"Believe me, it's not just this city." I stood, taking a deep breath after what seemed like an eternity of talking. "Kiin trusts you, so I do too. Just don't make me regret it."

Ildes bowed her head. "You will not, Lady Otylia." She whistled and flicked her hand toward Ta-naro. "Show the Earth Mother's granddaughter to her chambers and guard the door until she's ready to free her friends from the Winter Witch's men."

"What?" Ta-naro exclaimed. "I just told you I haven't slept!"

"Stop spending so much time with people you shouldn't and maybe you'd be awake with the sun." Ildes waved for the other szeptuchy to leave before stepping closer and smiling again. "Forgive her. She has only seen thirteen years and has much to learn, despite her considerable skill with channeling."

I nodded. "I was an initiate once…"

"Indeed, we all were." She hesitated, lowering her voice. "You have quite the story, but I must ask about this demon, Wacław. Is your relationship with him romantic?"

"It *was*," I replied, failing to hold back my flushed cheeks.

"Good. Then you have the wisdom to understand what will happen to him, and what must be done."

Anger flashed within me, but I bit my tongue. She meant well. "It wasn't wisdom that led me away from him but cowardice."

Her hands fell lightly on my shoulders. "Oh child, no coward could face what you have. If you have stayed with this płanetnik for so long, then you have done all you can. You must now let him go for both of your sakes."

"I didn't face the past moons alone," I said, furrowing my brow. "And don't tell me what I must do."

Bravery hadn't led me across Krowikie lands, through the Mangled Woods, and from Nawia's choking vines. I'd never truly been alone. Be it Mother—as both mortal and goddess—or Mokosz, Wacław or Ara, Sabina or Kiin, there had always been those who'd stood by my side and walked with me through the darkest of times. Wacław had been barred from seeing me, but he'd watched from a distance during my initiation and had given me the hellebore flower.

I remembered standing beneath Perun's Oak, holding the sacrificial knife to my palm yet unable to draw blood. Even then, there had been a presence with me. I didn't know whether that had been

Mother's soul or Wacław in his soul-form. The result, though, had been the same. With their support, then and now, I was strong.

Ildes bowed her head. "My apologies, Lady Otylia. I did not wish to offend you." I knew she was sincere, but I couldn't bring myself to forgive her.

"I should head to my room to rest. If that is all?" I turned to follow Ta-naro, but Kiin caught my gloved hand.

"I'm sorry we lost track of each other. These tunnels are danger-ous. By the time I fended off a second group of guards, you were gone."

"It's not your fault the fox's instincts took over."

"It was my responsibility to—"

"I'm no one's responsibility but my own." I pulled my gloved hand free, the voices from her wisp dangerously close. I'd seen enough of her endings. "It's time for me to stop being a burden on the Daughters."

Ildes drew closer with fluid motions that made nearly no sound. Even her gray dress embroidered with indigo upon the sleeveless shoulders did not flap with her steps. "You are no burden. Among us all, Kiin would be the first to admit if you were. She has quite the habit of saying exactly what she thinks." She chuckled. "Perhaps you two are alike in this."

Kiin bowed her head to her fellow szeptucha. " 'The Earth Mother values kindness as much as honesty.' That is what you always taught me."

"It seems you didn't take that lesson to heart. This is good. The Earth Mother needs both those with tender touches and firm hands at times. My own nature may be to blame for Ta-naro's disobedience, but I don't have the will to punish her too harshly after all she's lost."

"What happened?" I asked, catching the girl out of the corner of my eye as she waited to escort me.

Ildes's joy faded to sorrow. "Between the Earth Mother's demands and the slaughters of the Winter Witch, no one in Vastroth has gone without losing someone they love. Ask her if you wish to know. She could use someone youthful to speak with, even a goddess."

"I will talk to her."

"Good." She looked at Kiin, an unsaid message in her eyes. "Let her rest for some time while we prepare."

Kiin dropped her own gaze. "Of course."

Leaving the pair behind, I joined Ta-naro at the opening in the wall the other szeptuchy had gone through. It was still jarring to see the stone move at their touch, but I figured the same could be said for them watching my power. They hadn't seen End's wisps or the smoky figures in my dreams. Would their trust in me change if they knew I could so easily speak with the dead?

"I'd say you look like you've seen a demon," Ta-naro said as we walked further down the back hall of the Daughters' hideout, "but you obviously have experience with that."

Appearances were rarely my concern, but her comment made me self-aware. I instinctively touched my face, pushing away one of the many mangled strands of hair falling across it. Worse was how I felt. I'd been so focused on trying to find Kiin that time had passed as a blur. Besides a few hours sleeping in my fox form, I'd had no rest, and it hit me hard now that I had the chance to think of myself. From my aching knees to my pounding head, I was done with consciousness.

We reached a tapestry woven with images of a great boat passing through the Elder Cliffs of Sheresy. Men stood upon the ship's deck holding spears which they jabbed into the water below, fighting off dark figures who clawed their way from the depths. There was little detail in their expressions. I imagined their fear, though, as what I assumed to be demons swarmed them, more rising with each scene. Too many. And when winged figures dropped from the sky amid a barrage of arrows, the tapestry ended without concluding the battle.

"What is this?" I asked, running my fingers along the fabric. Even with gloves, the texture was so defined that each sewn ridge seemed to tell a story of its own.

Ta-naro shrugged. "Dunno. Ildes probably could tell you, but I'm not one for history. Bunch of idiots tried to sail through the canyons. They're dead. Men do that. At least I assume they do, seeing as boys never seem to grow up."

I managed a smirk as my fingers stopped over the winged creatures in the final scene. Chały or something else? Behind them, the sun was a dark circle. The other images had roaring light, but here, darkness consumed the sky like a veil. I pulled away with Serapis's warnings in my mind. "Sometimes men do change, and then you find yourself wishing they'd stayed those stupid boys."

She scratched her head. "You all right?"

"What?"

Tears stung my eyes, and I cursed myself as I turned away. They'd come without warning, my exhaustion weakening my will to fight the hurt. No matter how much I tried to hope, Wacław was still controlled by the demon. He'd never be that caring, hesitant boy again. We'd never run through the woods with the dirt between our toes and fake weapons in our hands as we played until dusk. No, even if I could help him retake control, he'd grown since then. We both had. But while figuring out what it was to become a woman and man was hard enough, now we had to discover what it meant to be a goddess and demon. How to love. How to forgive. And how to keep going as all we knew ended around us.

"Each end is a new beginning. The day, the night, the moon's cycle, and even death." I tried to cling to Rod's voice as he'd told me the power of the force I held, but it wasn't enough if I couldn't save the Wašek I knew.

"I'm fine," I replied, wiping away the tears. Sometimes, *fine* was the best I could muster. Even that was a lie today, but I didn't want to talk about it with a stranger, let alone one so young.

"*Fine*, then," Ta-naro said with a roll of her eyes. "Don't tell me."

She switched to the old tongue and placed her hand on the tapestry. "*Dviži.*" Move.

The stone obeyed, allowing us to push our way beneath the boat's demise and into the hidden room beyond. Small and entirely deep red sandstone like the others, a bed filled its center, and a mirror rested upon the wall to our right. Memories of my chambers in Nawia washed over to me as I stepped to the plane of glass and touched its perfect surface. The work of szeptuchy, surely. Had those in Weles's palace been the same?

After all I'd seen and experienced, I feared my reflection. I'd been strong and dedicated to both Dziewanna and Mokosz when I'd jumped the fire the night of the equinox. They had given me purpose, direction. It had been easy when they had chosen the path, but it was my own decision now. End's force was mine alone, but its visions and whispers seemed like mere coincidences at best. Destiny would say otherwise. But if this was Wacław and my fate, then I would face it with all my power.

The woman in the mirror was no longer a child. She'd seen battle and died, faced demons and gods, fallen in love and struggled to keep it, completed the Trials and Ascended, and yet, despite it all, I still recognized her—me.

I traced the crescent scar arcing from my lips to my left cheekbone, a reminder of Yuliya's ambush moons before. There were many like it scattered across my body as well as beneath the skin. Pain and fear lingered behind my stern gaze too, and even the soft glow of my skin when I breathed out *żityje* couldn't hide the dark circles below my eyes. Yes, I had changed. I'd suffered and gained for Mother, for Wacław, for friends both old and new, and for myself.

For myself.

Ever since we'd left Dwie Rzeki, my goal had been to save Dziewanna from whatever her sister was inflicting upon her. I'd done so as her szeptucha, her servant. But her Bowmark no longer graced my neck. My decisions were my own, and now, this journey was about more than saving a goddess and ending winter. It was about me, about *who* I was, not just *what* I was. I'd let being a szeptucha define me for too long. That decision had always been mine, even if I could only see it now.

I was more than a goddess. I was more than the Silver Fox of Nawia or the Lady of Endings and Moon. Those titles had been woven into my being and soul, but they weren't who I was.

Then who am I?

The answer was obvious as I stared at the woman before me. I was determined and strong. I was jagged at times, forcing away those bothered to love me. But beneath it all, I cared. Gods, I *cared*. Not just about Dziewanna and Mokosz but about people—about children who'd lost their parents and those who'd never found their place—about the animals and plants of the wilds that withered under Marzanna's grip, and about the boy who'd never abandoned me, who'd suffered so that I could live free from exile.

That care, that love, made me vulnerable. It had opened a hole in the wall around my heart and allowed pain to rush in like a great army, burning and pillaging everything in its way. Without it, though, I was lost and empty. I needed love to remind me why I fought. I needed pain to remind me that I was strong. And I needed others to remind me I wasn't alone.

"Tell me, Ta-naro," I said, glancing over my shoulder at the girl. *Maybe I could use the company.* "What do you know about demons and Nawie?"

"Uh…" She scratched the back of her head. "Only what Ildes and the other have told me, so not much."

I smiled and gestured to the bed. "Sit. You're stuck with me for a while, so you might as well know who you're protecting."

27

Wacław

Even in sleep, I can't escape you.

SHADOWS SHIFTED ACROSS MY DREAMSCAPE like great giants, staring down upon the realm below with malice and disdain. The gods. Distant and strong, they controlled the living, dead, and those trapped between while claiming to simply guide mankind. Only the szeptucha were their hands and feet on Jawia's plains. Nature's forces were theirs, but man was free to act according to our wills.

All of it was lies.

I drifted between the gods, too insignificant in the night sky to be of note to them. Oh, how they failed to grasp my strength.

"Their pride will be their demise," a dark figure said beside me—in *my* voice. He cast a shadow too, but unlike the gods, he was no larger than me. Such a shadow was nothing to them or the world. Yet.

"It always is," I replied with a deep breath of the cool northwestern wind. Kyustendil had died to free Otylia from Weles, as Kuba had given himself so that I could fight on. Selfless, heroic. "Father believed he could unite the Krowikie under his rule so that he would be remembered as the greatest chief. It was for his glory. We were just an inconvenience, so he cast us out and tore us from Otylia. Then he sent us east, hoping we died."

A thrill rose within him and me alike. "And we killed him."

"Marzanna killed him."

He scoffed. "She gave us the bow, but we released the arrow. For *her*, you probably think. Foolishness! Father made us what we are, so we wanted him dead. Marzanna just provided the excuse."

"Why did you join with me?" I enveloped him in the winds, preventing him from fleeing. Not that he tried. "Why did you possess my mind at birth?"

"Possess?"

"We saw my birth in the Lake of Reflection. I was born beneath the partial blood moon."

Slowly, he nodded his shadowed head. "You were, but the eclipse only granted you a second soul. Your corruption came after, when Father abandoned you."

"Then what are you?" I yelled, tightening my grip, but that only made him grin.

"You may not remember, Wacław, but I joined you in that moment. A Naw's dead soul is open to spirits, and Father's betrayal called me to you, making us one. That doesn't mean you control me. I've been with you for nearly your entire life, growing stronger with the anger you hid. Every strike from Father. Every word of mockery from our tribe. You fed me with your hatred."

The winds broke from my control, and I dropped until the Płanetnik called them to catch me. He crossed his arms, his dark eyes boring into mine.

"But I don't need you anymore," he snarled, "because I am us. You admitted it yourself when we attacked the tower. Otylia finally abandoned us, and you not only accepted our rage, you embraced it. You gave me control to destroy the weakness in us. Unfortunately, *you* are the core of our weakness, so it is best for us for you to die— forever."

The Thunderstone dagger was in his hand before I could reply. Its black blade glinted in the moonlight, enough for me to notice and dodge, breaking his hold just as he stabbed. But the winds were still his, and I tumbled through the clouds with his grin haunting me from above.

"You can't escape, Wacław! No matter how hard you fight or how fast you flee, your mind will succumb to our *need* for power and revenge."

He lunged, streaking toward me with the speed of a hawk hungry for its kill. That eternal craving for *żityje*, for life, rushed through my own veins too. For he was right about this: we were one, and I knew his every feeling. I always had. The urges within me had influenced my life for longer than I'd known, but those same sensations exposed the demon's strikes.

Left.

He jabbed at my side as I rolled. Despite no longer controlling the winds, I knew the air like a fish knew the sea. All it took was the right push and I shifted enough to dodge, but I couldn't defeat him. Even with foresight, I'd barely survived his first attacks, and his fury ignited a speed that no mortal could match.

"We are one," I shouted as he attacked again, my palm catching his forearm and deflecting another strike. "So you can't kill me."

The Płanetnik's eyes widened for a moment. He stopped, allowing me to fall and gain a sense of security. A trick. I sensed it before his arm even twitched, but his winds tightened around me. In my evasion, I'd become too confident. He knew my deceit. And this time, I wouldn't get away with it.

I didn't look away as the blade cut through the night. Silent, almost invisible in the dark sky, it seemed a creation of my imagination until it struck my chest at the heart. Relief came with it. The end of the struggle that had consumed me for moons. I was tired beyond what I could've believed once, and even picturing Otylia, Mom, and Kuba took the last of my remaining strength. They would mourn me, but though I'd lost, a part of me would live on forever in my płanetnik soul—a soul that had lived within me my entire life. The truth was obvious now that I'd joined my mind with his.

The Płanetnik was a demonic spirit, but he'd been part of me for all but my first minute of life. He *was* me. Corrupted by Oblivion, broken, but me all the same. I hadn't surrendered to his possession. I hadn't surrendered to an undead's will.

I'd surrendered to my own darkness.

28

Otylia

What's happened to you, Wašek?

A COOL BREEZE RUSHED THROUGH THE CANYON splitting Sheresy in two. It brought with it the smell of wet stone as the light snowfall gave way to freezing rain that covered my coat and scorpion-carapace breastplate, sending a shiver down my spine as I descended the stairs with Kiin and Ta-naro. Dawn would soon arrive, but it was still dark this deep. We needed it to stay that way.

Kiin had insisted I waste no more *žityje* on guards who showed interest in us. We had no idea what lay in the Frostmarked dungeon at Bottom Slate, the lowest level of the city and the only one below river level. I needed all my strength to fight any guards. With the shadowy faces circling me again, just focusing was hard enough.

"I can't give you what you want," I hissed at the demonic souls, tugging up my hood at the sight of Frostmarked ahead. "There's no way to save you from Oblivion."

They continued their pleas as Ta-naro glanced back at me with her brow raised. "You one of those people who talks to themselves?" she asked. "It's okay if you are."

I held my finger to my lips and nodded to the approaching guards. Three women traveling alone, all in trousers, would draw attention already. My pale skin and armor would only make things worse if they got a close enough look, so I kept to the young szeptucha's side with my gaze averted and my coat pulled shut over my breastplate. Killing them would be easy for us. The last thing we needed, though, was the entire Frostmarked guard of Sheresy discovering us because of a fight in the open.

For a few excruciating moments, I held my breath and ran my gloved fingers along the cliff's jagged stones. 'Riverstone' the Vastrothie called these layers. They were a reminder of Mokosz's strength, and as we passed the guards, I silently prayed for her to shield us from their suspicion.

"Oy!" One of them barked from out of my sight. "You, girl."

Ta-naro yelped as he dragged her from my side, but I held my calm, hoping they would ignore me as Kiin intercepted the girl. "What's this?" she said, arms crossed. "My daughter's done nothing wrong."

"Daughter, eh?" another guard asked. All five were focused on the pair, so I continued ahead slowly. "Fine, what are you doing heading to the river? You don't have buckets or nothing."

"None of your business," Ta-naro replied.

Kiin faked a laugh. "What she *means* to say is that we work at the forge on First Copper and were sent to pick up a shipment of leather for hilts. Please, we were already late yesterday, and if we don't return with the supplies before the sun hits the river…"

The lead guard scoffed as I reached the next landing and turned, giving me a visual of them again. I breathed a sigh of relief. Two of the guards had continued on, and those that remained had lost interest.

Until they saw me.

"And who is this?" one shouted, gripping his two-ended spear. "Trying to sneak past us, were you?"

I called my *żityje* as two headed toward me, but Kiin's gaze told me to remain calm. I was anything but. My instincts told me to fight. My anger told me to punish them for their loyalty to Marzanna. They would only punish those weaker than us if they lived, but something held back my flash of aggression. A memory of Wacław when he'd first shown me his Frostmark. His fear. His ignorance. Did these men truly understand who they served, or had they simply followed the path that kept them alive? Once, Wacław would've told me they had families who they did everything for. That boy was gone, but his voice echoed in my mind as a reminder that someone had to stop the bloodshed.

"I'm sorry," I said, raising my arms and removing my hood. No use in covering my head when they could clearly see I wasn't Vastrothie. "These people aren't with me."

The guards stopped with their spearheads pointed at me. "Likely story!" the tall one snapped. "Who are you, and why are you here?"

"My name is Vlatka." I made my voice as shaky as possible—a simple feat with my short breaths. "My master, the scorpion hunter Amten, sent me to examine Bottom Slate and capture any deathstalkers I see. Apparently it's riddled with them."

He looked me up and down. "You don't look like a scorpion hunter."

"She's got the armor, eh?" the other, fat necked one, said. "Never seen anything like it, 'cept at old Amten's stall."

"So she has," the first replied with a grunt before pulling back his spear. "Bottom Slate is off limits to anyone not part of the guard. We'll take you to make sure you get in, and that you're actually who you say you are."

I bowed my head, catching Kiin's glare as I did. We'd be separated, but my power would be stronger closer to the river. Its changing tides would leave mold and fungi behind. Decay was one type of ending I could wield, and the spores had already helped me escape Nawia. Now, they would help me save my friends.

"Of course," I said. "Please, lead the way. I'm unfamiliar with the Slate levels anyway."

The guards swapped smirks, oddly, and the tall, bulky leader walked ahead while the pudgy one followed me. I fought the temptation to look back at Kiin. My cover story was a thin one at best, and all the Frostmarked needed was a hint that I was with Kiin for them to turn on me. Even now, I doubted they believed me fully. The dungeon was, however, the most convenient place for them to catch me, as they just needed to throw me in with the others who they intended to sacrifice to Marzanna. Images of Huebia's blood-covered market filled my mind. Ildes had confirmed that my friends were alive as of a few days ago, but all I could do now was hope we weren't too late.

As we walked, the guards tried to ask me questions about where I came from. My replies were dismissive at best, as the shadowed figures grew in number and volume the closer we got to the river. Souls trapped in bodies beneath its flow. They'd become water de-mons—likely rusałki and utopiecs—that Father had sometimes re-ferred to as "drowners" because of their deaths. I'd killed one of both in recent moons. Why was that easier than saving them? Hun-dreds cried out for me, but it was no use. Even if I could help, I doubted I had the *żityje* to save so many.

But I remembered the lines that had come from them in my dreams. Bright and taut, almost like string that pulsed with *żityje*, they had connected the demons to each other and things far beyond the swamp. Could I see them now?

With at least three more levels to go until we reached the river, I took a deep breath and reached into my power as I had in the dream. *Show me how to save them.*

The tethers of every color came in a blink, connecting to both the demonic souls and guards before shooting in every direction. Most veered into the cliffs on either side of the river, but others bound pairs of the shadowy figures. What were they? A tether like the one between Wacław and me? I'd never *seen* that one, but when I looked down, I let out a gasp that caused the lead guard to stop and look back.

Another line extended from my chest. It glowed a bright green and wrapped around my torso before its different ends joined the sea of lines traveling elsewhere. Four went north, toward Huebia and Krowikie lands beyond. Another draped over the edge of the stairs and into the river below. The last led down the path we followed, but with the demons' own dark tethers crisscrossing the canyon, I lost sight of it a few strides ahead.

"Oy!" The lead guard grabbed hold of my arm and pulled me along. "Never seen the drop before or something?"

I didn't reply. The lines were too mesmerizing to look away from, and I found myself wondering about each one's end. Did they show who we were bound to, by choice or not? Why could I see them? Rod had said my power extended far beyond just literal endings, but what could these tethers have to do with the forces I wielded?

Our footsteps against the stone were distant as I searched my memories for any explanation of the lines. Father had only spoken of the Sudiczki, the three goddesses of fate, and Destiny had confirmed his stories during her Trial. They were said to weave a newborn's story into that of the Three Realms. I'd thought *weaving* to be a metaphor for something far harder to describe with mortal language, but now I wondered whether Destiny had chosen that word on purpose. It would explain why each strand held *żityje* within it—they were the Sudiczki's Threads of Life. Our bonds of love and blood woven by them at our life's beginning and evolving every moment since. Will and Destiny.

My Thread shifted when I raised my hand to brush the strand before me. Despite hanging over much of my body, it was loose and didn't interfere with my strides, nor did it seem to hinder the guards. The Thread adjusted to my every movement, drifting between my gloved fingers as I examined it. Finally, something that seemed to lead somewhere!

I had no idea what use I had for these Threads, but their existence alone gave me hope. These demons had come to me for a reason. Was this it? Could I somehow manipulate their Threads of Life? My heart jumped at that. If I could save them, then I could save Wacław too. And if these connected us to our loved ones, maybe it would show me the way to Mother.

I need to free my friends first, I told the demons in my mind, hoping they heard. *I promise I'll help, but let me focus.*

Their voices turned to a muddled clump. Some hissed and others cowered, but as the guards lost their patience and dragged me on, the male demon who'd spoken first in the swamp nodded. He faded along with the others, leaving behind reality's dull silence. Even the cliffs stretching above seemed boring with all their dark Threads gone. Only the guards' and mine remained, and I took note of the fact they had loved ones close.

The absence of the other Threads also made it clear where my own went. We were one flight away from the river level, and the glowing green line turned right at the base, heading directly into the guarded cliff face.

Sabina?

During my moon in Nawia, the forest nymph had become one of my closest confidants. Had that truly been enough to bind us through a Thread of Life? I had no idea, but I'd find out soon anyway, as we stepped onto the flaking ground of the Top Shale level. The river must've grown and receded with time like the Krowik. Except here, it met stone instead of dirt, creating a steady slope down to another set of piers further downstream from the one we'd stopped at the day before.

Among the fishermen throwing their nets into the water, one dropped to his knees and wept. He called out to the Earth Mother, but in seconds, a Frostmarked whip met his back. His cries continued regardless, and the guards dragged him into the caverns as the other fisherman watched, helpless to stop the inevitable.

"Another loyal one, eh?" the pudgy guard said. "Should've learned his lesson when she took the children. The Earth Mother don't care 'bout us."

The taller one shushed him. "Don't speak her name around here! The Winter Witch's chosen will sure as stone bleed you out next if they hear."

"Sorry, sir."

"Bah!" The tall one pushed me on and pointed for the other to follow. "Just get her in there and have them check she's where she belongs. If she ain't, throw her in along with the fisher."

We passed the crowd of fishermen and men carrying various

tools. The latter group came and went from downstream, but before I could get a better look at what they were doing, the guards guarding Top Shale neared.

"Who's the girl?" their leader, a square-chinned brute, said with an accent that made it sound like he'd just bit his tongue. He glanced from my face to my armor before focusing on Kwiecień in its amulet form.

Pudgy scratched the back of his neck. "Err, she said some scorpion hunter sent her to capture the deathstalkers 'round here."

I crossed my arms. "Amten. He said they've had problems with the stalkers lately. Something about them killing prisoners before they can be sacrificed."

"Wear you hear that, huh?" the brute asked. "People aren't supposed to know about the offerings."

"The Winter Witch has ruled here long enough for us to figure out people don't come back." I shrugged. "Not my problem. Just here for the deathstalkers."

Sabina's thread led directly into the tunnel behind them, and I gritted my teeth as the brute scratched his stubbled jaw. "No one told me you were coming. We can't just let anyone in there."

I smirked, stepping toward him with my brow furrowed. *Żityje* seeped from my soul as I let my skin glow. Kwiecień's hilt fell into my hand, and the guard staggered back at the sight of its tip cutting through the stone at my side. "I'm not just anyone," I said. "Trust me. Neither of us wants this to be more difficult than it has to be."

"Sure, fine…" he muttered. "Let me show you where the scorpions have been. You're going to need that blade."

Amten's claims of defeating scorpions as large as me had seemed ridiculous before. From the fear in the guard's eyes, though, I began to doubt my first impression. *What have I gotten myself into?*

Ten other guards joined Brute and Pudgy in escorting me through the tunnel entrance. A bronze gate hung above it on tracks, clearly rigged to drop and trap prisoners. It would do little to stop Vlatka's spells and my channeling, but the guards had mentioned szeptuchy too. Any extra problem could lead to the deaths of the mortals in our group. I couldn't let that happen.

As we traveled through a dimly lit maze of turns, I wished I could focus only on my Threads of Life. There were dozens of guards in the tunnels, and their Threads obscured the path to Sabina. I silenced the power completely. Though my headache from the demons had faded, the constantly shifting lights had brought it back in greater force—strong enough to impede me if it came down to a fight. I'd have to find Sabina on my own.

"I thought this was just a dungeon," I said as we reached the stairs down to what I assumed to be Bottom Shale. My breaths fogged the air this deep, and it took everything I had not to shiver this far from the sun.

Brute glanced over his shoulder with a hand on his short sword. "Dungeon's beneath the barracks. It's not far now. The scorpions like the less trafficked tunnels around there, and you're on your own once we arrive. Lost too many good men to those bastards already."

So the deathstalkers have earned their name.

I tightened my grip on Kwiecień, thankful for its golden glow. Without it, I'd barely have been able to see Brute two strides ahead, but the Moonblade was a sword, not a beacon. Everything beyond the guards was pitch black. I imagined giant scorpions scurrying within it and awaited a strike from their venomous tails.

"Surprised she hasn't run yet," Brute said with a laugh as we reached the bottom and turned down a hall lit by a single torch. "She'll regret it."

We entered a long room at the hall's end. Torches lined the wall at least fifty strides ahead, but there was no other light besides the dual torches at the end of the tunnel we'd just left. The torches, though, were enough to show open doorways into many smaller rooms. Faces watched us from each.

One was Sabina's.

I smiled at her, but her typically wide eyes were the size of fists. Before I could question why she was afraid or why the guards hadn't bothered to block the prisoners' exits, noises came from ahead. Scuttling. Rapid, like spearheads striking the stone. It was everywhere and growing louder.

Someone pushed me from behind, sending me stumbling forward as the guards laughed. My shoulder struck the ground with *pop*, but *žityje* rushed from my soul to heal the wound. A dislocated shoulder was the least of my problems.

Thousands of dark eyes watched me from the edge of Kwiecień's dim light. Deathstalkers, both large and small, their deep yellow carapaces clicking with each movement. As I pushed myself to my feet, they waited.

"You see, girl," Brute shouted from the tunnel entrance. "When you're the predators, you don't need a hunter."

Then he whistled, and every torch extinguished as the scorpions lunged.

29

The Płanetnik

I will escape. I will free myself from this tomb. Then, I will defeat all those who doubted and scorned me. With their final breath, they will realize how wrong they were…

WITH THE FRAGILE BOY GONE FOR GOOD, I awoke with a new hunger. Not for *żityje*. Not for power. Those cravings still lurked in my chest, but this was stronger, primal.

I needed the winds.

The sky was my domain to conquer. In it, I could wield storms, fly to distant lands, and call lightning from the clouds. None of that was possible in this stone prison, and I wouldn't allow it to confine me any longer. Kiin and Otylia would rather let me starve than kill Marzanna's men. Fools.

Excitement filled me as I held my hands to the wall. Many times already, I had tried to slice it with the Thunderstone dagger to no effect. What I hadn't considered was the air in my prison. The room was only two strides wide by three long, but in that small space was air. Not much. Compressed against the wall at a single point, though, even that was enough to crack stone. I was far from the sky. I was far from the winds. Kiin had believed that separated me from my power, but where there was air, there was wind.

Exhaustion washed over me as I released all the *żityje* I had left, sending it into stone beneath my hands. Air rushed past me. My lungs screamed at the sudden void. But I pushed on and drove it into the wall until it cracked with a deafening noise and sent rubble spewing into the basement beyond.

I grinned and wiped the sweat from my brow. That single use of my power had taken too much out of me, but freedom was worth it. Besides, beyond the Daughters' hideout, there were hundreds of Frostmarked I could drain for *żityje*.

The basement was empty, only one torch lighting the space at the bottom of the stairs. *Perfect.*

Even without *żityje*, I could return to my soul-form's natural state of invisibility, and no one noticed me emerging into the sleeping hall. Not that there was anyone who could stop me. Faarax was busy waddling around, muttering to himself with various supplies in hand, and the others here during daylight hours were just refugees looking for safety from the Frostmarked. They huddled in a corner and nibbled on stale bread as a small figure appeared in the doorway of the room holding Kiin's model of Huebia.

Look away, little scion.

But Darixa's haunting gaze followed me from among the crowd. Those eyes had seen more death than any child should've, and they held a weight that fell upon my shoulders. Otylia had insisted we protect her instead of returning to our friends north of Perun's Crown. Was it worth it? Helping the scions retake control of Vastroth could gain us an allied army, but every day wasted in the south was one the Frostmarked Horde spent destroying all in their path. Soon, Astiw would crumble. Krowik would endure the same if we couldn't stop them.

If I couldn't.

I ignored the girl's gaze, grabbing my wide-brimmed płanetnik hat before climbing the stairs to the alley above. Something centered in me when the straw touched my head. In the Lake of Reflection, I'd finally admitted to myself what I was, taking Eryk's old hat with it. It was more than just a protection from rain and snow. With it came an understanding that I was part of the storm, its fury surging through my veins and cracking at my fingertips, waiting to be unleashed.

The morning air was chilly outside, but compared to the cramped confines of the hideout, it felt like the sky embraced me and called me to it. Soon.

My cloak flapped at my heels as I rushed down the next alley. Hunger panged both my soul and stomach. Though I'd hardly considered my enemy's hearts a meal before, a few quick kills would satiate my cravings. Luckily, one was never far from a Frostmarked patrol in Huebia.

The search took longer than I would've liked without the winds to guide me, but after a few minutes, shouts from across a nearby square were enough to bring a smile to my face.

I jumped at a sprint, pushing past confused people in the tight alley. They'd hopefully think I was nothing more than a sharp gust of wind. If they didn't... well, I didn't care about them spreading tales of an invisible force in the alleys. I'd made my presence known already.

I soon arrived at the scene of the scuffle. Guards fought with a group of men wielding masonry hammers and fire irons at the intersection of three small alleys. Two of the men lay dead. The rest huddled behind another, who shouted curses at a guard gripping a woman's arm. I took heart in seeing some Vastrothie fight back. According to Kiin, Grudzień had smothered their anger with fear, but they had hope now. I'd ignited that flame.

The guard holding the woman barked an order to his three comrades before darting down the alley to the left. Cries echoed from the rebel men. They rushed forward, but the guards blocked the narrow path with their spears, slicing down the first four to arrive.

They've gotten smarter.

Badly outnumbered, the Frostmarked had apparently decided on a skirmish tactic similar to Father's favored one. Strike quickly and eliminate the target. Then run before the enemy has a chance to gather strength. Except in Huebia, Marzanna's men intended to capture sacrifices, not slaughter the Vastrothie who could resist. They needed the laborers to keep the city moving, but how long could they hold back the tide of anger against them?

I knew the answer: until Grudzień was taken. It was the only way.

The Thunderstone dagger hummed in my grasp as I charged the guards' right flank. They were too focused on the advancing men to notice my footfalls. Only when my blade found the first's throat did they move from their positions, and by then, they were too late. I dove away as their curved blades slashed at the place I'd been moments before. Blind, they had no hope of striking me, and I plunged my dagger into the second's back with ease.

Confusion spread among the Vastrothie men, but the final kill was theirs. I needed them to believe they could defeat the Frostmarked if I was to attack the tower alone. It was a slow process. With each victory, though, they came closer to revolution—the perfect distraction.

I dropped my invisibility and pointed at the guard. "Finish him. I'll get the woman back."

Fear filled the guard's eyes as the men swarmed him. I felt satisfaction in that. Despite not taking the kill for myself, his heart would be mine, and these men would hail me as a hero. All I had to do was find where the last guard had taken the woman.

The snowfall was light this morning, but the fine dusting revealed fresh tracks twisting through the alleys with another trail beside them. The guard had likely dragged her, slowing his retreat. A new thrill filled me as I made chase. He and his fellow Frostmarked had spent moons as the predators of Huebia's streets. Now, he would feel what it was like to be the prey.

Black blood streamed down my cheeks with each stride. I had no *żityje* left. In minutes, Oblivion would take me, but the danger only added to my excitement. Death was no rival of mine. He served *me*.

I found the exhausted guard struggling with the woman in a main street not far from the city center. People whispered from a distance but did nothing. *Cowards.* Grudzień strengthened their strongest emotion—fear—and, for most, even their disgust at the Frost-marked couldn't overcome it. Not yet.

The guard froze when he saw me. He'd been gripping the woman's hair, but his fingers loosened in that moment, allowing her to slip away. Instead of grabbing her again, the guard drew a sword. "Nawie," he muttered.

Instincts took over as I charged him. All I felt was hunger and rage. Each movement pursued his death, and I fought like a hungry wolf, desperate and lethal.

I needed *žityje*. I needed to feed.

My vision turned red the moment the dagger pierced his skin. Blood poured from the wound, but it wasn't enough. His heart still beat. Rapid, frantic, I heard its desperate fight to live as I crawled on all fours. My blade scraped against the stone and screams surrounded me, but the heart drowned all noise. Only its *žityje* mattered.

The guard wept as I sliced open his chest without hesitation. In his last breaths, I recognized three words, "…you, Earth Mother…" but hunger consumed my mind too much to care.

By my next blink, I had his heart between my teeth. Not invisible. Not hidden. I simply devoured the guard's heart before the gathered crowd, shaking with desperation and snarling at anyone who dared approach. His *žityje* was mine! I had earned my feast in combat.

It wasn't enough.

Blood dripped from my fingertips when I finished. My own blood no longer trickled from my eyes, but I barely felt the winds, their sensations nothing more than a tickle against my skin. And the hunger… Oh, the hunger…

Deep in my power, I sensed the *žityje* in everything around me, as I had when I'd drained that boar a moon before. I'd been strong enough then to know the difference between Ara and the beast—to resist the craving. In that street, though, I smelled blood. And I yearned for its taste.

What control I had faded in an instant. I moved with the speed of the mighty winds, slicing with my blade and launching gusts at anyone in my way. Screams filled the alley as crimson coated the stone. People slipped in puddles, tripped over the fallen and dead. They made easy targets, but the true thrill came from those who believed they could escape. A bolt of lightning in their backs ended their attempts as I consumed another heart, then another. Each death blurred into the next, hunger and anger fueling my pursuit of *žityje*. Here, I was an immortal god, and no one could stop me.

More Frostmarked arrived as I ripped my teeth into what could've been the fifth or fiftieth heart. *Žityje* coursed through me. Power. Life. It was intoxicating, raw, and even now, I craved more. If I was this strong now, what was I capable of?

The winds rushed through the alley as hail pelted my skin. I tossed aside my torn cloak, returned my invisibility, and advanced toward the guards, the hail and cold only pricks of pain that strengthened my hatred. Of Marzanna. Of her Frostmarked. Of the living who would see Nawia's paradise. The blood moon had damned me to Oblivion through no fault of my own, but these people had let a woman be dragged to Marzanna's altar. Why shouldn't they suffer for *their* corruption?

Wolves and guards rushed from the Frostmarked ranks. In the blizzard, I had no idea of my enemy's numbers, but it didn't matter. They were too weak to kill me.

The men fell quickly, unable to see my invisible form. The wolves, though, were endowed with Marzanna's power and struck with precision. One's teeth caught my arm in the same place another had in the Mangled Woods. Scarring remained, and I clenched my jaw at the rush of pain before calling lighting to my skin. It cracked across my body with a deafening noise. The wolf yelped and flew back into the wall, falling as nothing more than a charred ball.

Instead of stopping the lightning there, I plunged my *žityje* into it until bolts shot from my body for a stride in each direction. The other wolves charged, but I dropped to a knee and threw out my arms.

What lightning didn't strike, the gales did. Eight wolves lay dead around me. The smell of charred meat met my nose, and blood's iron taste lingered on my tongue. Even the air snapped with static as I approached the Frostmarked. They held the narrowest part of the street, jabbing out with their two-ended spears, but like those fighting before, they simply had to buy time. I'd sensed the demons flying from the tower already. The chały would be here in seconds—plenty of time to fill my *žityje* reserves.

I took the hearts of the closest dead, not bothering to remember if they had been man, woman, or wolf. We were all the same in the end. Animals driven by our own desires and hungers. I'd finally embraced my own, and as the chały dove from above, I knew that, this time, I wouldn't fail.

30

Otylia

Why is nothing ever easy?

BLUE BLOOD SPILLED OVER ME as I plunged Kwiecień through the face of the first giant scorpion, embedding the blade up to the hilt and taking its light with it. I cursed as hundreds of smaller death-stalkers swarmed over my boots. My sword was stuck, but the moon had yet to leave Jawia.

I launched myself onto the ceiling as burning pain surged through my legs. Scorpions clung on to my trousers and stabbed again and again with their tails. Even in the air, there were too many, and the giant ones could still reach me here.

Żityje seeped from my soul to heal the wounds, but I stopped it. To strike these beasts, I needed every bit of the life force I had left. Fatigue and nausea struck me as their venom spread through my body. Running wouldn't work. I had to kill the scorpions to survive, let alone release my friends, so I took a deep breath and shouted in to the old tongue, "*Svět!*"

Blinding light tore from me and illuminated a sea of scorpions covering the entire room. Eight giant ones remained, close enough to strike soon. Panic filled me at the sight.

You've done this before, I told myself. *Remember the forest with Wašek.*

Remember fighting the utopiec and keeping the crowd from Darixa. You were afraid then. Use that.

My heart jumped as the largest scorpions arrived. There was no time left to think or plan. The smallest deathstalkers alone would kill me with their venom if I stayed here, so I released the moon's pull. Doubt hammered my chest, but moments before I struck the ground, I summoned my silver spear, calling my *żityje* into it and demanding the moon's force throw the scorpions away. In the spell, I released my anxieties about Mother, Wacław, and Sabina. For them, I would suffer the pain and worry of love, because without it, I was lost.

Stone cracked beneath me as I slammed my spear into it, my scream echoing through the room. The blast that followed struck like a charging horse. I dropped to my knees, clutching the spear to keep myself from collapsing.

My light dimmed. Sweat glistened on my skin. Each breath was raspy and weak as my stomach churned from the venom. The moonblast had taken everything I'd needed to heal, but I'd succeeded. The scorpions surely couldn't have survived that. Nothing could've. Channeling was impossible to measure, but that spell had been deadly when I'd accidentally used it before. Now that I'd Ascended, it was unlike anything I'd ever felt. The very earth beneath my feet seemed to cower as I rose.

Eight dark eyes met me.

"Why won't you just die?" I asked the solitary scorpion as it crept over the corpses of its kind. Cracked and broken carapaces covered the ground—enough to make Amten an ecstatic salesman—yet there wasn't a single mark on this one's pure white carapace.

It stepped toward me with its eight terrifying legs. Its pinchers were wide, ready to strike, but when its maw moved, it spoke in the Vastrothie tongue. "You are quite the surprise, Lady Otylia."

I know that voice…

"Serapis!" I spat, jabbing at him with my spear, but he scuttled aside with his eyes always fixed on me. My blood boiled.

"It was actually a cunning plan, if I do say so myself," he replied. "I was excited to see you lose the Alatyr shard so quickly, but I did not expect you to be capable of such destruction this soon. Neither did Master Jaryło."

That name sparked a new rage inside me. I charged, swatting aside one of his pincers with the butt of my spear before stabbing his chest. He cried out, but as I pulled my spear free, his other pincer closed around my arm. Hard. The bone cracked, and I dropped my spear when his second pincer crushed my other arm too.

Blood trickled from Serapis's wound, but he showed no visible pain. His tail curled. With its stinger pointed at my chest, I winced, waiting for the onslaught of venom to get even worse. "Jaryło just won't leave me alone!"

"You stole what is rightfully his. During our conversation, you admitted as much!"

"I thought you don't believe in the gods. Why-Why serve him?" I coughed as bile rose up my throat.

He laughed, and my vision blackened as he squeezed me harder. "You aren't gods. Alatyr was the true deity, and it chose Swaróg's lineage to utilize its power. Perun was his eldest son, and Jaryło is the next in line, so Alatyr is his."

I cocked my head, trying to understand the sorcerer-turned-beast. How could he communicate with Jaryło? The god had surely survived our fight in Nawia with the help of the Maj Moonblade, but was he here? Had he found us that quickly?

"Your confusion is endearing, young Otylia," Serapis said. "However, I have no reason to hide the truth from you now. I bear Master Jaryło's Springmark on my neck—as you once bore your so-called goddesses'. With Marzanna violating the natural order, the gods' agreements regarding the ones you call szeptuchy no longer seemed relevant. Why would my master bind himself to only choosing women when his enemy claims demons as her own chosen? I had already been in pursuit of the Alatyr Stone, so Jaryło's offer aligned with my own goals perfectly."

There's something he's not saying.

Serapis had me trapped. With my *żityje* all but gone and arms crushed, I had little hope of escape, yet he held me, unmoving. Either he was an idiot or waiting for Jaryło himself, and from what I'd seen, this sorcerer was no fool. I needed to do something fast.

"What if I let you take Kwiecień for yourself?" I asked, grinning. "You said you want nothing more than to hold Alatyr yourself, so take it! The Moonblade is just strides away. Jaryło would never give you that much, no matter how long you served him."

His carapace feet tapped against the stone as he turned toward the scorpion that I'd left Kwiecień within. In the process, his grip loosened slightly, and I opened my mind again to the Threads of Life.

The brightly colored lines wrapped around each of us and spread in every direction. One of mine headed directly into the closest cell, where Sabina watched me with her hands held to her chest. There had appeared to be no door blocking their escape at first, but I sensed the spell upon the doorway now. Whatever it was, it had to be strong to hold back Vlatka witchcraft and Sabina's nymph magic.

My Threads weren't what mattered, though. Serapis's did.

Most of his Threads headed west toward his homeland of Anvora, but a single one wound its way through the corpses to the room's entrance. Jaryło's bond to Serapis. The odd sorcerer was telling the truth. For now, the Thread was loose, but I assumed that would soon change.

"Your offer is tempting," Serapis said, his feet still anxiously tapping, "but we are both aware of the restrictions placed upon szeptuchy and male chosen—whom your people once called szeptuny. Betraying my master would destroy me. I have searched far too long to lose my hold on the Alatyr shards now."

I ignored his rambling as the wisps of those near circled around us. Among them, Vlatka's voice pierced the whispers, *"You see the Threads, don't you? Don't reply. Serapis is notorious among sorcerers for his desperate search, and he'll realize you're up to something. If the force of endings is what the gods predicted it to be, then you can get out of this."*

How? I asked in my mind, despite her being unable to hear me. The pain grew each second, and the Thread leading to Jaryło had begun to shift.

"You wore those gloves to protect yourself." Vlatka clicked her tongue. *"Of course you did. Silly girl. Your mother was much the same, but she realized in time that she had to join with her force to be a true goddess. Now, so must you. Take off the gloves if you can and touch Serapis's Thread. You are the goddess of endings, and with his life in your grasp, you can cut it short."*

When she stopped, only the whispers of the other prisoners' memories remained among the trails of color around me. I tried to force them away, but they lingered. Vlatka was right. This power was mine. It would have to obey my commands if I let myself take control and no longer let my fear define me, but how? Between the Threads, whispers on the swirling colors, and demons appearing like smoke, it felt like I was losing my mind every waking moment. Not to mention the visions when I slept.

Could I even kill Serapis by touching the thread? Rod had insisted I wasn't the goddess of death, and unlike the man I'd allowed to pass into Nawia during my Ascension, Serapis was far from his natural end. Was such a violent use of my power against my role?

There's no choice, one part of my mind said.

There's always a choice, another replied.

So I decided.

The glove rubbed against my wrist as I wriggled my hand within Serapis's grip. It was well fit, though, and I winced knowing how long this would take.

"I find it fascinating," Serapis continued in his rant, "that young whisperers like you insist on releasing your *żityje* in such exorbitant displays when you have such little of it. A failure of your mentors, I believe. And look at you now! An Ascended so-called goddess who is drained after a single spell. Control, little one, is how you become powerful."

I just glared at him in response, too focused on removing the glove to care about his mockery. He was right about my overuse of *żityje,* but that wasn't my fault. No one had taught me the extent of my powers as Dziewanna's szeptucha. And even when I'd discovered I was a goddess, Weles had been too concerned about marrying me to Jaryło to bother actually training me. The skill I had was my own—both the strengths and faults.

Serapis's rambling continued until I coughed, spraying it at his face to disguise my right hand sliding free from its glove. I grinned at my small success. With his pincers holding my broken arms, I still had no way to reach to his Thread, but all I needed was to get one arm free.

"Jaryło won't want me dead," I said, noting the small tunnels the scorpions had emerged from. They must've used them to travel through the city, and with the deathstalkers dead, another creature could fill the space. "Release me. I don't even have the *žityje* to heal my arms, let alone fight you."

He just tightened his grip. My entire body spasmed from the pain as blood pooled at my feet, but I had no intention of healing. Serapis had made his choice and so had I.

I reached for the distant ants that had been forced out by the scorpions' superior numbers. They were hungry, eager to retake their lost tunnels. Their need joined with my hatred of Jaryło and now of Serapis, and in seconds, their silver forms burst into the dim room, swarming over Serapis's carapace by the thousands without me even expending *žityje*. Unlike before, I wasn't commanding them. They *wanted* this. I'd just told them how to get it.

"What is this?" Serapis shouted.

The ants' mandibles couldn't pierce his armor, but as he spun to try and throw them off, his grip loosened on me. I tumbled to the ground, weak but alive.

Wisps and threads danced around me. I rose, fighting against my body's insistence I stop. I was a disaster. Blood of blue and red coated my clothes, and my arms hung broken at my sides.

I charged anyway, gritting my teeth with each movement, but there wasn't time for pain or fear. The giant white beast before me struck and ripped apart the ants. I embraced my anger to avenge my creatures of decay. They were despised by many. To me, though, they were the essential conclusion to nature's cycle, allowing new life to be created again, and they'd given me a fighting chance.

I screamed in pain and dove for a segment of Thread draped over Serapis's right pincer. Skirting along his side, it fell into my ungloved hand easily as he spun, but he'd noticed my advance. His stinger shot toward my chest, far too fast to dodge. I braced for the venom.

It didn't come.

The stinger struck my carapace armor and bounced off without leaving a dent. Of course the deathstalkers had chitin strong enough to protect them from their own tail, and Amten had used that against them. I promised myself I'd thank the scorpion hunter later, but first, I had to survive.

Serapis's Thread hummed in my grasp. It seemed so delicate despite the *žityje* coursing through it. I'd needed to remove my glove's protection, but now, his life was at my mercy, and his memories rushed through me as they had when I'd found the old man with Rod. Moment after moment came and went in a stream of voices and images. Too many. I'd thought nothing could overwhelm me more than what I'd felt during my Ascension, but Serapis had lived a long, eventful life full of strange encounters and places unlike any I'd seen. In his heart, he truly believed he was doing what was right. He trusted Alatyr like an infant did their mother, and he saw Jaryło's unity with me as Jawia's only hope.

He was wrong.

Reality tore through the vision as I released my last shreds of *žityje* into the Thread, unleashing my hatred in a burst. Its glow dissolved, and Serapis released a horrific scream. I took a relieved breath watching him die. Then the pain struck.

Burning rushed across my skin. It seared my eyes and filled my lungs with ash. I collapsed as the writhing deathstalker transformed back into a man, his jeweled orange wig dropping from his bald scalp and clanging against the floor beside me. Serapis fell prone and hissed up at me. Darkness consumed his eyes, spreading across his body until it was wrinkled and decayed. His limbs contorted. Cracking echoed through the room with his cries for what seemed an eternity, and only when footsteps approached from the hall did his head drop to the floor, his fight over.

The pain didn't dull with his death. I'd drawn too much *żityje*, and I trembled staring down at his disfigured corpse. Unfortunately, being drained was the least of my worries.

What have I done?

Rod had warned me of manipulating Destiny's will for people. This death I'd inflicted upon Serapis wasn't natural. Deep in my chest, it felt like my heart had been ripped out and left vacant. No, this wasn't simply death but something darker, as if I'd destroyed his soul.

Slow clapping rang from the room's entrance. My light had diminished to nothing more than a faint glow from my skin, just enough to illuminate Serapis's face, but even in the darkness, I knew the visitor. I sensed his power. I saw his Thread of Life binding him to Serapis and many more beyond. And when he drew the radiant orange Moonblade of Maj, an aura hung over him like the hue of a great wildfire.

Jaryło—god of spring, of war, of the harvest—had come for revenge, and there was nothing I could do to stop him.

31

The Płanetnik

The storm is mine.

DARK CHAŁY STREAKED THROUGH THE MORNING SKY, their claws flashing beneath their wings. Ten of them descended upon me at once, but I anticipated their strike.

The winds whirled violently between my hands. They yearned to be released, but I waited until the demons reached the tops of the buildings. When I let go, they rushed free, throwing the beasts into the walls of the alley. It wasn't enough to kill them, but while they were stunned, I launched my Thunderstone dagger into the nearest one's head before spinning with the gales. They whipped into a searing whirlwind that trapped the chały within.

Their bones cracked, their muscles ripping as they scrambled for footing in the slick snow. Each time one advanced, I called the blizzard to fling it back. *Žityje* poured from my soul with the extended effort, but bodies lay everywhere in the alley—a feast of life force for me to consume. An undead demon couldn't match a Naw, and my whirlwind would hold longer than they could fight it. It was only a matter of time.

Then a shriek came from above.

Three lightning chały charged as bolts, forcing me to drop my whirlwind and dodge. That gave the grounded chały a chance to re-cover. There were too many, and they lunged at me in a tide of ooz-ing black blood and razor-sharp claws that raked across my legs. I called my dagger and took flight, narrowly missing their teeth.

This is why I'm in charge, I told the mortal, dead part of me. *Your hesitation would've killed us.*

But I wasn't out of danger yet. The dark chały flew after me with wicked speed as their lightning sisters attacked. Bolts burned my skin, chaining between the trio and growing into a constant surge that ripped through my core. I sliced at them with my blade, but they were too quick. Each cut found only air.

Hail pelted us as we rose into the clouds, obscuring any sight of the chały except for their flashes of light. The heart of the blizzard. I'd defeated a chała like these in the Lake of Reflection, and I closed my eyes, remembering its lighting coursing through me. I shut out the pain. I shut out the demons' cackling. And I shut out my bond with Otylia. All that mattered was the storm boiling in my chest.

The lightning chały shrieked in excitement and escalated their surge. Futile. Pure, raw power flashed through my veins as I ab-sorbed their lightning into my own. Then I sent it back.

Static snapped across me as a *boom* cracked through the air itself. All the strength of the chały's strikes combined with my own and set the sky ablaze. Before they could even scream, their bodies turned a charred black, and they dropped with only a faint trail of ash drifting behind.

I grinned watching the remaining dark chały rush toward me. *Żityje* healed my burns, but the life force of a countless number of hearts still swelled within me.. Because of the lightning I'd absorbed, my strike had taken little energy for the power it had generated.

While I balled lightning in my hands, the decrepit demons swept at me. Their dark wings blocked all light as their claws and sharp tails drew blood, but I didn't need sight. The winds guided my strike as I un-leashed my lightning into the chest of the nearest three. They shrieked, dropping through the clouds and giving the remaining four pause.

"You can't win this!" I snarled with lightning arcing between my fingers. "Marzanna lied to you. She won't give you what you want!"

"She's given us everything," one hissed from a mouth of sharp teeth, demonic blood seeping from her gums. "The queen of winter has freed us from our hunger and let us feast. When the scions doomed us to Oblivion, she kept us in her protection, so we bring her blizzards in return. Why do you betray her?"

"Because all she does is slaughter." I clenched my fists as visions of the Astiwie ambush and dead villagers of Bustelintin filled my mind. Though Boz had acted much on his own accord, it had been Marzanna who'd led Bidaês to the mad king's aid. Without her, thousands more would have survived.

The demon curled her lip. Much of her blackened skin had decayed, exposing muscles that twitched and spasmed beneath the dark shroud that consumed this chała form. "Do you not?" she asked. "The blood of Vastrothie people covers the alley because of you."

My stomach churned as I followed her gaze to the place I'd stood moments before. All I'd wanted was to save the kidnapped woman, but the hunger in my soul had been too much. I'd fallen into a frenzy. A terrifying, destructive, glorious frenzy that filled me with *žityje* and a pleasure unmatched by anything a mortal could experience. In the span of a few minutes, I'd killed at least twenty innocent people, and I didn't even know if the woman had made it out safely.

Yet I felt no regret.

"You despise the living," Marzanna's voice whispered, her mark burning on my palm. *"It is they who mock us, scorn us. They see us as nothing more than monsters, when we are only creations of their selfishness."*

Get out of my head!

Reality slipped away, and a dark horizon rose to replace it. The air was colder than the worst depths of winter. Frozen, black sand cracked beneath my boots as I knelt alongside a river that flowed like the night. I sensed a pull within it. To surrender. To die.

"You and I want the same thing," Marzanna's voice said.

I turned sharply with my dagger drawn, meeting the gaze of the goddess of winter and death. A simple white cremation dress draped over her frail frame. Her cheekbones pushed her pale skin to the brink, and her eyes were sunken and pure white. Beneath the ends of her embroidered sleeves, funeral wrappings covered her arms as blood dripped from the sickle in her grasp.

"Though you blame me for your father's death," she hissed, "it was needed for you to transform. He corrupted and then controlled you, like Perun and his son did to me. But we are more than our fathers or those who rejected us. Jaryło cast me aside for lust, and Otylia abandoned you when she saw the truth of your soul—even when she was the one who ignited your final transformation into a corrupted Naw."

"I was cursed at birth!" I yelled. "The blood moon made me a beast. Father corrupted me!"

"Don't you understand, my pet?" she continued, her voice carrying a power such a gaunt figure shouldn't have held. "You and I, we were born special, but we were betrayed. We were broken. Indeed, the blood moon allowed for you to become a Naw, but it was Jacek who tore Destiny's calling for you. He lured the demon to join with your second soul when he rejected you. Do you remember it? Do you remember the power rushing into you for the first time?"

I lowered my blade. "I do. That force…" During my vision in the Lake of Reflection, it had filled the longhouse when Mom had fled with me in her arms.

Now, a hatred burned inside me. Father had abandoned me, beaten me, and torn me from my only childhood friend, but to know that *he'd* been the reason for my corruption…

I shouted into the void, releasing my anger with a great whirlwind. My veins seared and turned a luminescent blue as lightning danced across my skin. Never before had I hated someone so much. Its fire devoured all else, and I shook violently, every muscle in my body eager to fight, to make him pay.

"Nawia was too kind an end for him," I snarled.

Marzanna nodded. "It was, but his death had to be your choice: the girl you believed you loved or the man who had destroyed your fate. I helped you down this path, and now that you are a fully demonic Naw, you are capable of helping me in spite of your disobedience." She neared me, her clawed fingers tracing the air with wisps of white. "I showed you the goddess I once was, but like you, Destiny's plan for me was ripped away. For centuries, I believed there was nothing I could do but continue the cycle, exacting my revenge on Jaryło each autumn and dying at Dziewanna's hand each spring. But then I discovered Alatyr's hidden truth."

"Alatyr?" I asked. "What do you mean? And why would I ever help you? All you've done is trick me and slaughter those I care about."

She held out her free hand, holding a pulsing brown rock within it. "I often forget how little you know. The twelve Moonstones are the largest shards of Alatyr, the stone Swaróg used to create the first gods. He believed Alatyr should remain his, but the others did not believe he should hold its power forever. They fought, and Alatyr dropped, shattering in Jawia to create żmije, demons, Nawie, and spirits. Swaróg hated them. So, he reunited the largest Alatyr shards and exiled the strongest of these creations to Oblivion. Those shards have been passed down through generations as the Moonstones until Jaryło and I possessed them. United, they sealed the barrier between the Three Realms and Oblivion."

I stared down at the stone in her hand, jagged and broken. "But then Jaryło betrayed you."

"Yes." She sighed, and I actually felt her sorrow as she stopped beside the river to stare into its depths. "Our split shattered Alatyr further, but much of the veil held until the most powerful żmij returned, bringing with him the spirits that granted those like us a chance for revenge."

"I don't need you for revenge. Father is dead. My tribe is scattered. They will unite behind me when they understand my power."

My palm seared, and I scowled as she swung her sickle to my neck. "Why do you insist on defying me? The other gods have told you that I am evil, that I only desire Jawia's destruction. Lies. The gods destroyed Alatyr in the first place, creating us through their pride and greed, and now they wish to grant Jawia to Jaryło when he shattered Alatyr again. War was inevitable. And if I am to reunite the Moonstones, death must come to those that protect the corruption."

I held her gaze. Even with the sickle cutting into my skin, I refused to flinch. Marzanna had proven that she couldn't be trusted, but there was truth in her words.

It was a long time before she lowered the sickle. Blood trickled from the wound, and she ran her finger through its black flow, licking it from her fingertip like it was the vibrant *żityje* of a sacrifice. A flash of excitement filled her eyes. *Does she feel the hunger too? Is she somehow part goddess and part demon?*

"Join with me, Wacław," she continued, stepping back. "You may hate me for doing what was necessary to reveal your true strength, but together, we can mend what has been broken and give us the life force that we lost. Jaryło will ally with Perun and Weles to destroy us—those doomed to Oblivion because we were wronged in life."

"And you would free demons?" I took a deep breath, wondering what life would be like without the fear of Oblivion. "If I help you reunite the Alatyr shards, we could exact our revenge before following our ancestors to Nawia?"

She hummed for a moment. The burning in my palm faded with it. "I swear it and all that I promised you shall be done. In the lands we conquer, we will complete our purge. No longer will demons created by unnatural deaths be confined to Oblivion in death. They will see Nawia, while those guilty of corrupting them will be trapped in the despair they inflicted upon their victims. Perun claims to be the god of justice, but only we can fix what his son has wrought."

"You'll honor your promise after the weakling failed you?" I shook my head. "Why?"

"For the same reason I gave Wacław that dagger—to kill a god. Do what I ask, and I will grant you rule over the lands north of Perun's Crown with Grudzień to control the tribes. All the demons and Nawie who we free will need a home as well as someone to lead them. Who better than the one who pierced the betrayer's heart with a blade crafted from his father's own Thunderstone?"

King of the demons…

I stepped back. My heart raced as I tried to comprehend what Marzanna was offering. Surely she would try to twist me to her own ends, but I was no longer the foolish boy she'd found in Dwie Rzeki. This deal, even if broken, would grant me access to Grudzień and the power I sought.

Not only could I take my place as high chief of Krowik, but I could also lead those like me forward into a new world—one where those corrupted by mortals could have justice. They could live an eternal life as a demon under my command, enter Nawia's embrace once slain in battle. *I* would rule. *I* would make those who scorned me suffer. And *I* would never again let myself be controlled. Though I hated Marzanna for the pain she'd brought upon me and those I'd thought I'd loved, my hunger was stronger. For power and *żityje* alike. She was a means to my ends—one I could be rid of when I ruled my lands. An imperfect one, but in a world tainted by selfishness, brokenness, and death, nothing was pure.

"Talk," I said, holding up the dagger that had started my fall. "Who must I kill?"

A wicked grin crossed her face, half shadowed in the dim glow of her Moonstone. "I came to you once because I knew you could get close to Jaryło. You did not steal his blades, but you slayed him all the same, granting me precious time to recover my strength. Now, you must do the same to the single goddess who can shift the balance of the war to come. Kill Otylia, take Kwiecień in my name, and then we shall defeat Jaryło together, forging a new world from ice and ash."

I released a sharp breath and stared at my dark reflection in the dagger's flat. Otylia had abandoned me, cast me out like Father after using me to Ascend. Yet, a flame still flickered in my heart for her. My first love. My only love. In our childish imaginations, all the Three Realms had once been ours to explore together, but that had been a different life—a life she'd stolen from me.

A part of me had loved her. He was dead. All that remained was a hatred that ravaged love's fading ember.

"I'll do it, on one condition."

"Name it."

I stepped toward her, my lip curling with rage. "When this is over, *never* call me your pet again."

32

Otylia

Why must you ruin everything?

JARYŁO'S ROBES SWEPT OVER THE SCORPION CARCASSES as he studied me. Sleeveless, they revealed his built arms and now darkened skin that appeared burnt like copper in the light of his orange Moonblade. His hair remained gold, though, and an eternal smirk pulled at the ends of his mouth. I'd thought that expression to be nothing more than cockiness. Now, I saw the menace in it.

"Finally crawled free from Weles's cradle?" I muttered, my broken arms and venom-filled body fighting every word. Even kneeling took more strength than I had left. But I wouldn't show Jaryło my weakness.

The god sneered before stopping to stare down Serapis's decayed corpse. Weles had claimed gods could alter their appearance depending on their location, but it was unsettling to see Jaryło in a different form. "Father made so many mistakes with you in such little time. Allowing you to keep your rebellious tongue was chief among them." He shook his head. "It is a shame how much you and Dziewanna are alike in your disloyalty to your fathers, foolishly believing you could do better."

"Because you're so perfect? Don't speak to me about loyalty! You betraying Marzanna caused this, and now you call the god who kidnapped you 'Father.' "

His voice turned mocking. "Ah, is your loyalty the reason I have heard rumors of a Naw płanetnik in Huebia? Oh yes, dear sister, I know you pushed him away. Why else would a *caring, cautious* boy like that choose destruction over peace?"

I shuddered. Wacław's anger had become so constant through our connection that it was impossible to tell what else he felt. It had been a mistake to leave him in Kiin's cage of rock, but even now, I didn't know a better option. I had been Wacław's tether in his darkest moments. Rejecting him had cut the last thread of hope he had, and until I could figure out how to pull him back, it was better for him to be where he couldn't hurt anyone—Frostmarked or not.

I'm sorry, I whispered through our bond. *We both have our darkness, and I should've never let you face yours alone.*

But I had, and now, my own darkness was laid out before me. With the force of endings, I'd cut Serapis's Thread of Life in something far worse than death. *Żityje* lingered in most corpses. He had none. That alone was paralyzing, but I had to deal with Jaryło before I could figure out what End was doing to me.

"I was trying to protect Wacław," I breathed. "But I was wrong. At least I'm willing to admit it."

Jaryło huffed, nudging Serapis's body with his foot. "The goddess of endings indeed. Were you trying to protect my szeptun too, or was severing his soul too alluring an opportunity?"

Severing his soul?

"You seem surprised," he said. "I thought you were so well prepared for Ascension that you did not need Father's help or mine? How childish of you to believe you could master a god's power in a few moons' time when we spend an eternity bonding with the forces we wield. Just because you seek to rescue Dziewanna doesn't mean you should emulate her failures."

I spat at his feet. "What do you want? Dziewanna dies in Marzanna's grasp and the Horde is conquering Jawia, but you're spending your time tricking me."

"I want my birthright. Jawia is mine to rule, and I will rule."

He approached and crouched before me, smiling wryly as his fingers traced my neck to my chin, pushing it up for me to meet his eyes. Such a touch felt intimate, tender, and my pain softened with it. I tried to look away. He forced my gaze back, the gentleness gone in an instance. This close, it was impossible to deny the beauty in his radiant eyes and the sharp cut of his jaw. Any girl in the tribe would've swooned into his arms. Many probably had. But I saw the rot beneath the glow.

"More than that, though," he whispered intently, "I want to mend the tear Marzanna has created between the Three Realms and Oblivion. Demons and Nawie are unnatural. They must be put where they cannot curse the living or the dead."

Visions pulled at my mind with his hand held against my cheek. As they threatened to take me away, I remembered why I wore those gloves. Just the thought of what I would see made me want to curl up in a ball and hide. They offered so much insight into someone's passions, regrets, and potential future—too much. When I could barely handle my own problems, how was I supposed to use my visions to help others? To find Mother?

"Serapis claimed he needed my help to fix the veil…" I managed, coughing. "He meant through you."

Jaryło released me, and I cried out at the onslaught of pain without his power. His fingers left a warmth on my cheek despite the frigid cavern air. I imagined it burning away the skin like acid. "He did. Poor sod had searched so hard for the Moonstones, only for you to kill him when he'd finally found one." He rose sharply, spinning toward the scorpions. "Speaking of Moonstones: Where is Kwiecień? I sensed it upon my arrival, but it's been dampened by the *horrific* act you just committed."

My head dropped to the cold stone, both from exhaustion and guilt. How long could I survive this torture? "What did severing his soul do?"

"What does it sound like?" he asked mockingly.

"Just tell me for once."

"Wacław's further corruption truly has wounded you. It is a shame, but such is the lot we face as immortal gods. While those whom we love die, we live on long enough for their faces to become little more than distant memories. But that is not what you asked." He pursed his lips, searching through the scorpions for his blade. "I am sorry to say that you broke the natural order of death. Instead of allowing Serapis's body to be burned or buried, releasing his soul to wander until traveling to Nawia, you have torn his soul from his mind. Typically, these elements of mortals are linked, the mind simply reflecting the soul, but his soul is now trapped in Jawia without direction. He will haunt these tunnels as a spirit until he is cast out to Oblivion."

I fell against the wall, barely upright. My broken arms ached from the angle, but I lacked the strength to reposition. "Rod said I'm supposed to help show people naturally to Nawia. Not this…"

"It is our decision how we wield our forces. In your case, however, I suspect Destiny will not look fondly upon you creating severed souls. If the force of endings is what I believe it to be, your role is to end the natural cycle the unity of the Alatyr shards. I fear that them splitting into the Moonstones again tore the veil to Oblivion, leading to Marzanna's corruption."

He paced over to the room's center, near where I'd first been thrown into the fray. Carapaces cracked beneath his boots with each step. Thousands of deathstalkers killed in a single moonblast, but I still barely understood that spell, let alone my ability to sever souls.

Kneeling there, I felt more alone than ever. More than when Wacław had first walked away. More than when I'd believed Mother had succumbed to Marzanna's Curse. And more than when I'd first awoken in that dark room surrounded by Nawia's vines. Friends and allies alike were strides away yet so far, and the boy I needed more than anything had lost himself because of me. Even with them, though, I had changed. Ascension had brought with it a force I had to explore on my own. That was terrifying.

Jaryło sighed and rolled his head in my direction. "This is ridiculous. Save me the effort and tell me where Kwiecień is. I'll mend those arms of yours in return, perhaps saving you another visit to Father. We both know how messy that was last time."

As if confirming his claim, my body spasmed, making it impossible to even speak for what seemed like minutes. The scorpion venom was taking roots in my blood, and pain ran from my arms to my head. It pierced my skull, my thoughts. I hated him for holding me at his mercy, but I needed his aid.

"The giant scorpion to your left," I admitted. It hurt to raise my head enough to see him.

"Ah, I see. First rule of swordsmanship," he said, wagging a finger as he pulled Kwiecień free, sending a brighter light through the room, "never stick your blade into something you can't get it out of. Actually, it may have been the third rule… Regardless! You are lucky the moon hasn't set yet."

I nodded slowly. The moon's pulsing presence lingered, but its fading power wasn't enough to restore my *žityje* quickly. Even drained, though, the Threads of Life remained as a constant reminder of life that leads to death, like you do with the moon to end the day. A severed soul doomed to Oblivion will never be reborn. Therefore, the cycle has been broken, and we all suffer when nature's balance is violated."

"Like when you betrayed Marzanna."

Regret filled his eyes for the first time, and he hesitated before standing and examining the corpses. "Yes."

Silence hung over us. I took a long breath, reaching into my power to see if Serapis's wisp would return. Sabina, Kuba, Vlatka, and the other prisoners appeared in the images with their whispers carrying memories and futures. Even Jaryło was among them. Flashes of his visions washed over me from our brief touch. Too many to grasp fully, yet I sensed something within them that I hadn't seen in him before. A hurt. Deep, hidden. It suffocated me.

"You're actually admitting fault?" I asked. "How mature of you."

"There is more to my relationship with Marzanna than you could ever understand, but, yes, I admit my lust ended our marriage and

of what I'd done. "If you're not here to take me back to Nawia,"

I muttered, "why are you still talking?" My patience was thinner than my hope. Each wave of throbbing pain wasn't helping either.

"Why would we return to that stuffy old realm?" He sheathed his swords at his back and returned to me, crouching again. "No, you are of much more use to me here, helping me take back the Moonstones. Besides, with my centuries-long separation from Marzanna, I need another wife."

I scoffed. "No."

"As if you have a choice."

"I'd rather suffer an eternity of demonic corruption. Go bed someone who isn't your family for once."

He stood swiftly and cracked his knuckles. "It is truly a shame that I'll have to kill every single person who fled with you from Nawia. Father may be more rebellious than Perun, but he does not look highly upon treason. Particularly *that* one." He pointed at Sabina, his finger almost touching whatever barrier separated their cell from the rest of the room.

"Don't touch her!" I snapped, forcing myself to stand. My legs wobbled but barely held as I used the wall for support, and I glared at Jaryło with all the fury surging through my connection to Wacław. "I swear upon Mokosz's name, I'll kill you every moon if you touch even a hair on Sabina's head."

"See, that is where you're wrong." With his finger still extended, he dragged it along the stone wall as he walked. "While Perun and I are not… close… Mother has always favored me. *She* is intelligent enough to understand the hope I bring to mortals, that I am the one who must save this realm from the abyss my sister drags it toward with each day."

"Sister? You abandoned the sister that could stop Marzanna." I staggered toward the invisible barrier. Sabina's wide eyes watched me from her side, her palm pressed against it. "Dziewanna is our hope, not you, and all you've done is stop me from saving her."

"You speak like a mortal."

I rested my forehead on the barrier across from Sabina. So close. "Because I was one. You've lived for longer than I can even grasp, and still, you don't understand what it's like. The fear of death. The sorrow of losing someone who just you hope to see in Nawia someday. The anger at life's futility when you feel too weak to change anything."

Jaryło's strides slowed and his voice softened as he approached me from behind. "Perhaps Dziewanna believed she was protecting you when she stole you from Father. What is obvious now, however, is that she let Jawia break you. She never taught you what it means to be a god. The responsibility when those prayers ring in your mind and blood pools at your altar."

When his hand rested on my shoulder, my weakness faded again. I took advantage, spinning and kicking at his groin. But he swept my leg from under me.

"My patience is running thin, Otylia," he continued, crouching before me as I writhed in agony. Part of me actually begged for his touch. To heal. To be free of the pain. "In return for me releasing your traitorous friends, helping you use your power to find Dziewanna, and sparing Wacław after he *burned down* my father's palace, I will take Kwiecień and you will become my wife."

His eyes grew distant as he held his arms to the side and took a long breath. "The newest goddess, mine! Our wedding will be the greatest celebration for centuries, and I will parade you before Perun, Father, Swaróg, and the rest. Once they finally see that I deserve respect, they will grant me their armies to rid this realm of Marzanna and her demonic Horde. That is only possible with us bound by marriage."

His gaze returned to me. The passion in his eyes made me shudder. "Accept my offer, or die and suffer a long recovery in Nawia while Wacław and everyone else you love endure the punishment *you* deserve."

The prisoners' wisps surrounded me like a swarm of hornets. I couldn't fight it anymore, and their voices swelled, speaking of starvation and torture. Worst of all were the images. With my bare hand clutched behind my gloved one, the wisps couldn't draw me into their visions, but as each streak of color passed, I saw my friends' deaths. Souls freed for mere days before being sent back to Nawia. Nymphs who hadn't seen the forces they were bound to in Jawia for so many years. The witch Vlatka, still standing defiant after executing Mother's plan for my escape. And poor, loving Sabina. She'd been the truest friend I could've had in Weles's palace, despite my aggression toward her during our initial meetings.

One-by-one they died before me in the wisps' images. The colors of each framed Jaryło's shadowy form as he sliced and stabbed with Maj, moving like a dancer more than a swordsman, but the slaughter was unmistakable. This was what he was capable of. A god able to kill anyone he pleased, not because a demonic hunger was eating at his sanity, but because he wanted to.

"You're more a demon than Wacław," I stammered, fighting both the physical and mental pain. Committing to be his wife would destroy me. An eternity of torture if I couldn't break free.

As I raised my head, I saw my Thread of Life. Love entrapped me through it, wrapping around both my body and soul. Serapis's death had come when I'd cut his thread, but it had been more than death as his soul was ripped from those he loved. Even demons' souls were linked to their loved ones. Why? Did it mean some part of them remained in their decaying, *żityje* craving forms? If that was what separated them from severed souls, did that mean the bonds we held with others kept us alive? Father had always said the ancestors were part of us, but it wasn't until that moment that I realized how much they were. Apart from love, we were only wandering souls, cursed to spend eternity searching for something we could never find. Gods, that was frighteningly familiar.

"You'll help me find Mother?" I asked, my tongue heavy as I dreaded every word. "And you swear to never harm Wacław or any of my friends?"

He extended his hand to me. "You need not rely on my word. This oath we will seal in blood, unbreakable by even a god, and it is the only thing that can protect Wacław from me."

Now my stomach turned, but I held back the urge to vomit. "What's the cost if you break it?"

"Imagine all the *žityje* in your veins boiling for an eternity. There is a reason blood pacts are incredibly rare among us. They endure forever, like Father's agreement with Perun."

"Neither Weles nor Perun can rule Jawia in its entirety," I said.

He nodded. "The last destruction of Jawia scared them both, but they seek ways around the pact."

"You."

"*Us.* You are Weles's firstborn and I am Perun's. Despite my strained relationship with Perun, Mother will convince him to respect my desire to rule Jawia, and together, we can ensure there is balance between the Three Realms."

I shuddered but rose to meet him. Every part of me hated what I was about to do, but I focused on my Thread connecting me to Sabina, Mother, Wacław, Ara, and Father. Each of them had loved me in their own way. So often, I'd failed to do the same. Now, though, I would return all I owed by protecting them from Jaryło's wrath. I would suffer forever for them.

If any of you is left, I'm sorry Wašek.

"I'll never love you," I said.

He nodded. "Love is not a requirement of this pact, but you will serve me."

"Then I'll despise you every moment." I paused. Even with his healing, my breaths were weak, and each word was a battle against myself. "I'll do what I must to find Mother and stop you from killing those I love. Nothing more."

Jaryło smiled and tilted up my chin, running his fingers over my lips. "Well then, my wife to be, let us draw blood before we free Jawia from Marzanna's icy hand."

Maj shrunk to the size of a dagger as he raised his palm to its point. He dragged the blade from his wrist to the tip of his middle finger, his blue eyes seeming to darken with each passing moment. When he finished, he took my hand.

The Moonblade's sharp edge met my skin. Pain and fear tightened around my chest, but I refused to succumb. Mother had been strong when Perun had forced her to marry Weles. I would be the same. No matter whether I wore my hair in a maiden's braid or a wife's headscarf, I was untamable, and one day, I would make Jaryło pay for what he'd done. With each beat of my broken heart, that promise to myself would keep me living, no matter how long it took.

Blood trickled from the wound as Jaryło pulled back the dagger and held his bleeding palm to mine. "Say what you ask of me," he said, "and then I will do the same."

I swallowed, fighting my trembling. *Żityje* flowed between our joined hands, and my arms finished healing as the venom's bite faded from my blood. My mind cleared for only a moment. Visions replaced the pain. Centuries. They swirled among my own memories, and my words slurred as my legs wobbled.

"Jaryło Perowicz, god of spring, agriculture, and war, you will aid me in my search for the goddess Dziewanna, you will allow those who escaped with me from Nawia to go free, you will not harm them or any of my loved ones, and you will not harm me."

The god bowed his head. "This, I swear." He looked to me again, intent. "And you, Otylia Welesiakówna, swear to become Otylia Perowiczowa, my wife until time's end or either of our souls finds eternal death, to follow my commands, aid me in my reign over Jawia, and to never attempt harm upon me."

My words caught in my throat as I stared at the god who would become my husband. The god who'd deceived me, killed me, trapped me, and now manipulated me. He'd asked me never to attempt harm upon him, but I prayed to Mokosz that she tear her son's heart from his body. For both my sake and Marzanna's. For all the women who'd been controlled by fiends like Jaryło.

I will kill you. "This, I swear."

Then the visions overtook me, and I dropped into End's grasp.

33

Otylia

I am a slave.

KNEELING IN DEEP SNOW, I finally wept as the trees creaked beneath the weight of the howling northern wind. End had pulled me into a vision of Jaryło. I wanted none of it. My gloves had protected me from seeing the endings of allies and strangers alike, and I had no desire to see my enemy's.

Yet there I knelt. Cold, defeated. Frozen tears stung my cheek as I refused to look up at the vision. For a few moments, all I wanted was isolation.

End had different plans.

Riders approached, their horses' huffs carrying on the gales. Something tightened within me as they neared. I opened my eyes to the Threads of Life, and my breaths quickened at the taut line connecting me to the lead rider.

"Mother…" I whispered with my mended hand closed around her amulet.

Dziewanna burst through the snowfall, a long cape of leaves draped over her steed and a crown of antlers rising above her willow-brown hair. She rode bareback and reinless as she guided the chestnut mare through their bond and scanned the woods with a single arrow nocked on her elaborately carved bow. She held herself with strength and poise. And when the second rider stopped alongside her, he bowed his head in submission.

"Sister, you should rest," Jaryło said, Kwiecień's Moonblade casting a golden hue over them, revealing gnarled trees similar to those of the Mangled Woods. "Facing the dark żmij alone was foolish, and if you continue, I fear—"

"I don't want to hear your fears, Brother," Dziewanna replied with her eyes fixed ahead. "Marzanna betrayed us when she called Czarnobóg from Oblivion, but her corruption is because of you. She is our blood. If we have any hope of stopping him before she falls to his control, then we must try."

"The equinox is not until tomorrow. Please, rest. This fight may last until the Marzec moon is finished, so we must not act with haste."

Dziewanna shook her head. "Sleep however long you wish. I will go alone."

Then she trotted off with her beast of a horse carving a path through the snow. Jaryło just watched for a moment, shaking his head as Zofia, his pure white horse, stood ready beneath him. The stones embedded in each Moonblade's hilt glowed from his back. Kwiecień's in his grasp was strongest of all, and as he raised it into the moonlight and examined his reflection, it gave his eyes a deep gold hue. Marzec, the third moon of the year, may have been Marzanna's, but it too would be her last.

"You're too soon, Sister," he whispered. "Why couldn't you just listen for once? I didn't want to do this…"

Jaryło sighed and sheathed the Moonblade, pulling on Zofia's reins. "Come on. Let's finish this before she ruins everything."

The vision shifted in a swirling mist. My mind spun with it until my boots met a solid surface. The air here was still, and I stared in awe as End's wisps crafted a towering room of ice around me. Elaborate designs carved crevices into the walls and ceiling. Within them, decrepit creatures watched me with eyes of black. Demonic blood oozed from gouges scattered across their bodies, revealing bones and rotting muscle alike. Zmory, chały, and others I didn't recognize.

Light shone through the translucent ceiling to reveal a long hall of spiraled ice pillars. At its end, Dziewanna knelt before a woman in a white dress trimmed with patterns of a light blue. The woman gripped a pulsing, blue-green stone whose power was familiar—Moonstone.

I hadn't realized until then that I'd never actually seen Marzanna. Wacław's encounter with the winter goddess had come the night after the equinox, away from me. He'd described her well, though, and from her sharp brow to the claws arcing from her fingers, this had to be her.

"I never thought I would see my wild sister bowing to me," the winter goddess said, her frosty voice echoing through the hall as she glared at Dziewanna.

"Where are your weapons, Mother?" I asked as I approached the pair. Dziewanna had her bow hung over her back, and I saw no blades on her form.

Dziewanna's head dropped. "Neither did I, but I have seen the truth now, far too late."

"And what truth is that?" Marzanna replied.

"You couldn't have released Czarnobóg with only five of the Moonstones. The dark dragon remained trapped for centuries after Alatyr shattered again, but only now did he escape." Dziewanna rose slowly, her fists clenched at her side. "I knew you were trying to tear the veil to Oblivion when I saw a demon corrupt one of a Naw boy's souls in Dwie Rzeki. It wasn't until Weles told me about the barrier, though, that I realized its strength. Even after all these years, you had only managed to slip a few dark spirits at a time through your tear. But then Czarnobóg escaped. What changed?"

Marzanna scowled as Dziewanna advanced, but she motioned for her demons to remain still. "How I released Czarnobóg is irrelevant. He is free, and I can finally have my revenge. With his power, I will reunite Alatyr. Those corrupted by gods and mortals alike will be free from Oblivion! The dead shall return."

"Sister, Czarnobóg won't give you these things, but I can."

My jaw dropped. *What are you doing?*

"I'm listening…" Marzanna said.

Dziewanna stopped beside the throne, offering Marzanna her hand. "When I arrived on Jawia, I believed you had discovered a dark power to aid you. I was furious. But I have fought your żmij each day since and, in that time, have come to a single conclusion: There is no power you could wield that is greater than Alatyr."

"What are you saying?"

"Our brother has deceived us both. Releasing Czarnobóg requires the twelve Moonstones to be together, for Alatyr to be complete—or at least aligned. Jaryło—"

"Enough!"

Jaryło's shout from the hall's entrance sprung the demons into action. Chały swept from above, their deafening shrieks paralyzing me as their lightning cousins shot at the spring god. He focused on them, but zmory stalked forward with hunger in their eyes. Dziewanna pulled her bow; Marzanna pushed it down.

"Let them fight," Marzanna hissed.

Kwiecień flashed as the chały arrived, slicing them down faster than my eyes could comprehend. They fell by the dozens. Cries of death joined their demonic fury, and I shuddered at the sight of Jaryło's power. In Nawia, he'd only just recovered. He was still weakened by his shared curse with Marzanna, but this warrior was unlike any mortal swordsman. No number of Marzanna's demons could match him.

If he needs Mother to kill Marzanna on the equinox, how powerful is she?

Black pooled over the ice as Jaryło cleaned his Moonblade, a satisfied smile crossing his face. "You never cared for your pets, my love."

Marzanna bared her teeth. "And you never cared for me!"

A sickle formed in her free hand, and she rushed him, shooting shards of ice from her Moonstone. He deflected each with Kwiecień's flat. Then, as her curved blade arced toward his neck, he ducked and spun clear.

"Tut-tut. That is no way to greet your former lover."

"Is it true?" Marzanna asked, circling him. "Did you help me summon Czarnobóg through Oblivion's barrier?"

Jaryło looked from her to Dziewanna. "I never should have let you return before the equinox."

"Together, we can take his Moonblades," Dziewanna told her sister as she advanced on Jaryło with her bow drawn, "and then I promise you, we will fix what he's broken. Your soul, the corrupted who deserve to see Nawia, all of it. Just let me have the shards."

"No!" Marzanna snapped. "You have killed me every year for centuries. Why would I trust anything you say?" She shifted to the hall's entrance, her blade ready with each step. "Czarnobóg is all I need to take the Moonblades for myself."

A deep roar shook the ground. Dziewanna loosed an arrow as cracks spread through the ice. But Jaryło raised his arm, a golden shield forming from his bracer, and batted the arrow away. "You actually believed she would help you, Dziewka?"

"To hope for my sister's redemption was no more foolish than trusting you," Dziewanna replied. "You've doomed Jawia."

He grinned. "No, I will be the one to save it. Father and Perun will finally realize they must unite behind me when they learn the dark dragon has returned. Jawia will be mine!"

"You fiend!"

Laughter filled the hall, tearing the siblings from their argument. A young man strode to Marzanna's side with only loose trousers and a spiked, scaled shoulder plate covering his body. Beneath, demonic veins spread across his muscled form before ending at a glowing mark upon his chest. Shadows rose from him and blocked out the light from half the room. In the darkness, his black hair and empty eyes seemed to swallow Jawia itself.

"Swaróg couldn't even bother to meet me himself?" the man said. "A shame. I would have loved to punish him first for what he inflicted upon me and every mortal since."

Dziewanna screamed and loosed another arrow, but the man threw out his arms. Dark wisps shot from him, throwing aside the missile as if it were nothing. "Marzanna has told me of your plight, Dziewanna. The gods entrapped you too, in their own way. You believed the Three Realms could be more, but Perun and Weles would rather control all beings, both dead and alive. What lurks in the darkness is a corruption to them. The unknown. Why should they allow change and power beyond their manipulation when it only threatens their rule? No, only those *chosen* by the gods should wield the *żityje* that resides in every soul. Pitiful!"

"You will destroy Jawia when you claim to save it," Dziewanna spat, her fingers still wrapped around her bowstring. "Czarnobóg, I do not love what my father has done, nor what my husband wishes to, but this is not the way. Let us free the wild spirits without sending the Three Realms into darkness."

"There's no time to talk!" Jaryło shouted. Panic filled his eyes as he clutched Kwiecień and waved for Dziewanna to come to him. "Kill Marzanna before it's too late!"

Death and winter surrounded Dziewanna, but in her gaze, a blaze burned. "The only one who should perish is you, brother. I *will* fix this with your Moonstones. We will finally end our family's war!"

Czarnobóg shook his head. "There will be no peace until Swaróg and his sons suffer as we have. Each day, they will fight to confine us to Oblivion forever. Only when Marzanna holds Alatyr in its entirety will we be free."

"Sister, he's using you!" Dziewanna pled. "Don't you see? He will take Alatyr for himself and destroy the Three Realms. All that you once loved will be gone."

The walls cracked further as Marzanna raised her Moonstone. More *żityje* than I'd ever felt rushed from her, and veins of black crept up her neck as she hissed, "I have no love left to give."

The palace erupted, its castle of ice showering upon us in a cascade of deadly shards. Jaryło raised his shield as they struck, but Dziewanna stood with no protection. I screamed for her to run. It was too late. Marzanna and Czarnobóg watched with glee as she collapsed beneath the rubble.

Then the beast shifted.

Black scales stretched from Czarnobóg's shoulder plate and over his torso as great wings grew from his back. His teeth turned to daggers, his fingers to claws, and soon, he filled half of where the palace had once been. Three heads breathed fire into the night sky above.

The black dragon. I shuddered at the memory of Death's Trial.

"It was you…"

Czarnóbog had guarded Mother in the ring of ice. He'd nearly killed me as I'd tried to reach her. Now, fear froze me in place as he rose above us. This ring was the place where I'd found Mother. It was where Marzanna had drained her, and as Jaryło pushed himself free of the rubble before me, I realized the worst truth he had hidden.

This was where he'd left Dziewanna to die.

The god took one glance at where his sister had stood, his chin held high and the moonlight casting him in a silhouette against the distant cliffs of ice. Only a glance. Without bothering to search for her, Jaryło took flight. Czarnóbog made chase, but Marzanna raised her pale hand.

"Stay. Jaryło is no threat to me without Dziewanna, and I need you to ensure she doesn't escape until your brothers return."

Czarnóbog released a dissatisfied roar but descended, striking the ice just strides from where Dziewanna had fallen. I cowered back beneath his giant form. All żmije were powerful, but if the gods truly feared the dark dragon enough to lock him in Oblivion for eternity, what was he capable of? And what chance did I have of rescuing Mother from *that*?

Czarnóbog dragged Dziewanna from the sea of ice. Blood streamed from her face and torso, and though she twitched, words in the old tongue slipping from her lips, she was no match for Czarnóbog's strength.

I dropped to my knees. My chest burned watching him carry her to the goddess of death. End's power had brought me here to see the end of Dziewanna and Jaryło's bond, not to change it. I hated that, but more than anything, I hated Jaryło for betraying Mother like he had me. Demonic corruption had dragged Marzanna into her obsession for revenge. Jaryło had no such excuse.

"I'll avenge you," I whispered to Dziewanna, to Mother, the vision fading as Marzanna placed the Moonstone over her sister's heart. "And then I'll do whatever it takes to bring you back."

34

Otylia

What hope do we have when the gods war for their own power?

REALITY RETURNED ALL TOO QUICKLY, its harsh, still air suddenly warm compared to the world of frost I'd endured. My rage remained.

Jaryło stared down at me with his eyes alight. He'd claimed me as his future wife, but in his gaze, all I saw was deception. His palm was still pressed against mine. Blood pooled between us, joining us by our oaths. Opening End's power, I studied the Thread of Life wrapped over Jaryło's shoulders and its glowing lines spreading into the distance. Another had joined it now. Red, it stretched from his chest to mine.

"You saw something, did you not?" he asked, his voice soft. "My own forces do not grant me visions, but Mother says time passes differently in them."

I drew back my hand to Dziewanna's amulet at my chest. Blood streaked across the bone bow, but it felt appropriate after what I'd just seen. Czarnobóg terrified me, as did Marzanna. Fear meant little, though, in the face of the god who had betrayed both mother and daughter. End's gift had shown me Jaryło's greatest error yet, and even if *I* could not harm him, revealing the truth to Perun or Weles would surely ensure they did not lend him the aid he desperately desired. *Jawia won't be yours, traitor.*

"I didn't swear to share my thoughts with you." My heart sank for a moment, thinking of Wacław. I stiffened and met his gaze with a glare.

"Very well, my dear." He gave a sarcastic bow before approaching the first doorway and waving for Sabina and the others to back away. Then, he placed his hands upon the invisible barrier and released a burst of *żityje*.

A *snap* echoed through the room, and End's wisps scattered as pain stabbed at my chest. I lost my breath. *What is this?* Though the air vibrated in a rapid shrill, Jaryło appeared unfazed, and he glanced back at me with a smirk. "A basic barrier. The shock will pass."

Sabina peeked her head out from behind the wall. "Is it down?" she peeped.

I rushed to her without waiting for Jaryło's reply, wrapping my arms around the tall nymph as she released another squeal that sounded like a combination of pain and glee. "Thank the gods you're alive!" I said with a relieved laugh. "When Kiin said you'd been captured…"

"We are well, Otylia." She looked back at the fifteen others in the room—too many for such a small space. "Well, those of us who survived are."

I cocked my head at the scruffy brown and black animal in the corner. Resembling a small wolf, it had tall ears that were directed toward me as a golden eagle looked out from behind it.

"What happened?" I asked, my joy fading as I held her hand in my gloved one. There had been a hundred souls and nymphs on the volcano's island willing to fight their way out of Nawia. So few had made it… "And what's with the animals?"

She winced. "Some fought when the Frostmarked found us… For the animals, well, Vlatka can tell you more."

"Vlatka?" I asked. The stout witch was nowhere to be seen. Neither was Kuba.

The eagle flapped its wings, sweeping across the room to land on Sabina's shoulder. But it was no small bird and she no warrior, so she wobbled before catching her balance with a considerable lean. "It's… uh… It's complicated."

"Little in the Three Realms isn't," Vlatka's voice said from the eagle, sitting tall.

"What… What happened?" I stammered. "And who's the wolf?"

The wolf-thing released a whine and ran to me, hitting at full stride and sending a fresh wave of pain through my bruised chest. "It's me, Kuba! In the flesh… or well, not *my* flesh."

What in the Three Realms?

Vlatka chuckled. "You are an adorable girl when you're confused. It wipes that scowl off your face for a few… Oh no, it's back…"

"Are you going to explain why you're animals?" I asked, patting Kuba's wolf head, which prompted him to stick out his tongue and sit next to me. The emotions of seeing them again clashed with my shock from the vision. What was I supposed to think?

"A force pulled us to this land when we passed through the Heart of Nawia," Vlatka replied. "Considering you are here too, I assume the same happened to you."

I looked from her to Kuba, still trying to comprehend their animal forms. "Yes, but we ended up near Huebia in the north. What happened? Where are the others, and why are you in these forms?"

"The spirits and still living souls you guided back to Jawia kept their human or nymph forms. Kuba and I have already lost our lives, and therefore, our mortal bodies. Our forms in Nawia were simply manifestations of our soul. When we went through the Heart, they could not hold in the living realm."

"What does that mean?"

Kuba yapped and popped to his feet… er… paws. "It means we needed new bodies!"

I raised my brow at Vlatka.

"Let me explain," she said, stifling another laugh. "In Nawia, deceased souls manifest their appearance from some time in their life. This was why Ivan could choose to be a bear or a man, as he'd been both on Jawia during one period or another. The rituals to send a soul back to Jawia grant them a new body and life. By passing through the Heart, we avoided this, leaving our souls unattached."

"So I found a dog!" Kuba said, shouting for no reason.

Vlatka gave him what I assumed to be an eagle's version of a glare. "Your form is a jackal, Kuba. Hunting dogs are similar, but they aren't the same."

My heart sunk. "You can't be human?"

"No. When we take the form of these animals, we are inhabiting their bodies, but we don't fully become them. People have souls which we can't simply force out. Though I'm a witch, so most people would expect me to do something like that."

Jaryło huffed from behind me, and the clustered prisoners sneered, the nymphs glowing as they readied their magic. "Father should have foreseen your betrayal, Vlatka. He allowed too many servants to run free of his control. Kyustendil and Ivan paid the price, so be glad I swore not to harm you."

Kuba growled, but Vlatka shook her head. "Don't let him get to you, Kuba. He is nothing more than a boy with a wounded ego because he couldn't live up to Perun's expectations."

The god rolled his eyes and stepped to the side. "I have released you, have I not? Come and be free of Marzanna's dungeon. Her Frostmarked will soon discover what has happened here, and I do not believe fighting them a good use of my *žityje*. There are more important things for me to do than wither in this desert." Then he sauntered off toward the tunnels, darkening our side of the room.

I waited with Sabina as Vlatka and Kuba led the others after him. She squeezed my hand. Silent, firm, and exactly what I needed. *Gods, what would I have done without her in Nawia?*

"You don't have to marry him," she whispered. "We'll find a way."

"This time, I don't think there is one…"

Another squeeze. "Have hope. There's little a goddess, a witch, a nymph, a płanetnik, and a fool in the form of a jackal can't solve."

My laugh came without my approval, but whatever weight it had lifted from my heart returned at the thought of Wacław. His emotions were unsettling—somehow even darker than before. "After everything that's happened, I've got no hope left. Wacław…" I shook my head. "Too much has happened since we left Nawia."

Kuba sniffed through the scorpions as Vlatka swooped over to the other, larger cell. Vastrothie were trapped behind its barrier, and she quipped back to Jaryło, "Oh kind and mighty god of spring and war, won't you release these humble people?"

"Mockery won't make me feel mercy," Jaryło replied. "I have honored my end of the blood pact, and there is much I must do to prepare for our grand wedding. Let Otylia free them if she's feeling so generous."

I furrowed my brow, stepping out of the first cell. "Your servant stole too much of my *żityje*!"

He tapped his chin. "If only Father had granted you a tool to free them."

If only you didn't betray everyone who trusted you…

I stiffened, touching Weles's silver and wooden armband on my arm. It had failed to stop Serapis's scorpion strikes, but energy remained within it. I hoped it was enough.

My lingering pain made me woozy as I approached the second doorway. Gritting my teeth was all I had to avoid toppling over, and I prayed to Mokosz that I could recover fast enough to return to Huebia and save Wacław. But only more *żityje* could mend the last of my wounds. That meant earning worshippers…

Wisps representing each of the prisoners surrounded me. They whispered of fear and betrayal, warriors dragging them away while their loved ones wept. I should've seen them as the innocents they were. Instead, my selfish mind saw the life in their blood, and I shivered in anticipation of feeling my true power. Nothing had been like it when I'd risen from the volcano, but in the time since, my lack of *żityje* had made that moment seem a distant dream. No longer.

I pressed my fingers against the invisible barrier, feeling its steady vibration. Raw energy coursed through it, and the harder I pushed, the more it resisted. *Who did this?* The channeler had been skilled. That much was obvious, and frustration boiled in my chest at how little I knew.

"One step at a time," I whispered to myself before holding

Weles's armband to the barrier. When it touched, the barrier's vibrations quickened, crackling like Wacław's lightning before dissipating.

I leaned against the wall to catch my breath. It felt like I'd been struck in the gut—again. But I forced a gentle smile to my face as the first prisoner stepped free, dropping to his knees before me.

"Thank you!" he cried with his forehead to the floor. "What can I ever do to thank you?"

Thirty more followed. Women, men, and children, each with their own thanks as they reached to touch my clothes. *Just like the demons,* I thought as I forced myself not to back away. A goddess needed to appear strong and worthy of worship. I *was* strong. Just… Earning the favor of others wasn't exactly my specialty.

"I am Otylia," I said, purposely leaving out my second name, "granddaughter of the Earth Mother, goddess of endings and the moon. When people ask how you escaped the Winter Witch, tell them I've come to defeat her. Then, sacrifice a portion of your food in my name, praying to me by whispering at the moment the day passes to night. I will hear you."

Their thanks carried on for some time, but noises from the tunnel silenced their chorus. I eyed the exit, searching for Jaryło. The god had vanished.

"Oblivion take him," I cursed, staggering toward the hall.

Fighting rang out ahead, and End's shadowed faces shouted as guards fell to Vlatka and Sabina's magic. I couldn't quiet the voices. No matter how hard I tried, they multiplied, and I released a shout of frustration before reaching the fighting myself. It was all a blur of wisps and blades. Stone seemed to shift beneath my feet. Standing was too difficult, let alone finding and swinging a sword.

The skirmish only grew louder with the voices. Bolts of *żityje* flashed through the tunnels, both nymph magic and szeptuchy. I had no intention of discovering the full force of Marzanna's chosen in the city.

"Lady Otylia!" Sabina gasped, suddenly at my side as Kuba intercepted a guard who'd been lumbering toward me, ripping through his neck with all the excitement of a predator. "Are you drained?"

I clenched my jaw. "What does it look like?"

"Oh… uh… yes!" She threw my arm over her shoulder before realizing she wasn't built to carry someone even as light as me. One of the men from Nawia noticed her peril and took over, allowing her to focus on her magic instead.

Our allies pushed their way down the tunnel. The torches cast inconstant light over the corpses as we followed. One freed prisoner had taken a spearhead to the neck and four others limped along, but it was a miracle so few were dead. *Not a miracle*, I realized as flames danced ahead. A witch like Vlatka would be offended by such a term.

We followed Vlatka and the warriors with the women and children. Unlike the Zurgowie, Vastrothie women not chosen by Mokosz did not fight alongside the men. They ruled as scions, built cities as szeptuchy, and organized trade, leaving the fighting to the men. Was that Mokosz's standard or their own?

My head spun from the voices and pounding of sorcery and blades. The freed man handed me off to another, his face familiar as Sabina guarded me. A song flowed quietly from her lips. She'd never explained her nymph magic before, and the more I watched her kind, the more curious I became. Weles had claimed words themselves had power. Szeptuchy were named after their whispers. Though channeling was possible without them, it was easier to align *žityje* with my wishes when I used the old tongue. Nymph magic felt similar, yet the tone of it was entirely different.

A *crack* jolted me from my thoughts. Bits of dark shale sprayed over me, filling my mouth with dust. I coughed, but before I could ask what had happened, we were running deeper into the tunnels.

"Wait," I mumbled. "We're going the wrong way!"

Sabina had disappeared, though, and the man hadn't heard me over the noise of battle. Or was it quiet? End's voices had merged with the world. Frostmarked and rescued prisoners cried out as metal pierced their hearts, their screams echoing into the afterlife and their shadowy hands reaching for me. But I couldn't save them, even if I'd wanted to. *Žityje* seeped from my soul. I needed more just to live.

"Sabina…"

The tunnels grew darker. My steps felt light as air… No, I wasn't walking at all. The man had lifted me, and as the sounds of battle faded away, I shuddered with each breath. Voices remained in my head, quieter than before. One was probably the man's. He seemed so familiar, but what was his name? Everyone had told me theirs on that black island, but there had been so many, and my mind was foggy. Ivan would've remembered. The old bear had known how to lead by example—until he died to save me.

I'll make you proud, somehow.

Time ebbed and flowed as we traversed the tunnels until beginning to rise. Stairs? The man huffed after what felt like a hundred flights. Still, though, he pushed on.

It was on what I thought was the fifth level that I realized Sabina was by my side again. Those deep brown eyes of hers never left me, and a calm fell over me as she sang a quiet song. When she noticed me looking at her, she laid a hand on my cheek. "It'll be okay. Mokosz's szeptuchy are here. They know how to get us out."

"Keep singing," I replied as my pain returned. "Whatever magic was in it worked."

So she sang. It was a sweet tune that reminded me of the willows along the Krowik River. Their branches would hang over the current, as if trying to stretch to the other side. In the spring, their catkins would float free in a strong wind, and Wacław had always run after them, diving into the shallows to catch one for me to place over my ear. "It's not a flower wreath yet," he'd say, "but someday I'll catch yours on Noc Kupały."

I'd thought his words to be nothing at the time. We hadn't even turned twelve, and thoughts of marriage and love were distant dreams for children our age. Those dreams had never come to me, though. Mother's marriage had seemed so *constraining*. The last thing I'd wanted was to be trapped like her instead of running free through Dziewanna's wilds, but now… I didn't know what I wanted. To save Mother, obviously. But what else? Did I simply hate Jaryło, or did I still despise marriage's lifelong commitment? Did nothing matter but becoming my own woman, my own goddess? The twinge in my heart gave me an uncomfortable answer.

"Otylia!" the voices cried around me.

I ignored them, resisting what was surely more calls for my help. Didn't they understand? I'd given all the *žityje* in my soul just to free myself and the prisoners. The moon had only given me so much, and without worshippers, I was nothing more than a crippled version of a szeptucha.

Then a cold hand touched my face.

I yelped at the onslaught of chill as a vision tried to steal me away. My flailing flung me free from the man's arms, though, and I crashed back to reality with my face to the floor, the throbbing from my wounds enough to draw tears from my eyes.

"Oh dear…" Ildes's voice said from above. "Get Ta-naro to prepare the altar. Under whose authority? Bah! The granddaughter of the Earth Mother is here and you question me now?"

Muffled complaints trailed away along with footsteps, leaving me in painful silence until someone pulled me onto a bed—my bed, I realized as my vision cleared. "Amten?" I asked, unable to hold up my head.

"Kiin said ya might need my help," the scorpion hunter said with a big smile. His cracked teeth would've looked like a demon's if he weren't… well… him. "I hear ya already got the deathstalkers, though. A shame. Them giants would've made a great couple helms. Been wanting to try 'em."

"Yes, yes, your scorpions are very nice," Kiin said, waving him away. "Lady Otylia is *very* grateful for your help, but now, let the chosen work."

The massive man shrugged and gave me a smile before turning to leave. I called after him, "Wait, Amten!"

I couldn't see him, but his footsteps stopped. "What can I do ya for, little goddess?"

"Nothing. I…" I coughed. Each word sent an ache through my chest, but I spoke through the pain. "I just want to thank you. Your armor saved my life. I don't know what you did in the battle, but I don't deserve your bravery."

"Ma lady," he said shakily. Then he left.

Kiin sat alongside me on the bed. All I could see was half her face with my body all but paralyzed from the pain—enough to see her furrowed brow. "I don't trust that man."

"I like him," I said. "He's the most honest person I've met in Vastroth, but I think I offended him."

Ildes chuckled. "No, you did not cause him offense. You must understand that for those not chosen, interacting with a goddess is quite unusual. They fear us as channelers enough, but you… Well, let's just say that many who believe do not truly realize how much they doubted until an immortal is standing before them."

"What about lying before them, crippled?"

Her footsteps rounded the bed, and glass clinked as she fiddled with something nearby. "You are a fledgling goddess who is learning to fly. They told us what you did in that dungeon in order to save the imprisoned."

Sorrow and rage struck me together, sending my stomach into flips. "Don't make me talk about it." The reality of my pact with Jaryło made me want to surrender to Oblivion.

"Running from your fears won't make them go away," Kiin said.

"I'm not running."

She huffed. "Then what do you call letting the boy you love die a slow, painful death as a demon consumes him?"

"*You* trapped him." I bit my cheek hard enough to draw blood. The taste was too familiar already. "But I'm responsible for Wašek losing himself this fast. You're right… I fled at first. All I'm trying to do now is fix it."

"And if you can't?"

"What's your problem?" I snapped, a fresh wave of pain striking me as I tried to sit up. "Gah! Why do you hate him so much? *He* didn't take Yesike from you. That was the Earth Mother!"

Żityje rushed from Kiin's hands. Her wisp shot past my head, and I sucked in a breath as the wall cracked behind me. But before she could do anything else, Ildes whispered sharply. The wall mended in a blink, the air vibrating with the clashing of their spells.

"Find your core," the old szeptucha said with all the force of the north's brutal storms. "Kiin, I taught you better than this."

Kiin grumbled to herself and spun away, stomping to the entrance. "We all have our failures. That demon… Know when it's time to stop fighting for him, when putting him down is better for the greater good."

When I didn't reply, she left with a huff. Ildes watched her go before releasing a sigh and circling the bed to me. "The Earth Mother's demands weigh heavy upon all who lost a child. So, too, do they burden her szeptuchy each day, as it was us who carried out the collection."

"I thought the scions took the children?" I replied, remembering Kiin kneeling before the cave as the scions carried away her son.

"Take this." She held a glass vial before me in her veiny hand. Though it had been a command, her voice was comforting, and I did as she said. "Now drink all of it. Quickly is best if you don't wish to choke. Earth Mother knows neither of us needs another problem."

I downed the dark liquid in one gulp, its sharp flavor leaving a trail of searing pain down my throat and spurring me into a cough. The next vial met my lips without her asking.

"Yes, yes, it burns. This should remedy it."

The substance left a bitter coating on my tongue, but she was right. The pain was gone in seconds—*all* of my pain. "What is this?" I asked, suddenly able to sit up. Everything felt distant. I ran my fingers down my arm and could barely even feel them. "Mother taught me potions, but I've never seen one like this."

She grinned, revealing her deep dimples as she gently pushed me back down. "I suspect not. The roots used for both of these potions are found only in these cliffs. Stonecreeper, it is called, for its growth is slow as it works its way through the many layers. Do not be misguided by its effects. You must rest, as it only makes you forget your wounds, not heal them."

Her words made sense. Their meanings, though, were lost as my head grew light, a calm unlike any I'd felt taking away my mental pains as well as my physical ones. No distractions. No fears. As I took a deep breath, the wisps' voices ended at my silent command, and I felt at ease for the first time in weeks. End's force asked to be wielded. Like a child's endless desire, it pushed at my soul. Except I had no *żityje*. That wasn't reassuring, but at least my power wasn't trying to control me for once. Why?

"Lady Otylia," Ildes said, laying a hand softly on my shoulder. "Your expression is that of a boy seeing a beautiful woman for the first time. What has happened?"

"I…" Even my breaths were slowed as I hesitated. Normally, I would've panicked, but something was pure about this sensation, as if my soul, body, and mind were aligned. "This is the first time since I left Nawia that my power makes sense."

When I closed my eyes, I willed the Threads of Life to appear, and their colorful glows met me without even needing to expend *żityje*. They wrapped themselves around Ildes tightly. Her movements seemed slow now, burdened beneath their pull as they stretched in every direction. I'd never seen so many on anyone but Jaryło, but his had been loose. These were taut, like all of mine except the one reaching to Weles.

"Connection is what gives us the ability to channel the god who chooses us," Ildes said with her fingers tracing Mokosz's Mothermark at her neck. "You are a goddess. Perhaps, to channel your own power, you must first find connection with yourself."

That made me squirm. *Connection with myself? What is that supposed to mean?* I didn't know, so I deflected, "You love them, don't you? The Daughters."

Her brow wrinkled even more than before. "Do not flee your own heart, my child. It will guide you to who you are and who you desire to become. No one else can decide that for you. Not even the Earth Mother's son."

"Thank you," was all I could reply.

"Rest and think on it. Perhaps find your core too. Ta-naro will return soon with Kiin if her head has drained of its venom, and once you have your life force back, we will discuss more." She bowed her head and swept to the tapestry covering the entrance. Before she pushed it aside, though, she took a portion in her hand, closing her eyes tight. "Yes, I do."

"You do what?"

"Love them." She released the tapestry and took a heavy breath.

"The Earth Mother did not grant me the ability to bear children, but because of the girls here, I have never needed to. Family need not be by blood but by bond." Then she left.

I watched the tapestry drift for a long time, allowing End's wisps to return. Images of szeptuchy aiding the ill and hurting came with them. Births and deaths alike, each an end within life's cycle. But there was more. Relationships forged with the strength of the Threads and the dismay of those broken. The Thread between the pairs never severed. Instead, it grew limp and dull, never lost completely but no longer binding them like the tether between Wacław and me. I took heart in how tight that line remained.

He's not gone. Not yet.

The stone was cold against my feet as I pushed myself free from the bed. Some feeling had returned, but my previous agony was now nothing more than a dull throb. I conveniently ignored it. Ildes's stonecreeper root had done its job so well that I hadn't even realized I was barefoot until I felt that chill. Familiar, it was a reminder of the enemy I faced. Marzanna was under Czarnobóg's sway, but she had been the one to capture Mother. Nothing I'd seen had changed that.

I shuffled across the room. My force called me to the tapestry with a tug on my soul, similar to my pull to Wacław. This focus would fade in time, and I intended to listen if End had something to tell me.

The whispers grew as I stopped before the tapestry. Nothing happened, so I studied the woven artwork and the story of the attacked boat along the Tiop River. The last panel drew me in again, and I focused on the dark, winged figures that swept from the sky. Suddenly, I understood what End wanted.

My numbness dulled my fear, and I raised my ungloved hand without resistance to the pull. Something about this tapestry mattered. End needed me to see its secrets, and when I laid my hand against its rough texture, tracing the demons, the voices pulled me away. Light blurred past me.

Then I fell through the clouds.

35

The Płanetník

It feeds my soul… I must have it.

FROST HUNG IN THE AIR. A thin coat of it covered every surface in the Glasstone Tower, turning the already precarious glass staircase curving up its center into a death march for those without powers to aid them. Luckily, I had no such problem.

The winds steadied my balance as I reached the highest floor. They surged through me with every stride, begging to be controlled, to be manipulated into a storm. How had I missed that urgency within them before? The eight grandchildren of Strzybóg were not the masters of the gales. I was. And they would bend to my will.

A pair of Frostmarked Vastrothie guards met me upon the final step. I admired their two-ended spears, the classic spearhead on one end and a curved blade on the other. An effective weapon for the quick, sweeping style they fought with. The dual ends gave them a versatility to fight with or without a shield, and I grinned knowing how Kuba would have envied such a weapon.

He doesn't matter anymore, I reminded myself before matching the gaze of the first guard.

"State your business, corrupted one," he said.

I held out my Frostmarked palm to him. The mark glowed

brightly upon it—a signal from Marzanna herself. "The Scarred Lady is expecting me."

The second guard huffed. "Lady Minna is not in the mood today."

"And I'm not in the mood for waiting."

"Fine." The first waved me on. "Guess we won't tell you 'bout the beasts she let loose earlier."

I furrowed my brow, releasing a low growl.

"No," he continued. "Get on up there, storm summoner. Would hate for you to be—"

My Thunderstone dagger was at his throat before he finished. Its sharp black edge pierced the skin ever-so-slightly, drawing blood and devouring his *żityje* like a parched traveler. The guard quivered, and his partner didn't dare move.

"Tell me," I snarled as a gust blew through the room. The black rising from me joined with it, spiraling around us both. "Or I'll drain both of you."

He stammered his reply, but I just made out enough. "The Lady… chały… endings…"

I released him, my mind spinning. He pled for his life, but I didn't even hear his words as I stormed into the room beyond. A force pushed against my mind. I refused to let the weakling retake control, not when I was so close to capturing Grudzień and ruling the lands I desired. That was all that mattered—not the goddess who scorned me like everyone else.

Floored with sandstone and adorned with elaborate statues of colored glass, the Hall of Scions was by far the grandest room I'd ever seen. Chandeliers carefully placed throughout the hall scattered the light from the high windows. It illuminated only the statues and the path leading to the stone altar. All else was shadows. Seven figures hid in that darkness—split by the aisle. They believed no one knew of their presence, but the winds needed no eyes. Nor did I fear them. Marzanna had given me my task, and none would dare confront me while I claimed to serve her.

A szeptucha knelt before the altar in a light blue robe. It draped behind her, down the two steps separating the altar from the rest of the hall. The altar rose from the floor without any cracks or seams, and I assumed it had once been in honor of Mokosz. Now, though, an image of Marzanna rose behind it. Chiseled from some parts black glass, other parts ice, every crevice of her body was jagged and sharp. I despised her.

"Wacław Lubiewicz," Minna said in the Krowikie tongue, rising to face me with a bloodied dagger in one hand and a staff in the other, a black stone radiating power from its peak.

We'll take it. Soon.

I approached without replying as my Frostmark pulsed in tandem with the one sliced over Minna's left eye. Her skin was tan and her hair a deep brown, unlike the people of Vastroth. *Żityje* radiated from all things alive and undead, but the power in her soul was unlike any I'd sensed in a szeptucha. It swirled with darkness. All too familiar.

The light was greatest around the altar, revealing a man of middle age lying upon it. A violet Mothermark was painted upon his brow, copying that of Darixa. The rest of him was sheer white as his blood flowed into the altar's cracks.

"You've reaffirmed your loyalty to Lady Marzanna and enjoyed her hospitality," Minna said, stomping her staff into the ground and sending an echo through the hall, "but you do not bow."

A force emanated from Grudzień and pushed upon my rage, but I stifled my growl. The stone shifted from a sphere to a cube with a crack down its center. When it changed again, it struck me with a new wave of anger.

"I did not come here to worship Marzanna," I said as I glared up at the idol.

"No, you came out of fear."

For a moment, I froze, remembering Otylia's pleas. *Ignore the weakness. She couldn't love us, so we left. Now, she must die.*

I swallowed. "Yes."

Minna scowled, her one unscarred eye looking me up and down. "You're lucky she's tolerated you for this long."

"I said I didn't come to worship. That doesn't mean I don't intend to do her bidding, as long as she honors our agreement." The lie excited me. Yes, I would kill Otylia, but I was no slave to winter. All I needed was that Moonstone to grant me the control I needed over the tribes.

A shuffling noise came from the shadows. Someone less adept wouldn't have heard, but the winds carried the smallest of sounds to my ear. *I have them.*

"Why should you be rewarded with Grudzień and all the lands north of Perun's Crown when you've defied Lady Marzanna?" Minna asked, circling me. "Her ice is endless, her wrath unyielding. And you, son of Jacek, deserve the worst of her wrath."

I threw out my arms, sending the gales into the szeptucha and throwing her into a stone column lining the hall's center. Her shoulder snapped as she struck, and before she could rise, I stood over her with the Thunderstone dagger in hand.

"Do not speak of him! That man was never my father. Nawia is too kind an end for him."

She grinned in spite of her mangled arm. "Our queen sees how far you've come. She's taken Jacek and your mother—though you stole her back. Normally, she would kill you just for taking a soul she'd claimed, but it's unheard of for a Naw to wield a Moonstone's *żityje.* So, perhaps you've earned this final chance. That is, if you can actually kill the goddess."

"I can." Something deep within me twinged again. I forced it away. "What is your plan? The Daughters of the Earth will rebel when Otylia returns."

Slowly, Minna pushed herself to her feet, pressing her shoulder back into its socket with a *crack* before stepping far too close to me. The cold itself seemed to radiate from her, but I invited the pain. It only fed my hatred.

"Are you sure you're ready?" she asked, her voice challenging. "Once we begin, you will complete your mission, or Lady Marzanna will devour your soul for eternity. You'll beg for Oblivion."

"Do you doubt your goddess? Marzanna chose me to kill Otylia, not you. Tell me the plan, or I'll make sure your warriors die like the rest."

She smirked. "So, the demon truly has won. Good. It would be a shame for that poor mortal boy to endure the pain of slaughtering his beloved Otylka."

Another twinge. "He's gone, forever."

Her fingers pulled down my chin, forcing me to look into her eyes. "Lady Marzanna understands what it is to be betrayed by your lover. You will have your vengeance and the lands she promised you. She's granted me new life twice, and she shall remake you too."

"And what of the chały you sent after Otylia?"

"Her? No, the chały are not meant for your little goddess."

"Then who?"

She scowled. "Mokosz's loyal 'Daughters' must be dealt with. They remain hidden here, but Otylia has drawn out those in Sheresy. We will cut off the organization's heads like the serpents they are."

"Kiin? The one who locked me in a stole cell for days?" When she nodded, I smirked. I could feel my anger igniting at Grudzień's shift. "I hope the chały make her suffer before the rebellion."

Minna stepped closer, studying me with an unsettling intensity in her eye. "You say the Daughters will rebel—good. Let them. Once those foolish enough to join them have taken up arms, we will slaughter them until the streets are stained with sacrificial blood for our goddess."

"That's it?" I asked. "No other plan?"

She raised her bloodied dagger and licked its flat clean. "Return to the Daughters. If they have heard what you did to those people in the alley, tell them it was the chały. You saved those you could."

"They won't believe me unless I have something to prove I fought them." I nodded to the staff, fighting its push as it shifted again. "Give me Grudzień. Marzanna has promised it to me any-way."

More shuffling from the shadows. I couldn't sense sorcerers and szeptuchy like Otylia, but my hunger alerted me to the figures' fresh *żitγje* drawing closer as Minna's skin began to glow. "Don't overstep your bounds, Naw," she snapped. "Lady Marzanna has given you a final chance, but we are not your servants. We will confront the Daughters. How you kill Otylia, however, is up to you."

Without replying, I returned to the stairs, my steps echoing across the Hall of Scions and darkness swirling at my heels. Minna believed her goddess had turned me. She'd believed I'd chosen Marzanna's side over Dziewanna's. What a fool.

The only side that mattered was mine.

Part 3
Redemption & Ruin

36

Narcyz

Can I tell him?

ANDRIJ SHIELDED HIS EYES as Mikołaj's army passed from Solga's forests near the Krowik River to the western hills. Trees were sparser here, not that the dead ones had provided much cover anyway. I preferred the slopes to the shadows. Better to face the enemy head-on, Pa always said.

"You've been thinking a lot lately," Andrij said, raising his brow at me. "I wouldn't be concerned if you were anyone else."

Stop being perceptive.

I gripped my horse's reins. They rubbed against my callouses, formed from years of working iron in Pa's smithy, but that familiar pain grounded me in reality. When the world was a nightmare, I needed that. "I told you Wacław talked through his mark."

He nodded. "Our friends being alive usually wouldn't bring you this much anxiety."

"I'm not anxious!" I insisted before glancing at the warriors around us. Besides Mikołaj, none rode, and they were too weary from days of walking to pay attention to us. Still, I guided Andrij away. None could hear what I was about to say. "There was more."

"All right. Tell me."

I sighed and looked to the hilltop to our left. The long grasses upon it had browned, and snow drifted from the sky as I forced my-self to speak. "Wacław wants Mikołaj to duel Chief Serwacy for con-trol of the army. It's my job to make sure he wins and kills Miec-zysław when we return to Dwie Rzeki."

Andrij's expression hardened. "Why hide this from me? I thought we were meant to negotiate."

"Negotiation won't work. You saw how aggressive Mieczysław is."

"It surprises me that Wacław would propose such cruelty." He shook his head, holding his temples. "This divisiveness will just lead to more death. I haven't known him for long, but this doesn't sound like a plan he'd come up with."

I shrugged. "Dunno. He sounded weird. Like him, but… you know… angrier. Guess a god stealing your woman will do that to you."

"Or surrendering to your demonic soul."

"Yeah, that too." Worry made my gut do flips, but I settled into my riding pad and rode taller, trying to look confident. "It doesn't sound like *his* plan, but it makes sense. Kill the chiefs unwilling to support Mikołaj and unite the tribe behind him. Warriors respect strength."

As we crested a large hill, Mikołaj stopped the march with a raised fist. He waved for someone to join him, and Albin's bald head emerged from the crowd. A tattoo crept from the infamous warrior's neck to beneath his clothes, barely visible from a distance. None knew what it represented. Some claimed to have seen it, but Albin had dueled each to prove their lies. He'd lived. They hadn't.

"Warriors also admire loyalty," Andrij said.

I nodded. "They do."

Albin had been fiercely loyal to Jacek until his death. That loyalty had apparently carried over to Mikołaj now that he was chief of Dwie Rzeki. Even if the other chiefs had made Mieczysław high chief, Mikołaj appeared strong like his father on the surface, and Albin could help convince Krowik's men he was worth following. The election of a high chief was the art of diplomacy. This, though, was about prestige and respect. What Mikołaj lacked with his tongue, he could make up for with brute strength. That was good for wartime.

"We'll convince Mikołaj to march north," I said, watching him argue with Albin, "and he'll challenge Serwacy when we arrive. By siding with Mieczysław, Serwacy broke his alliance of blood with Mikołaj."

"Because of his daughter?" Andrij asked. "We have no such pacts among my people."

I scoffed. "Well, Boz is an idiot. It's supposed to stop the chiefs from killing each other, and the broken marriage alliance gives Mikołaj a reason to challenge him."

"The high chief won't approve."

"We're away from Mieczysław. Who's going to tell him until he's surrounded by Mikołaj's men? It's not like we're planning to be pals with him anyway."

Andrij didn't reply, and before I could speak again, Albin stomped down the slope to us with his mouth in a tight grimace. "Narcyz!" he barked. "Chief wants you."

"What for?" I asked.

Albin crossed his bulging arms, enough to make me swallow and silently push my horse on. Andrij followed on Oleh with a nod at the warrior. Albin didn't return it, and only the muttering of the warriors we passed broke the tension as we climbed the hill.

Mikołaj had dismounted. Running his thumb across his fingers, he stared to the west, where two paths diverged: one toward the south and the other north. Despite being far more broad-shouldered than Wacław, I realized now how much he resembled his younger half-brother. *Had* resembled him. Mikołaj lacked the creepy black veins and spark of lightning in his eyes. Just two moons had been enough to make Wacław look like an entirely different person.

"I have considered your proposal," the young chief said as we dismounted beside him. Albin kept his distance but watched us with a disapproving glare.

"And?" I pried.

His cloak caught on the grasses as he turned to me, but he gave it no heed. His thoughts were obviously elsewhere. "If we return to Dwie Rzeki, will our people be safe? How do we know the Solgawi won't rush across the Krowik while we're focused on the east?"

"We have a storm demon and a goddess," I replied.

Andrij stepped forward. "*And* you need not completely abandon the west. The Krowik River is the most obviously defensible place. Leave a garrison along the bridges and shallow passes and build fortifications where necessary. If taking the east bank of the river costs too many lives, the Solgawi may decide it unwise to continue the war."

Mikołaj smiled and patted him on the shoulder. "You speak like a chief."

"Just a commander. Boz is a madman at times, but he understands the importance of tactics in war."

"Fine," Mikołaj said. "Then assume I wish to follow your plan to head east. How do we convince Serwacy and his allied chiefs to join us?" He pointed to the northern path. "That trail heads to where his men should be. We could find them in a few days, but I can't look like a fool when we do." He nodded south. "Rolika lies that way. We could be heroes by taking it before the Solgawi have time to respond."

"Take what you're owed," I said flatly, crossing my arms and meeting the taller man's gaze. Andrij flinched beside me, but I ignored him. "Kinga is Serwacy's daughter, so he should be your ally."

His eyes widened before he smiled eagerly. "You suggest I duel my wife's father?"

I flexed my arm, slapping the muscle. "You're young and fit! He's an old man. It'll be an easy fight, and you can prove you're the chief Jacek was. The warriors will follow you. Then Mieczysław will have to listen to *you*."

"Many may follow me, yes, but what about the high chief himself?" He circled away with his head bowed in thought. "Mieczysław will not die easily. He has loyalists."

"Then kill them! How many people did Jacek kill to 'unite' the tribes? Just win the duel and march back to Dwie Rzeki. Mieczysław can't resist the entire Krowikie army."

"There are possibilities here… But what gave you this idea? You bear what you claim is Wacław's demonic mark. Has he spoken to you?"

I nodded.

"Ah, so it's my brother's plot to get me killed?" Mikołaj scowled before glancing at Albin. "What do you think? Half-Chief wants to become my father's heir?"

Albin's expression was unreadable as he stared at me for longer than was comforting. "I never liked you. Ignorant little twat too desperate to strike with his spear. Gets more than you killed in battle."

My jaw clenched, but I held my ground. His words were like a punch to my gut. We'd all looked up to Albin as kids, watching him train as he bested all others in the sparring ring. Even Xobas had never beat the tattooed giant. Why had I believed I could prove myself to him?

"Narcyz is often blunt and rash, yes," Andrij said, gesturing down softly with his hand. "What he lacks in patience, though, he makes up for in determination. This plan is not my ideal situation, but if it is our way forward, then don't doubt his ability to fight for what matters." He looked at me with a solemn smile. "And I'll fight by his side."

"Thanks," I said, "but I can speak for myself." I went toe-to-toe with Albin, matching the intensity of his gaze. "I don't care what you think of me. I've fought more terrifying beasts in three moons than you have in your whole life. Believe me or not, whatever. The Frost-marked are coming regardless, and we have the chance to stop them if Mikołaj takes his father's title back. Or are *you* too afraid?"

Albin spat in my face and grabbed hold of my tunic, winding up for a punch. Mikołaj appealed for him to stop, but it landed with the force of a smith's hammer.

I collapsed. Blood poured from my nose. Or, at least, I thought it did. My head was spinning, and something coated my upper lip, filling my mouth with an iron taste. All else was pain. Dull but heavy, it swallowed my other senses as I gasped for air.

The bastard broke my nose. I raised my arm to wipe away the blood, but it just kept coming. *He'll pay for that.*

I was up a heartbeat later with all the rage of a wounded wolf. Someone shouted my name. They grabbed at my shoulder, at my arm, but my fist was already flying. Albin dodged to the side. A quick move. He was cocky, though, and let his guard down. I took advantage.

Feinting as if I'd lost my balance on the first strike, I put all my weight onto my front leg and kicked back at his knee. A *crack* broke through the chaos. More shouting followed, but I wasn't done. I rolled with my momentum. My shoulder complained at the sloppy move, but more pain just stoked my anger. Pa said to always strike when the iron is hot.

Albin growled as I rose from the roll at his flank. We exchanged body jabs, blocking more than hit. He was skilled, but the kick had done its job. When he lunged right, it slowed him and weakened the resulting punch.

So I did it again.

I let him catch my face shot, taking away his defense. Then, as he tried to throw me to the ground, I jumped and threw all my strength into a two-legged kick at his injured knee. His grip loosened. We fell together, and he dared not strike me again.

Andrij pulled me to my feet and brushed the dirt off my tunic. "What was the point of that?" he whispered.

"Respect," I muttered, checking my broken nose. It would need to be set later, but it felt bad. Even that would likely not be enough. "I told you, warriors respect strength."

Mikołaj tapped his foot. "Done injuring my commander?"

I spat out blood to the side before dropping to a knee in front of him. "Yes, Chief. Think I can help you beat some fat old men now?"

"You fight dirty," Albin growled. His leg was twisted, and he staggered on it as he returned to Mikołaj's side.

"When your enemy is stronger," I said, "you either fight smarter than them or die. We're outnumbered by both Mieczysław and Marzanna. But numbers slow them down. If we strike fast and smart, we can take over the Krowikie army and face the Horde." I bowed my head to Mikołaj. "It is your choice, my chief. All I know is that I'd rather fight dirty and live than die because I was too weak to do what had to be done."

Arms crossed, Mikołaj chuckled. He gestured for me to rise before striding to his horse and throwing himself onto its back. "We ride north!" he shouted for all to hear. "Serwacy betrayed my father and he betrayed me. I think it's time I paid him a visit."

Cheers broke through the army's grumbles. They raised spears and shields, their grime-covered faces full of hatred at their chief's rival, and as Mikołaj led them on, I smiled at their fresh determination.

"You did it," Andrij said with a shake of his head and a laugh, lightly touching my crooked nose. His joy faded, and he snapped it back into place with more force than necessary. "Are you ready to actually assassinate your own tribe's high chief?"

I bit my cheek with the pain as my eyes watered. I resisted the childish will to cry. *Don't lose the respect you gained so quickly.*

Blinking away the tears, I looked to the horizon. The sun had begun to set, and a red hue covered the hills of dead grasses and scattered trees. An ill omen. "I don't know," I answered honestly. "But if I have to, I'll make sure I crack Mieczysław's skull with a strike worthy of Swaróg's hammer."

37

The Płanetnik

We never dreamed before... Why must we now?

FACES HAUNTED MY DREAMS.

A storm whipped through the desert, swirling around me with their dark eyes watching my every move. Their screams battered my ears. They swallowed my mind and forced me to my knees until my own cries joined them.

"Why?" I pled. "Why are you doing this?"

Their terror turned to rage as they shrieked and dove. Their claws like razors ripped through my tunic, slicing my ribs and sending my black blood seeping into the sand below. A trickle that became a flood. I lashed out at the spirits, but my blade found only air as their wisp-like forms vanished and reformed, unharmed.

Then the ground sank.

Tendrils wrapped around my calves, gripping my thighs and pulling me to the depths of the earth. Still the spirits struck. I choked on sand and blood as the winds defied my calls. What were they? Why did they make me suffer?

I dropped through the sand for an eternity. No air met my lungs, nor did the screams fade. Death had tortured me at Oblivion's edge and had tried to drag me away multiple times, but nothing could compare to this horror. It took my mind. It beat my body. But I wouldn't surrender. I wouldn't give in to whatever force that wished to wrestle this new, unshackled life from me. Agony meant nothing in the face of power.

Frigid water struck my skin like a thousand needles, but with it came breaths full of air.

Dreams were irrational places I'd discovered in recent weeks. The sky could suffocate and the water could fill my lungs with life. Voices needed no tongues. Light required neither fire nor sun.

These voices had a source, though. Or more, thousands of them. They watched me in those dark, shadowy forms as stray beams of light illuminated their ranks. Above, they had been aggressive and impossible to understand, but the sea gave clarity to what were desperate cries. Not to kill me. Not to tear me apart or rip away my power. For help.

Then they fell silent.

"Wacław, second son of Jacek, first and only of Lubena, exile of Krowik, lover of the Lady of Endings…" a stern yet youthful voice said from among them. "You have made quite the name for yourself among the Three Realms in such a short time."

I growled, gripping my Thunderstone dagger as *żityje* mended my wounds. "Show yourself, coward!"

"Coward?" The voice laughed as it drew closer. "Płanetniks rarely have the gall to throw such accusations around. Your kind typically prefer to flee instead of facing Death, but not you."

The figures parted, their eyes downturned and their cries muffled. A man strode on the water. Dark veins shattered his pale skin, and a mark of sharp, interlocked triangular shapes pulsed upon his chest. On his shoulder rested black interlocking armor, almost like the aspid's scales in Boz's longhouse, and his fiery eyes were the vertical slits of a snake. They were fixed upon me.

I drew upon my power. Even here, the winds had reach, and darkness swirled defensively around me. "I have met Death. He has no hold on me."

"Because *you* are strong," the man said, his own wisps of darkness rising from his skin. The figures around him seemed to weep at the showing of power. "Unlike your father, unlike your brother, you have the power to lead your people to greatness. You were right to accept Marzanna's offer, but know that she has her own intentions. As do I."

"I don't trust her." I raised my blade toward him. "But she can help free the Nawie from Oblivion, from our hunger. She can give me the power I need."

He grinned, exposing jagged teeth as he circled me. "Perhaps."

"What are you talking about?"

"Alatyr created the true powers of the Three Realms, and Alatyr can destroy them. It cannot magically grant each of us everything we desire." His eyes dropped to the Thunderstone dagger, and he shook his head. "The gods have made man distrustful of man. They have allowed injustice to reign, blinding demons and Nawie alike to what corrupted you. Within each of us—man, beast, demon, god, or even żmij—there is a craving for the pure power of the *żityje* that gives us life. That hunger is not a burden but a gift. Something to be embraced, to feed upon in order to push forward."

Slowly, I nodded. "It's given me more than I could've dreamed of just moons ago."

"And that is why I only appear to you now, when you are ready. This bond you hold with Otylia makes you more than any Naw before you and any that will come after. A slice of divinity resides in your soul, and you don't need her to access it." He pushed upon the flat of the dagger, but I held my ground. "Wacław, you and I are more alike than you believe. Instead of receiving the praise and honor we deserved, we were cast out. We can change that now."

That stupid weakling deep inside me twitched again, but this time, I lowered the blade. "How? And why are you telling me this?"

"The real question is not my intentions but Marzanna's. What does she gain from Otylia's death?"

"Otylia is the only one who can save Dziewanna." I looked to the sea of dark figures surrounding us. Some still watched me with desperation in their gazes. "It will ensure Jaryło has no hope of stopping her."

He sighed. "Then you do not know. Unfortunate."

"Know what?" I growled, my impatience growing with each word.

"That she has accepted his blood oath. The two are to be wed, and with their marriage will come the greatest alliance of gods ever seen: Perun and Weles's armies united behind their children." His wisps snapped around him as he turned away, his voice growing in intensity. "Together, they will crush Marzanna and any hope we have of freeing those who have been corrupted by their injustice! We must end the gods' reign before they succeed."

My heart stopped. I staggered back, drifting through the waters without direction. *She's marrying him?* Despite all my hatred for Otylia, some fragment of me had held onto hope that she'd never marry that fiend of a god. But she'd chosen him. In the end, I was nothing but a demon to her, and she had chosen control, order over all else. Why?

"What are your intentions, then?" I stuttered. The shock held me in place as I tried to find my words and shove away my weakness. How could she betray me so?

"You listen well," the man replied. "I see the Three Realms as they should have been: dynamic, without the gods to rule their forces. I see a world where people, spirits, and demons alike can choose their own destiny without it being foretold." He turned, balling darkness between his hands with a greedy smile pulling at the ends of his mouth. "Darkness resides in us both. Wield it, boy, and we will reshape these lands into our own."

A thousand thoughts swam through my mind, but only one came out as the dream began to fade. "Who are you?"

The man held out his arms, the dark wisps dancing over the figures as the armor on his shoulder crept across his skin. Flesh transformed into scales. His neck turned to three with gaping maws full of teeth and flames upon each. The figures cowered beneath his black wings as the dragon's roar shook me to my core.

"I am called Czarnobóg, first of the żmij. Go forth, Wacław. Obey *none* of the traitorous gods, and do as I will."

I awoke to the stale, chilled air of the Daughters' sleeping hall. A startled yelp rang out as Faarax, the bearded caretaker of the hideout, stumbled back with his mouth covered.

"Forgive me, Master Wacław," he stammered. "I had believed Lady Kiin to have… er… detained you until her return. The rubble in the basement caused *quite* the stir when we attempted to hold our typical supper festivities."

With a groan, I rubbed my eyes. The last day had seemed a dream. From finding my chance to take Grudzień to being tasked with killing Otylia, I still didn't know what to make of it. There were plans beyond what I could see, but did they matter? I would fulfill my destiny. Krowik would finally see what I was capable of.

"I'm not going back in that cage," I replied, letting a snap of lightning dance between my fingers. "Get it?"

"Oh, yes!" he exclaimed with glorious terror flashing in his eyes. "Having you to aid us is far more important, indeed."

"Good."

As I stood and grabbed my straw płanetnik hat, he examined my bloodied shirt with a twitching lip. "If I may…"

I pushed past him. "You may not. Blood is part of my work. It doesn't matter what I look like when I spend most of my time invisible anyway."

"Yes, of course, Master—"

"When will Kiin return with Otylia?"

Faarax's cheeks turned red. He removed his simple cap and scratched the bald head beneath. The man was far out of his depth, but I had little pity for him. We'd all chosen our sides. Czarnobóg's words made me wonder if I was actually alone on mine. "I do not know. The Lady Otylia intended to fly your friends back, but they may have run into trouble."

Worry was evident on his face. I didn't share the feeling. Chały were worse than simple trouble, but they wouldn't succeed in killing Otylia. Only Thunderstone or Moonstone could do that.

Otylia, I said through our bond, walking away from the stout man without a parting word. *You there?*

"*Oh, now you reply.*"

This isn't a reply. I'd heard her pleas for my condition while she'd been gone, but I hadn't bothered to reply. Her rejection had revealed how she felt about me. Now, her blood pact with Jaryło confirmed it. *How long until you return? The Frostmarked are planning something.*

Discomfort flowed from her along with a sharp pain. I flashed my *žityje* to dull it, not that I'd actually been hurt. "*You escaped? Wašek, please tell me you didn't do something you'll regret.*"

Blood. The smell of it returned me to the alley, screams carried by the howling gales feeding my rage. I tasted it on my lips and felt it flowing down my throat. Most of all, though, I sensed it filling my soul with power. The thrill consumed all.

Nothing I'll regret, I said. *I escaped, yes, and be glad. I discovered the Frost-marked intend to begin a new wave of sacrifices. It'll be far worse than Mokosz had ever demanded.*

"*Send them to Oblivion,*" she muttered. "*I'm trying Wašek. We found Kuba and the others. Half of them didn't make it—and Kuba returned as an animal—but we rescued those we could.*"

Once, I would've been overjoyed to hear of Kuba's survival, even if it was as an animal. Instead, I felt nothing except a single spark that extinguished in an instant. *Good. We'll need their help.* I closed my eyes and stopped at the first step of the stairs up. *You're hurt.* Why did I care? I was to kill her anyway.

"*The Frostmarked had an army of scorpions guarding the dungeon.*" A chain of emotions followed. Shame. Anger. Then embarrassment. "*Jaryło's sorcerer was planted among them, and, well, he got me. It was so stupid. I should've seen it coming, but he trapped me long enough for Jaryło to arrive.*" Her voice cracked. "*He threatened to kill our friends if I didn't agree to marry him… I'm sorry. Gods, I hate him!*"

I had no reply. What could I say to the woman who'd rejected me? It didn't matter who she tried to wed. My blade would find her regardless.

Another twinge in my chest.

"*I feel your pain,*" she said. "*It's okay to admit you still hurt.*"

Whatever I once felt for you is gone, but it doesn't matter. You've chosen Jaryło to get Dziewanna back. She's all that matters to you anyway. She's all that ever mattered to you.

"*You know that's not true.*"

I opened my eyes and stared up the stairs, leading to the freedom of the winds outside. *I'm only sure of myself and my power. Return soon, or I'll face the Frostmarked alone.*

Sorrow was the only reply, so I huffed and flung myself up into the fake tavern. No one batted an eye. Invisibility still amazed me at times. For years, I had failed to use it to its pure potential. No longer. Pulling down my hat, I took off at a sprint and burst into the snow-covered city.

Soon, I would fight a goddess, but first, I needed to feed.

38

Otylia

I need to stop him. But how?

WACŁAW'S WORDS REPEATED THROUGH MY HEAD as I sat upon the wooden deck of the large riverboat from the Daughters' dark tapestry. I'd fallen into the river depicted in it, and now, lukewarm water trickled down my face and body, forming an ever-expanding puddle around me. A few passing men showed concern, but I was the least of their worries.

The boat rocked as a creature's head appeared over the railing to my right. With long green hair and a horrific, mangled face, the rusałka grabbed hold of one of the men, holding him tight and digging her fangs into his neck before pulling him overboard. He didn't even scream. Dozens more surrounded the ship, rocking it and luring in men who came too near to the edge.

Idiots. All of them.

Men were so easily manipulated. Bat your eyes and show some cleavage and he wouldn't notice the dagger in your hand. The rusałka hadn't cared about me when I'd dropped into their waters. Those stupid men were their targets, and apparently, it was up to me to save them.

If only I had *żityje*.

Screeching demonic souls encircled me on End's wisps. Faces

and images flashed within them, of suicidal mothers, rejected maidens, and raped women who couldn't prove their accusations. Rusałki lurked forever in their waters, seeking revenge against all men. After dealing with Wacław's corruption, I was starting to get the appeal, but each man's death only created more water demons—utopiecs. I'd had enough of those after defeating the one by Dziewanna's altar on the equinox.

So I stood. Sopping wet and drained, I stared down at the nearest of the rusałki. The man had dropped his spear before he'd died. I snatched it and charged when her head appeared, driving it into her forehead.

A snap of pain struck me with her death, but what else could I do? These demons were doomed to Oblivion now or eventually. Better they go down without creating more of their kind.

"Don't trust their beautiful faces!" I shouted to the men. Women could see through rusałki disguises, but these poor fools were likely traveling merchants. They hadn't held a woman for too long. "They're demons who just want to eat your hearts for their blood!"

The men stared at me with a reasonable mix of "Who is this woman?" and "Why is she bossing us around?" but the one with a strand of colored rope wrapped from one shoulder to the opposite armpit repeated the order.

"Listen to her, whoever she is," he shouted. "Kill the beasts!"

"Ay, ay!" the men called in response to the man I assumed was their captain.

Female screams rang out as most of the men recovered their wits and stabbed the assailants. One rusałka, though, clambered over the rails and grabbed hold of my ankle. "You betray us!" she hissed. "You are the one who could save us, but you side with *them*!"

"Save you?" I asked, kicking free of her grasp. "Why do you demons keep saying that?"

A harpoon shot into the rusałka's head. She dropped to the deck in a pool of black blood, and I cursed as a sailor grinned at me, probably believing he'd saved my life. *Idiot.* But there was no time to worry about him or question another rusałka as familiar shrieks came from above.

"You need to reach land, now!" I called to the captain as the chały's storm hit, sending waves crashing into the boat's side. "The chały will rip you apart."

He waved away my claim, pointing instead to the rusałki. "Keep your focus on the mermaids, lads. Ain't nowhere to go if they sink us!"

"Fine, die then," I muttered. Without *żityje*, I couldn't aid their fight, and they were doomed if those chały arrived unharmed. Well, *when* they arrived. The tapestry had already warned me of the inevitable ending.

Exhaustion clutched me as I stepped back and watched a hundred of the winged beasts dive with their claws and jagged tails tearing through the sailors. If they saw me, they didn't care about my presence, and I couldn't get close enough to jab with my spear. Not that I had the energy. It had taken all my strength just to stumble to the tapestry. Now, with Wacław's demonic voice striking my heart and Ildes's potion flooding my veins, I struggled to stand. I'd done all I could for these men.

It wasn't enough.

The screams and their echoes seemed endless in the tight canyon. When they finished, their souls' terrors continued in End's flashes around me, pounding both my ears and heart. The sky turned black as the wings of the storm demons blocked all that remained of the clouds and sun alike. They smothered the world in death and darkness, and time rushed past as the desert heat fell into a heavy hill.

Chały picked through the dead, devouring their hearts and fighting among themselves for weapons and blood. Rusałki cowered. Many remained on the boat, naked and frightening as always, yet there was a frailty to them now.

They fear the chały…

It was odd to think the demons could have ranks, but Wacław had said płanetniks had levels, ranging from chiefs—like he and Eryk—to the weaker płanetnikami forms that Eryk had led into the battle in the Mangled Woods. There seemed like something more, though. I couldn't explain it, but a feeling of dread hung over me in the chały's presence. No other demon had the same effect.

Soon, time slowed again as the boat reached Sheresy. It was an entirely different city to the one I'd left, and I gasped at its golden, spiraling towers and elaborate designs of glass weaving their way up the western cliffs. Each entrance and building were part of the various layers, molding it into a city of a thousand colors. And on the winding staircase, szeptuchy and szeptuny stood behind an army of archers, *żityje* snapping at their fingers.

How long ago was this? I'd never seen a city this grand nor heard stories of so many demons striking at once, at least, none since Weles's tales of the devastation of Jawia. Could this have been part of that last war of the gods? Or had it happened even before that?

My mind spun at the possibilities, but before I could ponder further, a roar shook the canyon. Boulders dropped into the river and caused great waves as glass shattered along the city's cliffs.

Then he appeared.

Czarnobóg's great wings sent sand and water swirling beneath him as he descended over me. My armband burned at just the sight of him, but this time, I wasn't the żmij's target. Instead, he laughed as the channelers launched their strikes at him, doing no visible damage, no matter their spells. He threw his three heads back. An orange hue radiated from their mouths, and I winced as he lunged and breathed flames that cascaded over the cliffs.

Men and women burned by the hundreds. Both channelers and warriors alike had no hope against the dark dragon's power. Those that survived the initial strike cowered, but chały followed their master.

The voices of the dead were too much. I dropped to the boat's deck, screaming as they rushed over me. Demons begged for me to save their souls. Mortals cried for me to rescue their loved ones. And szeptuchy asked why their gods had forsaken them.

I had no answers. I had no power. Before me, the world burned, and despite being a goddess, all I could do was watch as death reigned and the sun turned black.

I awoke in the bedroom Ta-naro had prepared for me, panting like a dog and feeling somehow worse than when I'd arrived in Amten's arms. The vision's horrors ran through my mind. Demons, death, flames, and darkness consuming the world. Wacław's voice hovered over it all.

"That must have been some nightmare to startle you," someone said from above.

I yelped. The room was nearly completely dark, but my skin glowed softly with the moon's power, revealing a bird on the bed's headboard. "Vlatka?"

The golden eagle seemed to smile. "Of course! Your mother tasked me with guarding you, but it appears I must spar with Sabina for that honor. She has only stepped away for a short while to see nature's life—such a thing seems important for nymphs. Likely, she will return soon. I am glad to have you alone until then."

"It's going to take time for me to get used to you in this form," I said. "Kuba acts like a jackal anyway, but you're a witch. How much does this affect your power?"

"Hmm." I sensed her *žityje* swell for a moment before a ball of light fluttered from her, hovering between us with a soft yellow glow. "To cast my spells I need many elements. Some are simple, like this, but it will be difficult to collect the herbs and other materials required for more complex acts. I imagine it is not unlike your own power while you reside in your silver fox form. Far weaker, of course, but similar."

"How are you weaker? I'm lying here, useless, while the boy whose soul I stole is falling to his darkness. All my life, I just wanted to choose my destiny, but now I'm bound to Jaryło by this stupid blood pact." I curled into a ball, gripping my legs to my chest and staring down at nothing. The stonecreeper had worn off completely by now. Pain followed each movement, but I stubbornly ignored it. "I wish I could've just stayed a szeptucha. Maybe I wouldn't have messed everything up…"

"You are who you choose to be, Otylia." With a flap of her wings, Vlatka hopped down next to me. I didn't look up at her. "I became a witch because I wished to serve the forces I chose to serve. No god or spirit could influence me… So I thought."

"It was better when Dziewanna and Mokosz told me what to do. Their influence helped the world make sense. Now, everything is spiraling out of my control." I groaned and buried my face in the pillow. "Even demons are begging me to save them, but I can't even figure out how to save Wacław or even myself. How in Oblivion am I supposed to help everyone else?"

She pondered for a moment, her ball of light casting a consistent glow that made me wish for the solitude of darkness. "What did you feel when Ildes gave you that potion?"

"It was like I was numb. My worries were gone, at least for a bit."

"And? What of your power?"

I looked up at her, furrowing my brow. "It was easier to reach, even with my lack of *żityje*. Why?"

"Wielding life itself requires an understanding of who we are." She chuckled, igniting my frustration further, but she just pecked at my hand when I frowned. "Now, now. I'm trying to be light-hearted—gods know someone has to be around here. I laugh, child, because I know how much your mother struggled with the same thing. She was so determined to not be 'tamed' by others that she didn't truly know her own heart. Like you, she let the noise of the Three Realms swallow the voice within her. That potion was meant to dull the pain of your wound, but it also calms you, allowing you to listen to that voice. Find that calm if you want to understand the heart of your force. Endings are significant. Perhaps you will find you are capable of more than you know. Many whisper that you are, but we shall not know until you prove it."

Before I could reply, a yap came from the entrance as the wall shifted, revealing the tapestry and Kuba's nose sniffing beneath. "Wake up time! Unless you're, like, changing in there or something?"

Gods, I missed that fool. "Come in, Kuba."

He released another excited yap and rushed in with Sabina ducking through behind them. A knot loosened in my core. It was impossible to be tense with such good company. That thought would've startled me just moons ago, but I needed my friends more than I'd ever known. Sure, I'd Ascended. All that seemed to mean was that I needed them even more.

"And if it isn't my favorite nymph," I said, leaning up against the headboard, still with my legs tucked in. I realized then that tears wetted my cheeks. Again, I wished for the dark. "What happened to the others we rescued?"

Sabina smiled sweetly and sat beside me. I'd left little space on the edge of the bed, but she was thin and nuzzled into me anyway, laying her head on my shoulder. "*You* saved them, Otylia. And they're safe… as safe as they can be in a city ruled by Marzanna. In fact, Kiin said they have a surprise for you when you're ready."

"I hate surprises."

"What?" Kuba said, aghast as he hopped onto the bed too. "Surprises are the best!"

The bed was getting far too crowded for me, but when I tried to wriggle free, Sabina held on harder. "You need to rest. It's okay."

"Since when do you tell me what to do?" I muttered.

"I… uh…" She glanced at Vlatka, who nodded her eagle head. "Right! Vlatka said I need to be more assertive. Of course, only if that's okay with you…"

I let myself laugh at her blush. "You're not my servant anymore. If you want to be more assertive, then do it."

"I'm trying to teach her," Kuba replied, "but she says there's a difference between my jokes and being taken seriously."

"That's because there is."

Sabina blushed again. "I didn't mean it like that."

Kuba cocked his head. "Didn't take offense. You never know what someone wants until you ask. I do my best to ask."

"Repeatedly," I said.

"Don't get me started on you. After all that's happened to you and Wacław, I can see through you about as well as I can through the old northern swamp." He waited a second, shuddering beneath my glare. "Get it? It means you don't make sense. Girls are supposed to like flowers and warriors and weaving and stuff. You had mud up to your neck and more burrs in your hair than flowers, but Wacław couldn't keep his eyes off you anyway. Believe me, I tried to find him another girl."

My heart sunk at the reminder of Wacław, of our years apart. I'd thought Destiny cruel then. Now, I'd discovered how truly brutal of a mistress she could be. *I miss you, Wašek.*

Kuba popped to his feet or, well, paws. "Ah Weles, that was dumb. I meant to say I *had* told him to find another girl, but you two are good now. For sure. I mean, you know how to make him actually do things instead of hesitating all the time, and he gets all protective and tough around you, and then you're—"

"Kuba, stop," I mumbled through my tears. I couldn't take it. "I don't know what you all have heard, but Wacław's demonic soul is taking over. The Płanetnik… Wacław isn't himself anymore. I pushed him away, trying to protect him from what I'd done, but it made everything worse."

A little whine escaped his throat. "Oh…"

He paced across the bed with his head down as Sabina took my one gloved hand. The other I held to Mother's Bowmark. *No more visions today.* I could barely face reality, let alone the horrors of the past and possible future.

"So, that's it?" Kuba asked, his voice suddenly tense. "You just left him in Huebia? Are you even trying to fix it, or did you already get what you needed? Take his soul and run?"

"It's not that."

He sighed and hopped to the ground. "Sure sounds like it is. And now you're marrying Jaryło because—"

"Shut up!" I spat, anger surging through me stronger. It burned deep in my soul, all my desperation and anguish boiling over at once. "I messed up. I know. But I love him. And I failed him. I thought getting him away from me would protect him. I thought…" I shook my head. "It doesn't matter what I thought. All I've done since then is try to fix what happened to his soul, but I can't do that without allies and worshippers to ensure I have *żityje*. All of that would've been destroyed if Jaryło killed you. Not to mention you're my friends."

"Is there a way? You know, to save him?"

I looked to Vlatka with a shake of my head. "I don't know. Demons have been speaking to me, saying I can help them, but it's been hard to figure out End's force without *żityje*. I'm only now starting to understand the basics."

A little jackal whine was Kuba's only reply before he sulked out of the room, taking the little joy I'd found with him. Vlatka returned to her perch as he did, and when his footsteps had faded, she huffed. "There is no way for one of such a simple mind could understand what you've faced."

"No," I said. "Kuba saved my life. Even if I died anyway, he didn't know I was a goddess when he ran in front of Yuliya's ice bolt. We've both faced death and come back, so if anyone understands what I've faced, it's him." My heart ached as I remembered the celebrations after we'd jumped the fire on the equinox. "He left the girl he loved for this, you know. Gods, he'll never be able to wed Maja now…"

"He will see her because of you," Vlatka replied. "Nature commands that he must reside in Nawia, but you brought him back—brought us back."

Sabina squeezed my hand. "All things are a cycle."

Something stirred within me at her words. A pulse in my chest, rising to my skull until I shuddered and pushed myself up. "It's all a cycle. That's it!"

I flung myself from the bed. Each step was weak, and I had to catch myself on the wall, but excitement rushed through me. An answer. Finally, an answer!

"Otylia!" Sabina called after me. "What's going on?"

With my first hopeful smile in what felt like forever, I looked back at her, our Threads of Life connecting us with a vibrant glow. "I know how to save Wacław and the demons. But first, I need *żityje*. A lot of it."

39

Ara

Otlezd, give me strength. I'm about to hurl.

ZAKIR'S FOOT TAPPING AGAINST THE SNOW sounded like a stampede as I stood beside him. I didn't know if he was clutching my hand or I was clutching his. Probably both. The remnants of our clans watched us expectantly, and neither of us were prepared for what came next.

Xobas approached. As the Simukie held only their bond to their horse as sacred, they had no priests. That left the highest-ranking commander to conduct the marzban induction ritual, and he looked no more prepared than us.

"I never thought I'd be the one doing this." Xobas scratched the back of his head, a bead of sweat trickling down his brow despite the frost that had fallen upon us. "An exile inducting a marzban."

"My father respected you more than anyone," Zakir replied. "He understood people. I never grasped how." He looked to me with his brows forming a crease. "Potions are simple. They follow a formula that I can track, but people are too complex."

I forced a reassuring smile. "We'll ensure you're not alone. I promise."

People were complex, but I had a feeling he didn't think he understood himself. Maybe that was what I could do for him. Beyond making sure his quiet, straightforward nature didn't alienate the Simukie, I would try to help him lead with his unique strengths. That would be difficult. Someone had to do it, though, if our clans had any chance.

Even as Zakir nodded, his stance was stiff, his face stoic. He wore a deerskin cloak draped over his loose steppe shirt and trousers. It wasn't enough to protect him from the cold—not that any of the clansmen were used to winter's heavy chill—but he didn't shiver.

"You both will die," he said flatly. "After they slaughter the Astiwie, the Horde will search for the clan warlords first."

Xobas crossed his arms, the tattoo of his fallen horse exposed on his forearm. "I don't wish to disobey you so soon, but I am not leaving. Not again."

"Me neither." I took his hand in both of mine and kissed his knuckles. They were cracked from the cold, but they were mine. All of him was mine, and that was all that mattered. "Your brother abandoned you out of his selfishness. I won't do the same."

Sorrow filled his gaze as he slid his hand free. "There had to be a potion… Never mind now. Bidaês is gone. These people are alive."

"And impatient," Xobas added.

"Yes. Proceed with the ceremony then."

Zakir gave me one last nod, then followed Xobas to the hilltop, the blizzard dropping white into his curled black locks. Those winds howled with all the pain of an anguished mother. With every moment, the storm seemed to grow, and I could barely see the first line of clansmen. They huddled closer to hear Xobas's speech. I couldn't.

Either fear or awe held me in place as Zakir placed a hand on his horse, Eliastr, who a warrior had brought while we'd spoken, and repeated after Xobas. The exact words were lost to the winds, but I didn't care about them. Instead, I watched his lips as he spoke each with precision and care. Not because he felt them in his soul, but because he knew it had to be done to finish his induction. He had completed his required journey to become marzban. Now, all he had to do was repeat a few simple phrases. Of course he believed it to be trivial, yet he did it anyway. For his people.

The ritual ended as quickly as it had begun. After another long day of traveling west through the hills of southern Astiw toward Krowikie lands, we were all frozen to our cores and had little energy for celebration. Nor did we have the food. We'd recruited more Astiwie to join our caravan with each passing day, but the frost had covered their crops and starved many of their animals. Over three hundred of them walked or rode with us now.

"More mouths to feed," High Priestess Zhaleh had said with a scoff. "We should protect our own kind before saving those whose king slaughtered us."

Zakir had been hesitant too with our resources draining, but after speaking with the commanders, he'd decided we needed everyone who could hold a spear or blade. A game of numbers. Though I hated the thought of that, his mind had come to the conclusion my heart had. The Astiwie villagers who wished to come could, even if it slowed our journey.

Those pale faces seemed to disappear quickly in the snow as the crowd dispersed with nothing more than a few cheers and raised canteens of the remaining alcohol. Whatever form it took, it wasn't enough to drown the caravan's sorrows. Zakir's induction would give some of them joy. It would take more than a new marzban, though, to renew hope among people who had been driven from their homeland into what appeared to be eternal winter.

Those were problems for later, for night had come, and after accepting the congratulations of the Simukie, Zakir returned to me with a solemn look in his eye. The trials ahead never left his mind, so it was up to me to ensure he didn't drown in them. All the Simukie clansmen and Astiwie refugees were his responsibility. He was mine.

"You did well," I said, offering him a hug.

He neither rejected nor returned it, and we stood in an awkward stance, my arms around him for a moment before he spoke. "Let's return to the tent. It's cold, and I have a potion I would like to tinker with."

I stepped back and brushed the stray hairs from my face. "Did you talk to Zhaleh? Now that you're officially marzban, she'll want to negotiate how we go forward."

"She is irrational."

"But she leads my people. The Zurgowie won't keep marching if she tells them to stop. Like it or not, we need her on our side, and that means taking to time to speak with her."

"Tomorrow, when we ride." He drew a pattern in the snow with his heel, whispering something to himself.

I stifled my disappointed sigh and nodded instead. It was something at least.

Only the winds and the crunching of snow underfoot broke our silence as we returned to our tent. Like all of the clans', it was rounded with a wooden frame and covered with felt and sheepskin. Unfortunately, those thin layers struggled to keep out the cold. Our breaths fogged the air, and even our blankets would provide little comfort. His warmth would've…

"You should rest," I said, lying on my bedroll and pulling the blankets over me. "The blizzard will only make people more anxious. They'll need you awake to lead them."

Zakir knelt on a wool rug nearby. He'd arranged a portion of his alchemical supplies before him in an order I failed to understand but that was *very* important to him. Little upset him. When I'd tripped and disturbed those vials the day before, though, it had sent him into a frenzy. Half the words that had followed were either from another tongue or so technical I didn't know them. Either way, I'd learned my lesson.

"This work is crucial," he said. "Affection can wait."

My cheeks burned, and I rolled over to face away from him. "Because I'm just a girl who wants you? Is that it?"

A vial clanked against the hard ground. He released a sharp breath. "No."

"Then what?"

"Is this mad? I find it difficult to tell when you're mad or flirting."

I wrinkled my toes, tension running down my spine. *Patience.* Why was he so difficult sometimes? Was I nothing more than another project for him, fascinating for his mind but little else? "I'm not mad, but you've been working on this potion most nights since we left Dwie Rzeki."

"I see." A harsh smell met my nose as he poured something, the liquid's trickling just loud enough to hear. "It is an important formula." When I didn't reply, he continued, "Would you like to know more about it?"

Turning back to face him, I let myself smile. "Sure, but only if you explain it using words I'd understand."

"A challenge…"

"Luckily, you like those."

His eyes shone in the candlelight of his work station as he returned my smile—if a small tug on his lips could be considered a smile. "You always know how to challenge me. Thank you for that, Ara. I am sorry I have not joined you in recent days. I just… This potion could have saved Bidaês if I had figured it out in time. I must hurry to finish it for Wacław."

"What does it do?"

"It is supposed to help a demon resist their hunger. From my observations, they grow more desperate during great swings of emotion. This is likely due to the demonic element of their souls feeding upon negative emotions, so I have devised a potion that can be drunk when the demon believes they are losing control. It calms them and brings with it an infusion of the life force they desire. I intend to ask the other płanetnik, Eryk, to test it."

"That's brilliant!" I threw back the blankets and crouched beside him, examining his work. Without my boots, my toes were freezing, but this was the most exciting thing I'd heard from his alchemy. "How do you get *žityje* into a potion?"

He held up a vial. "Blood."

"Oh…"

"It is not much, but Wacław eating the boar heart gave me an idea. The heart holds most of the life force, so blood has the remnant fragments. Enough of it could satiate the demon before they attack anyone." He turned his head away. "I am sorry. The use of blood like this is probably disgusting to you."

I laid a hand on his back. "You're trying to solve a problem. If a little animal blood in these potions can save Wacław's sanity, then I'll sleep alone for as long as it takes."

"It is a temporary fix. He will still be a demon."

"It's something to help, though, and I adore you for trying."

His muscles relaxed beneath my hand, and he tilted his head toward me. I took my opportunity to kiss him slowly, trying to lure him away for even a moment. Something shifted in his touch. He pulled me to him and, for the first time, *he* initiated the next kiss. It was only that one before he returned to his work, but it was enough. The man, the marzban, I'd fallen for had shown some passion toward me. He had compromised, so I would too.

"Show me," I whispered, resting my head on his shoulder. "I don't understand how you mix your potions and poisons."

He paused. "You actually want to know?"

"I do."

"Then fetch me another candle," he said with the widest smile I'd ever seen from him. "We will need fire to finish it."

I kissed him again. "And then we save Wacław."

"As many would say, I hope so."

40

Otylia

How'd I not see this sooner?

IT TOOK ALL MY PATIENCE AND MORE NOT TO CHARGE out of my room as Sabina insisted that I change into clothes not covered in blood. She'd brought a variety of options from the Daughters, but I replaced my shirt, trousers, and half-missing pair of gloves with another set of black ones, throwing Amten's breastplate and Kiin's coat over them.

Black just felt right. It had my entire life, but now more so than ever. Still, despite the simple outfit, Sabina brushed off every speck of dust or strand of hair until I was ready to burst. Vlatka watched the whole ordeal with what I assumed was an eagle's equivalent of a smirk.

"The people you saved will be waiting for your appearance," she said, landing on my shoulder as Sabina finished. "They willingly have given you sacrifices of blood and possessions, so you must appear to them as the savior they're hoping for. It's a shame you lack the *žityje* to conjure the illusion of a kokoshnik crown at the least."

I winced with her added weight. My body was still battered. "Why does it matter? They saw me surrender to Jaryło. They know how weak I am."

"You aren't weak."

"Yes, I am," I replied, stepping away from Sabina's constant straightening of Dziewanna's Bowmark necklace. Enough was enough. "But I needed to understand my weakness to realize I can't do this alone. My entire life I've pretended to be strong, even when I wanted to run and cry. I claimed I was better by myself—that only following Dziewanna and Mokosz's commands gave me purpose. I was wrong. I get that now."

"Wise words, child," Vlatka said. "Will you tell us, then, why you wanted to rush off? You're right that you can't do this alone, but we can't help if you don't tell us."

"Fine. Just follow as I talk. The sooner I get *żityje*, the sooner we fix Wacław and find a way out of this godsforsaken blood pact."

After tightening my gloves to avoid another vision, I pushed through the tapestry into the hall of the hideout with Sabina following and Vlatka riding on my shoulder. There was an itch in my soul. An irritation. I'd followed the wrong path too often in recent weeks. It had been accidental, but intentions were irrelevant when I'd alienated the boy I loved and turned him into a beast.

Ta-naro was waiting beyond the tapestry. Likely, she'd heard everything, but I pushed away my embarrassment and waved for her to join us. "Sabina, you said everything is a cycle," I began without glancing back at her. "Rod and Weles implied the same, and my force… I still don't understand it, but End's visions have been showing me demons begging for my help. Whether by coincidence or destiny, it's showing me something. I finally get it."

"Get what?" Ta-naro asked. "I'm lost."

"Catch up," I quipped. "We're talking about Wacław and demonic corruption. More importantly, I think I figured out a way. There's a cycle for mortals: life, death, rebirth. Demons and Nawie break that. They can never be reborn, so they become trapped in their own cycle: wholeness, brokenness, and then a third step I couldn't understand until now. It's mending, redemption!"

The young szeptucha shook her head. "Nope. Don't get it."

"You're saying demons can be redeemed?" Sabina asked. "How?"

I thought back to the Lake of Reflection. When Jacek had held Wacław for the first time, he'd promised to protect him, to love him. Chieftess Natasza convincing him to break that promise had sent some type of force through the room when Lubena fled with her child. Had *that* been his moment of corruption, not birth itself? Had the blood moon simply allowed Jacek's betrayal to corrupt him?

"Demons are created when people die or live unnaturally and their bodies aren't burned," I continued. "That much we know, but what about Nawie? Even Jaryło thought it was Wacław's blood moon birth that had corrupted him. It wasn't. At least, if my idea is right it wasn't."

"His father?" Sabina asked. "You said in Nawia that the high chief had thrown him away."

"Exactly. What if that corrupted him? Demons usually lurk in the place they were killed. Rusałki, for example, attack men in the river where they drowned, usually looking for the man that was the reason for their death and never finding him. Why are they doing that? Probably some for blood and *żityje*, but there has to be more. They're *looking* for something. Maybe, finding it cures them."

Vlatka sighed upon my shoulder as we entered the main room, where Ildes and Kiin were whispering to each other. They stopped when they noticed us, and Kiin crossed her arms. "You should be resting."

I shook my head. "There's no time. I might've figured out a way to save Wacław and maybe even the other demons."

Kiin's eyes widened, and Ildes stepped closer with a hand pressed to her chest. "You have?" She shuddered. "Is that for the best? The Earth Mother allows demons to remain in their state for a reason."

"Oh, yeah?" I asked, gritting my teeth. "Why?"

"The goddess's secrets—"

"I'm a goddess, so it's not a secret to me. Besides, the gods are far from perfect. They've destroyed Jawia more than once, and I'm not going to let them do it another time." Ildes tried to stutter a reply, but I advanced, meeting her gaze with the fire growing in my soul. "I am the goddess of endings—*natural* endings. Demons are a break from the natural order. If I can mend their souls and ensure they return to life's cycle, then I have to try."

Before Ildes could speak again, Kiin pulled her back. "Otylia's right. It's at least worth listening to what she has to say. She's proven that much to me."

"Unfortunately," Vlatka replied, "her solution seems a far stretch. Demons are created by unnatural lives and deaths, but you can't fix that simply by them having revenge."

I fought my frustration, pacing the room with my breaths fogging the chilled air. My coat did a wonderful job of keeping my core warm, but Vastrothie attire left my arms exposed and cold. It didn't matter. No clothes could fix the death that would come from the desert's unwelcomed winter. "Revenge may only be a part of their search for justice. Wacław chose to save me over Jacek, but his father's death didn't change his soul because it didn't mend what he was missing— a father's unconditional love. A rusałka might find peace by drowning the man who caused their demise. Others will be different."

Ta-naro stuck her tongue out. "Really? *Love* is the answer?"

"The girl has a point," Kiin added. "Haven't you already admitted to Wacław that you loved him? Why didn't that fix it?"

My heart sunk, and I leaned against the wall in my weariness as, no longer dulled by my excitement, my broken arm throbbed again. "I said that as part of the Trials of Ascension. I meant it, but it's hard to claim it was unconditional when I stole his mortal soul moments later."

"That's it?" Kiin spun her fingers, as if telling me to continue. "There's more."

I groaned but nodded. "Then I pushed him away. I thought it would help to give him space after what I'd done to him, but the demon in him took over quickly."

"Another broken love…" Vlatka said to herself before raising her voice and taking flight. "This is fascinating!"

"Glad you think so, because it's been agony for me."

Kiin began to speak again, but Sabina swooped in front of her, throwing my good arm over her shoulders. "Speaking of agony, perhaps we should allow Otylia to regain her *žityje* before we continue. She is still injured after all, and—"

"I'm fine."

With a graceful wave toward the far doorway, Ildes gave an amused smile. "You are not. Go, ensure that *you* are mended, and then we will speak further about demons."

I reluctantly pushed myself off the wall and walked to the cloth-covered doorway with Sabina's help, taking my arm from around her when we arrived. *Appear strong, even if you aren't.* Those I'd rescued from the dungeon would be watching.

"Please, stay by my side," I said to Sabina. "I've missed having you there."

Her wings fluttered. "Of course!"

Another set of wings flapped above, and Vlatka returned to my shoulder now that I was standing again. "Your first worshippers… Soon, you'll have enough to make Jaryło quiver in his fancy boots."

"Glad to have you too, Vlatka." I chuckled. "Your talons can rip his face off for all I care. I promised not to seriously harm him, but that doesn't stop any of you from doing it for me."

"I like the way you think."

As I pushed aside the cloth, I spared a glance back at the szeptuchy. Only Ta-naro had followed as Kiin and Ildes returned to their hushed conversation. Kiin had been forthright with me after our initial confrontations, so I had no reason to mistrust her now. Yet I did. What secret was significant enough to hide from a goddess who could aid the Daughters more than anyone?

Nothing was hushed in the room beyond. The freed prisoners erupted in cheers at my entrance, some of them dropping to their knees and holding their foreheads to the floor. Awe filled the eyes of others as they touched my coat in hopes of transferring some power or luck to themselves. A foolish belief, but I couldn't blame them. I'd once dreamed of what it would be like to see a goddess. The confidence in her stride. The endless impact of her magic. And the way nature itself would bend around her feet, making way for her.

None of it was true. If anything, it felt like life had become far more difficult since my Ascension, the world entrapping me in thorny vines instead of clearing my path.

These worshippers, though, created an aisle to the altar of stone at the far wall. Mokosz's Mothermark was carved upon its front, and a small glass statue rested on its left side. I rolled my eyes at her unrealistically proportioned body. It had been annoying enough for male Krowikie priests to depict her as their perception of the ideal woman, but for her own szeptuchy to do the same was ridiculous. Hadn't they met her as I had? Mokosz was beautiful, yes, but her presence was supposed to be a comfort for women, not a figure for men to gawk at.

More important than the statue was the bowl across the altar from it. For blood…

I took a relieved breath at the sight of four lambs, a basket full of fish, and—mostly rotten—vegetables. My first offerings from true worshippers wouldn't be *their* blood at least. These people trusted in me, needed me, and as a goddess, I needed them just as much. This was the natural balance Weles had spoken of. But if it was right, why did I feel like an imposter?

"A szeptucha must accept the gifts for the most *żityje* to be extracted," Vlatka whispered from my shoulder as I rounded the altar. "Unless you intend to conduct the sacrifices yourself and drink blood before your worshippers."

I looked down at the offerings. What would they think of me if they saw what a goddess did to gain her power? Sacrificing animals and plants to my goddesses had been a simple duty as a szeptucha, but it was so much more now. After seeking to become a szeptucha my whole life, I'd never considered the possibility of choosing my own channelers. To take on that responsibility was something I'd never demand of anyone. It meant service for life. Such a role could only be pursued willingly, not imposed.

A hand fell upon my shoulder.

"No," I whispered as I raised my gaze to Sabina's.

Ironically, the frail nymph towered over me, and I was at her mercy now. The weight of what it had meant for Dziewanna, for Mother, to take me as her only szeptucha fell upon me. Without channelers to prepare sacrifices, a god was vulnerable. That gave the szeptucha more power than any of us had realized. Yet another balance…

Sabina's wide eyes were wrinkled with her smile. One of genuine joy as she fell to her knees before me. She was one of my few true friends, my confidant, and now she wished to serve me. I'd known she'd never let go of her mindset in Nawia, despite my attempts to ensure she saw me as her equal, but I'd hoped this wouldn't happen. Who else, though, would give their life for me? Wacław—when he was sane—and Ara. That was it. And neither of them were here.

"I haven't completed the rituals," Sabina said, her voice fighting her trembling, "but I am ready, my lady."

I held her hands in my gloved ones. Our eyes met, uncertain and hesitant, but though I hated her for her selflessness, she was right. Losing these worshippers by appearing like a monster would ruin my chance to gain followers and save Mother. It felt like lying. It felt like I was enslaving a friend. But I took a deep breath and nodded, fighting the tears that stung my eyes. No, I wouldn't command her. Sabina would be free, as Dziewanna and Mokosz had largely allowed me to be. That was that.

"Sabina," I began with my voice raised for the crowd, "daughter of the wilds and born of both nymph and mortal, I take you as my szeptucha, my chosen. You shall be my priestess and my voice among the people of Jawia."

I removed my glove and held my hand to her neck. Her pulse raced against my fingers. End's wisps had filled the room before with dozens of voices begging for salvation, but they faded to silence as I allowed my mind to turn inward, to seek myself as Ildes had said. To be calm. In that place, I found the Thread of Life binding me to Sabina, its glow vibrant and strong, like how I felt with her support. The pounding of her heart reverberated within me. I reached for it and the visions within her bright green wisp. It took form as I did, and visions flashed before me while I chanted aloud in the old tongue.

Few would understand my lyrics. Mother had taught me to recite it when I was young and seeking help, claiming it would mean I was never alone. As memories and endings of Sabina's life flashed before me, it only seemed more relevant. She'd been isolated for so long. Away from her family. Away from her people. Away from anyone who cared for her.

Then I'd appeared.

The endings at first had been of childhood memories, but they jumped forward quickly to when she'd met me. I threatened her at first. Soon, though, her loneliness faded as my skepticism did the same, and tears streamed down my cheeks seeing our time together through her eyes. It was just a glimpse—the endings—but it was enough. Unfortunately, it wasn't the last vision.

My chant reached its final verse as Sabina's form wept in the wisp. She clutched a tree with black slashes upon its bark and decay tearing at its branches. A pain gnawed at her core. Dull at first, it grew more frenzied with each second until she was ripped apart as the tree tumbled beneath the strain of disease and endless snowfall. With her last breath, she held a quivering hand to her neck, where a mark pulsed in radiant white.

I gasped at reality's sharp return. The vision had ended with my chant, and the crowd waited in anticipation for what came next. I didn't know. Then I looked down at my hand on Sabina's neck.

Pure light burst from our connection. Sabina winced as blood trickled down her neck, but the pride on her face never faded. Her gaunt cheeks were still fixed in a smile, and when I stepped back, she rose with her head bowed.

"My goddess, I will serve you with all my honor."

"I know you will," I whispered, another spurt of exhaustion washing over me. Marking her had taken another piece of *žityje* that I couldn't afford, and the world seemed to spin around me as I tried to catch my breath. I wondered at my mark. What would my symbol be? But my vision betrayed me.

Sabina tugged at my arm and nodded towards the door with that new dose of certainty I was starting to love in her. "The people have seen you. Let me do the rest. I promise I'll meet you in your room when I'm finished."

"Thank you, Sabina. You have no idea how much this means to me."

"No," she said with a gentle urge for me to keep walking. "You have no idea how much this means to *me*."

41

Wacław

FOUR YEARS EARLIER

Peace.

DOGODA'S WARM WESTERN WIND BLEW THROUGH MY HAIR as I dangled upside down from an oak branch with my arms free. A dare from Kuba that I couldn't reject. Well, I *could've*, but what was the fun of that?

"I'm getting dizzy," I said with a laugh. "Is that supposed to happen?"

Kuba just shrugged and kicked a rock, sending it skidding into the bushes nearby. "Dunno, but it happened to me too."

"Then it's definitely wrong!"

"Hey!" He jumped at me, grabbing hold of my arms and dislodging me from the tree. We fell in a heap, and my skull struck the ground hard enough to make my head spin. It was better than remembering…

With a groan, Kuba pushed himself to his feet, not bothering to dust off his tunic. I did. Mom worked to keep our clothes as clean as they could be. Disappointing her was a worse feeling than Father's beatings. At least she cared.

Kuba rapped his knuckles across my head. "Oi! What's with your long face lately? Not thinking about Otylia again, are you?"

I pushed him away. "Not now, Kuba."

"So you are." He huffed and leaped for the branch I'd fallen from, grabbing hold and hanging there at full stretch. "C'mon, she's just a girl. Those stupid witch rituals don't mean anything compared to us." He hauled himself into a seated position on the branch and gripped the rabbit's foot he wore at the end of his twine necklace. "I caught this rabbit myself! She couldn't do that."

My shoulders slumped. The ritual of a boy's first haircut happened when we each turned twelve, and we had to hunt on our own to pass the trial and be claimed by our fathers. I'd tracked a deer for what'd seemed like a moon, my stomach grumbling for much of it. In the end, I'd succeeded. Father hadn't cared.

"Jacek will see," Kuba continued, swinging his legs with a boyish joy I'd lost. Things just weren't the same without Otylia. "You'll prove him wrong."

I took a strong breath and nodded. "I will."

"So you're definitely not going to see her again, right?" He rolled his eyes. "Oh come on, I know you went to watch her in the swamp. It's been days. She's not coming back, like that other witch, Vida. Probably for the best."

"No."

"That's it? Just 'no'? You know I'm right and that you should spend the dusk sparring with me instead. Would be more fun."

I turned away, my heart aching. How could I just abandon her? Otylia had been my best friend for so long, and she'd saved me from those wolves on the equinox. With *magic*. I still didn't understand what had happened that day. She didn't either, but my wounds had been enough for Father to believe she was dangerous. Though he could ensure I would never speak to her again, he didn't need to know I'd knelt alongside the pond, waiting for her to emerge with a god's blessing.

"One last night," I finally replied over my shoulder. "I have to try one more... time." I caught on that last word, remembering saying that before, but I hadn't. Had I? *Why does this all feel so familiar? Am I really that tired?*

A *thud* tore me from my thoughts, and Kuba brushed off his dirt-covered hands as he stopped at my side. "Fine, but if she doesn't come tonight, promise me you'll move on? There's other girls. More importantly, there's other girls that aren't witches who can kill you with just a glare."

He ended his joke with a slap on my back, but I couldn't laugh. Not when Otylia's life was on the line.

The sun reached the horizon as he passed me walking backwards. "Four years, Wacław. We've got four years 'til one of them long-haired girls is allowed to take us forever. Might as well enjoy freedom while we can."

There's no freedom in loneliness.

We parted ways, and I headed toward the swamps, my fingers drifting across the trunks of each tree along the way. They kept me grounded in the moment and stopped me from wondering about my odd recollection. Mom had told me many stories of the leszy, miawki, and other demons that lurked in these woods at night. She wouldn't be happy about me being out again, but some days it had seemed like she liked Otylia even more than me. If Otylia had passed her initiation, Mom would want to know too. If she'd failed… I shuddered. Life was hard enough with the distance between us already. I'd given up our friendship so Father wouldn't exile her, but her death would be so much worse.

But she wouldn't die. Even an angry bear couldn't kill Otylia if it tried, and the forest was her home. It was more likely that she'd boil the pond with her spite than drown in it. Unfortunately, that spite had been directed at me lately.

As I neared the place Dariusz had led her to, I pulled a few spare heads of grain out of the pouch hanging from my belt. Not much, but I needed something to offer to Dziewanna. Otylia had said the gods prefer offerings of animals or food. Between working the fields and helping Mom with chores, I'd had no time to hunt, so grain would have to do.

The remaining light gave the pond a murky hue, and a muddy smell met my nose as bugs swarmed me, biting at my exposed skin. I pushed on anyway until I reached the pond's edge. Its waters seemed almost black as I knelt beside it and released the grain into its depths, whispering a prayer to Dziewanna and asking her to save Otylia. I had no idea if it would work. Kuba's doubts lingered in my mind as the grain disappeared, but I held onto hope. She *would* rise.

Time passed slowly there. I remained still as the sun disappeared, replaced by the moon's soft glow. Tears threatened my eyes, but I refused to weep. Otylia wouldn't tolerate that. She would've been strong, so I would be too.

My eyes were heavy by the time I heard a sloshy footstep in the muck behind me. I scrambled to my feet, stumbling on the uneven ground as Dariusz's cold glare met me.

"You shouldn't be here, boy."

I hung my head. "I'm sorry. I was just trying to help her."

"Help her, you say?" He stopped before me, his staff digging deep into the ground as his eyes did the same to my soul. The scent of ash hung over him like a fire long extinguished. "The most *helpful* thing you could do for my daughter is to leave and never see her again. Jacek rarely speaks with wisdom, but I am grateful for whatever he said to force you away from her." He touched his fingers reverently to the iron Forgemark of Swaróg on his headband. "The gods will not abandon Otylia. They are not mortal boys."

I cowered past him but stopped at the first tree. Running my hand along its bark, I found a last bit of courage. "Why do you hate me? Father is your rival, but you don't scorn Mikołaj or my other siblings for sharing his blood."

Dariusz stared over the water with his staff held between his palms. Then he spun it slowly in the shallows, sending a ripple through the pond. "Your father and I will never see eye-to-eye. However, it is not he nor his sons with Natasza whom I fear. Each break in nature's balance is like this staff. At first it seems nothing more than a tiny shift, but that turn sends a tide across the Three Realms, severing more than you could ever know."

"I… I don't understand."

"Nor would I expect you to. You are a child, not yet able to grasp what it means to be a man. How could you understand the world of spirits and beasts?" He waved a hand dismissively. "Leave me. I believe Otylia will rise this night, and your presence would stain the initiation rituals. Do not come to Perun's Oak in the morning."

"But—"

He spun, deep crimson robes sweeping around him as he raised his staff like a spear. "Listen, boy. There are forces far beyond the both of us in this world, and interfering with them could threaten Otylia's initiation. Nod if these words reached through your thick skull."

Reluctantly, burning with shame, I did.

"Good. Now run along. Lubena is surely worried about you. Gods know you have done enough to make that woman suffer, and no one will help her if she searches for you. Hurry! Neither of us needs her straying from the trails and finding demons."

Without another look back at the pond, I ran with all the energy left in my legs. They were heavy after the day's work and my time playing with Kuba, but something in Dariusz's tone told me he was serious. Many stories of demons were for children. That much I knew. Others, though, even the adults feared, and I wondered why.

An image invaded my mind with each step. Of an older and taller Otylia alongside the pond with me. She was scarred yet pretty, and she looked at me with sorrow and resentment. Somehow, that *me* wasn't the boy kneeling on the shore but one of greater height than even her.

What is happening to me?

The door was already open when I hopped down our house's wooden steps. A single candle sat upon the table, illuminating little, but our home was small. It was enough to show Mom sitting upon her bed in a sleeved blue drees, her boot rapidly tapping against the dirt floor. Her concerned expression turned to relief as I stepped into the room.

"Oh, thank the Great Mother!" she exclaimed, wrapping me in a tight hug. "Wašek, I was worried about you."

I hugged her back. "Sorry, *Matka*."

Her worries were about more than me disappearing to visit the pond. Ever since the equinox, I'd been different, I knew it, and sorrow filled her eyes whenever I refused to laugh or smile like normal. I wanted to—I just couldn't. It hurt to pretend everything was fine, especially after Otylia's mother had died from Marzanna's Curse. I should've been there for her.

Mom crouched before me, cupping my cheeks in her hands. I hated it when she did that. It wasn't like I was a child anymore, but I let her do it anyway. She needed to know she could still care for me.

"Otylia stayed under?" she asked.

All of a sudden, the wall I'd built to hold back my tears gave in. I closed my eyes, but they broke through as I leaned into her embrace.

"Now it's my turn to be sorry," she whispered. "I know you loved her." I squirmed at her use of *love*, but she just chuckled through tears of her own and brushed the stray hairs from my face. "You did love her, Wašek, and that's okay, no matter what your father says."

"I wish I died instead," I mumbled into her shoulder. "Everything's better without me."

She clung tighter to me. "Never say that. I love you, and I'd be lost without you. Your father revealed who he truly is when he threw us out of the longhouse. He might still try to control you, but we're better off on our own, you and I. Understand? You mean the world to me. I'm sorry the world hurts you so."

For a long while, we stayed in that embrace. She didn't release me in spite of my tears running over her dress and the still open door flapping against the wall. Part of me didn't want to feel better, but I did. Her love had always made things better. She was more than just my mother. She'd been my confidant and ally against those who mocked me in the village, and no matter how hurt I'd been, she'd always found the right words.

I eventually pulled away and wiped my remaining tears with my sleeve. To sob so heavily was childish. Father would have hit me for doing so in front of him, but Mom never scorned me for emotions—even when I was embarrassed to admit them.

"High Priest Dariusz said she'll be chosen tonight," I said. "Do you think he's right?"

Her eyes narrowed for a moment before she smiled. "Dariusz knows the wills of the gods more than any other, spare szeptuchy with their individual god. If he says she'll live, then she'll live. You know what happens after that, right?"

"The other girl had a ritual with those candles around Perun's Oak."

She nodded. "That's right. Otylia will have one too, and we can be there for her."

I crossed my arms and released a huff. "Dariusz said I can't."

"Why not?"

"I'm a 'stain' that could threaten her initiation." To distract myself from the next wave of sorrow, I sauntered to the door and shut it. The winds died. Only our sniffled breaths and the crackling of the candle broke the silence, but a voice echoed in my head, telling me Dariusz was right. I *was* dangerous. Why?

She stood and circled the table, dragging her fingers over its surface in thought. "That man's lies are why we're here in the first place. You're not…" She shook her head. "You're not a threat, Wacław. Don't allow anyone to tell you otherwise."

I flopped onto my bed and burrowed my head into my pillow. "You're my mom. You're supposed to say that."

"I am also supposed to tell you to listen to priests, but don't."

That pulled me from my despair. I stared up at her, the flickering candlelight casting half her face in shadow. "What are you saying?"

"Use your soul-form and go." She paced to my bed and crouched again. Her hands were firm as they took mine. "Dariusz won't know then, and neither will your father. If Otylia does return, then she deserves to have you there during the choosing ritual, even if she doesn't see you either."

"But she hates me now. She doesn't care if I'm there."

She pursed her lips, pain filling her gaze. "The gods will know, and so will the two of us. Maybe that's enough."

I let myself smile, and I hugged her in thanks. "I promise I'll come right back after the ritual."

"Good. Please, just be careful while you're there. The ritual must involve the power of the gods, and I don't want you to get hurt."

"I won't."

Standing, she gave me one last look and blew out the candle. "I hope you're right."

Sleep came easily most nights, but not this one. I tossed and turned with anxious thoughts filling my head. Otylia and I had looked forward to her initiation for years. Now that it had come, all I felt was fear and regret, and I spent hours staring at the thatched ceiling with my feet drumming the air.

Eventually, exhaustion did overtake me, allowing me to rise in my invisible soul-form. It was refreshing, as if I'd escaped the real world and stepped into another where I could be free. Each step was lighter too. I felt bonded with the eight winds, and with Dogoda's western one gently brushing over my face, I ran toward the village center.

Dadźbóg had yet to bring the sun, but I sensed him coming by the air's warmth. The nights were often chilly, even in summer. His heat, though, would have sweat dripping from every farmer's brow soon.

The guard at the eastern gate was one of Father's more gullible ones, Lucjan. Before dawn, the gate was typically shut but not barred from the inside. All I needed to do was distract him and slip past. That was hard with Albin or other well-trained warriors, but not with Lucjan.

I grabbed a decently sized stick not far into the woods and snapped it against the nearest tree, following it up with my best imitation of a demon—or at least what I imagined one sounded like.

"Not you again!" Lucjan called as he rushed to the tree line. "They call me crazy, but I'll get you this time."

I smirked, holding back my laughter and slipping through the gate. *Silly Lucjan.* Warriors told stories about how well he held a shield wall in battle, but I was glad his skills stopped there. I had enough nerves without having to deal with a real guard.

Lucjan continued his unnecessarily loud shouting as I headed down the trail toward the village center. Surely, he'd wake people with that racket, but they would be waiting near their doors anyway. It wasn't often one of Dwie Rzeki's own girls was initiated, let alone one who had channeled before being chosen. Everyone was on edge after Vida's failed initiation, but Otylia had survived. No one would want to miss her approaching Perun's Oak.

A chill ran up my arms when I reached the village center. Despite the moon still ruling the sky, the space was aglow with torches and rings of candles around the great tree. Men gathered with low murmurs about girls being allowed to use magic and not them. Women tightened their headscarves as children hid behind their skirts, only peeking out when the commotion began behind me.

My heart jumped. *She's coming…*

Dariusz led Otylia through the gathered crowd with the winds blowing his long, gray-streaked black hair. He looked weathered, leaning upon his staff more than he should've. Otylia couldn't have been more different.

She stood tall, defiant, her sharp green eyes fixed on the path ahead as people accused her of being a witch under their breaths. Though she'd always hated jewelry, she wore the headband her mother often had. Its green and brown designs wove across the fabric, and silver temple rings the shape of moons hung from it over each of her ears. She looked… grown. Like the girls at sixteen who jumped the fire to become women. And as she passed by, I was too shy to reveal myself to her. She'd seen me in my soul-form many times, but I'd hidden myself once again after our separation. It was better that way. Right?

The ache in my heart said I was wrong. It begged me to disobey Father and return to my best friend, but something held me back. Whether it was duty to my father and chief, cowardice, or a faint hope that I could still prove myself apart from her, I didn't know. It didn't matter. I watched all the same, invisible and alone in the crowd.

The bones in the branches of Perun's Oak swayed in the breeze as Otylia advanced through the rings of light, passing from the torches to the candles. A diviner of Mokosz awaited her before the tree and an altar of bones.

Is that a dragon skull?

An odd force seemed to radiate from within that innermost circle of candles. Without another thought, I drew nearer, stopping beside Otylia and staring in awe at the massive skull. Legends claimed żmije were real, but to see one's skull… I shuddered. At least it was dead.

Otylia bowed her head to the diviner but hesitated before kneeling. She glanced in my direction, as if by instinct. Her eyes met mine. I could've sworn for a moment that she'd seen me, but there was no recognition in her gaze. Pain jabbed my heart as she knelt, allowing the diviner to begin the ritual, and as she gave Otylia a knife I'd seen Dariusz use in sacrifices before, I began to back away.

She doesn't need me. She's strong enough alone.

But I hesitated as the diviner waved for a shaman of Weles to bring a goat to them. Then, she commanded Otylia to draw the goat's blood.

My breaths caught watching Otylia slice through it with precision. This was a szeptucha's role, but I'd never seen her kill an animal. Instead of hesitating, she'd been quick, giving it to the gods with no doubt—at least, none that I could see.

She shut her eyes as the diviner ran the goat's blood down the right side of her face. The old woman's chant filled the now silent village center, and my hair stood on end with the power of that inner circle leaking into the world beyond. It seemed to push me away. I was a stranger to this ritual, a soul that didn't deserve to see the secrets of the gods' chosen, yet I stayed. Until Otylia entered the final circle, I would be by her side. I owed her more.

Another feeling of remembrance washed over me. That dragon skull, the sacrifice… I'd seen this all before. Not just during the initiation of the other girl, Radojka. I swore that I'd lived this very moment. How?

Otylia's first hesitation came when the diviner held the dagger to her palm. To serve the gods, she needed to understand what it meant to give her own blood, but she froze, staring down at the iron tip against her skin. I could almost feel her fear. Not just of piercing her hand but of what came next, of finding which god had chosen her, so I stepped to her side. Had I been wrong? Was she strong enough to do it alone, without both her mother and best friend to support her? The pain in my chest was enough of an answer.

Slowly, I laid my hand on the back of the dagger, trying to avoid touching her. My pinky finger brushed against her knuckles, though, and she released a sharp breath. I didn't push. This had to be her decision, but something in me hoped she would sense my presence. Whether she did or not, it worked. She sliced open her hand.

The diviner smiled at Otylia's success, but before I could celebrate with her, a force struck my chest. I staggered back. Each breath was harder than the one before it. And as I suffocated in that circle, invisible to the entire village, a voice echoed in my mind.

"Wake up, Wašek."

42

Otylia

My first szeptucha. My first worshippers. Does it ever get easier?

THE ISOLATION OF MY ROOM CALMED MY MIND as Vlatka sat on the headboard above me. Marking Sabina had taken the last of my *żityje*. I felt my strength dwindling, eating away my body slowly until Ildes led Sabina, Kiin, and Ta-naro past the tapestry, their footsteps worsening my headache.

"You did well for one untrained in the art of being a szeptucha," Ildes said to Sabina with a warm smile.

As I sat up, it took all my willpower not to stare at the mark on Sabina's neck. My Moonmark. Fresh, it pulsed a bright white in the shape of a downward crescent with converging diagonal lines splitting it into pieces. The design warmed my heart, and the curved scar on my cheek tingled at the sight.

"I am blessed to have her," I added, rising and extending my uninjured hand for the bowl containing the blood offering. "What will happen to these people after this? I have my *żityje*, but they're still trapped."

Ildes clicked her tongue. In the short time since I'd spoken with her and Kiin, her hair seemed to have grayed and her brow had become more wrinkled. Surely, it was just a figment of my imagination. "Lady Otylia, it is our duty to protect these innocents," she said with her head bowed. "We will defend them as we would the worshippers of the Earth Mother, and once you are restored to health, we can discuss what lies ahead."

I nodded, relief washing away a sliver of my anxiety. "Thank you. The generosity of the Daughters of the Earth has been far more than I could ever ask for."

"You can end the Winter Witch's rule," Kiin replied. Arms cross, she paced with her gaze fixed on the floor. "Whatever it takes to get the scions back is yours."

Ta-naro grinned. "The ice brains won't know what hit 'em now."

Sabina placed the bowl in my hand. "It… It all should be prepared. I think it might be different when you have an altar, but—"

"You did well, Sabina," I said. "Thank you."

She blushed as I raised the bowl to my lips. The quicker I got this over with, the better. Beyond my desire for *żityje* to restore my power and heal my wounds, I felt more whole with it in my soul. Completion.

My throat spasmed as I drank, but I forced myself to swallow. Like always, the taste was entirely revolting, and the sensation of blood coating my tongue was enough to make me want to writhe in discomfort. I didn't. My friends and allies were watching. Though they weren't my worshippers, they needed to know I'd do what was necessary. Gods, I wished it wasn't.

But the *żityje*…

Few things were as amazing as it filling my soul. Since my Ascension, I'd been keenly aware of every bit of it, and as the blood steadily refilled my supply, I realized this was more than I'd ever had. Szeptuchy held only their own small amount, channeling some of their god's life force to use magic. I had no idea how much gods could actually hold. Based on the aura I'd sensed around Weles and Jaryło, though, it was immense.

The world came alive around me as I took the last sip. Wisps of every soul near circled me, both mortal and immortal, in shadowed but colored forms. So many potential visions. So many colors and experiences laid out before me.

They were nothing compared to the Threads of Life.

Streaks of every shade swept across the room and beyond, shooting from each person's chest. The web seemed incomprehensible, yet as I lowered the bowl, they all became clear. I could track their beginnings to ends that were near. I could sense the bond's strength by the vibrancy of the thread's glow. My instincts told me that I could know so much more if I touched any of them, but after seeing how I'd severed Serapis's soul, I wanted no part of it.

Kuba's excited bark tore me from my thoughts. I hadn't heard him enter the room, and he jumped into my bruised side before it healed, sending a shot of pain through me. I gritted my teeth. *He means well,* I told myself. That didn't make me want to punch him any less.

"That glow is awesome!" he exclaimed.

Light burst from my skin and filled the room before I could ask what he meant. Once lit by just a solitary torch opposite the cloth-covered opening, it was almost blinding now. The glow had started to become familiar. This, though, was more than ever before, and I grinned knowing the power that came with it. The moon beating with my heart. The creatures of decay at my command. And the whispers of living and dead souls at my ear. I forced myself to be calm and confident, to control my power instead of allowing it to wield me. In that moment, it felt like I could charge into the sky and taken on an entire army with just my force—because I could. I was a goddess, an immortal.

I see how this power goes to their heads.

It was intoxicating, and this *żityje* was a mere fragment of what Perun and Weles held. The temptation to use it for my own will was strong. Why did Vastroth or Krowik matter when their mortals would perish while I lived on? I pushed away that thought. My role was to help protect the balance of life, not selfishly use my force for my own standing. If only Jaryło had understood that.

The pain from my wounds faded quickly as I released *żityje* to mend it. After a few moments, I sighed in relief and twisted my torso to test it. "Finally, I'm free of Serapis's punishment. All of this would've been easier if Jaryło hadn't gotten involved and then disappeared after enslaving me!"

"We'll figure it out," Kuba said. "We always do—even if the result is *super* weird like becoming a dog."

Vlatka groaned. "Jackal…"

"Yeah, that!"

I laughed and patted him on the head. "I don't remember much from our escape from Bottom Slate, but I know you bit a guard before he could attack me. Thanks."

"Wait." He narrowed his eyes. "Are you actually being nice to me?"

"Regretfully."

Ta-naro yawned in the corner, leaning against the wall with one leg propped up behind her. "Hate to ruin the moment, but what are we doing next? This swimming with rusałki stuff sounds way more exciting than standing around this stuffy room." Her gaze dropped, and she stiffened. "We've gotta try, right?"

"Ta, this is not your place," Ildes said. "Saving the demons is simply an idea. Lady Otylia lacks evidence, and though I admire her for her hope, the risks involved in trying to tame demons are too high."

"Don't silence her," Kiin replied. "The child seeks to help advance our mission."

The young szeptucha lunged forward suddenly, grabbing hold of my arm like a feral animal. "Ildes doesn't get it! All those people the Winter Witch's men sacrificed weren't sent to the afterlife. I've been watchin' the ice brains!"

The river!

The demons that had invaded my dreams through End's force had said they were trapped in the Tiop River. How many had been sacrificed? Could we free them to fight against the Frostmarked? I had no idea what happened to demons after they were uncorrupted, but the possibility excited me.

Ildes sighed, pinching the bridge of her nose. "Your parents cannot return, Ta. I'm sorry."

"Otylia says they can!" She pulled on my arm again and looked up at me. "Right?"

"I—" I began, but Ildes interrupted me.

"Don't trap Lady Otylia. She is here to free us from the Frostmarked, not to raise the dead."

Ta-naro stomped her boot into the ground and darted out of the room. I watched her go before shooting a glare at Ildes. "You don't speak for me. *I* am the goddess of endings, and I will determine what's worth my time."

Before Ildes replied, I followed Ta-naro in hopes of catching her before she got too far. The girl's pain was obvious. Ildes had said that she'd lost a lot, but I hadn't pressed Ta-naro during the conversation my first night in the hideout. If her parents had been sacrificed by the Frostmarked, I couldn't blame her for fighting to save the demons. I was doing the same for Wacław.

I followed her footsteps to a room further down the hideout's winding halls. It wasn't far from my own, and when I pushed aside the tapestry covering it, the room was nearly an exact match—except for the smaller bed and scattered glass shards across the floor.

"Go away, Ildes," Ta-naro muttered, sprawled on the bed with her face buried in the pillow.

I circled alongside the bed. Some would've avoided the broken glass and cracked stone statues, but I just crushed them under my boots. Obviously, she hadn't thought them a success. She'd probably believed their destruction was better than finishing a failure, so I was simply helping the process. "They took your parents?"

Her head shot up. "Otylia?"

"Thank Dziewanna someone didn't call me 'lady' for once."

"Why are you here?" She pushed her short hair over her ear and averted her gaze. "Usually it's just Ildes barging in to complain about my 'lack of decorum' or something stupid like that."

I chuckled. "Decorum is nothing but a tool for powerful men to silence their opposition."

"Never thought I'd hear a goddess say something like that."

"You've never met my mother." I nodded to the bed. "Can I sit?"

"Yeah, but it's not all that comfortable."

It was hard not to keep smiling around her, and I smirked so hard my cheeks hurt as I sat beside her. Gods, she was so similar to me at her age—lost and desperate, pushing away anyone who dared to care about her. Except me. That made her acceptance of me all the more meaningful.

"You're tough, you know that?" I said. "It was never a choice for us, but that's the point. You either become strong enough to live on your own, or you die."

Again, she looked away, tucking in her legs close to her chest. "I didn't live on my own. Scary, it was. Sand brains everywhere tryna' take your stuff. Everyone said the scions were stopping it, but they didn't see the Deeps."

"Deeps?"

There's that smile. It disappeared as quickly as it had come, but I found some pride in bringing it out. "The tunnels far from the cliff face. Poor ones like 'em. So do the sand brains."

"Like the ice brains?" I quipped.

"Yup." She rolled over and reached out for a shard of glass near my feet. I nudged it to her, and she snatched it greedily. "Too much sand in yer head drives you cliff mad. That's what mother said before…"

With a sharp sniffle, she spun away. I let her. The last thing a girl like her needed was another person telling her what to do. There were enough bastards thinking they ruled the world already.

I took a shard of the glass for myself, holding it in the torchlight. It was a burnt orange with a slight curve. What had she wanted to make of it? A sculpture? A weapon? When she didn't talk for a few minutes, I decided to find out. "You've got a nice collection here. No one's ever going to sneak up on you with all this on the floor. Smart."

"Ildes checks on me," she said, barely louder than a whisper. "I don't like it."

I remembered the Thread of Life connecting Ildes to Ta-naro. The eldest szeptucha had bonds with most of her fellow Daughters, but that one had pulsed brighter than any other. "She loves you. Her way of showing that might be flawed, but I can see the tethers between people. Ildes probably sees you as her daughter."

She scoffed.

"I hated my father—well both of my fathers," I continued, accidentally closing my fist around the glass hard enough to cut my palm. A bad habit I'd picked up from squeezing Dziewanna's Bowmark as a child. "The man who raised me could never relate to me, and at times, he was harsh with Mother. We fought endlessly after she died. I was a pest to him, uncontrollable and disobedient, and he was a menace. When I found out the truth about my parents, though, something changed. I realized that he didn't need to raise me as his own. But he did."

"You said he was mean," Ta-naro said with her flat piece of glass in her open hand. Almost turquoise, its blue and green shades spiraled around each other before joining in its core.

I shrugged and dropped my shard into her hand, alongside the first. "Dariusz was never good at being a father—many men aren't. He tried anyway. His sharp tongue and criticism were his ways of showing love, pushing me to be better than I was, because he knew I could be. Despite knowing I would someday Ascend to become a goddess, he treated me like a mortal child. That gave me something neither Jaryło nor any other god has."

"What?"

"An understanding of mortal struggle." I took her hand, intertwining our fingers. Surprisingly, she let me, and her smile returned despite the glass between our palms. "To be human is to fear death, to fight for things to be better for yourself and the people you love, and to find joy in the smallest moments. When you're immortal, each day means nothing. You can move slowly and plan for decades. Mortals don't have that luxury, so each moment is crucial, even if you don't realize it at the time."

Ta-naro tucked her tongue into her cheek as she thought. Then she released my hand, hopping to the floor and rummaging through the other shards. "Forever's a long time. Never wanted it."

"Not sure I want it either."

That gave her pause, and she looked up at me with a furrowed brow. "But the powers you get are cool, right? Flyin' and stuff."

I sat back, remembering my first flight over the volcano in Nawia. There had been more than just power in it. With my dress's tassels fluttering around me and the wisps of light at my command, I'd felt truly alive, beautiful, whole, especially when I'd joined with Wacław. "Living forever is torture if you have to do it alone. The demon has controlled Wacław for only a couple weeks, but it's felt like an eternity. I can't imagine how Marzanna felt when her husband betrayed her after hundreds of years."

"Oh…"

"I'm sorry." I shook my head to myself. "I got distracted. I was trying to tell a story about my father to say I understand your relationship with Ildes—that she loves you in her own way, even if she's not great at it. There's just so much on my mind."

"Can't blame you." She crouched, still sifting through the pieces. "Sometimes, this glass is like my head. All broken and jagged. Grab one of 'em wrong and it'll cut you."

"I get it. My father used to describe me the same way, except like a poisonous flower."

For a moment, there was no reply, but then Ta-naro finally pulled a shard free from the pile. Clear with black streaks through it, the piece gave me an eerie feeling, like the first time I'd seen Marzanna's dagger. It contrasted sharply with the wry smile on her face. "That's the best kind of beauty," she said. "*They* can't take that away."

A crack filled the air as she stood. *Żityje* rushed from her, and the shards in her hand joined together, creating three curved blades arcing from a circled center. Each was a different color that merged with the others in the ring. A sleek weapon unlike any I'd seen.

She chucked it against the wall.

The blade shattered upon impact, sending glass spewing over the floor and bed. Ta-naro just glared at the rainbow of shards with her fists clenched. She showed no care that her hair was a mess and blood trickled from her hand, cut by the odd weapon. I doubted she even remembered I was there. The process she'd followed was a ritual not of religion but anger, a sacrifice to the fire burning in her chest, tearing her apart day by day.

I knew that cycle too well. Mother's hellebore upon my nightstand had channeled my sorrow for years. We expressed our pain differently, but it didn't matter. Pain was pain. It bled us from the inside, invisible to those around us until we lashed out.

"I'll bring your parents back, Ta-naro," I declared, standing. "Whatever it takes, I promise you, I'll figure out how to save the demons."

She wiped the blood on her coat and looked up at me, a new passion in her eyes. "And then we're going to make those ice brains pay."

43

Wacław

ELEVEN MONTHS EARLIER

I can fix it.

I AWOKE TO THE SMELL OF WARM BREAD and the choking heat of the Czerwiec sun. Usually, I was slow to wake after my night wanderings. Not today. The summer solstice had come, and with it, Noc Kupały, the most exciting festival of the year.

"You seem eager this morning," Mom quipped, laying out the bread on the table as I quickly changed into my forest green work tunic. "Remember, you haven't jumped the fire yet."

I lunged for a slice of bread and devoured it while replying, "I know, but that's less than a year away! I'm sixteen already."

She raised her brow. "Yes, far too old to be speaking and chewing at the same time. I know I'm not as exciting as the girls, but come and sit with your mother for a moment. The fires won't start until nightfall anyway."

"Yes, *Matka*," I replied, sliding onto the stool across from her.

To fight the heat, we left the door open during daylight hours, and Dadźbóg gave her hair a golden glow. Even brighter was her smile. Mom's happiness was often fleeting, so I clung to the few times we could share a moment of joy. Gods, she deserved all the Three Realms after what she'd given up for me. A conversation over her wonderful bread was the least I could do.

Her fingers drummed against the table as I ate another slice. How was she so good at baking? Kuba kept complaining that his mother could barely make an edible meal, let alone the warm loaf of Prawia sitting before me now. We had little outside Dwie Rzeki's gates, but Mom had always done her best to raise me by herself.

"So," she finally said. "You're obviously excited to see a girl. Which one?"

I blushed, trying and failing to hide my embarrassment behind the food. "Maybe I'm just excited for the dancing and rituals."

"You've mentioned that blonde girl, Genowefa, a lot recently. Is it her? Otylia?"

"Mom…" I groaned, but before she replied, an odd feeling washed over me. Images came with it. Like memories, but ones I'd never experienced. I saw the wreaths of Noc Kupały and wept as Otylia screamed at me in the woods. I felt the winds at my fingertips as I clashed with a dark beast. I endured the sting of snow-covered sand from a far-off land. And I suffered the rage burning in my soul, the taste of blood lingering on my lips.

I'm going insane!

In an instant, all of it disappeared. I sucked in a breath, stumbling back from my stool and falling into the wall beside my bed. Sweat beaded on my brow as my lungs heaved for air. At once, I was both sweltering and frozen, a force trapping me between two realities. It was as if I could sense a place far away from here. Another time. Another me.

"Wašek?" Mom asked, rushing to me with a waterskin. "What happened? Is it the heat? You haven't drunk anything yet."

I drank greedily. The sensations faded slowly, but part of me didn't want them to. In them had been a semblance of something more than I knew, somewhere I belonged. Why had I seen the future? Had I? Those visions had been terrible, destroying my excitement for the ritual. Otylia had appeared in all of them. She'd been bitter, angry. But there had been something else in her gaze in the later visions, something I couldn't explain. They felt like memories—and from the pain in my chest, not kind ones—but I'd never done those things.

"I… I'm fine," I mumbled. My mind was only half in the present, but it was enough for me to understand that Mom couldn't know. She worried enough about me already. If she knew I was having visions of the future…

"Boys and their wayward heads," she said with a laugh, offering a hand to help me up. "You think about girls for one moment and you're falling in the dirt. Best you tend to Tanek and the fields before you spend the day down there."

So I went to the pasture, making sure my chestnut horse Tanek was fed before going about the rest of the day's typical chores. That unsettling feeling lingered with me the whole way. I remembered bits of each vision so vividly that I could taste the moisture in the forest air. Unnerving at the very least, it had me looking over my shoulder until it came time for me to head into Dwie Rzeki for the festival, and even then, my heart no longer fluttered with anticipation. One of the visions had shown Otylia shouting at me this night. Would it come true, or was my mind playing tricks on me?

Mom gave me a kiss on the cheek once I'd changed into my traditional white and red-trimmed tunic and pants. She wouldn't join the rest of the village for the Noc Kupały festival. To her, it was no longer home, as its people had never bothered to push back against Father's rejection of me. She meant nothing to it, so it meant nothing to her. Despite her feelings toward Dwie Rzeki, though, she never denied my requests to visit it myself.

Smoke already filled the air by the time I passed through the eastern gate. Down the path to the left lay Otylia and her father's house, and I wondered if she would come this time.

Unlike the other szeptuchy who honored the holy summer solstice with the tribe, Otylia had instead ventured into the woods on her own each year since our separation. We were both sixteen now. That gave me hope, even if seeing her would only jab at the old wound in my heart.

The hours that followed went by in a blur. From Kuba forcing a horn of oskoła into my hand—then another—to the ritual dances around the bonfires and more food than we had on any other day, it was exhilarating.

As we danced, the priests chanted, claiming the spirits of the world joined with us. Maybe they were right. Maybe it had been those spirits in my head this morning. Mom claimed demons' and spirits' whispers could drive a man mad, and they were more powerful than ever on the solstice, when the Three Realms collided and unleashed fresh waves of magic over Jawia's forests and plains. Surely, that was it. A spirit's influence, nothing more.

I lost myself in the music and my ever-increasing drunkenness. We painted our faces in honor of the gods as the girls donned flower wreaths they would soon send into the river, sending the eligible boys on a chase. Beautiful things, they seemed like crowns upon their heads. The Drowning of Marzanna was the first time each year the girls wore them, but tonight was the most important. A boy who retrieved an eligible girl's wreath was by tradition bound to wed her. Often it was a rigged game. That didn't stop the excitement from spreading through the crowd in anticipation of the wreath release, fire jump, and venture into the woods that followed.

Kuba and I joined the other boys in the rush to the river. We weren't yet eligible, but people of every age participated in the fun of releasing the wreaths or catching them. It was important to remember who'd worn what wreath. At the very least, we could have a moment with her when we returned wearing it.

Before the girls disappeared upstream, I scanned for Otylia among them. She was nowhere to be found, but there were plenty of other girls from both Dwie Rzeki and nearby villages. I noted a few girls and their wreaths. I'd never successfully caught one before, and I prayed to Jaryło that he aid me tonight.

"Hey, Half-Chief!" a shout came from ahead. The familiar square-jawed face of Narcyz appeared, and I groaned, anticipating the mockery to come. "You actually think a girl *wants* you to catch her wreath? Any of 'em would rather become a rusałka than wed you."

I stuttered, searching for a reply, but Kuba beat me to it. "Don't you have a pile of muck to roll in, you hog? Sure as iron smells like you've done it already."

Thank the gods for him.

Father had scolded me enough times for fighting with Narcyz. We'd both ended up bruised for a week after our last bout, and another one would end up with me wounded from Father's fist as well as his. Kuba had no such care.

"Need your lackey to defend you, huh?" Narcyz spat, going toe-to-toe with me. He was shorter, but his wide shoulders and arms had me on my back foot. "What? You scared after I sent you crying to Lubena last time?"

I gritted my teeth. *Don't let him get to you.* But he had, and my training with Xobas kicked in by instinct. With a quick sweep, I took his legs out from under him, sending him into the soft earth and covering him with mud. "You were right, Kuba. He does smell like muck."

We made for the river before more of Narcyz's friends showed up, but they'd already heard. Four of them emerged from the darkness with their chins held high as Narcyz staggered to his feet. This was exactly what Father hadn't wanted. In the moment, though, I didn't care. Narcyz had insulted my mom. I could tolerate a lot, but never that.

Unfortunately, my anger didn't change that we were outnumbered.

The boys beat us badly before the horns had even signaled for the release of the wreaths. I heaved on the ground, searching for air as Narcyz sent a kick into my stomach. "Go find that stupid witch, Half-Chief. She's your only shot."

One of the other boys laughed. "Nah. She hates him too."

"Good." Narcyz spat in my face. He kicked me once more before leaving with his thugs.

For a long time, I lay there, clutching my ribs. "I had him," I mumbled to Kuba, who was pulling himself up a nearby maple.

"Yeah, we *really* had them." He wiped the blood from his chin. "Maja ain't going to be impressed by this. Gods, what are we doing picking fights with them?"

"Xobas has been training me."

"One fancy move, woo-hoo. I'm sorry, Wacław, but if you're going to find a girl, you've got to move on. Forget Otylia. Forget Narcyz. Make something for yourself, or both of us are going to be alone next year."

I opened my mouth to reply, but he'd already stumbled his way back toward the village center. Even Kuba had given up on me. Just like Father. No matter how hard I worked in the fields or trained with Xobas, it wasn't enough. I'd never be Mikołaj. I'd never be the heir Father had always wanted.

Soon, a horn blast signaled the beginning of the boys' search. I didn't join them. With my ribs bruised if not broken, I could barely stand, let alone forge through the Krowik's deep waters. The wreaths' arrivals, though, had me entranced. A hundred candles illuminating flowers of blue and violet, red and yellow, representing each girl in our region. None would care that I'd failed.

I caught my breath against a tree as the boys swam. Some whooped in joy quickly, holding aloft their prizes. Others still fought and searched, but the flow carried many of the wreaths away as others became caught along the opposite shore. A bad omen for those girls.

As I stumbled my way back up the trail, the successful boys ran past with their wreaths. Their laughter felt like another kick in the gut. Only some of it was directed at me, but even a portion was enough. The couples exchanged their celebrations and prepared to jump the fire together, marking an official declaration of their relationship. I hadn't the strength to watch. Next year I would have my first chance to do so, but what hope did I have? The pairs seemed so *happy*, like they belonged. Could I ever feel like that?

Something pulled me to the woods beyond the eastern gate. It was a force I'd felt before, one guiding me wordlessly, but after a terrible night, I went after it. The visions from the morning returned as I did. So did the pain.

What is happening to me?

"Please, Wašek," a whisper replied in my head. *"I know you're in there somewhere. Come back!"*

"Otylia?" I breathed. Her voice sent a shiver down a spine, and I pushed into the dark trees with a renewed fervor. All that led me was that pull in my chest and that distant feeling that there was something I was missing. I needed to know more.

The winds grew the deeper I traversed into the woods. Unlike on the equinox years before, I stuck to familiar trails as much as possible, but each creak and crack had me on edge. Dariusz and Mom's warnings about demons and spirits haunted me with each step. Somewhere deep in the forests lay the Fern Flower—the magical flower that only bloomed during the Noc Kupały solstice. The spirits protected it from the unworthy, the one who cowered. But tonight, it was not what I sought.

Near the Wyzra River, the ground softened. I stopped to roll up my pants. Mom complained often about me returning with my clothes covered in dirt and mud, and both she and Father would rave if I ruined my festival attire. Then, when I looked up, the pull in my chest snapped taut.

Roots twisted around my ankles, trapping me in place as a figure swept past. Trees shifted. The figure's braided black hair flew behind her, and she whispered in the szeptuchy old tongue, her magic swelling around us. I tried to call out to her. My voice faltered, and instead, I succumbed to the hold of the roots as she stopped before me, her thick brows furrowed in a frown as jagged as a knife.

"Why are you here, Half-Chief?" Otylia growled.

I tried to step back, but the roots tightened around my calves at the effort, sending pain shooting up my legs. "You weren't at Noc Kupały."

"So? I never go. The festival's for drunkards and lustful girls."

"What about me?"

She rolled her eyes and stepped closer, a hand raised with her fingers flexed. "You reek of oskoła, just like Narcyz and those foolish warriors. They turn a festival for the gods into an orgy." She closed her fist, and I cried out as the roots squeezed my injured ribs. "Answer me! Why are you here?"

"I…"

"Gods, you never change." The roots released me as she turned away sharply. "Except that's the problem. You did."

Another force struck me again. I dropped to my knees as a vision surged through my head. Otylia striking me and forcing me away in a strange hall of stone, her tone sharp and her green eyes longing. Though I couldn't understand every word, the brokenness I felt said enough. So did the hatred that followed.

In the present, Otylia scoffed. "Get up. The roots didn't hurt you *that* much."

"I came because a force led me here," I said. My ribs ached, and I gripped them as I stood and met her gaze. "Something weird is happening to me."

"Why should I care? You've proven for years you want nothing to do with me."

"That's not true."

"Liar!"

The earth seemed to shift with her rage, throwing me into a nearby tree. Her channeling brought a glow to her skin, and though she wore neither a wreath nor a dress with elaborate woven patterns, I couldn't look away. The stench of swamp and sweat followed her. It added to her menacing presence as anger, pain, and regret clashed within me—the vision's emotions and my own. How could I trust my own thoughts?

"Wašek, I love you," Otylia said in my head. A different voice yet hers. This one was lighter, more caring than the girl before me. *"Come back to me."*

"I don't understand!" I shouted at the world and at nothing. "Why are you talking in my head?"

Otylia shook her head. "What are you talking about? I don't need to get in your head, Half-Chief, to know what you think. You're just like everyone else, calling me a witch."

"I'm coming back. Be strong."

"Get away from me," Otylia snapped, throwing up her arms and calling forth a wall of roots between us. "Don't pretend to care about me anymore, and don't *ever* try to find me again."

44

Otylia

This better work.

THE CHILL BREEZE SWEEPING SNOW AND SAND through the canyon sent a jolt through my body. As did the light. I'd spent too long in the darkness of Sheresy's western cliff, planning my attack with the Daughters of the Earth, but I was finally free. With *žityje* surging in my soul, now I could free Marzanna's victims too.

Sabina and Ta-naro flanked me as I climbed the steps towards Third Limestone and the highest bridge across the river. They'd joined me despite my objections. My position in the fight to come would be the most dangerous of all, and neither of them were immortal. Instead of being dismayed, my threats had only empowered them. That didn't surprise me coming from Ta-naro. Sabina was a different story.

Come on, I thought, surveying the path ahead. *Someone try to stop us. Make this fun from the start.*

I needed the distraction more than anything right now. An itch in the back of my mind constantly reminded me of the shift I'd felt in Wacław the last night. Small but there. He'd reacted to my call for the first time that felt truly like him, but something had been different. As if he was trapped within himself.

Few people walked the winding trail up the cliff at dusk, and those that did gave us as wide a berth as the narrow path allowed. I smirked. My silver fox pelt, Ascension dress—now covered in scorpion carapace armor—and cape would already be quite the sight. The forest nymph and brazen Mothermarked szeptucha alongside me only made us stand out more. So, it wasn't long before we drew a patrol's attention.

"Hey you! Sto—"

The Frostmarked guard's throat spewed blood as a spiraled glass blade stuck from it. Ta-naro examined her cuticles beside me. "Thought this would be harder."

I called my light spear. Even in my gloved hand, I felt its cold silver. "Do that a hundred times and we'll see."

The four remaining guards were smarter. They approached steadily with the straight end of their spears extended toward us. An effective tactic in traditional battle, I assumed, but we weren't traditional.

Sabina took flight as I swung my spear and yelled in the old tongue, "*Metl*!"

The moon's power swept before me with my spear, crashing into the guards. The impact threw three off the cliff before they could react. In a last-ditch effort, the final guard dropped his spear and grabbed hold of the path as his feet dangled over the edge. His shouts echoed through the canyon as he fought to pull himself up, but Sabina was faster.

Light flashed in her hands before a blast rocked the cliff. Chunks of rock slid from the path, sending the guard to his demise, and awe filled me as Sabina landed at my side once again.

"That was insane!" I laughed. "I felt the *žityje* leave me when you channeled."

"Sorry…"

"Don't be. This bond is why szeptuchy are powerful. You combine your own strength with mine, drawing *žityje* from both of us."

Ta-naro nudged me. "Enough with the girl talk. They're coming."

A horn echoed around us as guards spilled out of every passage-way in the cliff faces. Most filed toward the river, where Kiin and Ildes organized the ambush with the others. "It's working," I said. "Let's go!"

We were close to the bridge, but the guards that hadn't gone to the river had blocked off the path above and below. I found some relief knowing they didn't understand my powers yet. Our advantages were few, and even that could make all the difference in the battle to come. Grabbing Ta-naro, I leaped from the ledge.

"What the sand dragon!" she hissed.

I caught us with the moon's pull a moment later, grinning. "Don't worry, we'll kill the Frostmarked, but your parents and the other rusałki and utopiecs come first."

Ta-naro stopped fighting as we landed on the Third Limestone bridge—thank Mokosz. My footing was unsteady enough without a squirming child in my arms. On a two-stride wide bridge far above the river, one slip would mean death for a mortal. The gales didn't help, and even with my ability to fly, I shuddered looking over the edge at the gathered Daughters of the Earth below.

It's time.

"Hold off the guards," I ordered the girls. "This will take all my focus."

Sabina gave a soft smile. "Do what you do best."

"Threaten to stab everyone I care about?"

"Free them."

Then Sabina took flight, leaving Ta-naro to draw her glass throwing blades and face the opposite end of the bridge. As the first guards stepped onto it, she glanced over her shoulder. "If we die, you can call me Ta I guess."

"I can't call you anything if we're dead."

"Bah. Ildes was right. Not very funny…"

I offered her a wry smile before turning my attention to the river. Hundreds of souls lurked within it. Undead, demonic, the Frostmarked had sacrificed them to empower their goddess and grant her a power far greater than what I wielded now. Their lives had been nothing more than a tool to her. Blood was all.

"Show me their lives," I told End with my eyes shut. "Show me the Threads that remain."

When I opened them again, the river burst with thousands of colorful Threads of Life. Black wisps floated among them, carrying faint whispers in their wake. Demons, yes, but they weren't dead. The bonds they'd made in life remained. So did their souls. All they needed was to be set free from the curse that corrupted them—no, that *broke* them. These people weren't corrupt or evil. They were hurt. For years, Mother had trained me as a healer, and though mending their souls involved neither potions nor salves, it required the same care.

I reached for the wisps and called them to me. We'd chosen this point because it had the only unobstructed view of nearly the entire city, and I gasped at the wave of souls that rose from both the river and cliffs. Black streaks weaving their way through the flurry of snow. I'd never seen anything like it.

Before they arrived, the clanging of combat rang out below. The battle had begun, and I needed to do my part. "Come," I said to the demons. "I can save you."

"So you can," said the woman who'd appeared in my dream. Her figure remained misty and dark, but her smooth voice was too distinct to forget. "Show us how we can be free."

I pulled my hands free from Kiin's gloves, fighting the fear that came with the exposure. They'd shielded me from End's visions, but that same protection had separated me from the Threads. Hiding from my power wouldn't save the demons… wouldn't save Wacław.

The demons' Threads pulsed in my grasp. I grabbed as many as I could, clutching them until they filled my hands. Even then, I stepped forward onto the air, allowing them to entangle me as I released my power into them. Visions pricked at my mind, but I fought them, focusing only on the forms of the demons around me. Their faces were there in those shadows. Just like their souls, part of them lived.

"I know the injustice Marzanna has inflicted upon you," I shouted. "She claims to free Jawia from the reign of gods and men, but nothing matters to her except power and revenge. Her Frostmarked slit your throats. They bled you dry and threw you into the river so that *she* could bring blizzards and death upon your land. But today, we bring back the balance she broke!"

"How?" they cried around me, their passion flooding through the Threads that touched my exposed skin.

"Justice." I turned my gaze to the gathered Frostmarked as they fought with Mokosz's loyalists. "We've lured out the warriors and the priestesses. I grant you my strength. Take it and restore the balance. Kill those who sacrificed you, and then you will be free from the demonic toils you endure."

I held my spear aloft and released a burst of light from it. "Go!"

The figures dropped in an instant, their Threads releasing me as they swept to their bodies. My light had been the signal, and now, the Daughters' szeptuchy flung rocks below and crafted the earth to bend the river toward Marzanna's men on Top Shale. Frostmarked channelers fought among the Frostmarked ranks too, but we'd hoped for that. Those priestesses had done the sacrificing. The demons needed them most.

"Done yet?" Ta called from my left as she sent a stone shooting from the bridge and into a guard's throat. "I mean, how long can you talk to demons, right?"

"I'm done. We can join the others."

"Finally!" She threw up a barrier of stone with the remaining parts of the bridge before her. "That'll hold 'em." But as she dusted off her hands and took a running start toward me, the bridge cracked beneath her. Its material had fueled her channeling, and now it had thinned far too much.

"Jump!" I shouted.

She didn't have the chance. A third of the bridge tumbled into the ravine below, taking Ta and a dozen guards with it.

Rubble crashed into me as I dove after her. *Žityje* healed my wounds quickly, but I worried for Ta amid the shards. She couldn't fly or heal so easily, and the ground was approaching fast.

A gash bled on her temple as I closed in, cursing and grabbing her arm to stop our fall. That allowed the rocks above to crash towards us. There was no time to dodge or channel, so I raised Weles's armband and shielded Ta's body. Even then, shards slipped through the band's protection. They sliced at my arms and battered my torso, but Amten's armor ensured none impaled me. I silently thanked the scorpion hunter.

The fluttering of wings approached once the debris had passed, and Sabina gasped at Ta in my arms. "Oh my! Is she all right?"

"I don't know. Her heart's still beating—that much I can sense—but she's knocked out." I shook my head. Foolish girl. One of the first rules of becoming a szeptucha was learning that you had to be one with the force you were wielding. Anything more would damage the very thing you were supposed to be protecting.

With a glance at the chaos below, I handed Ta to Sabina. She grunted from the weight on her slim frame but held. "Take her away from the fighting," I said. "Protect her until it's over and I find her parents."

She bowed her head. "Yes, Lady Otylia."

"Don't say that like I'm your master."

"You are, but I chose this." She smiled. "I know that look. You're mad but can't justify an argument."

"Get out of here, then, my *servant*," I quipped.

Her bright eyes released the tension in my heart, only for a moment. By the river, the Daughters were outnumbered on the sloping shores. A few of the demons had joined the fight, but it wasn't enough with Marzanna's szeptuchy fighting down the cliffs and flooding from the Top Shale tunnels. The river needed to be higher if more of the demons could reach them.

Or the Frostmarked need to be lower...

I flew toward the western cliff face. Guards had formed a line upon it, trying to force their way into the fight below, but it was far too crowded for the narrow stairs. They were trapped with only a single szeptucha to guard their rear. Easy.

The szeptucha drew back her hood and shot bolts of ice in my path. Maneuvering with the moon's power was still new to me, so I dodged too slowly. Some struck my limbs and face, drawing just enough blood to be annoying. I bit my cheek and called my spear as she threw up an ice shield. Guards swarmed us, trying to stab my sides. Idiots.

I drove my spear through the szeptucha's shield. It shattered into a thousand pieces, and when I shouted, the shards became daggers within my moonblast that flew into the surrounding Frostmarked.

Screams echoed even louder than my ringing ears. Deep in my soul, a part of me felt a thrill at their suffering. That excitement only grew as my spear ripped through the szeptucha's sternum. The shards had sliced her enough to kill her slowly, but a dying channeler was still a channeler. She would've been dangerous until her final breath.

With me blocking the guards' route up the stairs, they charged into the Mothermarked szeptuchy's rising waters. Fear dominated their gazes, but their glances weren't directed at the demons lurking in the shallows. A goddess faced them now. Even a rusałka's embrace was kinder than my wrath.

Ahead of them, the battle turned to slaughter as the demons advanced with the tide. Where there had once been tactical lines of Frostmarked, there were now men fleeing into their charging allies. Those in the front hadn't seen my appearance. How could they have? Amid the shattered rocks and swarming rusałki and utopiecs, they'd been swallowed by the confusion. Cries of agony echoed through the chasm as demonic snarls took over.

"Where is your goddess?" I spat at the Frostmarked that dared to face me. Unfettered bravery led them on, but they found only my spear and the swarm of silver ants I called from the cliffs. *Finish them!*

As I neared the river, Kiin called to me from atop the Daughters' makeshift bank that protected them from their own flood, "Otylia, the demons! They're turning on us!"

I struck down another guard and leaped into the air to see exactly that. Decayed forms had begun to climb up the bank, their bony fingers grabbing for the legs of our warriors and szeptuchy. Others swarmed the surviving Frostmarked who hadn't fled into the cliffs, but most had turned to the greater feast.

"Stop!" I shouted, diving to the bank alongside Kiin, her hands raised before her as she crafted the earth to her will. A horde of demons were climbing over themselves to try and reach us now. But there was a different look on their face. Not the bloodlust I'd seen on many demons' faces, but fear.

"Lady Otylia!" Ildes reached my side. Sweat beaded from her brow despite the cold, and her legs shook from overuse of *żityje*. "I insisted before, and now I must again. Give them the mercy of death. They are demons, nothing more."

I spun on the szeptucha, grabbing hold of her as her Threads of Life spiraled around me. So many szeptucha she loved. So many who she'd trained. But in her eyes, I saw my fathers. Both Weles and Dariusz had commanded me as if I were their warrior, not a daughter. Was she no different, claiming to protect the Daughters of the Earth while neglecting the most rejected of daughters before her?

"These rusałki are Mokosz's daughters too!" I yelled for all to hear. Battle still raged between the demons and both the Daughters and the Frostmarked, but my voice carried with a strength greater than the chaos. "We all create these demons through our selfishness and our pride, and then we scorn *them* for what we've turned them into. We punish *them* for the brokenness we caused." I extended my free hand toward the demons and released my power at them. "Those who corrupted you are dead. Be free!"

Ildes pried at my now exposed fingers, but I held on to her with all the bitterness in my heart. Years of pain and rejection spilled over me like alcohol over a flame. So much hatred.

"Let her go!" Kiin snapped, still extending one hand to mold the bank against the demons.

They'd stopped, though. The ones attacking us had ceased their fighting and their vicious snarls. Instead, they stared down at themselves, the black of their eyes fading to white and brown, and in End's wisps, dark shadows turned to a rainbow of colors amid the snowfall.

"We did it…" I whispered.

All my rage vanished, and I released Ildes as the freed demons looked at each other in shock. Their appearances remained the same besides their eyes. It didn't matter. The dancing of their souls brought me a rare joy. Life. Raw and pure, it surged from them in an aura of *żityje* that warmed the air, if only for a moment.

"Lady Otylia," Ildes stammered, "I—"

"Was wrong, yes," I said, but I gave her no attention. In all her wisdom, she'd shown no belief in the redemption of the demons. Kiin had, and she embraced me with tears in her eyes.

"We can save them. All of them!"

"Save?" I held the back of her head, cradling it against mine. "I don't understand. We just did."

Her whole body trembled, and she pushed back quickly, a familiar determination on her face. "The children… The children we sacrificed to the Earth Mother."

"But they aren't demons." I looked from her to Ildes. "They were sacrificed and given final rites according to the gods, so they should be in Nawia."

Kiin dropped to her knees. She held her hands over her heart, barely able to whimper her reply. "No… The scions said the Earth Mother demanded they remain as a remembrance of our failure."

I stepped back as a new fear filled me. All the stories the Daughters had told about the time before the scions' falls finally made sense. Mokosz's apparent anger, the Behmir River flowing red, and the goddess's demand for sacrifices. None of it had been her. It couldn't have been. No matter what we called her, Mokosz was the Great Mother, and she would never have allowed those children to become demons.

"I knew something was wrong with the stories," I said once I'd regained my bearings. Looking from the now awakened demons in the water below to Kiin's mournful face, all the joy I'd had from our victory perished in an instant.

"What do you mean?" Kiin asked.

"Marzanna tricked the scions. They weren't szeptuchy, so her voice likely sounded similar to Mokosz's when they heard the demand." I shook my head. It was hard to imagine hating Marzanna more than I had, but turning children into demons for her own gain was unforgivable. "She gained control of the Dominion of Vastroth because the people lost trust in the scions. Why face a realm at its peak when you can force it to crumble from the inside first?"

Ildes sucked in a sharp breath, *žityje* rising around her. "You dare question the scions' devotion to the Earth Mother? They served her until the Frostmarked slaughtered them!"

"We never saw their bodies..." Kiin whispered before scrambling to her feet. Her curled hair was wild and her own magic cracked the stone at her feet. "We assumed them dead when the Frostmarked took the Glasstone Tower and Mokosz sent us visions about Darixa."

"The Earth Mother would not tell us of a new scion if the previous ones weren't dead," Ildes said.

Kiin stepped to the elder szeptucha, her voice sharpening. "She would if those scions had betrayed her... betrayed *us*. My Yesike could've died for nothing! Don't you want to know the truth, even if there's the slightest chance we were wrong?"

Ildes wavered. "I... The Earth Mother did not interfere."

"She is the patron of all women," I replied. "Thousands call to her every day, so what if her force was too divided to stop Marzanna?"

"Or she truly has rejected us after our people's failures," Kiin said. "None of us—besides Otylia—have heard from her for some time." She turned away, hands held palm down before her. "Mother of the Earth, forgive our failures. Bring back my son. Please..."

I pointed to the rusałki and utopiecs. They looked at us for guidance with Marzanna's warriors and szeptuchy slaughtered around them, the river a rust brown from the mix of mortal and demonic blood. "We saved these people, Kiin. We'll do the same for the children, and then we'll free Huebia from Marzanna's grip."

Ildes shook her head. "They're demons!" she screamed loud enough for them to hear. "Look at them. Their bodies reveal that the corruption remains."

Murmurs spread through both the Daughters and the demons until I stepped to the ledge and slammed the butt of my spear into the stone. "Don't listen to her! She is a szeptucha, yes, but the blood of the Earth Mother flows in my veins. I am the Lady of Endings, and I say that your end is your own choice. Pass to Nawia as a mortal would or stay on Jawia, remaining free of mind and soul but trapped in your demonic forms until you choose to move to the next realm. I will not force either upon you. Know that if you stay, however, the power of your forms may aid us in the battle ahead. The Winter Witch threatens all our lands."

"Lady Otylia speaks for the Earth Mother more than we ever could," Kiin declared at my side. Her eyes were reddened and her cheeks still wet with tears, but no more came. The warrior I'd met in Huebia's streets had returned. "I believe the Earth Mother sent her granddaughter to aid us in freeing Vastroth from death and corruption. The Daughters will fight beside her, and each of you is welcomed among our ranks."

No cheers erupted from the awakened demons. Instead, they stood in silence for what seemed an eternity until a tall rusałka stepped forward. Though her skin remained decayed and her face warped, there was an aura of confidence in her stride, and I recognized her soul as the one who had met me upon the shore of the swamp in my dream.

"The Winter Witch took everyone I loved," she said, locking eyes with me as Sabina flew down from the cliffs with Ta floating alongside her.

"Not everyone," Ta said, dropping into the water. "Mother?"

The rusałka gasped along with a towering utopiec beside her. "Ta?" she asked as she dropped to her knees. "My little troublemaker! Thank the Earth Mother you're safe."

Ta rushed to the rusałka and wrapped her arms around her neck. "Nah," she said, her voice stifled by tears as she smiled up at me over her mother's shoulder. "Was the Lady of Endings that saved me. Her lanky nymph too."

"Then the Lady of Endings has done more than free just us," the rusałka said, turning to me as Ta moved on to hug her father. "If the Winter Witch truly manipulated the scions to kill our children, then

I will do whatever I can to ensure her influence is burned from each grain of sand on Jawia. It matters not whether I must remain hideous and cursed. You, Lady of Endings, have granted me a new life, a new chance with my family. I shall not waste it."

Then she dropped to a knee in the shallows. Naked and bowing, she held more strength than I did as a goddess. I hurt for her. Never before had my heart bled so strongly for a stranger, and I acted without thought, descending into the waters myself.

I reached out to her. "Don't bow to me."

Blood and muck coated my Ascension dress, but even if my power wouldn't clean it with ease, I wasn't the pure and bright figure I'd been rising from that volcano. Yes, I was a goddess. To move forward, though, I would do it my own way. As Otylia. Not as Father had wanted or even how Mother had. It was time for me to become my own goddess, my own person, and that started now.

Ta's mother took my hand, standing slowly. Her wisp of bright green swirled before me. Images of her children's birth flashed through my mind, followed by her death at the hands of the Frost-marked. The scions had already sacrificed her other child, another girl. She'd endured so much pain, but it was hope that filled her gaze now.

"We will make Marzanna wish she never broke winter's bounds," I said. "But first, we need to free your people and those she has corrupted."

45

Narcyz

"YOU WERE ALWAYS A THORN IN MY SIDE, boy," Chief Serwacy yelled across the clearing his and Mikołaj's armies had formed.

A plain with only a steady hill and shin-high snow separated Mikołaj from the father-in-law who'd betrayed him. It offered little protection from the northern wind that ruffled Serwacy's gray hair and filled it with speckles of white.

Mikołaj held his hands behind his back, his posture straight and his face hiding all emotion. A layer of frost covered his brows, but he didn't bother to brush it away. Nor did he wear furs over his tunic, despite the last day's blizzard. Comfort didn't matter. Not when he was about to fight for control of his dead father's army.

"I'd thought us closer than that," Mikołaj replied. "When I first pursued Kinga, she warned me that you were a stern but rational man. You had turned down many suitors for her hand, and the first thing you told me when I declared my intentions was that I reminded you of my father."

"I remember well enough."

Mikołaj advanced, keeping his hands away from the blade at his hip. "Then what changed? In the years since then, all I've done is grow and learn."

"You still remind me of Jacek, Mikołaj. Arrogant. Stubborn. Prideful. Your father claimed to unite the Krowikie clans into a single tribe, but he only did so by crushing those who dared to oppose him. I respected his power, not him."

"So you chose even more rashness and brutality?"

Serwacy scoffed, mirroring his opponent's march toward the top of the hill. Unlike Mikołaj, he trudged through the heavy snow with labored breaths before he stopped to reply, "I chose a leader. Mieczysław has a streak of anger greater than even that of your father. That is why I voted for him. Do I respect him more than you or your late father? No, but we are in a time of war. Victory requires sacrifices greater than a boy with his chin held too high to get it bloody is capable of."

"You believe me weak?" Mikołaj clenched his jaw. Even from my position with Andrij and the rest of the warriors, I could see his muscles tensing. His hand twitched along his blade's pommel. "Weak men violate their oaths! They turn their backs on their families for power!"

They were no more than six strides from each other now. Mikołaj reached the hilltop first, towering like a leszy over his prey. His sword made the chilling sound of iron rubbing against well-oiled leather as he drew it from its sheath.

"I challenge you, Serwacy Stojaczak, to a duel to the death. For defying tradition's right. For choosing pride over blood. With all of Krowik's fighting men as my witnesses, I declare to you now that I will take my birthright. I will protect my father's honor and my own, and I will lead our tribe against winter's Horde."

Serwacy's expression shifted from disgust to rage. He threw out his arms, releasing a great roar that echoed across the plain with the shouts of many, but not all, of his warriors. I noted the chiefs that remained silent, as their men had done so with them.

They doubt the old man.

"I'll gut you!" Serwacy growled as he pulled his two-handed ax from his back. Carvings raced up its wooden handle, and Perun's Thundermark glinted on its head. All warriors believed the war gods fought with them, Perun above all. I'd met a god… and a goddess… but I still had no more understanding than anyone else who each god actually favored. Did Perun care which chief's blood stained the snow?

Serwacy charged and swung in a raging sweep. Mikołaj was ready, his block chipping Serwacy's pristine ax head.

I shook my head. No skilled ironsmith would craft such a fragile ax. It had been smithed for show, not use, and when Mikołaj struck its handle, nearly splitting it in half with a single blow, I let out a laugh.

"Amateur."

Andrij nudged me as the sparks flew again, iron striking iron with a glorious ring. "Who's an amateur? Chief Serwacy appears slow, but he moves with power. Any mistake and Chief Mikołaj will fall."

I smirked, stuffing down any uncertainty, and watched Mikołaj's continued advance. He'd quickly gained the high ground. Each step forward unsettled his rival even more. The duel had barely begun, but it was already over. Unless Perun truly favored Serwacy, he wouldn't survive until dusk.

"The ironsmith of Klist, Serwacy's village," I whispered, leaning over to him. "Pa always claimed he rushed his work, making the blades too brittle. They might shine like a bald man's sweaty head but they're useless."

"A bald man's sweaty head?" Andrij crossed his arms and gave me a side-eye. "I wonder what happens in *your* head sometimes."

"What? They don't have bald men in Astiw? Or is King Lunatic too busy decapitating people?"

His head dropped. "Just watch the fight, all right? I'd rather not think about home right now. The Horde has likely begun their attack. Soon…"

"I know. But we warned them. Boz made his choice, and Ara and Zakir will try to get out the Astiwie they can. Wacław said they've got a lot."

"Not enough. Thousands will die, and I'm left wondering if I could've stopped Boz somehow instead of trying to persuade him."

Andrij turned his attention back to the fight, refusing to answer further questions. I followed his gaze as Mikołaj sliced Serwacy's side, sending the first drops of red over the hillside. The snow had begun to fall thicker now, and Serwacy's only attacks were wild swings with his long ax. It kept Mikołaj at a distance much of the time. Didn't matter. Those jabs would slow him down eventually.

"You did what you thought would work," I said with a shrug. "Not your fault a crazy goddess is conquering Jawia and your king would rather massacre every bear in sight."

He frowned at my insistence but chuckled. "You know Boz didn't kill the aspid, right?"

"Had no doubt. No way he hunted a dragon by himself. Might not be a żmij, but doesn't matter. A dragon's a dragon."

"Boz didn't even go on the expedition. Neither did I, but at least I don't claim to have killed it." He sighed. "What I wouldn't have done to take one of those scales."

Before I could reply, Mikołaj sliced Serwacy again, this time in the thigh. The elder chief released a shout and charged with what strength he had left, throwing Mikołaj to the ground. I gritted my teeth. Mikołaj had gotten cocky. We couldn't afford that. If our army stayed in the west...

Serwacy's ax snapped up and down in quick succession. The hill blocked my view of Mikołaj on the ground, and I winced when it struck. But no cheers came from the opposing warriors. Instead, Serwacy groaned, pulling on his ax. It didn't budge, and my fear turned to excitement at the flash of blond over the crest. Serwacy was too slow.

Mikołaj's perfectly sharpened blade found its final mark.

The crowd went silent as Mikołaj tried to pull his sword free from his victim's neck, but he'd cut to the spine. It remained trapped, sending blood over his face and tunic until he released the hilt, causing Serwacy to collapse. Not a pretty blow. Albin and the other warriors had told me deadly ones rarely were. Tales of melee combat resembling a dance between two lovers were fantasies, but I preferred it better this way. War wasn't meant to be romantic. It was raw, disgusting, and I loved the thrill, the way my body put everything into killing to survive. Nothing was like it.

A mighty shout finally erupted around us as Mikołaj crested the hill and raised his bloodied fist. His breaths were heavy, his tunic slashed, but a fire burned behind his eyes.

I joined in the chorus. Pride filled me knowing I'd made this happen. Andrij and I had neither magic nor an army of our own, but together, we'd turned Krowik's power toward Mikołaj. Soon, we would face the Horde.

First came the dissenters.

"Are you really willing to help Mikołaj kill those who oppose him?" Andrij asked, grabbing my arm as the warriors rushed to their chief. Across the field, Serwacy's army stood in wait. They'd seen Mikołaj's victory over Krowik's third most powerful chief and wouldn't dare interfere with tradition. Unless their own chief said otherwise.

"Krowik has to be united," I replied, shielding my gut with iron. Nerves would only make it harder. "Any chiefs who defy Mikołaj are only helping Marzanna. They have to pay for that. Hopefully, there won't be any."

"Wacław's instructions still don't feel like him."

"No, they don't."

He raised his brow. "Yet you'll execute your own chiefs anyway? What if the demon influenced Wacław? Please, for me, at least ask him again before going ahead with this. Maybe there needn't be more bloodshed."

I pulled myself from his grip and started toward Albin, who watched the celebrations nearby with his arms crossed. "You're a commander, Andrij. Blood is part of war."

"So are people."

That left a sting in my chest as I left. Wacław's messages *had* sounded weird, but that didn't mean anything. He'd gone to Nawia as a demon and somehow returned. I'd be pissed too.

"You're not celebrating?" I asked Albin with a slap on his back.

The giant of a man just grunted.

"What? Mikołaj won. Should be happy, shouldn't we?"

"I fought by Serwacy's side for years." He looked down at me, and for the first time, I saw pain in his eyes. Then it was gone, a stern glare taking its place. "You better know what you're doing. The tribe will be in chaos when they learn what we've done."

"At least we'll have an army against the Horde."

He shook his head. "Da, an army, but how loyal? Kill the opposing chiefs and their brothers—by blood or by sword—will come for you."

"We'll do what we have to."

The cheers had quieted. Mikołaj now headed toward the opposing chiefs with his allies covering the hills behind him. Andrij was among them, so I joined him with a hand tight around my spear's shaft. It was cold against my calloused fingers. Heat was familiar at the forge, but this frost had me on edge. Attacking any rebellious chiefs was just duty. I wasn't afraid of duty.

Andrij didn't look at me when he spoke. "Did Albin try to talk sense into you, or did he preach for unnecessary death too?"

"He warned me against it," I muttered.

"Hmm."

"That's it?"

With a roll of his eyes, he sighed. "I've said my part. You're a better person than you think you are, Narcyz. Just... Remember that when you're preparing to send another member of your tribe to Nawia."

"Chiefs of Krowik!" Mikołaj shouted before I could reply. "I come to you today bringing justice, not turmoil. Serwacy violated a bond of marriage, but he was not the true threat to our people."

A stout, bald chief I didn't recognize scoffed. He gripped a spear and had a large round shield strapped to his back. His tunic was ratty and stained, his boots no better cared for. I grinned. His feet would freeze before I had the chance to get to him.

"Yer right!" he snapped, his words slurring. "The threat's you! We're at war and you'd rather fight your quarrels than the Solgawi."

Mikołaj approached, locking his hands behind his back again as his breaths fogged the air. "I tolerated Serwacy's betrayal initially, but then I discovered the truth of my brother's warning. We thought the diviners had foreseen the clan attack on the equinox. The true army is far greater."

"None of these lies!" another chief replied. His hair a deep black, he wore it shaved on the sides, as was tradition when our tribe marched to war. He wasn't familiar to me either. That was a good sign. Most major chiefs came through Father's forge when they were in Dwie Rzeki for festivals, and if I didn't recognize them, they likely commanded few men.

"I don't lie to you, Boleslav," Mikołaj replied. "The Horde of Marzanna has slaughtered the clans of the east and reached the Narrow Pass. Astiw cannot hold them back." He circled close to the chiefs, looking each of them in the eye. "If we stay here, fighting for our ancient lands, we lose everything. They will sack our villages and take our women. Would you have your men sit in the Solgawi hills when Klist burns? While blizzards starve the eastern plains?"

"Superstition!" Boleslav exclaimed. "It is just snow."

Mikołaj stopped before him. He towered over the chief but kept a respectful distance. " 'Just snow'? The forests died! The crops have not taken root! Can you remember a time when Jaryło failed to bring life? I cannot."

The first chief stomped his spear into the snow. "You question the gods?"

"I can't claim to know what happened to Jaryło, Horacy. But I know that the Horde is coming. Mokosz's channelers showed us, and we failed to listen until now." Mikołaj tapped his nose for a moment, thinking. "Don't you have a young daughter? I'm sorry, I don't remember her name."

Horacy stiffened. "Ksenia."

"Good name that. Too bad she won't grow old enough to jump the fire because her father was too insolent to see his family was at risk."

"You bastard!" Horacy lunged, striking with his spear. But Mikołaj was faster. Without a blade, he sidestepped and grabbed hold of the shaft of the spear. Horacy spun on his toes to throw him back, and they both tumbled to the ground.

Arguing spread through the armies as the two wrestled in the snow. Most seemed to have joined our side, but even a few vocal chiefs were enough to cast doubt among others. Horacy and Boleslav's villages probably held less that fifty people combined. Call them chiefs and these bone-headed brutes listened anyway. I wondered which side I would've chosen had my life taken a different turn.

When Mikołaj staggered to his feet, he held Horacy by the scruff of his coat. "Hear me clearly," he declared to everyone. They quieted, waiting for him to finish. "Chief Horacy lives because I choose to show him mercy. This will be the last shred of it I offer until we reach Dwie Rzeki." He threw Horacy into the arms of his nearest warrior with blood trickling from the chief's brow. "You understand?"

Horacy nodded rapidly, but Boleslav just raised a hand in recognition and turned away.

He'll be trouble, I thought. *At least it's only one. Just one…*

"See," Andrij said. "Chief Mikołaj learned from Jacek how to handle the chiefs better than either of us could've. A single dissenter isn't a problem. Tell Wacław, and then we can march to Dwie Rzeki and get this over with."

"Mieczysław will die either way," I said. "This won't be bloodless. You saw how aggressive he is."

"Why must our high chiefs and kings be the closest to lunacy?"

I shrugged. "Nobody wants to fight a madman."

He chuckled and patted my shoulder, his expression still hard as stone. "True. Luckily, this madman wields only an ax. Let's hope the one whose mark burns your arm hasn't lost his mind yet."

46

Wacław

TWO WEEKS EARLIER

"Don't ever try to find me again."

"SHE HATES US."

My thoughts consumed me as we left the room holding Kiin's model of Huebia. Every word the szeptucha had said seemed like a distant whisper from the past, her coat sweeping behind her and vanishing into shadows beneath the knee. And that voice in my head…

"She always has."

Faarax, Kiin's short and overly respectful helper, blabbered on as my vision fell into a blur. Something inside me wanted to reach for Otylia's hand. I tried, but she snatched hers away without a word.

"You defy it, ignore it, but she's never forgotten. She's never forgiven." The voice cackled, its every sound tearing at my sanity like a zmora's claws raking through flesh. *"Otylia wants us dead. She sees the power growing within us, and now she hates us all the more."*

Does she?

I stumbled as my foot caught on an uneven stone—odd for a hideout managed by channelers capable of shifting rock to leave such a hazard exposed. In fact, the stones were everywhere. They rolled my ankles with each step, sending shooting pain up my leg and draining my *žityje* to heal.

Black swirls blurred the air beyond Otylia and me. Kiin, Faarax, the entire sleeping hall just vanished, as if lost in a heavy autumn mist. I growled at that. Mists meant a lack of wind, and the winds were all I had. Except for Otylia.

"We never had her," the voice continued. *"Otylia used us to Ascend, tricked us for power."*

But… She loves me.

"No, she doesn't."

Silence fell over us in that ever-blackening void. My hair stood on end. Something was wrong, but a force crushed my doubts. It strangled my mind, replacing confusion with anger and pain, memories of every fight I'd had with Otylia. Any will I had to resist it smoldered out until the darkness didn't matter. Only hatred did. Otylia had stolen my soul when I confessed my love for her, and now she feared my awoken power. All the gods did was manipulate us for their own wills…

"I can't do this," she whispered.

But I took her in my arms anyway, resisting the voice, desperate to prove it wrong. She refused to face me. Her body was rigid, her hands held tight to her chest as I apologized for fighting her in the model room, but the words weren't mine. None of this was right.

Then she screamed.

Reality shattered as her elbows struck me. I stumbled back, Father's rejection and hers hammering my head over and over. Rage burned away whatever love had beat with my heart. Otylia hated me.

You were right, I told the voice.

"We've always known the truth. Now we must kill her before she grows too powerful. Take our revenge. Take her power."

"We've changed…" Otylia continued. "I don't know who I am anymore, and I can't hurt you again. I can't…"

Time rushed forward until Kwiecień's cold hilt stung my fingers. I raised it, prepared to strike as the demon shoved me on with the strength of a storm, but something held me back. The voice grew to a roar. All else dropped into nothing except for the space between us. A stride that could've been miles, it was too far to bridge, yet the tip of my blade hovered so close to her face. Death's threat.

"End her! Take her power and become more than she could ever be!"

Kwiecień slid through her ribs. I'd stabbed out of instinct, almost to kill the voice instead of her, but the sword struck true. The sound was disgusting, horrifying. My cries were thick with anguish and rage. I couldn't hear her choking on her blood. I couldn't hear her whimper the name she'd called me since we were children. And I couldn't hear final breath before she fell limp at my feet.

I trembled, dropping the sword and falling to my knees. Tears stung my eyes. My heart seemed to stop in my chest.

"Wašek, wake up," Otylia whispered through our bond.

I'm not asleep, I replied. *I've just seen the truth.*

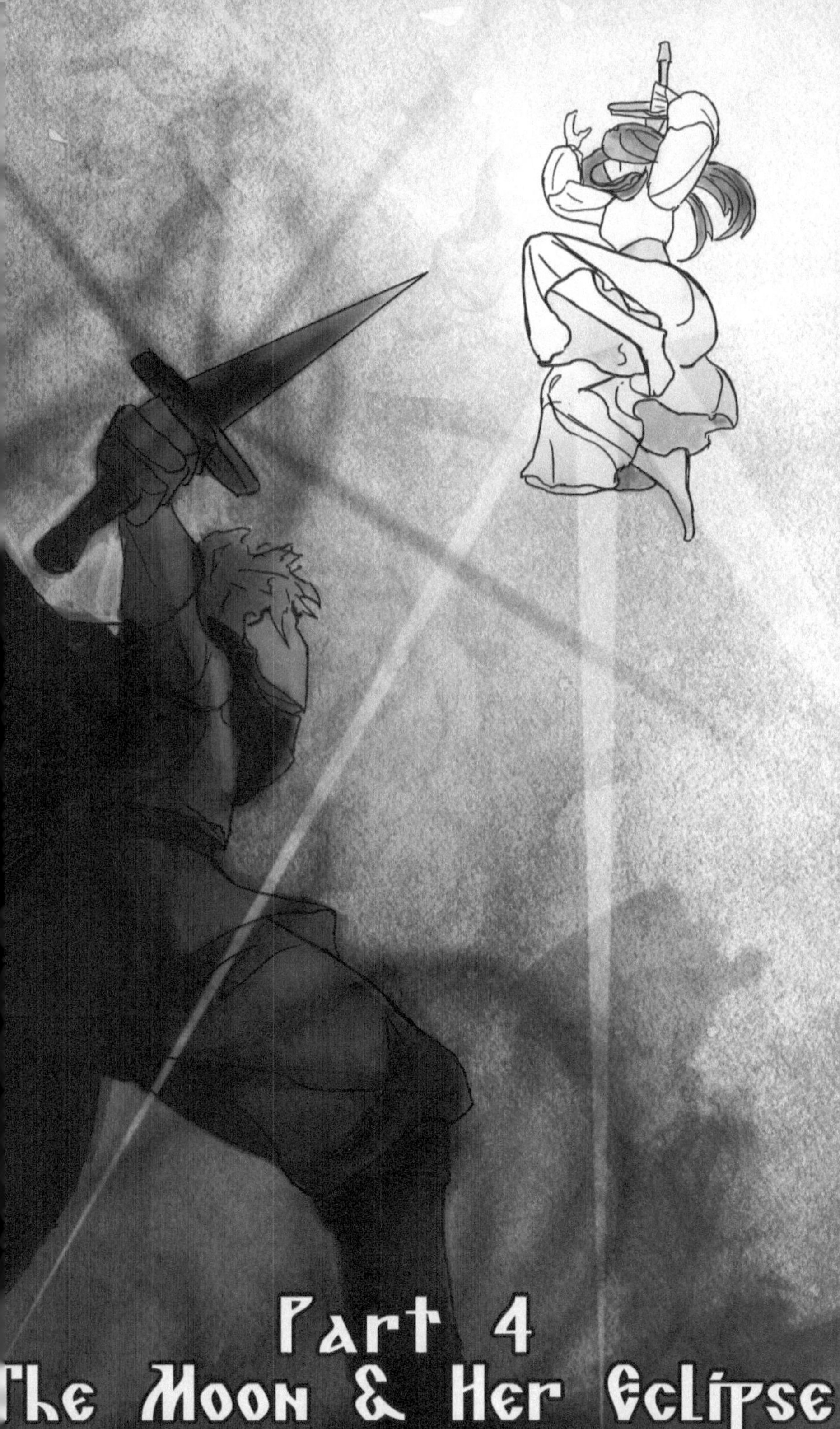
Part 4
The Moon & Her Eclipse

47

The Płanetnik

Otylia will come soon. We will end her when she does.

THE SCATTERED ROCK CRACKED BENEATH MY BOOTS as I entered the Daughters' hideout. Guards watched the door but failed to notice my invisible entrance—yet another mortal weakness. Otylia had freed me from that toil. If only she'd seen the truth.

A shred of the petty mortal had remained in me for a time, but he'd silenced finally… with some convincing. I'd simply reminded him of the pain Otylia had caused us. Oh, it would feel *good* to plunge Marzanna's Thunderstone dagger through her heart. Even watching the weakling kill her in our visions had me humming with anticipation. I'd have my victory soon.

First, I needed the scion girl.

My footsteps alerted two Daughters as I reached the base of the stairs in the second-floor sleeping hall. Faarax was speaking with a woman with wider shoulders than most warriors, but when I revealed myself to him, he swallowed and shuffled over with his head bowed. "M-Master Wacław… How may I be of service?"

Darkness curled around me as I stopped at the hall's center. Besides him and the woman, who raised her brow at Faarax speaking to an invisible figure, the hideout was empty. It often was at midday. Darixa was usually here, though. Where had she gone?

"Darixa," I said. "I need to see her."

"F-Forgive me, but Lady Kiin—"

I didn't let him finish. Cursing, I turned on my heel and started up the stairs. The creaking of a bowstring pulled taut came from behind, but I gave it no care. A simple arrow wouldn't stop me. Nor would Kiin's trickery.

"Master Wa—"

"Shut up if you want to live," I snapped, raising a hand and grabbing hold of the breath in Faarax's lungs. The winds lived in all of us. They could kill us as quickly as they wished. "You waste enough air that I wonder how anyone else can even breathe."

The bow released a *twang*. With a huff, I let go of Faarax and rolled to the edge of the stairs, dodging the woman's arrow and catching it with the winds just before it struck stone. It had been a good shot considering I was still invisible to her. But the glass-tipped arrow was light. It took little effort to hold and then spin its point back toward its source.

The woman had nocked another arrow, her chin raised as if it were a threat. "Kiin knew you'd turn."

"You think you can stop me?" I laughed. "You've already granted me one arrow. Send another and I'll pierce both your brow and chest. Better to ensure the job's finished. If only I'd bothered to learn your name before you suffocate on your own blood." I'd known it at one time, but recognizing the Daughters would make them more than enemies protecting my target.

"I don't have to stop you," she snapped. "Darixa's safe. You'll never find her before the Lady of Endings returns."

I looked from her to the arrow hovering at my side. "A shame."

A gust tore across the room. The arrow flew with it faster than the woman could move. She released her second missile just as the first struck her between the eyes, and with Faarax's whimper echoing through the hall, I continued up the stairs. A thrill rushed through me. There was no more regret or doubt, no voice that dared to name my victim as her soul's *žityje* faded. I was in control now.

The guards again paid little attention to the gust of wind sweeping through the old tavern. They had likely been warned about my return, but even after interacting with szeptuchy, magic was new to them. It would've been easy to kill them too. Another trio to add to Marzanna's growing pool of blood sacrifices or my own *žityje* reserves. I had no desire to strengthen the winter goddess more than necessary to achieve my ends, though, and there was more *žityje* in my soul than ever before. My recent escapades through the city had ensured that.

So much blood…

Each kill was intoxicating. It sent my heart racing as power coursed through my veins. And that was before I devoured my kill's heart. There was something natural in the melee itself. Victory was sweet no matter the opponent, but I was already growing bored with the random people of Huebia I found alone in the dark alleys. Their cowardice made them weak. I punished them for that, yes, but there was no challenge. Only demons and szeptuchy could grant me that—and gods of course.

Otylia's sorcery had frightened the mortal child I'd once been. It had been strange, wild. Though that same channeling had saved my life against those wolves, it was another thing entirely in the hands of the girl who despised me most.

Now, just when I'd finally gained an understanding of Otylia's power, her Ascension had given her insight into forces I could barely comprehend. She could *see* people's ends. Had she seen hers? Mine? Ours? Was that why she'd forced me away: fear of what she'd seen? I shook my head. No, Otylia had hated me for years, and my new strength was just an excuse to be rid of me now that I wasn't useful to her. Like Swaróg and Perun before her, she saw Nawie as menaces to be manipulated and then cast away to Oblivion. Tools. That's all we were to the gods—demons and mortals both.

Where did you hide her, Kiin?

I launched myself to the top of the nearest building, dropping swiftly onto the thick layer of snow and ice that covered its roof. Many had collapsed in on homes due to the unusual weight. Not all buildings were made of thick Mothermarked-crafted stone, and all the ruined buildings were in the poorer districts.

Mokosz claimed to protect all women. Why, then, did she allow her scions and szeptuchy to aid only the most well-connected in the city, abandoning the women who needed her aid the most? Many of them were demons now. The Daughters didn't seem to care.

Streams of black flowed through the snow at my feet. A reminder of my origin and true goal. Not just revenge on Otylia, but to rule the lands north of Perun's Crown. To prove I could be a greater chief than Father had ever been. For that, the Krowikie needed to survive. They'd be desperate upon my return and would see my power for what it was. None would dare defy me. Not after I'd slain one goddess and taken Grudzień from another. I'd need to kill Marzanna to truly secure my reign, but for now, using her to secure the Moonstone was enough.

Kiin had said there were three other hideouts the Daughters of the Earth had scattered throughout the city. They were obvious places to hide the young scion, but she'd refused to give me their locations. Where could they be?

I sat upon the building's edge, allowing my legs to hang into the narrow alley below.

This particular intersection rested on the highest ground in Huebia. The entire city sloped toward the river in the northeast, and from the opposite corner, I could see everything not blocked by the Glasstone Tower. My eyes, though, wouldn't be enough. Otylia could return at any time. I needed Darixa as my hostage—my bait—before then.

The winds darted through each street and crevice in search of clues. They carried people's whispers to my ears, but despite many mentioning the Daughters, none spoke of Darixa. More common were tales of the "Shadow Terror" who struck where the sun dared not touch. I smirked. Those stories had alerted the Daughters to my emergence, but they would've discovered it eventually. It had been inevitable once Kiin threw me in that cell.

A growl escaped my throat at the thought of my imprisonment. Yet another of Otylia's betrayals in quick succession. It had been torture, and now that I was free, I intended to ensure I was never trapped again.

My patience ran out.

In the time since my escape, they couldn't have taken Darixa far with the Frostmarked patrolling the streets. She was here. Faarax hadn't known where, but one of the Daughters would. With my ruse exposed, there was no more pretending I was still on their side. I could kill each of them until someone squawked.

The winds heard whispers between two Daughters near the northeast wall. They separated, and I took to the air, scanning the alleys until I found the man walking toward a particularly crowded cluster of buildings. Every few seconds, he glanced over his shoulder or tugged on his hood. If I hadn't found him, the guards would've soon enough.

He soon ducked into what appeared to be a typical house. A simple cloth covered its opening, but when I followed him, invisible, he pulled aside a chest to reveal a trap door like that in Kiin's hideout. Giving a once-over of the room, he climbed into it and disappeared. I waited. My instincts pushed me on, but it was better to catch them off-guard to reserve my *żityje* for the more important fights to come. I had more than ever. Otylia, though, was a goddess. To fulfill my side of Marzanna's deal, I would need every bit my soul could hold.

But the hunger…

That's long enough, I thought, jumping down the hatch and landing in a narrow hall with a kick of dust. The fall would've broken a mortal man's legs. Just a bit of wind had slowed me, and I kept a hold of them as I drew the Thunderstone dagger.

Conversation and laughter came from the torchlight room ahead. I approached, my confidence swelling with the darkness surrounding me. Yes, I'd find the scion girl.

Six people filled the chamber. Far smaller than the sleeping hall of Kiin's hideout, it connected to other rooms like it, where others continued to speak. The winds would be limited in the tight quarters. Fear, though, would aid me.

"Something's happening," the man who I'd followed said. "The guards have stopped the kidnappings."

A woman yelped, her palms held together before her lips. "That's a good thing, right? Maybe the Winter Witch is finished with us."

I dropped my invisibility and snarled, "I promise you she's not."

They screamed as the darkness swirled through the chamber, my blade following close behind. Two fell quickly, and the three others reached for their own daggers. I let them. Their trembling hands revealed enough.

"Where's the scion?" I snarled, sending the winds around me with the darkness. The Daughters huddled in the corner and watched it close in. "Where's Darixa?"

"I… I don't know," the woman stuttered.

The others repeated the same as people rushed from the other rooms bearing short, curved blades. Surrounding me, they remained silent until a shawled woman entered. Her face and neck coverings concealed her Mothermark, but I sensed her power.

"Mokosz is supposed to protect her people," I said, focusing on the szeptucha. "Tell me where Darixa is and I'll spare the others."

"You'll sacrifice her," she replied, the walls cracking as she flexed her fingers. There was a carnal rage in her gaze. *We're all capable of killing.*

"Not unless I have to."

"You're a demon. Killing isn't a choice. It's embedded in your soul as the earth is bound to ours."

"Then you've chosen." I spun and sent the dagger through the nearest Daughter's throat, calling it back into my grasp as the ground rose around my ankles. I leaped free before the rocks could grab hold.

The szeptucha launched shards from every surface, but a whirlwind burst from me. Holding us off the ground, it formed a barrier that deflected her attacks. Rock and glass cracked against the walls and ceiling as she tried to break through. When one of her allies cried out—a shard piercing her skull—the szeptucha stopped.

"I don't even need to kill your people," I said with a laugh. Her air was running out within the whirlwind, and her confident aura faded with it. "You're doing a fine job of that yourself."

She shuddered, releasing her power. I couldn't sense *żityje* usage as well as Otylia, but it was like a taut rope had loosened. My hunger grew at her vulnerability. Szeptuchy held elements of both their own *žityje* and their god's. So much to feast upon…

"You're a monster," she hissed. "Kiin should've never let a demon near a scion."

I raised my dagger to her neck. "Where is she?"

"For the sake of my sisters-in-arms, I will tell you, but you must release me. My breaths… They are difficult."

"Clear the room!" I ordered the others. They didn't wait for the szeptucha's permission, and when we were alone, I dropped the whirlwind.

The szeptucha struck the ground hard for someone literally in command of it. Then again, I'd barely had the chance to grasp their power before my imprisonment. Perhaps falling upon stone would hurt no matter how they shaped it?

"The Hidden Waters," she croaked. "Only a chosen can open the passage."

"Show me," I demanded, "and I'll let you live."

When she conceded, I pressed the dagger's tip against her back and pushed her on. She led me through a winding chain of halls and waved down anyone who dared to consider fighting. They knew what I was capable of. One life wasn't worth their entire rebellion, but I didn't care about the Daughters anyway. To take my birthright, I'd promised Marzanna I'd kill Otylia. When that was finished, I would take Grudzień north, and the Daughters could have Vastroth if they wanted. My job would be finished.

We eventually stopped before a wall covered by a tapestry. Once, I would've examined it and wondered of its meaning, but now, I tore it down. "There's nothing here!"

"The only way through is by moving the wall," the szeptucha replied.

"Then do it." I grabbed her arm and threw her into the wall.

Whispering in the old tongue, she raised her hand to the place where the tapestry had once been. The wall shifted like it had when Kiin had trapped me. This time, though, it revealed a crudely carved tunnel into a cavern. Perfect.

"Go," she szeptucha muttered, "but know that I'll close the—"

My dagger met her heart before she could finish. Better to tie up loose ends and end another threat before I faced Otylia. A single szeptucha was merely a pest now, but in numbers, they would outmatch me, especially in their homeland. I wasn't as powerful as a god. Not yet…

48

Otylia

Please tell me he didn't escape...

SWEAT BEADED ON MY BROW as I strained to keep my allies aloft after two nights of flying. I'd thought carrying myself across Nawia had been hard enough, but even with more *żityje* offerings to fill my soul, this tested my moon powers more than ever. What lay ahead would be worse.

We'd freed Sheresy from the Frostmarked. It was a secondary city, though, far from the core of Vastroth. Ildes and most of her faction's Daughters—except Ta—had remained to ensure order. She'd described it as preparing for the scions' returns, but how could she hope for that? Marzanna and Czarnobóg had manipulated the previous scions to sacrifice thousands of children in Huebia, turning them into demons to be wielded. I feared what I'd see when I entered the cave from my vision of Kiin. To mend what Marzanna had broken, I had to. Darkness had consumed Vastroth. If I could save it, maybe I could save Wacław too.

Despite the szeptuchy staying, Ta's parents and over fifty other rusałki and utopiecs had agreed to join us. A small army. Their weight, along with others such as Amten and those I'd brought from Nawia, was immense. I still couldn't believe my plan to free them of their demonic corruption had worked. Some of them had reported still feeling pangs of hunger for *żityje*, but their minds were theirs again. We could work with that.

"We can rest if you need to," Sabina said at my side. Her wings' fluttering broke the endless sound of the winds, and I welcomed her reassuring yet worried smile.

I shook my head. "There's no time. Each day Wacław spends controlled by the demon is another where he slips away. I'd felt a part of *him* before. It's just that godsforsaken płanetnik now."

"You freed the rusałki. I'm sure you can free him too!"

Ever the optimist.

I looked from the waning moon to the rolling dunes below. Ever-changing yet remarkably consistent in appearance, the landscape would've left me directionless without the Behmir River in the east. Nothing but a sea of sand. Gods, I missed Dziewanna's wilds.

"I'll do what I have to," I replied. She cocked her head, but I interrupted her before she could speak. "Don't remind me what that could mean."

"Of… Of course."

As if sensing I didn't want to talk, Vlatka swooped from above, drifting beside me. "Worried about the boy? I know I was at your age."

I gritted my teeth. "Not now."

"Avoiding the topic won't change that corrupted Nawie are different than undead demons," she said. "There's dark magic at play, and this won't be as easy as—"

"I know!"

Conversations quieted around us, all the demons turning to look at me as my blood boiled. Something deep within me reveled in the anger. It hadn't been a goddess's response, but I didn't need everyone telling me how hard it would be to fix Wacław after I'd broken him. This was *my* problem. This had been *my* error. And *I* would fix it. All they needed to do was help me retake the Glasstone Tower and the emotion-bending Moonstone within.

I sighed and shut my eyes. "You needn't tell me how hard this will be. I know. Just thinking about the state he's in is enough to make me want to turn back."

"You blame yourself," Vlatka said. "That is not unfair, considering you took his soul, but you said he willingly gave it, no?"

"He did."

"Because he loves you. When you were trapped in Nawia, he gave everything to break nature's laws and help you escape, even surrendering his mortal soul." She stretched a wing around my head in what I assumed was her eagle version of a hug. "The demon in him is his own, though. It is a battle that he would've fought regardless of your actions, but you are returning to aid *him* now. Love requires both of you to pick up the other when they're weak."

I swallowed, a panging striking my chest. "I barely understand my power. How can I save him when I don't know what to do next without my goddesses? So many people are looking to me for what's right, but Ascending didn't give me any answers."

"Does it feel right to fight for him, to not give up until he's gone completely?"

"Yes," I replied without thought.

Vlatka chuckled. "Then why are you worried about whom to follow? It seems your heart is plenty a guide."

"And you understand more about your magic than I do about mine," Sabina replied with a smile. "You connected with the demons. It was amazing!"

"You can see the Threads of Life?" I asked.

She nodded. "Nymphs just sense spirits and souls, but I saw them through your power. Something changed when you sent your *žityje* into them." Holding her hand over her heart, she giggled. "I think you purified their souls."

"No, I just showed them that they could be free."

"Isn't that a strong enough reason to trust yourself? So many of them came with us because of you, and I doubt Ta-naro would've come if you hadn't followed through on your promise to her."

I wrinkled my nose. "You think too highly of me."

Suddenly, Vlatka's wing went from comforting to tense. She batted the back of my head and took flight, positioning herself before me. "If you refuse to trust us because we're your friends, then trust me because your mother did. You are *good* Otylia. These struggles in your head wouldn't be there if you weren't. Yes, Dziewanna and Mokosz are no longer telling you exactly what to do, but they instilled their values in your soul. Follow them. Listen to them. And in the end, if you choose to see the Three Realms differently, then do so. They may be goddesses, but they are nothing more than the product of thousands of years of experience. Weles and Jaryło have lived many lifetimes themselves. They found different values. So, too, will you—that's okay."

"You make it sound easy."

She swept to my side and sighed. "Nothing is easy in these realms. I imagine even the gods struggle, and you are a confirmation of that suspicion. Rod didn't grant you omniscience during your Ascension, did he?"

What had the eldest god granted me? A bond with End's power—and through it the moon—but there was far more to it. I saw what would come and what had finished before, feeling the pain and glory of others in those moments. To the demons, I had become a hope of redemption, of mending. I wielded both creatures of decay and the moon's light in the night sky. Most of all, though, I'd become something far greater than myself through my Ascension: a protector. Of life. Of nature. Of the balance between change and stability, light and dark. Did that mean foreseeing death and pain and allowing it to happen because it was Destiny's will, or was I the one tasked with changing it for the better?

"He gave me power I couldn't understand," I said. "Then he sent me into the next war between the gods with only a warning to be mindful of the destruction I'm capable of if I alter the future. Maybe Serapis was right. We're not gods."

Vlatka looked back at me. "If gods can't learn from their mistakes over the eras, then how can mortals expect to? I find comfort knowing that even the gods don't know everything. It means we can still grow to become better than those before us."

I smirked. "A witch would be happy the gods aren't perfect."

"Witches pursue nature's truth. Unlike szeptuchy, we just don't believe it begins and ends with a single being, no matter how powerful they are."

Sabina cocked her head. "Wait, are you making fun of me?" She rubbed my Moonmark on her neck. *That's going to take far too long to get used to.*

"Of course not!" Vlatka explained, laughing and rolling with her wings tucked in. "Szeptuchy are needed to serve the gods, but we witches aren't the deviants the Krowikie and other tribes believe us to be. We channel magic from ourselves and nature, just as szeptuchy can do with elements related to their deity—Otylia saw this with plants."

"Demons can do the same," I said.

Vlatka stopped her roll. "Demons? They aren't capable of draining plants or other forces."

"Wacław can drain trees at least."

"Hmm." She hesitated, rare for how quickly she usually talked. "Then we have more in common with Nawie than I thought. Sorcerers, witches, corrupted, and channelers alike can draw life—the methods and limits are different, but the ends are the same. *Žityje.* Only gods cannot drain it from an unwilling source."

Sabina winced. "What about Marzanna's sacrifices?"

Vlatka landed upon the nymph's shoulder, narrowly avoiding being buffeted by her wings. "Her szeptuchy *willingly* gave the blood by killing their prisoners. Slight distinction but important. Marzanna couldn't drain their life force herself."

"What if she were Naw?" I asked.

"You surprise me again." Vlatka eyed me curiously. "Do you really think her transformation from a nature goddess was the same as corruption?"

"Corrupted Nawie and demons are created by people living and dying unnaturally. Since rusałki often come from men betraying their wives, why would Marzanna's change be any different?" I pictured Czarnobóg standing behind her. Was he controlling her, or was there something more? There was so much we didn't know.

Vlatka didn't offer a reply. Fighting Marzanna was frightening enough already, but if she was both goddess and Naw, none of us could comprehend what she was capable of. Even Jaryło, and I really didn't want to talk to him.

Deal with him later.

My hand ached at the thought of our blood pact. There would be a cost. I'd known that in the Frostmarked dungeon, but it was hard to know what I feared more: wedding that bastard or the repercussions of breaking the pact. Gods, I'd indebted myself to Death during his Trial and now had done the same with Jaryło. How much of myself could I give before I broke? Vlatka and Sabina claimed I was strong, but it sure as Oblivion didn't feel like I was.

Those doubts echoed in my mind as Kiin called for me to bring her closer. I did with the moon's power. An odd thing, it allowed me to pull people in a direction as if we were flying, unlike the push the winds gave Wacław. Rod hadn't explained why the moon had a pull, and I wondered if I'd ever know.

"We're close," Kiin said. "They'll spot us up here if we go much further."

Huebia's wall encircled the city before us, the Glasstone Tower like the center of a storm. And a storm we found. Dark clouds released a torrent of hail ahead, but while the rest of the group panicked, I laughed. "Marzanna's blizzard will cover our advance. She's given a gift on accident."

Kiin sucked in a breath. "She hasn't."

"What do you—"

A chorus of shrieks pierced the air. Dread clutched me as lightning flashed through the clouds, unlike any blizzard I'd ever seen. My senses detected a swarm of demonic *żityje* in its midst, and I brought us to a stop, calling my silver spear.

Vlatka circled above with her eyes on the storm. "Send the others to the ground," she said. "The sky is a chała's realm, not a rusałka's."

"No," Kiin replied. "Send us to the river. The underground tunnels connect to it through a route I can open, and the demons will be safer in a familiar element. You just need to keep the chały from chasing us."

I nodded. "Do it. I'll meet you at the hideout once I'm finished with them."

"Once *we're* finished with them," Vlatka said, landing on my shoulder again. "You may be a goddess, but my witchcraft can still aid you."

"Me too," Sabina said. "I'm not much of a swimmer anyway."

I wanted to object, but lightning cracked closer. In moments, clouds had consumed the sky, blocking out the moon and leaving us with only my own light to see. Chały were dangerous—that much I knew—so I pushed against my instincts and nodded. Becoming a goddess meant trusting my allies. Maybe I could face the chały alone, but it would be better with them at my side. Why did that hurt to admit?

I lowered the rest of the group toward the river as quickly as was safe. Balancing the moon's pull with their weight strained me further, but keeping them alive was worth the *żityje*. Even beyond Huebia's walls, I felt Grudzień igniting my fear. We needed to take it if there was any hope of freeing these lands from Marzanna, as it would be the Vastrothie attacking the tower while I dealt with Wacław.

"Vlatka, get ready," I said, gripping my spear and watching for a lightning bolt to streak toward us. "I'm going to strike the first that comes, and I need you to cover my back."

Sabina held out her hands. Moonlight pulsed at her fingertips, and I felt the trickle of *żityje* that she pulled from me grow stronger. Though she would draw from her own soul too—or whatever the equivalent was for a nymph—I would need to ensure she balanced her channeling. A szeptucha wasn't much use if she drained me first.

"I trust you, Sabina," I said. "The moon's power will be the most useful in the sky. I doubt End's wisps will do much."

She narrowed her eyes and watched the colored wisps of the freed demons and blackened ones of Marzanna's corrupted ones. "They're faint for me anyway. I wonder if their motions mean anything, though. Like, can they show us what is the next ending?"

"I'm not sure what you're asking."

"I'm not either. There's just a feeling I have…"

A *snap* tore my attention back to the storm. I barely had time to strike before the lighting chała burst into form, slicing at me. My armband burned. When its… *her*… claws struck my skin, it pulsed and released a short blast that repelled the demon away—right into the tip of my spear.

Well, used up that defense already.

The chała's shrieking ceased the moment my spear punctured her sternum. Silver shredded her being, and she dropped as I pulled the spear free. One down. But how many were there?

Wisps usually offered some insight into enemy numbers. Now, though, they shot around with such speed that they were impossible to track. The Threads of Life were no more helpful, blinding me as the chały shot forward on their lightning. As they did, Sabina's voice hung in my mind.

The wisps *were* trying to tell me something.

One had streaked closer with the first's attack. They were too quick to count, but could they show me when one was about to strike? Each was a female, a person corrupted. I held that in my mind as I took a long breath, closing my eyes and allowing only my power's senses to guide me. Something between sight and imagination found me there. It showed the wisps as shadowy figures, as they often appeared when they wished to show me a future. What if I asked them to show me the immediate ending—like the end of their next movement—as Sabina had asked?

The wisps shifted as I opened my eyes and released the silent command. One burst into a dark form to my left instantly. I trusted it, calling for Vlatka to attack as I released a moonblast with my free hand.

My blast and flames that billowed from Vlatka's eagle mouth met the winged chała. She had swept from above just as the wisp had shown, almost invisible in the darkness, but now her shrieks turned to terror as her decaying skin burned further. The moonblast amplified Vlatka's magic, sending it forth in a wave that consumed the chała and sent her reeling into the distance. If she didn't die, she would at least suffer for a long time before fighting again. I had no idea how to mend these demons' corruption. Until I did, this would have to do.

Sabina yelped behind me, and I spun to see a dark chała raking her claws over the nymph's face.

"Don't touch her!" I spat, striking at the demon, only to have her wings deflect my spear.

Call a light weapon, I told Sabina through my mark as I intercepted another dark chała. They wanted to isolate us. I couldn't let that happen. *Svĕt is the old tongue word for light. My power is yours, so it'll answer.*

My own spear exploded with light as the chała who'd stopped me swung a weapon with three spiked balls attached to the handle by a metal chain. Those ends wrapped around the spear's shaft, tearing it from my hand. I cursed and opened my vision to the Threads of Life.

This chała had few connections, but one Thread was close. I grabbed hold of it, letting her memories wash over me. Anger, pain, and a deep hunger filled her. Far greater than that of the rusałki and utopiecs at Sheresy, it engulfed her soul to the point that if she had ever been human, she didn't remember it. What did that mean?

There was no time to figure that out now. Her memories had proven she was corrupted beyond redemption, and severing her soul wouldn't make that worse. So I plunged my *žityje* into the Thread until she screamed like Serapis had. The thread dissolved to ash in my hand, and I moved away as the chała warped even more, her wings contorting to impossible angles and her body oozing puss and black blood.

Is she the dark one, or am I?

I turned back to Sabina before that dread could pull me down again. There was no time for doubts in combat. In that, Narcyz had been right. The boy was a brute, but his rants in the Mangled Woods about fighting had taught me at least that much.

Vlatka launched a blast of *žityje* at another chała behind me as I called my spear once again and charged. Sabina had been repeating *"Svĕt"* with her voice cracking more each time. It hadn't worked. Blood poured from her wounds, and the chała released a gleeful screech before trying to bite her exposed neck. I was too far to strike with my spear.

So I screamed.

Light shot from my extended hand in a beam. *Žityje* surged from me, draining far more than I'd wanted, but I didn't care as it cut through the hailstorm and shredded the chała's core until only its disconnected limbs remained. Sabina *had* to survive. She was my szeptucha. More than that, though, she was my friend, and I refused to let her die for me.

When my light beam faded, I caught Sabina in my arms. Her wings were sliced and useless, her body covered in both her blood and the chała's. I hated her for throwing herself into combat before she'd gained experience with channeling. Her nymph nature magic was weak in the desert, and she'd only been a szeptucha for a few days. But I'd let her stay. Why did needing her help have to put her at risk?

"I don't know why it didn't work," I said. "I'm sorry."

She had the gall to smile back, but her voice was little more than a squeak. "Don't worry. I'll be okay, I think. It's my job to fight with you."

"But your wings…"

Vlatka released a round of flames above us, sending another chała shrieking and swooping to prepare another strike. "Wounds can heal, Otylia! The chały are chasing the others to the river."

"I can lower myself with my channeling," Sabina whispered. "Release me and cover the others. My wings may mend, and if they don't, your mark can still allow me to fly. That is the only gift I need."

More shrieks followed, and Vlatka groaned as I sensed her magic draining her *žityje*. Yet another ally I'd pushed to her limit. "Hurry!" she shouted.

I relented and summoned my spear again. Its light flashed through the storm as hail pelted my skin, the winds whipping through my moon dress and autumn cloak. Fury ignited and distant future at once. I feared what that would mean once the battle was over, but all that mattered now was protecting my allies below.

Kiin, Ta, Amten, and Kuba had nearly led the others to the city by the time the remaining chały reached them. Luckily, the river provided protection for our water demons, and the two szeptuchy crafted defensive fortifications along the banks. But the chały channeled lightning. Though two utopiecs dealt significant damage to the attackers, their strength wasn't enough. I arrived just as they sank to the river's bed.

The remaining utopiecs and rusałki swarmed the chały, pulling them into the waters as I struck another. We fell into the cracked stone on the shore. It scraped at my already bruised body, but more pain couldn't slow me. By the time the chała could shoot a bolt into my chest, I'd already sent my spear through her throat.

Despite my victory, the bolt sent me to my knees. Its lightning paralyzed me for a few excruciating moments. Even *żityje* couldn't heal it fast enough, and I watched helplessly as the final chała plunged a blade of lightning through another rusałka. Then came a flash of fur.

"Kuba, no!" I shouted, sending a moonblast over the river.

It was too late. Kuba's jackal jaws closed around the chała's arm before she released a bolt lightning directly into him. When my moonblast arrived, it only knocked him further away, along with the other demons nearby. Only the chała was unaffected. She'd created a lightning shield somehow, and she grinned with her arms crossed before her.

Then she exploded.

I raised my hands and shouted, "*Prl!*" as the electrical blast struck.

A glowing shield of light hovered before me, deflecting its force from those nearby, but most had been on the chała's other side. The shield drew more precious *żityje* from my soul. I still had more than I'd ever wielded as a szeptucha, but I'd used a significant portion since we'd left Sheresy. That just fueled my anger.

something within me. I became the light, moving with the speed of End's wisps as I foresaw the chały's attacks in their shadowed forms.

Sabina had claimed I'd granted her a gift, but in this, she'd given me something far more powerful. End's wisps showed me the near

Once the blast passed, I dropped the shield and repeated the motion that had called the beam before, adding what seemed like the right old tongue word. "*Stridzi!*" Slice.

The beam didn't come. Instead, a sweeping pulse of light burst from my hand, its arc expanding until it struck the chała and cut straight through her torso. She dropped in two pieces, and just like that, it was over.

I heaved with each breath. Hands on my knees, I didn't want to look up and see the destruction her explosion had caused. My defense had cost me nothing more than *żityje*, but my allies lacked that reserve. Even if they'd had a goddess's life force, they couldn't use it to heal like I could. Hiding wouldn't change the truth, though. So I whispered a prayer to Mokosz and looked.

Bodies floated on the river's surface and lay scattered over the bank. At least fifteen utopiecs and rusałki had been killed in the battle—nearly a third of those we'd brought. Amten's arms bled, but his scorpion carapace had held strong over his chest, as had mine. He gave me a slow nod of respect before looking further downstream.

Kuba hobbled through the shallows in his jackal form, bleeding but very much alive as he licked the faces of the wounded and those who needed their spirits raised. How? Despite dying once and nearly doing so again, Kuba still put the joy of others before caring for himself. I mustered a smile. By bringing him back to Jawia, at least I'd done something right.

Then came the cry—Ta's cry.

I bolted into the river, pulling myself through its current with the moon's power. Ta was just a child. From the look in her eyes when she'd agreed to come, I knew she was here because of me. Her weeping continued as I ran, the darkness too much to see what had happened beyond a few strides. *If she's crying, she's alive,* I told myself. *Please, don't let her lose her parents again.*

My light soon illuminated her trudging to the riverbank with a body in tow. A woman's frame. At first, I sighed in relief at seeing her alive, but the corpse wasn't her mothers. It lacked the long hair and blackened skin, instead having curled hair that ended at the collar of a long coat.

"No!" I screamed, rushing to Ta and helping her lift the body onto shore. Some part of me still hoped it wasn't Kiin. It couldn't be. The szeptucha was invincible after all she'd been through.

Kiin's head turned toward me as we set her down, and I froze at the sight of her charred face. The explosion had struck her with her eyes open. Though lifeless, fear still filled them, replacing their usually dominating presence. That stabbed at my heart. We'd been so close to returning and saving the children who'd been sacrificed, so close to saving her son, Yesike. Why had Destiny chosen her to die now? Or had this been my failure? I'd altered the undead and seen the future. Had I doomed more to suffer in return?

"I'm sorry," I sobbed, clutching Kiin's body. "I was too slow…"

Ta fell back. Blood covered the top half of her coat, the rest washed away by the river. For the first time, I saw her tremble as she clawed at the mix of snow and sand beneath her. "What were those ice brains?" she babbled almost too quickly to understand. "How did that one do that?"

"Chały," I forced myself to reply. Failure dragged down my heart, but we weren't safe yet. These people needed me. "They're female storm demons. I've never seen one explode before…"

Ta wiped away tears. "Tried to pull Kiin out of the way, but nah, she had to 'protect' me. What's that supposed to mean? I can fight!" She touched her bandaged head, wincing. "She wouldn't have died if she'd just let me take it!"

I laid Kiin's body into the snow. Grudzień pushed on me, and I gritted my teeth just to think. Fear told me to run, to leave Vastroth's problems and find Dziewanna myself. I couldn't. Fleeing into the woods worked when I was alone, but I wasn't anymore.

"She considered the Daughters her responsibility," I whispered, touching the szeptucha's cheek. Kiin's ending was already different than the vision I'd foreseen during the battle to come. As my skin touched hers, more of her lost life overtook me. I slipped into them, watching the woman I'd failed to save with a single thought in my mind.

They're my responsibility now.

49

Ara

The Horde is close.

SMOKE ROSE IN THE EAST. Though barely visible at first through the constant snowfall, it now blanketed the sky in a haze. I tried not to look back, but most in our caravan lacked my willpower. The Astiwie among us stopped often to stare at their burning lands.

Alongside me, Zakir seemed unfazed. He refused to worry, as he believed the Horde's victory over the Astiwie to be inevitable. Sure, Xobas and the other commanders were convinced Astiw lacked the manpower and organization to hold the line, but *accepting* that it would happen and *not caring* were two entirely different things. My heart ached remembering every village we'd passed. So few had heeded our warning and joined us.

"We saved the ones smart enough to flee," Zakir said, noticing me glancing over my shoulder. "We cannot mourn a decision that was not ours."

"I can," I replied sharply. "Hundreds of Astiwie are with us now, so they're your people too. Otlezd knows Zhaleh won't protect them."

His gaze remained fixed on the next hill. "They will need to appoint one of their own. The lands ahead are familiar to none of us."

I shook my head but didn't object. We'd had enough disagreements over the last few days already. When we'd reached the Wyzra, we'd crossed west into Krowikie lands, following Wacław's instructions to Eryk. Wacław had either told the płanetnik little about why we were heading directly for Dwie Rzeki or they were hiding something. Fleeing to the southern hills—that belonged to the clans' as part of the treaty with Krowik—seemed the better option to avoid conflict. Xobas and Zakir, though, were convinced Wacław had a legitimate plan.

At least this leg of the journey has been quiet, I thought as I leaned back into Sosna for her warmth. The red fox yawned and snuggled closer, as I'd hoped.

Our clans weren't used to the winter, and many had grown weary from cold and sorrow. Thousands had died already. This snow made the path ahead feel little better than the destruction we left behind. Somehow, we needed to give them hope.

"A hunt," I whispered to myself before grabbing Zakir's arm excitedly. "That's it! There are woods ahead, and there's bound to be *something* to catch in them." We'd survived on grains and breads from the Astiwie and yogurt and cheese from the clan animals for now, but meat was scarce.

Zakir furrowed his brow. "You were worried about the fires. Now you would like to delay?"

"Give us two days. Eryk can update us on the Horde's progress while we're gone, and I promise you, people will be excited when we succeed."

"You are confident?"

I moved my hand to his, intertwining our fingers. Being so close to both him and his horse had the added bonus of providing heat. My own mount's bay coat now appeared completely white, and with so few blankets to warm even us, we had nothing to keep the thin-coated steppe mounts from freezing. The Simukie especially struggled watching their few remaining sacred horses slowly die with little grasses to graze upon and no place to sleep warmly.

"You did not reply," he said.

I smiled to myself, pushing away the hairs the wind had pushed over my face. "Not all replies are words, my dear."

"So, you are confident? Holding my hand is 'yes'?

"This time, yes."

His gaze went to a distant place before returning. "I'm sorry. It is difficult to understand people when they follow no patterns."

"Everyone has patterns." I squeezed his hand and raised it to my lips, planting a kiss. "Even me. Watch them, and you'll start to figure us out."

"I suppose Bidaês had a routine too. I studied it as a child, but I never understood why he left the tent at night. Then he betrayed us…" He picked at a stray thread on his deerskin cloak. Unlike the other commanders, he'd chosen not to take one of the few sets of fur we had because it was too itchy for him. Ironic, as I'd always considered wool the more irritating material. "I will watch more in order to understand. Would you like me to join the hunt for this purpose?"

"Stay. You need the time to work on your elixir for Wacław. Just watch people while we're gone and tell me what you noticed when I return. Maybe you'll learn something new."

My breaths slowed as I nocked an arrow and pulled on my bowstring. The cold permeated every part of me after sleeping without a tent, but this motion required no thought. When my fingers met the bow, we became one. All I saw was my prey.

Stay still, I willed the deer. A doe and her fawn grazed on a rare batch of foliage that wasn't covered shin-deep in snow. They were the first sizeable animals we'd seen any evidence of.

"Ready?" I asked the hunter beside me. A built, tall Zurgow, he'd proven himself a skilled shot with a duck kill early that morning. These deer would be far more substantial, and I could only hope the other groups nearby would find more.

He nodded slowly, his own bow ready.

We shot together, and exhilaration filled me watching my arrow fly through the air. I sucked in a sharp breath. *Go down easy, please.*

The iron tip punctured the doe's lungs, spurring her and her foe into a run, but she didn't get far. My second arrow pierced the neck. In seconds, she collapsed, choking. I slung my bow over my shoulder and pulled my knife, rushing to end her suffering, but a movement out of the corner of my eye stopped me in my tracks—a mass of brown fur and snarling teeth.

"Bear!" I called as it lunged at the hunter.

He turned too late. Before he could even draw his own knife, the bear's claws struck his throat, dropping him into the snow. Then the beast looked to me.

Its eyes burned blue.

"Everyone back to the camp!" I shouted to the other hunters nearby, but there was no time to check who'd heard.

The bear charged. It was far quicker than any I'd seen, and its claws raked across my thigh as I ducked into a roll. When I rose, I pulled my bow and reached for an arrow. One shot to the eye. That was all it would take to pierce the brain. But my leg crumpled as I pulled back the bowstring. The arrow slipped to the ground between us, useless.

Run!

My feet slipped as I tried to dash through the trees. Pain ran down my leg and fear paralyzed me. The bear was strides away. I had to fight, but all I had was a hunting knife for melee combat. I gripped its hilt and faced the beast. Marzanna's beast.

"Otylia save me…"

The bear's next swipe missed as I ducked onto my strong leg. On all fours, its chest was at head height, and I plunged my dagger deep into its ribs. Not deep enough.

Its teeth ripped through my archery bracer. I tried to pull away, but the bear threw me into an oak's trunk. Darkness nipped at the edges of my vision. Stinging, burning pain sliced across my wounded arm and leg. I'd been too slow. Father said a hunter always considered that another predator could be stalking the prey. Except this bear hadn't cared about simple deer.

I'd been the prey all along.

I struggled against the bear's weight, but it was no use as it lunged for my neck. For the kill. But before its teeth pierced skin, a great wind threw us to the ground.

The bear faltered back as clouds rolled overhead, and a graying man emerged from them in deep ashen robes and a staff that cracked with lightning. Eryk dove on his gales. Static followed, his lightning bolts snapping through the sky and making my hair stand on end. Though the bear turned to face his demonic attacker, he stood no chance. Three bolts wobbled him. The last sent him sprawling into a lump of brown fur and snow.

I drew an arrow from my quiver and met the bear's gaze. Its blue eyes seemed to flicker. Maybe it was just a foolish hope, but in that moment, I saw the life within it. Marzanna had claimed this beast that Krowik admired and Astiw feared, but it had not chosen. Death was a mercy.

I drove the arrow through its eye and into its brain, ending its suffering. It deserved to be free of Marzanna's wrath. We all did, but some of us passed from this land and into Otlezd's light sooner than others. I didn't know if I actually believed that anymore, but in truth, it didn't matter. Marzanna and her Horde's threat remained the same. Otlezd hadn't arrived to stop them.

With some effort, I yanked my arrow from the bear as Eryk descended before me, his robe torn to slits at its bottom. The winds sent those strands swarming around him like flies in the summer heat.

"How'd you know to find me?" I asked.

The płanetnik's face was normally pale, but he looked ghastly now, almost translucent. "Something is wrong with Master Wacław." He raised a hand to Wacław's Eclipsemark on his cheek. "A part of his energy is in this mark, and I've felt his thoughts change, as mine had under Marzanna's influence. A strange feeling came over me. He knows we're here, and now, so does Marzanna."

Before I could reply, a horse and rider approached at a canter. Xobas sighed with relief as he dismounted alongside us. "You have no idea how happy I am to see you alive. Eryk warned me about the bear, but he was faster with the winds it seems." He patted Eryk on the shoulder. "Thank you. I know you've struggled to retain *žityje* without people to drain."

"Good thing he came," I muttered, dropping at the base of a tree and gripping my leg. It was stiff but would be fine with some rest. "More importantly, though, he thinks Wacław had something to do with the attack."

Eryk nodded slowly. He held his hands behind his back, stiff. "Marzanna has attacked many before, but this was specific to you. Revenge, maybe? I don't understand why Master Wacław would help her, but she could only track us if there were Frostmarked among us."

A chill ran down my spine, and I held my legs close to my chest. "So Wacław is different now, aggressive. What if the demon took over and allied with Marzanna? He still bears her Frostmark, even if it's been dormant. Maybe he tracked your mark for her…"

"That isn't the boy I know," Xobas said. He reached into a pack strapped over his horse's side, grabbing a roll of ratty cloth before kneeling alongside me. As he talked, he wrapped my wounds. "Demons aren't my specialty, but if it changed him, he needs us. Someone needs to remind him who he is."

"Narcyz could be in danger too." I surveyed the woods around us. Even without leaves, the trees gave enough cover from the snowfall for me to see the other hunters waiting nearby. "Wacław's plan feels wrong the more I think about it. Heading to Dwie Rzeki is only going to anger Mieczysław, and now Marzanna lays a trap for us? It doesn't make sense." I forced myself to my feet, earning a scowl from Xobas as he tried to finish wrapping my leg. "If Wacław's turned, then Otylia will need us too. All of us. Eryk, I know your power is weaker, but Zakir has a potion he thinks can help tame a demon's hunger. Could that be enough for you to fly us to Dwie Rzeki and then to Huebia?"

"It should," Eryk replied. "That journey is lengthy, however, so I won't be of much use when we arrive."

Xobas paced before pausing with a hand on his horse's neck. "I know Wacław better than most. That boy is all heart. If the demon pushed hard enough on the pain of his past, especially now that he knows what Jacek did at his birth, he could've broken."

I winced. "That's harsh."

"No, it's the truth. Wacław is strong of heart and of will, but you and I have both seen demons. Their hunger must be immense to become such monstrous things. They feed on emotions, and we both know he has a lot of those." His shoulders dropped. "I wish I could be there to guide him, but what could I say to change it? The forces he fights are beyond my understanding. While I could teach him to hold a spear, this lesson, I fear, he must learn himself."

I hobbled toward him, and Xobas broke from his sorrow to help me to the horse. "What lesson is that?" I asked, climbing on behind him.

"Sometimes the heart isn't enough. It can follow dangerous desires when squeezed too hard."

"So how do we fix it?"

He glanced over his shoulder at Eryk. "We release the pressure. Luckily, we have another płanetnik to help us do exactly that."

50

Narcyz

HEAVY SNOWFALL OBSCURED OUR SIGHT of the four guards stationed on the Krowik River's west bank. It wasn't enough to hide their eyes, wide enough to make me think they'd soiled themselves in shock. They were strangers. Mieczysław had probably pulled more men from his northern village of Talis to prevent Jacek's loyalists from assassinating him. After he'd all but threatened civil war on the equinox, the bastard deserved it.

Mieczysław's men trembled in their shoddy boots as Mikołaj advanced. He rested his hand on his sword, and I wondered whether he'd have the guts to use it.

"I recommend you step aside," Mikołaj said, faking a deeper voice. I stifled a laugh from behind him, and Andrij elbowed me in the side.

One of the guards stepped forward with a glance at our gathered army. Krowikie warriors never wore armor, and he raised his wide circular shield like he knew how easy it would be for an archer to shoot him down. "You're supposed to be fighting Solga."

Mikołaj surveyed the chiefs to either side. They'd fallen in line so far, but the first test of loyalty would come soon. "I don't need to explain myself to the likes of you. Get out of the way, or I'll throw you in the Krowik so you can entertain the rusałki."

The lead guard grunted, gripping his spear. *Put it down, idiot.* We'd lost enough men already. The Horde would kill thousands more if Mieczysław's warriors lacked the brains to see they were outnumbered.

"Fine," another of the guards replied. "Go, but the high chief won't be happy."

Mikołaj raised his chin and gave a smug grin. "I've never seen a time when he was." Then he pushed his horse into a walk, skirting close enough to the first guard for his stirrup to clatter against his wooden shield.

Albin motioned for the army to follow, and Jacek's heir led the chiefs single-file across the bridge toward Dwie Rzeki. Andrij and I took the rear of the riders. We'd made this march back home happen, but we weren't chiefs or generals. The only important thing about me was Wacław's demonic mark burning on my arm.

The plan was almost complete.

Wacław's words rattled around in my head like a stone caught in a jar. *"Once you unite the Krowikie armies behind Mikołaj, march to Dwie Rzeki,"* he'd said in a creepy voice. *"Miko will try to convince Mieczysław to surrender his title, but he'll never agree to it."*

So we gotta kill him? I asked.

"Yes. Mieczysław will always be a thorn in our side while he lives, but he has one last use."

What?

He laughed, sounding far too excited about killing the high chief. *"First, he's going to kill my half-brother. Mieczysław is too hot-headed to give up his power* again *after Jacek took it from him once before. They'll fight—like Miko did with Serwacy—but Mieczysław isn't an old man. If all goes well, Mieczysław will kill him in his anger."*

Hold up! You want *Mikołaj to die? What's the point of dragging the army all the way to Dwie Rzeki just to kill your brother?*

"We need the Krowikie army… I need the Krowikie army… but I'm an exile. Mikołaj can unite the warriors and chiefs to his aid, and when Mieczysław

kills him, those allies will want revenge. Mieczysław will be executed for defying the chiefs."

I fell back against a tree with a sharp breath. It all clicked at once. *You want to become high chief.*

"Yes." He sighed, and the pulsing of his mark seared on my fore-arm. *"My father stole everything from me, but I have the power to take it back. Without Mieczysław, Mikołaj, and Serwacy, no single chief will be powerful enough to claim Jacek's title. I'll return home when you're finished. Then, they'll finally see they were fools to exile me."*

My chest tightened as I looked at Andrij's sleeping form. He'd never approve of such deceit. Before the demon's influence, Wacław wouldn't have either. But honesty didn't win wars. Marzanna was a goddess, and her Horde would destroy us if we let Mieczysław focus on Solga. They'd probably kill us anyway, but I wasn't about to die without making them suffer for it.

I'm in, I finally replied.

That conversation had been days before. Or had it been longer? Time had lost its meaning in the slog through the blizzards that had slowed our march east. There had been plenty of opportunities to tell Andrij the full scheme, but I hadn't. We'd grown closer, and I couldn't risk his scorn for betraying Mikołaj.

It's better this way.

We followed the winding snow-covered trails through Dwie Rzeki's outer farms before reaching the western gate. Guards stood here too, but they gave Mikołaj no hassle. Thousands of us passed into Krowik's capital without having to kill a single overly ambitious brute. A part of me hoped Mieczysław would be that smart. I'd have bet Swaróg's mighty hammer he wouldn't.

I took in the familiar smells and sights of home as we rode. Our sunken houses of wood with their sloped, thatched roofs were built to withstand the winter, but it was unsettling to see them covered by snow when the crops should've been rising. The fields lay fallow. Goats and cattle alike were thin. I was no farmer, but it didn't take one to see Marzanna was already making our tribe suffer. We'd make her pay for it.

Pa and Ma were nowhere to be seen, but other families were re-united. Children rushed into the army as women dropped baskets, threads, and leatherworks to hug their husbands, only for the men to urge them to leave. No blood had been spilled yet. That would change soon.

"WHAT IS THIS?"

Mieczysław's shout echoed from the base of Perun's Oak and through the trees and houses like a wilkołak's roar. I tensed at the memory of Bidaês's betrayal. I'd seen blood before, but that night…

I nearly jumped off my horse's back as a hand landed on my shoulder. "Don't worry," Andrij said. His smile was tender for a man who'd been an Astiwie commander under Boz's harsh reign. "We're here because of you, Narcyz. Don't forget that."

"Thanks," I muttered. *So this better go well.*

Mikołaj kept his head raised, glaring down at Mieczysław. "I've returned with our armies to face the true threat in the east."

I sat higher to get a better sight of Mieczysław and cursed at what I saw. I'd assumed he would carry his favorite battleax—a far better one than Serwacy's shiny piece of useless metal. No. The massive Thunderstone ax in his grasp wasn't his own.

It was a god's.

"Traitor!" Mieczysław stamped the heel of Perun's Ax into the snow. A gust of wind rattled the bone amulets in the oak's branches as he did. The god of thunder did not approve. "You turn my armies against me and threaten your high chief? Where is Serwacy?"

"Dead," the defiant Chief Horacy shouted from our right flank. Sweat beaded across his bald head, and he dared not look at Mikołaj as he spoke. "Jacek's boy killed him in cold blood."

"That's not true!" someone shouted from our army, but Mikołaj raised a hand to silence him.

"It is true that Serwacy fell by my blade," Mikołaj admitted. "However, it was not in cold blood as Chief Horacy claims, but by a duel. Chief Serwacy failed to uphold the alliance formed when I married Kinga, so it was my right."

Shuffling spread throughout the crowd. Horacy moved first,

spurring his horse to Mieczysław's side, followed by Chief Boleslav and a few dozen warriors. Hardly an army, but it was enough to make things ugly.

"We can't let this become a slaughter," Andrij whispered to me. "Death will only divide your tribe further, especially when your high chief wields Perun's Ax."

I gritted my teeth without reply. This was Wacław's plan. The chiefs needed to fight for him to be able to return and lead our armies east, but my stomach turned watching Mikołaj lead the army we'd united. That *he'd* united. He was cocky, arrogant, and often a drunkard, but he'd shown that he could lead. Was that enough?

Mieczysław advanced on foot. Ax held high, his voice carried for the entire army to hear. "I hold Perun's mighty weapon because I was chosen by our tribe to retake our ancestral lands and protect what Jacek lost. For the gods! For Krowik! Our traditions give us purpose, but you dare strike down a commander in a time of war? You steal my armies and march upon *my* throne?"

He was close enough for a single swing of his ax to reach his opponent's horse, but Mikołaj didn't flinch.

"Things have changed," Mikołaj said with his hands still on the reins. "Wacław was telling the truth, but you were too blind to hear it. Stolen lands mean nothing when Marzanna's Horde threatens to slaughter every one of us until they erase our tribe from the legends. Man, woman, and child are the same to her monsters." He turned to the army behind him and extended his arm. "These brave warriors have returned to fight for their families, their land. Best you listen to their will or stand aside so someone else can."

Mieczysław swung.

Thousands of voices shouted together as Mikołaj's mount collapsed. Blood covered him, and he cried out as his leg caught beneath the horse's weight.

It's actually happening. My heart raced. I couldn't find my voice or the will to reach for my spear and shield. Andrij was yelling something at my side, but I only stared at the ring of warriors forming at Mieczysław's flanks, buying him the time to take the final strides and raise that mighty ax for its killing blow. Jacek's firstborn would fall. The army would have its revenge.

And a demon would rule.

Wacław's mark burned like a branding iron as I made a choice. My hands found my weapons instinctively, and I threw my heels into my horse's sides. Wacław could rule. But each time I heard that command in my head, I didn't hear the Half-Chief who'd become my friend. I heard a monster.

My mount struck at speed, toppling the warriors daring to stop me. Mieczysław didn't see me coming. The kill was wide open, but I leapt instead, Andrij's voice replacing Wacław's.

Perun's Ax fell as I struck the ground and rolled. My shield covered Mikołaj a moment later, and all I saw was light reflecting off the ax until a deafening *boom* rocked the ground.

The impact threw me back into the army. My shield-arm went numb, and all sound became distant as I crashed into our first line of warriors with serious force. They would've fallen without their raised shields, but those same shields smacked my shoulder and face *hard*. I wished they'd been numb too as I collapsed to the snow-covered ground.

What was that?

Andrij was over me in a blink. The screeching in my ears drowned out his voice, and my head spun too much to read his lips. So I just stared up at the matted brown hair that fell over his face in waves. Pa would've scolded him for letting it tangle. I liked it.

He helped me up, and slowly, my hearing returned. Didn't mean much. The warriors just gawked. Some at Mieczysław. Others at me.

"What're they looking at?" I mumbled, throwing my arm over Andrij's shoulder. He grunted and leaned hard to his right to compensate, but he was tough enough to take it.

"You… Narcyz, you were hit by lightning. Did you channel Wacław's power?"

I shook my head to fight off the fogginess. Wacław's mark throbbed, but it didn't hurt any differently than before. My head was another story. "Didn't try to." Gods, what was that *stench*? It was rancid enough to feel like a punch in the face.

"Perun has spoken!" a gruff voice shouted over the commotion.

"Oh great," I muttered to Andrij. "High Priest Dariusz decided now is the best time to ramble about the gods."

Andrij gave me a knowing glance. "He raised a goddess and married another. I think he knows more about them than us."

Dariusz pushed his way to the front of our army, his deep gray robes trimmed in red sliding over the bloodstained ground. His leather headband kept his long gray hair in place and pressed Swaróg's iron Forgemark into his brow. I stared at that amulet. If Pa had believed the gods to care at all, he would've taught me to worship Swaróg each time I struck with my smith hammer. Instead, revering the eldest god was as strange as considering his existence. Even meeting Jaryło hadn't changed that.

"He condemns you, Mieczysław," Dariusz continued. "The god of thunder and justice declares you unfit to rule."

Mieczysław roared. Pained, like a wounded animal, it echoed through the village center. The mighty northern chief glared at Dariusz with malice, but he held no weapon. His hands and forearms were blackened and charred.

Perun's Ax was nowhere to be seen.

Dariusz looked back at Mikołaj, who'd finally picked himself up with Albin's help, before turning to Mieczysław again. "You dared to raise Perun's own weapon against Krowik's true heir. He has delivered his judgement to spare your life, but it is Chief Mikołaj's decision what to do with you now."

As Mikołaj advanced, I didn't know what to think. It hadn't felt like I'd channeled lightning—not that I'd have known. Wacław had claimed his power surged through him. All I'd done was dive with my shield raised. Did that mean Perun had actually stopped Mieczysław?

Mikołaj stopped toe-to-toe with his father's old rival. The priest by his side hadn't liked Jacek either, but at least he had enough of a brain to realize what we face. "My judgement should be the same one you gave Wacław a moon ago," Mikołaj announced, "but Marzanna's Frostmarked are too great a threat for us to face them divided. Follow me as your high chief and I'll forgive your opposition. Your lands in Talis will remain yours, as will your warriors. We both know this is a more generous offer than the one my father would've given."

"Generous?" Mieczysław spat at Mikołaj's feet. "You defy our tribe's traditions and use Jacek's priest to usurp my rule! You're nothing but a fraud."

"So you prefer death?" Mikołaj huffed and nodded toward his men, a cocky grin across his face. "I'm sure many of these warriors would enjoy watching your head roll. We could even use a dull blade to give more of them swings. Weles would surely love for your blood to trickle to his lands, and Perun would smile at this justice."

Horacy and Boleslav scrambled off their horses. Once defiant, the chiefs now knelt in the snow with their heads bowed, pleading for mercy. Mieczysław scowled at them, fists clenched, before taking a deep sigh. "My warriors will fight beside yours until this war is done. No longer. Talis will not suffer longer under Jacek's bloodline."

"You're a fool," Mikołaj said, "but I'd rather spend my life defending our tribe from Marzanna than waste it fighting you." Then he looked to the kneeling chiefs. "I spared you once. I gave you the same chance as Mieczysław, yet you chose not to listen. Face Weles. I'm done with you."

Horacy cried out, snatching at Mikołaj's cloak as he walked away, but Albin intercepted him. The massive warrior gripped an ax sharp enough to glint in the little light. He only needed one swing.

Gasps spread through the crowd as the chiefs' heads rolled. None protested. Not even Mieczysław dared to reject Mikołaj's word now, and he joined with the warriors from the north in a gruff silence. Even after being beaten down, he was a dominant presence. I just hoped I could stop him if he decided to stab Mikołaj in the back.

A harsh gust battered us as our new high chief neared. He studied me with amusement before laughing and smacking me on my shoulder. "Always thought you were a clod, but that was something. Come, let us talk in my father's keep."

After ordering one of his warriors to find both his family and mine, Mikołaj led us through the large doors and into the longhouse. Torches and candles dimly lit the space. Not enough. I blinked hard, trying to get my eyes to adjust as Mikołaj passed the long wooden table and settled on the fur-covered throne at the hall's head. Perun's Ax was missing from behind it. Pa would be a mess when he heard. From toe to knob, each part of it had been a masterpiece of carvings. He'd wanted to master smithing enough to create a similar ax someday, but no one could match its designs.

"I suppose I should thank you, Narcyz," Mikołaj began before waving his hand at Andrij, "and… Aleksander?"

Andrij just mumbled to himself, so I spoke for him, "He's Andrij, and he's the only reason you're alive."

"I don't understand."

I groaned and pulled my arm from around Andrij, limping toward Mikołaj with a glare. I'd defied Wacław. I'd saved his half-brother's life. That didn't mean I had to like Mikołaj. "Andrij urged me to stop Mieczysław before we broke into a war. I didn't want to."

Mikołaj raised his brow. "You went through all that for him to kill me?"

"No. Your men would've taken their revenge, and then maybe we could've found someone better. But that would take moons of war. Probably years. You're better than that." I looked back at Andrij with a solemn smile. "You have him to thank for what happened."

Andrij returned the gesture. "My people have been destroyed by Boz's pursuit of power. It would pain me to see Krowik end the same way."

"Then you have my thanks as well," Mikołaj replied, leaning on his knees, intent. "I do, however, need to ask you about that lightning."

I shrugged. "Don't know."

"So it wasn't my brother saving me through you? A shame."

I kept my mouth shut and shrugged again. *He wanted you dead, idiot.*

Andrij stepped to my side. His cheeks were tight, his lips pursed like he did when he was worried if he should speak. I didn't get why. Things he said made sense. My words just made people mad. "Isn't it significant Perun intervened, then?"

"It is." Dariusz's voice came from the longhouse doors, and he paced around us to a shadowed corner to Mikołaj's side. It was like Jacek had never left. "Perun and Weles swore to remove themselves from Jawia's politics unless the other agrees it is necessary. That means either Perun has broken that pact to interfere or the two have stopped their bickering."

A pit opened in my stomach. I glanced at Andrij with a single culprit in my head. *Jaryło.* Andrij hadn't been there when Jaryło betrayed us and killed Otylia, but he knew enough. If Jaryło had done something…

Life was better when I thought the gods stayed away.

"I don't know anything about the gods besides the legends," Mikołaj said. "What they do could change everything, but my role is with Krowik and Krowik alone. We will face Marzanna with the gods or without them."

A brutal gust flung open the doors behind us. It swept through us and around the throne before stopping at once, and Mikołaj stood at the sound of a commotion rose outside. I reached for my dagger. *Who we have to kill this time?*

Three figures and a fox pushed through the crowd beneath Perun's Oak and stepped into the longhouse. The dagger slipped from my fingers at the sight of the one in front.

"High Chief Mikołaj," Xobas said with a proud smile, flanked by Ara and Sosna. I didn't recognize the third figure—an elderly man wearing long gray robes and an Eclipsemark like mine on his cheek. "I see our friends have treated you well. Rare for Narcyz."

I crossed my arms but let the smile come. "Thought you were dead. Who's he?"

The robed man shifted before Xobas replied, "Eryk. He's the płanetnik Wacław marked in the Mangled Woods."

"The one that tried to kill us."

"My apologies for that," Eryk said, head lowered. "Marzanna used my need for revenge, but Wacław freed me from it."

"Time's short," Ara interjected. She advanced, looking from Andrij to me. "You fit to fight?"

No.

I checked my bruises from Perun's strike before cracking my knuckles. "Yeah, I'm ready. Whose skull we splitting?"

Ara smacked my injured shoulder, chuckling at my wince. "Good. We're leaving the moment Eryk has enough *žityje* to fly us south. Otylia awaits, and so does our demonic friend."

51

Otylia

"MY GREATEST APOLOGIES," FAARAX RAMBLED as I knelt before the hole Wacław had blown into the basement wall, my head bowed. "We tried to contain the demon… Master Wacław… but I am a simple man. And when he used his power, it was far too much. He escaped, killing recklessly and feeding upon the corpses like a fiend from the legends!"

"Legends are a mix of reality and mortals' childish minds," Vlatka said, examining the black blood spattered across the prison. Ta leaned against the wall nearby, silently tucking another glass throwing blade up her sleeve.

"He wouldn't do that!" Kuba yapped, the noise something between a shout and a cry. "Wacław 'bout threw up after killing his first person at Bustelintin, and that guy was trying to kill him."

"Power is a dangerous whisper," Vlatka replied from my shoulder. "Every witch feels it when we touch the immensity of life that breathes beyond our soul. Some of us fail. Others, like me, learn to face that darkness each day and proclaim that it shall not control us." She raised her eagle head to the ceiling, staring at something only she could see. "Even that pull is nothing compared to that which the

Nawie face. My darkness is mirrored in my own soul, but theirs is split between two until the demon devours the mortal. Imagine the worst parts of you gnawing at your mind until whatever memory you have of hope, of love, is gone."

"Otylia saved the demons at Sheresy," Kuba replied.

"Undead demons are weaker," Vlatka said. "Nawie are alive. That life gives them resilience—first against the demonic soul and then in protection of it once the corruption is complete."

"We agreed she can do this," Sabina said, kneeling beside me. I winced at the scrapes across her skin just beginning to close. Would she ever fly with her wings again?

"I do not doubt her," Vlatka said, "but some part of him must wish to be free for it to happen."

Sabina cocked her head. "Why wouldn't he?"

"Because I broke him!" I snapped, silencing the room.

I tilted my head back and soaked in the sea of voices drowning me through End's wisps. The conversation around me had been just another among hundreds. My inner dialogue was somewhere among them, but I let those thoughts become lost. The voices weren't direct prayers. In them, though, were desires, worries, and dreams. I needed to hear their pleas, to know there was something more than the fear and regret dragging me to the darkest recesses of my mind. Wacław had fled when I'd lashed out. Now, so much of me wished to do the same. To disappear and forget about the world for an eternity.

I couldn't.

Tears stung my eyes as I rose, not bothering to brush the dirt off my dress. Kiin had crafted this prison to prevent Wacław from slaughtering innocents. Except it had only pushed him further into the demon's grasp. Looking back, I realized I'd felt each slip but had been incapable of stopping it. Kiin was dead now, and I wouldn't let both of our mistakes lead to Huebia's demise.

"Kiin died fighting for Mokosz's people," I said. "Alive or undead, mortal or corrupted, everyone is a Daughter of the Great Mother, and Kiin realized that in the end. She saw her son, Yesike, in the utopiecs and her sisters-in-arms in the rusałki. Despite the

Vastrothie's failures, she gave Yesike to the scions so that each person in this dominion could have another chance. So that Mokosz would redeem her children. But she was deceived. All Marzanna does is lie, and Czarnobóg amplifies her corruption to the ends of Jawia— to even Wašek."

I turned from the wall to the empty firepit in the basement's center. "Kiin invited Wacław and me to this fire upon our arrival. We were desperate, weak, and I argued endlessly. She took us anyway…" My breaths fogged as I clutched my autumn leaf cloak around me for warmth. "I will honor her by releasing the demonic children sacrificed by the scions. When I return, I will right my wrong, and we will free this city from Marzanna and Grudzień."

The sound of a blade sliding from its sheath echoed through the space, followed by a white glow. I spun, scowling at the figure striding from the shadows. "You show up *now?*"

Jaryło smirked and glanced down at Czerwiec, the blade of the sixth moon. I hadn't even noticed Maj's completion with all that had happened, but when I shut my eyes, there was a slight difference in the moon's power. One I couldn't explain.

"I have my own priorities," he replied. "Vastroth is not one of them, but I heard what you did in Sheresy. Quite the feat, saving demons. Unfortunately, I won't help you do the same here. Marzanna is looking for me, and I have plenty of groundwork to lay before we wed and unite the gods."

What did Jaryło want? Dressed in a clean white open-front shirt, unbuttoned vest, and trousers that contrasted heavily with the dark skin of his Vastrothie form, he no longer appeared like a god of war. He was *almost* regal. Only his golden hair and eyes offered any color, and he was almost blinding in Czerwiec's light.

I turned away, pacing toward Ta. "Then leave. Why come now except to mock me?"

"I had been preparing for the extravagant event that will be our wedding, but I returned to warn you against continuing down this path. Are you prepared to kill Wacław? He is not like those rusałki, my darling." His purr with the final world made me tense. *Why'd I promise not to hurt you?* The god grinned at my discomfort. "The corruption that has taken him is far more powerful, and he must die if your plan fails—which it will—unless you choose to disturb Destiny's will further."

"I'll do what I have to," I lied. Every part of me burned at him calling me his *darling*, but my revenge would have to come later. When I was stronger. When I had Wacław's help.

"Good." His footstep approached, and I bit my cheek as his hand fell lightly on the small of my back, Czerwiec's blade cutting into the stone at my side. "Even if you can redeem him, he must be cast out. I don't want you distracted."

"Don't. Touch. Me."

Before Jaryło could reply, Vlatka squawked and flapped her wings at him. It caught him off guard, and I grinned at his cry of shock that followed, taking the chance to spin away from him. *I can't hurt him. That doesn't mean I can't have others do it for me…*

Jaryło held his hand to a nasty wound beneath his eye. Shadowed by only a single flickering torch and Czerwiec's glow, it seemed to bleed white before healing with a burst of *žiłyje*. His lip curled, and he swiped his blade through the space between us. "Will you never be grateful for all I have done for you? You discovered the truth of the boy's soul and yours because *I* showed you to the Lake of Reflection. Your friends survived the battle in the Mangled Woods because *I* killed the final Frostmarked. And you faced the Trials because *I* took you to Weles."

"Er… Master Jaryło," Faarax stuttered. "Perhaps we should avoid—"

"Not the time, fuzz chin," Ta muttered, creeping behind Jaryło and looking to me for a sign to attack. I shook my head. "Darn. No fun."

Jaryło turned on his heel and held the tip of Czerwiec to her neck. "If you would like to have 'fun,' then be stealthier on your feet." He studied her from head to toe. "I saw you in Sheresy but didn't consider you much then. My opinion hasn't changed."

Ta growled, but I stepped forward, a hand raised. "Throwing

your ego around like a cat that caught an already dead mouse isn't going to fix anything. Not that you've *ever* fixed things."

I circled him to Ta's side, listening to the wisps of those in the room. Jaryło tried to quiet his thoughts, but End exposed the fear in his wisp. Of failure. Of disappointing his father… or fathers. I could use that.

"You need me to help you unite Perun and Weles's forces behind you," I continued. "I'll do my part, but you betrayed me. You betrayed Perun too by choosing Weles. Why would the lord of Prawia support you now, after you've severed the veil between Jawia and Oblivion, sacrificing all he and Swaróg wished to do?"

"Congratulations. You have seen far more than I thought, oh Lady of Endings." He lowered Czerwiec but didn't sheathe it. "Perun will be difficult to convince, and that is why I need you. Mother despises me after what I did, but she is quite fond of you. With you as my wife, she will sway him to our side." He paced to the wall, running his fingers along the stone. "Some part of her is in this city."

"I know," I replied. "She talked to me in the Hidden Waters."

"Of course, she likely did so while you were in Nawia as well, skirting the blood pact between Father and her husband. This cave where the demonic children remain trapped… It sounds like a place she would stay in mourning. Go and speak with her. We will need her favor."

"For your plan?"

"For *our* plan, yes." He looked at the others, his smirk returning. "I will be gone before you return from the cave. And don't worry, I swore not to harm your friends—so long as the eagle knows her place and the child puts away that creative blade in her sleeve." Ta retreated as he approached. "*Tsk tsk.* You know I am partially a god of war, right? I have seen every possible way to kill someone and succeeded at most of them myself."

I stepped between him and Ta, shooting him a glare. "I will go to the cave. First, I want to speak with Darixa. She needs to know what's happened if the Daughters intend to have the scions rule when this is finished."

"Excuse me, Lady of Endings," Faarax said with his head bowed.

"I believe I should have mentioned this sooner, but Master Wacław declared his intent to capture the young scion before he left."

My eyes widened. "He did *what?*" I rushed to the short man, grabbing him at the chest. "How did you leave this out? Where is she?"

He shook in my grasp, fear in his gaze. "I… I do not know. My apologies. Lady Kiin intended for only the chosen to know her location."

"So Wacław hasn't found her?"

"It is unlikely. Lady Kiin was the only chosen here, and the others in the city are in hideouts Master Wacław would not know of."

Relief filled me as I released him and looked at Vlatka on my shoulder. "We need to find him, quickly."

"Go to Mokosz and the children," she replied, dropping to the floor before me. "I will search for our rogue płanetnik. He won't recognize me in this form."

Kuba brushed against my leg and sat beside me. Those jackal eyes of his never left Jaryło. "I'll stay here with Ta to bite Jaryło if he does anything we don't like."

"Wait, you want me to bite 'im?" Ta asked before smiling maniacally. "Yeah, why not? Can take my blades but not my teeth!"

I took a deep breath, shaking my head in hopes of pushing away my weariness. After the long journey and tiring days at Sheresy, I really didn't need this headache. "Whatever, I'll return soon. Sabina can contact me if something happens."

She held a hand over her Moonmark as I started toward the stairs. "I can? Right, of course I can!"

Mother help me…

Cold sand was an odd feeling. Coarse, unlike snow, it brought its own sting against my bare feet when I removed my boots outside the cave from Kiin's memories. There was little formality around shoes and holy altars, but it felt right to enter Mokosz's cave with a connection to the earth.

The pain also distracted from my fear.

My heartbeat echoed in my head as I held my cloak tight and approached the mouth. Like a shaman of Weles during a festival, it drummed on and on, growing faster with each step. I could handle demons. I had met Mokosz. But what lay in the darkness ahead was heavier than anything I'd faced. Marzanna and Czarnobóg had manipulated the people of Vastroth to sacrifice their children for their own selfish gains. Parents had complied out of hope of ending Mokosz's supposed wrath, but the Great Mother would never have done such a thing. I'd served her for years. She protected women, yes, but she loved all her children unconditionally. This… This had been no act of love.

The thin crescent moon gave little light to the desert, and beyond the first few steps into the cave, I could see nothing. So I calmed my breaths as Ildes had suggested.

Moonlight glowed from my skin as End's wisps hovered over me in a sea of black, winding streaks—slow, like they hadn't noticed me yet. When I searched for Threads of Life, I gasped at the thousands that stretched from the cave and into the living world beyond.

I remembered my meeting with Death as sand turned to stone beneath my heel. His appearance had been frightening by itself, but the dread that had hung over him was unlike anything else. Part of it had never left me. I'd promised him a gift of his choosing in return for Wacław's life, and in the back of my mind, a voice reminded me that offer would soon come due.

This was his domain.

The cave descended into the earth, my feet slipping upon stone that had been smoothed by channeling or years of rainwater finding the deepest crevice. Multiple forks met me along the way, but I kept my focus on the sources of those Threads. I was an intruder here. A sensation of being watched crept over me as my steps and nervous, inconstant breaths pierced the silence of the stale air. Even the children's dark wisps stirred after what seemed an eternity of walking. An infant boy's shadowed face appeared in one.

"Mama?" he asked, his brows angled up and cheeks puffed, as if he were holding his breath. Other faces joined his. A mix of worry and anticipation filled each of their expressions.

"No," I replied. My heart ached at his disappointment, but why would he believe me to be his mother? "My name is Otylia, goddess of endings and the moon. I'm here to help."

The boy just whimpered, and a girl's face moved before him. She had curled locks like Kiin's that drifted like smoke away from her wisp's ends. "It's so dark… But you're bright."

"Too bright!" another exclaimed. "Please, it hurts!"

Of course, their eyes have become so used to the darkness that I'm blinding them.

I forced myself to dim the moonlight from my skin. It reduced my field of vision, making the children appear like an endless array of shadows, but their wisps slowed, their movements growing less anxious. "Better?" I asked.

The girl nodded. "You're really a goddess?"

"I'm the Earth Mother's granddaughter, yes."

"Mother said she sacrificed us…"

"That's not true." I bent down to them, removing my glove and reaching out to touch the wisp. She didn't pull back, and visions met me of her weeping in the moments before her death, her mother's head turning away as she clawed at the scions. Abandonment. Hopelessness. Their weights were crushing, forcing me to pull back with a sharp inhale. "The Winter Witch lied to your parents. She used the scions to bring you to her, so she could take your lives and make herself more powerful."

She cocked her head. Of course she didn't understand. The battles between gods were often too complex for me to comprehend, let alone a child who'd been trapped for years as a demon. When she spoke, though, there was a faint hope in her voice.

"Will you take us home?"

I stuffed away my doubts and forced a smile to my face. "I will."

With a squeal of delight, she spun with the others and shot further down the slope, disappearing into the darkness. "Then follow us!"

I ran after them as fast as my legs would carry me. Each step was treacherous with only my dim light to expose steeper drops or crevices that could catch my bare feet, but it didn't matter. *Žityje* could mend a rolled ankle or stubbed toe. These children craved freedom, and I wouldn't delay that a moment longer than necessary.

The dry, dusty air soon gave way to must and a dampness that would've been inviting had Marzanna's chill not ruled this realm. I stepped into a chamber that stretched far beyond my light. Just at its edge, the children met me with their thrilled voices pulling me on, willing me to go faster. I followed, but not with haste. *Something* lurked in the darkness. I sensed it among the sea of mold and fungi feeding on whatever decayed in this moisture-filled room.

"Careful," the girl whispered, zipping past. "They wait."

I furrowed my brow. "Who waits?"

Before she replied, a maniacal laugh echoed through the cave. More and more followed until my ears throbbed and my mind spun from the noise. As I summoned my silver spear, creatures' wings beat the air, and the children whispered together.

"The skrzaki…"

52

Otylia

I've had enough of stupid flying beasts.

TWO HEARTBEATS PASSED between the spear's cold silver finding my hand and its tip plunging into the first skrzak's mouth. Except the mouth wasn't on its head.

Where the demon's head should've been was a stump pulsing with Czarnobóg's horrific mark. A dozen mouths covered its torso and the webbed wings jutting from its back. My spear had struck the one in the center of its chest, but despite the dark blood pouring over its purple-black skin, the laughter only grew louder. Then came its claws.

They raced toward my neck, but my silver and wooden armband burned and released a burst that deflected the blow as I raised my arm. The skrzak just screamed, pulling itself free from the spear with its other hand. I called my energy to my hands for a moonblast only for the air to vibrate around me.

What are these things?

Three more of the creatures appeared. Their laughs struck like a mighty wave, filling my ears with a ringing, and I gasped for air as a rib snapped in my chest. *Žityje* mended it quickly, but something trickled from my ear—*Blood?*

The laughter stopped, the world becoming deathly silent as the eyeless, headless skrzaki circled me with their razor-like teeth gnashing. I tried to recollect my strength, but the calm I needed in my core was gone. Only panic replaced it, forcing me to spin and jab with my spear to force the beasts away.

They were just toying with me. I'd seen predators do it before, as our cat Maryn did whenever she discovered a stray animal that snuck into our home. But I was a goddess. Why would they think they could—

Pain shot through my spine. A skrzak had flanked me in my deafness, and its teeth ripped through flesh and muscle as I spun and flailed with my spear like an untrained boy fighting in the woods. With the demon clutching to my back, it was little use, so I dismissed the spear and freed my hands for a magic strike, pooling the *żityje* in them as I screamed through the pain. The other skrzaki had to be near. Where? I should've heard their laughter and their wings striking out at me while my voice pierced all of it.

There was only silence.

My healing *żityje* fought with the demons as they bit at everything they could. I closed my eyes to avoid the agony, but the sharp pain sliced from my shoulders to my elbows and legs. They had shattered my confidence, my strength. But I kept my patience, stopping my healing and holding that *żityje* in my grasp as End's wisps flowed behind my eyelids. I saw the torture of the children within them—the cries of the eldest ones and the silent pain of those too young to have known their first full moon. Even in my deafness, I heard the mothers' screams as they lost their children, their babies. This torture was nothing compared to theirs. I could endure it. I *would* endure it. And I would free them, for Kiin, for Mokosz, and for my own mother who suffered in Marzanna and Czarnobóg's prison too.

My panic vanished, and with it, I released every bit of pain I'd felt in those visions. I plunged it into my power. Not out of rage. Not out of hatred. But out of a need to defend those who couldn't defend themselves. The broken, the corrupted. I would grant them salvation so that, together, we could destroy the corruptors that shadowed Jawia's life in Death's veil.

Light burst forth. Bright, pure, it flung back the darkness and the skrzaki with it. I didn't let them flee so easily.

Throwing out my arms, I grabbed hold of the elements of decay covering the cavern floor. Mold grew up the demons' legs as they tried to take flight. They squirmed and fought, but I sent another wave into the mold, releasing their spores into the skrzaki's many mouths until they choked.

Żityje repaired my hearing as I strode toward them, the fungi cushioning my steps like moss. I didn't take pleasure in their suffering. Surely, these demons were little different than the rusałki and utopiecs in Sheresy, just more lost. Their wisps were there among the children's, but when I searched for their Threads of Life, none came from them. Impossible. Everything had *some* connection through the Threads. How could they have nothing?

"What did Czarnobóg do to you?" I asked them, stopping between the poor creatures.

A haunting thought gripped me as I called back my spear and prepared to end their misery. *Is this what a severed soul looks like? Ruined, lost, disconnected from everything they've ever loved?*

I plunged the spear through the first until it fell limp. The others cowered, but the spores killed them slowly. Though I wished I could do more for them, bringing them back from this deep of corruption was impossible. Death was its own freedom for them. Wacław would be different. He had to be.

Each of their deaths distracted me from the implications of severed souls, both for my own power and Czarnobóg's. Jaryło had claimed I'd severed Serapis by destroying his Thread of Life. Was it true? I clenched my jaw as I finished the gruesome work and released my control of the mold. That power had been useful in my desperation, I decided, but I wouldn't use it again until I knew more. The cost was too great.

Then why didn't I regret what I'd done?

A question for later, as the children's wisps had returned. They danced among themselves and beamed at me like only children could. Joy they'd never had in life.

"Why didn't you warn me about the demons?" I asked.

"I don't know…" the girl replied. "They're nice to us but don't let us leave. Why don't they let you come?"

"They didn't want me to help you. Are there any more like them?"

She shook her head, then stared at me as if waiting for something.

I stepped closed. "Where are you? It's hard to see the tunnels without my light." It had dimmed after the initial burst, and the children seemed to think it wasn't too bright anymore.

"Close," she whispered. "C'mon!"

The children's wisps led me through the dark cavern and down one of the many tunnels branching from it. They quieted as it narrowed, the dropping ceiling forcing me to crouch, then crawl. Only my strained breaths broke the silence as I pushed on. Unlike the smooth stone above, here, everything was jagged, ripping my dress and drawing blood from my arms and knees. It mattered little. Such things were trifling to a goddess who could heal and reform her gown at will. Was that why Jaryło seemed not to care about people's suffering? Would I be like him soon, numb to pain and loss as I mended whatever I willed?

No, I told myself. *I'll never be like him.*

The tunnel only tightened more, trapping me if I dared to move too quickly. I sensed the children's impatience. That pushed me on, even as I gritted my teeth with each annoying jolt or blockage. Too many times I had failed as a goddess, but not today.

Just when I thought the tunnel couldn't get any tighter, it spat me out like a dog choking on a bone. I sprawled into a shallow pond and coughed out the water that splashed down my throat. Once I raised my head, though, my little light was enough to reveal what had become of the children. The sight alone froze me in place.

"She'll pay for this," I whispered, pushing myself to my feet as the decaying, infantile forms walked and crawled toward me.

Their eyes were black like the water and held some resemblance to children of various ages. But they were wrong, distorted. Their far too large heads weighed down their bodies, their legs twisted with their knees pointed the wrong direction, and umbilical cords wrapped around some like a snake constricting its prey. Children, broken and mangled by Marzanna and Czarnobóg's desperation for power. How could they claim to free Jawia when it required doing *this* to the innocent?

How am I going to save them?

The rusałki and utopiecs had pursued the death of the men that had killed them, but I knew nothing about the type of demon these children had become. Father had always ensured our village's dead children received the proper funeral rites.

Before I could wonder further, the water shifted around my feet. The children cooed and bobbed in the shallows as a figure formed before me. My instincts, prodded by Grudzień's manipulation, said to call my spear, but a new calm came over me. Threads of Life shot from the shifting form so bright that I had to shield my eyes. Between my fingers, I saw them connecting to every visible child and beyond, and as a gentle touch pulled my hand down, I knelt before the woman whose Thread joined with mine.

"Great Mother!" I exclaimed, suddenly shaking.

Mokosz narrowed her eyes, holding my hands in the soft yet reassuring way of only a mother's touch. Her skin was dark like the Vastrothie, her hair tied up in a bun with the stray strands falling before her face with the slightest curl. With her arms extended, her robe's drooping sleeves were long enough to cover my own tattered ones.

"You should know by now that a goddess does not kneel," she said. "Not even before her grandmother."

So I rose and met her gaze. "You didn't do this. You'd never ask mothers to sacrifice their children."

"No, I would not…" She released my hands, holding hers over her heart as tears welled in her eyes. "I would never force mothers to suffer as I have ever since the day Marzanna turned to the darkness, the day I was too dispersed, too weak to stop my Jaryło from breaking nature's balance—a balance I have brought you to restore. If only Jaryło hadn't been foolish enough to entrap you too."

"Balance? You mean saving the demons?"

She sighed and looked at the children. "How can I express such a complex phenomenon in such little time? These children are but one example of corruption's stain upon Jawia. Death is a necessity for mortals. It allows the natural cycle to continue, but with it must come balance, not this eternal decay that manipulates life instead of allowing its rightful end. Marzanna was a victim of this corruption. So, too, was Czarnobóg, I believe."

"Victim?" I spat. "Marzanna has slaughtered thousands and enslaved more. She captured Mother! When Dziewanna gave her a chance to free herself, Marzanna mocked her, and Czarnobóg only pushed her further into whatever evil this is."

"Is Wacław no different?" She cupped my cheek with her hand, sending a calm through me that could've been magic or simple care. Either way, it sharpened my clouded thoughts as I remembered Wacław's rebukes after I'd turned away from him. "The corrupted have fallen into a great darkness, most often not of their own making, and it is the responsibility of others to pull them free. Is that not love?"

Tears stung my eyes as I leaned into her hand, wishing I didn't have to be strong. Why were Jawia's problems mine? Vastroth's? Why couldn't I have a relationship that wasn't full of doubts and interference? "What if they're too far gone?"

Mokosz raised my chin and forced me to look into her eyes. They shone with her own tears, but her hands neither shook nor wavered. For a long time, we held that moment, sharing unspoken pain and fear between us. A heavy weight. I'd dreamed of the goddesses' powers as a child, but only now could I understand the struggle they held upon their shoulders—that *we* held upon our shoulders.

"This is your role," she breathed. "Goddess of endings, protector of the balance, the cycle. It will be up to you to decide whose darkness is essential to that balance and whose is an unnatural corruption. You have saved demons from Oblivion's abyss, and you can do the same for others. When even you are not enough, though, you must have the strength to know death is a mercy for those tortured by corruption."

"Me?" I shuddered, struggling to hold my weight. "I barely know who I am! You were always my guide. Mother was always my guide! How am I supposed to decide the balance when I broke it with Wašek?"

"Oh my child… You do not live countless years without regrets. I have many, not the least being my inability to stop the betrayal of my scions. Those failures haunt each of us, and over the centuries, it becomes difficult enough to forgive yourself, let alone those you love." She kissed my forehead softly, running her hands through my hair. "Despite this, our regrets do not define us. Chaos, order, good, and evil all live within the Three Realms. We must each serve our role among these forces, and you will find your way. I see your doubt. Fear is part of gods and mortals alike, Otylia, but so too is courage. You must fight to discover the heart of your power. And that starts now." With an arcing wave, she guided me toward the demons.

"These children have become poroniecs," she continued. "They would feed upon the mothers of this land, as they lost their own, but I have surrendered my own strength to them instead. Though this has weakened me, it is the cost I choose to bear for my failures."

I opened my mind to their Threads, letting them overwhelm me. "Demons are corrupted but still bound to their loved ones. Why?"

Mokosz held a hand over her heart. "There are some forces even I do not understand. Love is a mystery, and I hope that never changes."

"Then how do I save them? If they just need a mother, can't they have you or be returned to their families? Why wait for me to come?"

"Despite my perceived importance," she said with a sigh, "I lack the strength of many others of our kind. Their power is dispersed only through their szeptuchy, but mine is bound to every girl, every woman, and especially every mother. Even men hold a fragment of me, as a son holds a part of his mother. You speak of being lost in your power. Well, know that you are not alone in that."

I took a ragged breath, studying the goddess I'd once believed to be the most powerful of any. Maybe she still was. Her connection with the earth and its people was greater than Perun's lightning or

Marzanna's frost. A part of her was in each heart and soul, and I realized then that even when she'd been distant, she'd guided me through those she touched. I was grateful.

"Then tell me what I must do," I said, turning my resolve to iron.

My grandmother raised her chin. "Take the children's Threads and imbue them with your light. Redemption is powerful alone, but you can help strengthen their minds against the corruption. Then, you must find the scions who betrayed me. Bring them to justice. Once you are finished, the poroniecs will be at peace, and you will be ready to save Wacław and yourself."

53

The Płanetnik

She'll come for the girl… Yes… Then we'll finish this.

THE HIDDEN WATERS. The Daughters had spoken of such a spiritual place before, but they'd never admitted that it had been beneath our feet the entire time. A truth just waiting to be discovered. And the last true scion lay within.

I hated those caverns, their cramped spaces rejecting the winds and leaving only the stalest of air. It sought to smother my ambition and rage, but I was too close now. The power I'd been denied at birth would soon be mine. Krowik and Astiw, Solga and the clans, they would all bow before me and see for the first time that I'd never been the pathetic weakling they believed me to be. By slaying Otylia, I would gain Grudzień's influence, and none would resist me.

As I was immortal, so too would be my reign.

Instinct led me toward the power deep within the tunnels. With neither light nor the winds, that pull in my soul was my only guide, and I followed it with haste. The tether binding me to Otylia had tightened by the minute. Soon, she would discover my plot. I needed to capture Darixa before then.

Memories flashed before me of when we'd first met the girl. Sheer terror, as if I'd been her nightmare birthed to life. Otylia believed the young scion had Mokosz's gift of foresight, despite never becoming a szeptucha, so had she seen this moment? Had she known I'd accept my demonic core?

It didn't matter. Though the Daughters surely had at least one szeptucha guarding Darixa, I wouldn't allow them to stop me. Not now. Not after all I'd suffered.

My fingers twitched against the hilt of Marzanna's Thunderstone dagger. Soon, I would have my peace, but there could be no sympathy until then. Otylia had betrayed me, as had the Daughters. They would suffer Marzanna's eternal winter for my freedom. So be it. Regret and pain would only slow me, so I allowed them to feed my hatred, my craving for blood.

For some time, the only sound filling the caverns were my footsteps and the scattered drips of water from spikes of rock that jutted from the ceiling. Those droplets soon accumulated, though, forming a stream that rose to my ankles as I descended. I hadn't seen this much water beyond the Behmir River since our arrival in Vastroth. It reminded me of life—of its resilience despite all else.

If only I hadn't lost my chance to live…

Undeath was something far different than mortality. For years, I'd been confined by fear and hesitation, but not now. Allowing and then embracing my anger had released me from Father's binds, granting me a strength I'd always had but never known. That craving, that urge, in my chest had grown from a whisper to a roar. I would never silence it again.

The water had reached my knees by the time the first light appeared. Violet and dull, it barely split the darkness, reflecting off the stream to reveal the black wisps rising from me. Ever-present now, they circled like a viper around her nest.

I drew my dagger and trudged through the waters, heading toward the light. Each step made a loud sloshing noise, but stealth only mattered against a stronger opponent. Against whatever forces the Daughters had protecting Darixa, *I* held the advantage. I would defeat them and feast upon their hearts. Only Darixa would live, out of necessity alone, but she would die by my hand too once I dealt with Otylia. The scion was merely a means to draw her in. After that, she was nothing more than a mortal whose heart held the *żityje* I so badly desired.

"He's here," a trembling voice said from below as the light shone over the ledge ahead.

So Darixa did foresee this… I grinned. If she had, then her fear was a good sign, as it meant she'd seen my inevitable victory.

The stream poured from where I stood into a pool below, where two szeptuchy dressed in sleeveless shirts and golden-brown trousers had created a platform of rock. Illuminated by rows of glowing violet stones embedded in the walls of the cavern, they kept Darixa behind them as they glared up at me. One gripped a staff of stone like Kiin's. The other wielded a short sword, its blade glinting with copper's burnt orange hue.

"Leave, demon!" the one with the staff snapped. "This is a holy place, and you defile it with your presence."

I snarled and launched myself into the air as the rocks cracked beneath my feet. Stone rose like vines, grabbing at me, but I was quicker. The szeptuchy cursed as I soared between them and the ceiling, where an odd glass tube seemed to draw the water upward. That tube allowed the winds through. Just the slightest breeze, but enough to hold me aloft.

"You claim Mokosz as the Earth Mother," I said, "so isn't every rock holy for her? What place, then, don't I *defile?*"

"What an insight from one so thoughtless," the other replied, her dark skin releasing a dull glow with her use of *żityje*. "Your kind stain all of the Earth Mother's lands, and we shall protect them!"

A *crack* to the side alerted me, and I flipped back on the little gust of wind I had, narrowly avoiding a spire that sliced from the wall through where I'd been. The szeptuchy whispered the old tongue together and more followed—shards of rock that were difficult to track in the darkness. Without the full strength of the winds, I relied on instincts.

I *needed* Darixa. Each strike wasted time, and I gritted my teeth, patience running thin as I swung out of a dodge and grabbed hold of a spire. Pain arced through my back. I ignored it and pulled as hard as I could to throw myself at the szeptuchy's island.

But Mokosz's witches turned to more savage magic. Instead of spires, they launched swarms of shards from the walls. They cut me like a hundred daggers, and I screamed as I forced the winds to push me faster.

So weak. So slow.

My rage fueled the gales. I gave them more, taking my *žityje* from healing and focusing it all on my speed, my power. There was no lightning here to build from, but I didn't need it. Even in the slightest breeze, I was the storm.

Sparks arced from my fingers as my vision burned red. I hated the szeptuchy for the pain they'd inflicted. I hated them for siding with Otylia. I hated them for keeping me from my ultimate victory. They would suffer, and no matter how many of their puny stones they launched, I couldn't be stopped.

Darixa screamed as the szeptuchy threw her into the water moments before I struck. The first channeler's staff snapped against my side, sending a jolt through my torso. Black blood spewed from every part of me. What was a bit more of pain? Against my burgeoning supply of *žityje*, it was nothing, and I grabbed her staff before she could pull away. She shouted in the old tongue. I tried to release the staff, but it bent like rope, entrapping my hands as the second szeptucha swung her sword.

So I released my lightning.

Žityje drained from my soul, far too much with no natural storm to draw from, but time was short. Lightning blinded me as it snapped over the small island.

The szeptuchy screamed, the staff-wielding one collapsing in an instant as the other stumbled back, her blade held vertically. It deflected the bolts somehow, and a familiar hatred veiled her face as she countered.

Otylia had claimed few szeptuchy were trained with weapons. This one obviously was. While those new to a blade tended to jerk and strike with little precision, her blade moved sharply. It wasn't a dance like Jaryło's but a direct, focused style that caught me off guard with its ferocity. Only a quick block with my dagger stopped her from slicing my throat.

The szeptucha showed no hesitation standing over her comrade's charred corpse. Hilt held tightly in both hands and the old tongue ringing from her lips, she was more threatening than the strongest of warriors.

And she would've been a match if I were merely a warrior.

I kicked at her leg with the winds amplifying my speed. She hadn't expected a low strike, and my heel struck her shin with all the strength I had. Though it didn't break her bone, she staggered, slowing her slices that followed and giving me plenty of time to evade and draw in close. Her long blade was effective to keep me at range, but here, a dagger's quickness reigned. I held mine to her neck before she could bring her sword back for another swipe.

"Where's your goddess now?" I hissed, glaring into her eyes with the darkness swirling around me, tasting the death to come.

She opened her mouth to reply, but I didn't care to hear the response. Crimson sprayed over my face as I slit her throat from jugular to jugular, reveling in her choking on her own blood. The Thunderstone absorbed much of it on the blade. The rest I licked from its flat before taking a deep breath as a trickle of *žityje* entered my soul. I needed more.

Darixa whimpered nearby, splashing in the water before clinging to the island's edge. Why had the szeptuchy believed she could swim?

She can wait a few more seconds, I told myself. Leaving the szeptuchy to decay without draining their *žityje* first would be a waste.

"Why do you do this?" Darixa asked, her head turned as I devoured the first szeptucha's heart. The process had become so simple. How had I gagged just a moon before? This sensation was glorious—power igniting within me, burning with my rage.

I looked across the island at the soaked girl, her brown dress embroidered with violet across the front. Unlike a szeptucha, I couldn't detect the strength of a being, whether spirit or mortal, but I could sense the vibrant *žityje* pulsing within her as Mokosz's Mothermark glowed upon her forehead. She was special. That much was obvious.

"My father tore my future from me at birth," I replied. "My tribe is ruled by weak, greedy mortals, but they will follow me when I show them my strength. First, I must earn Marzanna's favor and take Grudzień."

"I saw you in my dreams."

I didn't reply as I pulled the second szeptucha's heart from her chest. This time, Darixa didn't look away.

"You don't hate Otylia," she continued. "You don't hate us either."

I hesitated, squeezing the heart so hard that the blood dripped between my fingers to the stone below. My own wounds had healed now, but a ring of black and red surrounded me. That would've frightened me once. "She abandoned me and agreed to wed Jaryło. She stole my soul!"

Darixa cocked her head. "You said your father did that."

"He did!" I took another bite of the heart, releasing a growl in frustration. "I've been Nawie my entire life, but I'd been *alive*. Otylia took that from me. I'm more powerful than ever, but she hates me."

My bond with her tightened at that moment. I shot to my feet, ripping one last bit from the heart before throwing it into the water. "We go now."

"She won't kill you," Darixa said.

"Then I'll kill her."

I reached down to grab her, but she stood willingly, her gaze contemplative for such a young girl. "One like you cannot kill a goddess. I follow you, but the Earth Mother protects me through the Lady of Endings. As a scion, I see what is to come."

"My destiny is my own to seize." I snatched her arm and took flight toward the tunnel. "And no goddess will stand in my way."

54

Otylia

The scions will pay for this.

YESIKE COOED IN MY ARMS as I carried him from the cave. Kiin's lost son, now mine to protect.

Many of the Huebia Daughters followed close behind, carrying the infants with the help of the poroniecs old enough to walk. I'd retrieved them as quickly as I could after Mokosz disappeared, and tears welled in each of their eyes. These little demons had never had a full chance at life. With my light radiating from their skin and the scions soon to be dead, at least they would find rest.

The late afternoon sun met us, not offering its usual summer warmth. Instead, the frost chilled me, and I covered Yesike's face with my free arm to protect him. His cries voiced his objection, though, only ending when I allowed the light to hit him.

They haven't seen the sun in so long…

I fought the sorrow that came with that realization. There would be time for tears when the poroniecs were laid to rest, Vastroth was safe, and Wacław was himself again. But gods… Yesike's wide eyes and giggling tore down the walls I'd built around my heart. Kiin would never see him again, and there was nothing I could do to change that. Why could I grant new life to rusałki and utopiecs but not these children or mortals? Mokosz had instructed me how to turn the poroniecs into friendly spirits called kłobuki who would protect their families, but I wished I could do more. It was impossible.

"The scions who killed these kids are in the tower?" Ta asked beside me, her brow furrowed as she stared at the sun for far longer than was healthy. "Huh. Ildes always said those ice brains were as gone as a stone dropped in the river."

"Kiin thought they were dead too," I replied. "But what we thought was true doesn't matter. We need to bring them to justice if we have any chance of redeeming these children."

Amten huffed from behind us. The massive scorpion hunter held a poroniec in each of his arms, their heads tucked into the crook of his elbows. Somehow, they'd managed to fall asleep. "Ha! Good for us that we're 'ttacking the tower anyway. Don't think my stomach could stand flying to another city so soon. Hear it? Still rumbling."

I couldn't muster a laugh. "Your carapace armor will be helpful for both of us."

We made our way back toward the tunnel entrance near the river. By winding between the dunes, we could stay out of sight of the guards on Huebia's walls. Nightfall would've made it easier, but Marzanna's Frostmarked could strike at any time. Each moment was another for her to plot and for Wacław to fall further into her grasp. I sensed my Thread of Life stretching to him, toward the city before disappearing. *Where are you?*

An eagle's call pulled me from my thoughts as we trudged through the river's shallows. Vlatka swooped down, and I tensed in anticipation of her scouting report. Part of me didn't want to know what Wacław had done to find Darixa, but the young scion needed me. End had shown me to her for a reason. I would follow through.

"I've found our rogue demon!" Vlatka exclaimed, taking a quick breath before looking down at the boy in my arms. "And it seems you've found the children."

Yesike tucked his head beneath my cloak, then tilted it so one eye peeked out at her. "Where?" I asked. "We need to stop him before he gets to Darixa."

The gathered crowd listened eagerly as we slowly made our way toward the tunnel. There was so much to do: protecting Darixa, defeating the disloyal scions, capturing Grudzień, and restoring Wacław's mind. I couldn't face every problem alone. Luckily, I didn't have to.

"The Hidden Waters," Vlatka said. "He attacked one of the hideouts and forced a szeptucha to let him in."

I clenched my jaw, swallowing my panic and handing Yesike to Ta, who struggled with the weight of two poroniecs in her arms. "Then I'll follow him. Sabina, take the children to the hideouts and start finding the homes of the ones from Huebia. Let the parents know the poroniecs will fully regain their minds when we're done."

Then I took off at a sprint.

My boots splashed into the Behmir's bank, but I ignored the water rushing into them as I entered the tunnels. The Daughters didn't need my help with the poroniecs for now. I'd helped them prepare defenses throughout the city to protect against the Frostmarked, and they could use those to keep the demons' families safe ahead of our assault on the Glasstone Tower. Wacław, though, was my burden to bear. Darixa was in danger as long as the Płanetnik controlled him.

I passed through the tunnels with only my power's light to guide me. Of course Kiin had instructed the szeptuchy Daughters to protect Darixa in the Hidden Waters. No one knew of it except for Mokosz's priestesses, but that secret had only gotten more Daughters killed for standing in Wacław's way. Those deaths were on me.

Footsteps caught up behind me when I stopped at a fork in the tunnel and tried to remember the correct path.

"Wait up, will you?" Ta huffed, hopping over a hunk of rock that looked sharp enough to pierce a boot. Thank the gods, she no longer held the demons as she did. "We can help."

"No—"

"Don't say that!" She skidded to a stop in front of me. "You got my parents back, so let me help you get your… you know, demon-lover-thing… back. That's what sisters do. Besides, your szeptucha and that jackal boy are too hurt."

I eyed the bandage still wrapped around her head as Vlatka landed on her shoulder. "And you're not?"

"Ta-naro is right," Vlatka said. "You're not alone in this, Otylia. We have all taken damage to get to this point, but we're with you."

"Fine." I held out my arm for her to jump to, and Ta sighed in relief when she did. "If you're going to be stubborn, then stay close. The tunnels to the Hidden Waters are a maze."

So we ran. The caverns seemed infinitely longer than our last passage through them, each twist and turn as unfamiliar as Huebia had been upon our arrival. My heart pounded the whole way and cold sweat stung my skin. No matter how hard I tried, I couldn't calm my mind. End's power had shown me Darixa a moon before. She'd been my responsibility, and I'd failed her. That trend was becoming all too familiar.

I was glad for Ta and Vlatka's company in those dark tunnels, and I wished Sabina and Kuba could've joined us. That hurt to admit, but knowing *they* believed in me gave me the hope I was more than my failings and the pain I'd caused. I was strong because I had them. Despite Mokosz's claims that I was supposed to bring balance to the realms, it was my friends that had somehow balanced the chaos in my own soul.

Ta gasped when we reached the violet pool of the Hidden Waters and rushed to the edge of the tunnel, staring over the ledge into the Hidden Waters below. She had her glass throwing blades ready, but I stopped strides behind. End's power told me all I needed to know.

"We're too late," I said.

Ta furrowed her brow back at me. "How'd you know? No way you can see that island from there."

She was right. But I didn't need to see, because a new terror crept over me, more potent than when I'd seen Koschei slaughtering on the steppe or Wacław's first storm. It swallowed that glimmer of hope in my heart, and my voice cracked as I clenched my fists, staring at the Threads of Life.

"His Thread is gone," I breathed, "and so is Darixa's wisp. Gods, I'm so stupid! I should've seen this sooner."

"Don't be so hasty." Vlatka pushed off my shoulder and glided through the stone spires that cut over the water. "There's two women on the island down there. Perhaps—"

The cavern shook, stopping her short. Dust rained from the ceiling as cracks sliced across the rock. I fought for my footing, barely catching hold of the wall as Ta and I exchanged worried looks.

"This it?" she asked. "The big one?"

Vlatka returned to my shoulder, her head lowered. "I assume so. The szeptuchy that protected Darixa are missing their hearts. Maybe the Frostmarked decided to strike first."

I turned back toward the tunnels with moonlight pulsing from my skin. All I saw each time I blinked was that little girl curled in the corner with a copper earring clutched in her grasp. Darixa needed me. Wacław needed me. And Vastroth needed me. "It doesn't matter who struck first. These people, those children, are depending on us, and I'm done failing them."

It was time to be strong.

55

Otylia

How can a city change so quickly?

HUEBIA WAS FROST AND FLAME, blizzard and ash.

Snow fell so thick that the normally looming Glasstone Tower was invisible behind the wall of white. Somewhere above, the crescent moon fed my power, almost silent compared to when it was at its fullest. A frigid wind whipped from the north, pulling a red-black haze over the southern section of the city and forcing me to cough before I took flight. Ta and Vlatka had stayed behind to help the Daughters bury the children and defend their families. As I rose, though, I had a sinking feeling mortal weapons and barricades wouldn't slow the Frostmarked, let alone stop them.

The silvery white tassels of my moon dress twirled around my legs. End's wisps followed in a crazed dance of colors, carrying screams and images of Vastrothie's final moments and prodding at my resolve. Another, stronger force pushed too. A foreign entity. Magical and imbued with power.

Grudzień.

I sensed it upon the Glasstone Tower's peak at the center of the storm. Its pulsing blackness arced across the sky once I reached a height equal to the tower's. Inconsistent, its pattern changed every few moments, sending the wisps into an increased frenzy as visions of my mistakes shot through my mind. But I held my arms before me and drew from my *žityje*. Weles's armband burned and released a pulse of energy that met the darkness and deflected it from me. I smiled. *At least he gave me something worth keeping.*

I burst through the blizzard as the sounds of battle rang out below. It was impossible to tell how the Daughters and our allied demons fared with my obscured sight, so I could only hope they could defend the innocents until I'd fixed Wacław and killed the scions.

Grudzień's pulses seemed to follow me the closer I got to the Glasstone Tower. With each, my armband burned hotter, and I could sense its store of power fading. This close, though, the snow thinned enough for me to see Grudzień's shifting form atop a cylinder of glass at the center of the tower's roof. Shards of violet hovered within the glass, scattering with each blast of its power before returning in fewer and fewer numbers.

A szeptucha stood before Grudzień. With the pale skin of the northern tribes, she grinned menacingly with her single unscarred eye fixed on me. A Frostmark glowed over the other as her robes, the color of crystalline ice, blew behind. Frozen daggers hung loosely from her fingers.

As I dove for a strike, a command from the old tongue slipped from her lips. "*Čuji.*" Feel.

A wave of black cut through the blizzard, dispersing it as Grudzień's grip tightened around my soul.

Visions flashed. Voices echoed. Both mine and those of every person I'd touched through my power. They called me weak, unloved, useless. I'd failed to save Mother, Ivan, Kuba, and so many of the Daughters. Why did I believe I could save Darixa? I'd slain countless demons, unable to redeem their lost souls, and hadn't rescued the rusałki and utopiecs from their decayed forms. Why did I believe I could remake Wacław into who he once was?

I'm nothing, my own voice said. *My friends support me because they think I can protect them. My worshippers grant me blood because they fear Marzanna. None of them know me. And the only one who does wants me dead.*

A violet wisp neared, a face forming within it. "I wish you'd never come."

"Kiin?" I asked.

Her jaw clenched as her curled locks hissed like vipers ready to strike. "My son will never see his mother because of you! You, Otylia, may be the Earth Mother's granddaughter, but you're as dangerous as the spawn of the deadly sun."

I shuddered, staring at my still raised arm. The searing of the armband pulled me from my thoughts. Each symbol seemed to weave a pattern in the air as they rose from the bands of silver and wood, words of the gods. Some were familiar and others not, but despite Kiin's continued shouts, they commanded all my attention. Time froze. The world's chill faded to a dull, breathless nothing.

Then the symbols dissolved with a *pop* in my ears. Grudzień's grip loosened, and I took advantage, charging toward the tower's rooftop as the szeptucha raised her blades. My silver spear fell into my grasp the moment Grudzień shifted again.

Silver met ice in a flash. The szeptucha spun just as quick, never taking her eye off me as she whispered a chant repeatedly in the old tongue, "The rivers shall freeze. Walls will crumble before her might. The lands shall fall."

"You must be Minna," I said in the Krowikie tongue as she circled me, far too confident in the face of a goddess. Kiin had told me of the northern channeler who led the Frostmarked from the tower's peak, undying and brutal.

She offered no reply but her chant, so I jabbed with my spear, only for her to spin away.

"I'd heard you were using Grudzień to manipulate people for Marzanna, but I didn't know you were insane."

"No!" she snapped in our tribe's tongue. "There is no madness once you've seen the truth. Marzanna's touch has remade me again and again. Death is no master to her, so he is no master to me."

I shook my head. "What in Oblivion are you—"

Another blast radiated from Grudzień, forcing me away as dark chały dropped from above. Their wings outstretched, the three of them covered the space between the roof's edge and Grudzień. Minna lurked behind with her one eye never leaving me.

"Chały do not take kindly to those who kill their sisters," she hissed before raising her hand to the sky. "Nor does their mother."

A mass of gray and black emerged from the storm with the speed of a falcon. Thunderclouds crafted her legless, dragon-like form, and a thousand jagged teeth filled her maw as lightning cracked within. I dove from the roof as her first bolt snapped through the sky.

The mother chała dove with a ferocious shriek, her children following as I tumbled in my panic. My shoulder throbbed in memory of the black dragon tearing me apart in Death's Trial. My ears rang from the brutal winds. Among it all, I couldn't find the calm in my soul, and my power felt as distant as Dziewanna's had in Nawia.

Sabina! I shouted through my power, aimless. *I know you're hurt, but I need you!*

If a reply came, I was too deaf to hear it or too shaken to understand. All I could do was hope my loyal nymph would find me. But there was no time for that. The ground was rushing toward me faster and faster. So I closed my eyes, searching for my center, for the balance Mokosz demanded I find in the world and in myself. I thought of Mother's potion lessons. Of our times venturing the woods and picking both edible and poisonous berries. Of her proud smile in her final moments.

I struck the ground.

My screams tore through the shred of calm I'd found, agony consuming me as my bones cracked and shattered. *Žityje* worked quickly, but my mind wavered. The sky above was a blurred tapestry. I tried to blink away the confusion, but the streaks of yellows and whites and blues refused to fade. It was beautiful. It was terrifying.

It's a demon!

I threw myself blindly to the side. Lightning blasted the spot a moment later, close enough for the heat to singe the hairs upon my raised arms. More pain. There was only so much my mind could handle, and I hid against a sandstone wall, watching the massive mother chała conquer my vision until I saw nothing but her serpent form. Her head was reared as she prepared another bolt.

But the earth shifted. Branching over me like the thick branches of a weeping willow, it absorbed the lightning as a deafening *boom* threw me to the ground.

I scrambled back to my feet, groaning in pain but holding back my healing *žityje* as I ran with the innocents who'd been hiding in nearby homes. The battle had only just begun. Jaryło would've chided me for using so much of my strength, and I had no idea how much I'd need to face Wacław and take Grudzień. First things first, though, I had to slay the mother chała before she charred someone who wasn't blessed with immortal healing.

"Otylia!" a voice called from nearby. "This way!"

Instinct pulled me after it. End's wisps swirled with renewed frenzy, and I barely saw the narrow alley where Ta's cocked head peeked from. She wasn't looking at me.

My hair rose with static as I spun and threw up my arms, yelling with all I had, "*Pri!*"

A shield of light shot from me as the lightning struck, pulling from my *žityje* and sending sparks cascading around the gathered people. Before me, the mother chała hovered over the buildings with hail and lightning falling from her flanks. Her children circled near before striking down at some victim I couldn't see, but I sensed the death in my soul. Panic, desperation. Then nothing. A light extinguished in the night, and the poor soul lacked even moonlight to grant them guidance.

"You got ants gnawing on your brain or somethin'?" Ta said. "You're lucky I stopped that lightning for you. C'mon. They've got the sky, but the earth's ours!"

That's it! I smirked at the young szeptucha. "Take these people. I'll distract the beast until you're back and then lure it closer to the ground. Make sure the Earth Mother's embrace meets it."

I launched into the air with the moon's pull, only to find Sabina sweeping to my side. Moonlight radiated from her skin. "Sorry, Lady Otylia. I figured you could use Ta-naro's help too."

"Glad you brought her, but—" We dodged opposite directions as a bolt shot between us, the mother diving our direction with her hungry eyes fixed upon Sabina. "Your wings!" They were still bandaged against Sabina's back, and I worried whether they'd heal after another battle.

"For once, I'm not afraid." she smiled. "That's because of you."

Her sentiment softened my heart's guard, but there was no time to talk. The mother chała lurched toward us on the wind, another bolt brewing in her mouth.

"Keep going!" I ordered Sabina. "Wrap around her other side and we'll moonblast her down together."

She nodded. Though an unsteady one, it was enough, and we took our flanks, fighting the winds and stinging hail with each movement.

The storm had its own roar beyond that of the demons. Pain seemed to fill it instead of rage, a desperate plea to be unchained that almost sounded like words. I looked to Sabina. She hadn't been lucky enough to find only the winds in her way, and the beast's spiked tail raked toward her, a hundred daggers searching for her heart. She darted quickly, but chały were part of the storm. They moved like rolling thunder and struck like lightning. When Sabina rose with the moon's power, the tail followed.

I released a moonblast at the mother chała's exposed underbelly. The angle wasn't what I'd hoped for, but Sabina needed the distraction. The serpent only shrieked louder when the blast hit, though, her attack uninterrupted until another sound met it.

Singing. Sweet and pure, it was quiet yet pushed back the people's screams and the demons' shrieks. It demanded to be heard but was not forceful. Counter to Grudzień, it calmed my fear and anger. It gave me clarity, strength.

And it came from Sabina.

The power in her voice wasn't caused by her Moonmark. I felt no pull on my *żityje* nor a tug on the Thread of Life binding us. No, this was nymph magic—a thing of spirits that few mortals understood. Even Weles had failed to grasp the nymphs' powers beyond their assigned roles as his servants. I'd seen it when Sabina had commanded the roots to release Wacław in his palace, and now, her lull-aby dulled the mother chała's demonic rage, granting me hope as the beast drifted downward, toward Ta.

The children shrieked at first and tried to charge Sabina to end the hold over their mother, but they too fell under her spell. I slowly moved toward them with *žityje* pooled in my hands. One powerful strike would end them, but awakening the mother chała now would be fatal for Sabina. She still hovered only strides from the beast's tail. Sweat beaded on her brow. A strange power flowed from her when I looked into End's wisps and Threads. It had neither the feel of *žityje* nor the harsh grip of Grudzień. What did that mean?

Even if she used some other energy, I lent her my *žityje* anyway. It was simple through our bond as goddess and szeptucha, and her arms rose again. Outstretched, each finger seemed to be reaching for the ends of the living realm as her words drifted away.

A spire shot from the ground when the mother chała reached the rooftops. Odd, twisted, it nearly missed the beast, impaling her side and spurring her to roll as black blood gushed from the wound. It was too loud to hear Ta curse, but I knew she did as more spires followed desperately, each frailer and less accurate than the one be-fore.

Sabina's song stopped too when the mother chała's tail whipped toward her. The mother was still slowed, though, her mind groggy from the song, so I took advantage, diving toward her mouth and releasing my held *žityje* directly into her gaping jaws as she shot her lightning.

Moonblast and lightning combined into an explosion that lit the sky. I flipped back, pulling myself away with the moon's strength as the force shredded the mother chała's body from the inside out.

The remaining chały shrieked at their mother's death. She had been a powerful beast, but there were hundreds more Frostmarked. From this low, I could see Marzanna's szeptuchy, warriors, and de-mons alike ravaging homes and slaughtering all who stood in their way. So many Vastrothie dropped their weapons and fled. Grudzień's grip still had them, and only I could release it.

I need to get to the top of the tower, I said to Sabina through my mark. *Can you and Ta handle the chały and guide the people away?*

She gave a small smile. *"We'll be only gone from your side for a moment. The redeemed demons from Sheresy are helping the Daughters well, even without us."*

Stay safe.

"You too."

We parted, her toward the chały and I into the raging storm. The lightning had ceased with the mother's death, but the blizzard's sting only grew. I'd suffered Krowik's bitter cold seventeen winters. This was worse than any of them, hail and an unbelievable chill striking to my bones, demanding I stop for cover and heat. None could be found in Huebia except for the fires of battle.

I covered myself with my *pri* moonshield as arrows rained from the tower's balconies. Archers lined its many levels, each focused on the goddess before them, but better they target me than the Daughters and innocents below.

Even when one of their arrows pierced my defenses and plunged into my shoulder, it was only pain that followed. *Žityje* mended the muscles and skin, pushing the arrow free as if I'd never been struck. How long would my reserves last? So quickly my Ascension had changed my view of injuries, but I had no idea how much *žityje* I could actually hold.

Grudzień's strikes strengthened when I neared the tower's peak, so I ducked toward a balcony two levels beneath, moonblasting away the archers guarding it before stumbling inside. My breaths caught. End's whispers battled with Grudzień's visions. They flashed so vividly that I barely took in the room beyond.

What is this place?

Draperies of violet hung over glass sculptures both large and small. A different color tinted each, surrounding a bed with rainbow blankets and spiraling pillars rising from its seven corners. Above, the ceiling created a dome that bore Mokosz's Mothermark in a spiral of colors, but someone had painted a Frostmark over it in blood.

Though the sculptures were cracked and the sheets slashed, there was a beauty to the space. But I had no time for admiration. Each wave of Grudzień's power made me wish to cower, and it already took all my focus just to push on to the open doorway ahead.

Guards filled the ringed chamber beyond, where another six open doorways led into what appeared to be bedrooms mirroring the one I'd left. The guards held their two-ended spears over those entrances with a glazed look in their eyes and black veins creeping up their necks. When they noticed me, they grunted and advanced. I struck first.

My moonblast shattered the glass lining the halls and sent the guards flying back into the rooms. None cried out. None tried to catch their fall or flee. They simply crashed through sculptures and furniture alike, their bodies limp like corpses, surely dead.

I turned to the spiraling stairs of glass at the chamber's center, but a creaking sound stopped me after the first step.

The bodies moved. Not rising like mortal men but hobbling to their feet with limbs contorted and twisted as they'd fallen. Some still wielded their spears. Others just limped silently with their cold gaze fixed upon me and their teeth bared. When I opened my mind to the Threads of Life, they were all empty, disconnected from the Three Realms like the skrzaki in the cave. Severed souls.

"Good pets," Minna's voice echoed from above as the guards entered the hall. "Lady Marzanna likes obedient pets, and your płanetnik gave her many."

Gods, what has he done?

The undead men were close now, so I released another moonblast, risking the *żityje* in hopes of finally killing them. Demonic or not, they were in my way. Some fell, their heads cracking against walls and doorways. Others just rose again with black blood spilling from their wounds. Still they advanced, unrelenting.

Fear struck me over and over as Grudzień shifted above. My grip loosened on my power, but I summoned my spear and sent it through each warrior's head in turn. They fell without complaint. Neither their strikes nor their defenses were anything more than wild flailing—easy for me to avoid but enough to tear apart untrained innocents. Had Minna released more of these 'pets' below? Wacław had killed hundreds of Frostmarked warriors. Could Marzanna bring each back as one of these beasts?

"All who serve shall rise again to worship," Minna chanted from above. "Death is the Lady's toy and life her gift. A new life, free from pain and fear."

I shot into the air, directly at the szeptucha. She only grinned and leaned into the railing upon the stair's edge. Her words stung like ice. They merged with Grudzień's call, pushing my fear for Wacław and my friends, but as I neared with my spear ready, she didn't move. Instead, she dropped her twin ice blades and extended her arms with Marzanna's chant on her lips.

The spear split her chest.

My momentum sent us tumbling into the hall beyond the top of the stairs. Silver jutted through the szeptucha's body, but no fear filled her gaze as she stared up at me. "You will experience her blessing soon. Death has his own pact with you, false one, and he always collects, but neither of us will see him yet."

Then she shattered like ice as laughter rang out from the dark room ahead. I drew back my spear, prepared for another fight. My heart raced and the tether in my chest tightened. It was Wacław. It had to be. But Grudzień's grip held me back from looking to the Threads. Could I really face him? Could I really mend what I'd broken? The voices said no.

I rose anyway. With doubts and self-hatred clutching every piece of my soul, I forced my legs to carry me toward him. Toward my failure. Toward my regret.

Toward my end.

56

The Płanetnik

I'll finally have my birthright, my throne.

DARIXA SQUIRMED IN MY GRASP as we landed on the roof of the Glasstone Tower. Black flashed across the sky of gray and white, Grudzień releasing its fury to terrify Huebia's futile revolutionaries.

Minna had descended to the market below with the seven dark figures who always accompanied her. Only a fake ice form remained to face Otylia, and that left the artifact's power for me to wield.

The little girl tried to scream, but I stole the words from her lungs with the winds. Seven of the gales howled in protest to my control, useless to resist the power surging through me. Only the northern aided me willingly now. Chorna, the rogue of Strzybóg's grandchildren, reveled in the chance to rain his destruction and rage upon the lands usually too far south for his rule. I didn't even need him. I was the storm, and combined with Marzanna's blizzard, no one could stop me.

That familiar thrill burned within me as I raised my hand to the shifting black Moonstone. Jagged and misshapen, its form never resembled anything real, just shapes with edges sharp enough to kill.

It tucked into my hand with ease, and Darixa averted her gaze as its power pulsed with my anger. Mine to wield. Mine to command. Mine to control, like the people I would soon rule. Yes, I was stealing

Grudzień from Marzanna's szeptucha, but the goddess would forgive me when I slayed Otylia. It didn't matter anyway. I'd soon kill her too for her own betrayals.

"You wanted to see Otylia?" I asked Darixa.

She nodded, wiping the tears from her eyes with her hand still clutching that stupid copper earring.

"I'll show you to her, then. Come."

The winds circled me in a swirl of darkness, blowing my cloak aside as I drew the Thunderstone dagger. It thirsted for godly blood. So did I.

Grudzień pressed upon that hunger in my grasp. Like a mighty flood, it swept away all else but my need to feed and the endless rage that lay beneath. It showed me how close I was to all I desired. My birthright. My revenge on all who had scorned me.

Only Otylia stood in my way.

I descended one of the two staircases leading to the Hall of Scions below, following its arc to the side of the altar that had once been Mokosz's. Blood for Marzanna coated its stone now.

Her szeptuchy had enslaved this city for moons, but apparently more sacrifices were needed. How much blood did Marzanna need to reach her full strength? A question for those who endured her wrath—I would not be one. Our deal would protect my lands north of Perun's Crown for long enough for me to build my army. Whatever happened to the rest of Jawia wasn't my problem. I would live forever if I wasn't killed by sorcery or blade.

The winds carried the sound of Minna's false form shattering from the stairs at the opposite end of the hall. I laughed, pulling Darixa with me to the altar and holding the dagger's edge to her throat.

Welcome to your doom.

Faint beams of light trickled from the glass windows above. Their glow revealed the red and black blood covering the approaching figure. Adorned in the sweeping white dress and cloak of autumn leaves she'd worn after her Ascension, Otylia looked like a princess caught out of her depths. I knew better. Behind the mat of black hair draped over her face was a glare striking enough to skewer a man, and beneath her thin frame was a strength greater than any warrior in Father's army. She'd been a wild witch once, untamable and alone. Ascended or not, some things never changed.

"So you do care about someone other than Dziewanna," I said, my voice carrying a thousand times through the stone and glass hall. "All it took was a child scarred by your grandmother."

Her nose wrinkled, predictably, but there was an unusual hesitance to her. *Ah, yes.* Her eyes exposed her worry as she stared at Grudzień in my off hand. Its blacked bursts spewed through the space with my own darkness. Each made her flinch, just as I had when I'd anticipated Father's strikes. Weakness. I'd purged mine, but she clung to hers like a child to their favorite toy.

"Let her go, Wašek." Even Otylia's voice was frail as she leaned upon her silver spear. They called us corrupted, but it was the mortals and the gods that believed themselves so pure who were truly broken.

But that name… Something twitched inside me, flashing memories before my eyes. *Lies.* Whatever I'd been, whoever I'd been, was gone. Otylia had killed him, but it was better this way. I'd shed mortality's decaying skin and become the master of the storms. It was with those storms that I would have my revenge.

At my will, Grudzień shifted to a longsword in my grasp. Black, the blade kept its Moonstone's jagged form with misshapen ridges like a sawblade's carved into its sharp edge. Instead of Kwiecień's golden glow and bright old tongue symbols inscribed along its flat, Grudzień seemed to suck away the light with its own inscription a hollow gray. I hungered for its immense store of *żityje*, but it was the Alatyr shard of the twelfth moon. This was far from its time.

"Surrender and I'll let her live," I said, reveling in Otylia's moment of pain as the Moonstone shifted within Grudzień's hilt. It was only a flinch, but it showed her that she was weak. "Throw her to Sabina or Jaryło or whoever else you've allied with. I don't care about them. Marzanna only sent me to kill you."

"Haven't you asked yourself why she wanted you to kill me?" she asked with a hand extended toward me. A gloved one. How pitiful.

"She's afraid of you and Dziewanna."

"Then why help her?"

I jabbed the dagger further into Darixa's throat, drawing blood. "Stop talking! All that matters is taking what I'm owed! *I* should lead Krowik, and now I can. I'll save them from Marzanna and show them I'm not the weakling they thought I was."

She winced as Grudzień pulsed again, but her eyes never left mine. "You were never weak, Wašek. Would a weakling have protected me against those wolves with only a makeshift spear? Would a weakling have turned away from his best friend to save her from exile? Would he have taken beating after beating from his father's fist and never lost his caring heart?" Slowly, she stepped closer, now less than six strides away. "The villagers were foolish to push us away, but using Grudzień won't save them from Marzanna or themselves."

She's too close!

I stepped back, forcing Darixa to follow and waving Grudzień to hold Otylia back. "One more step and she dies." *Why haven't I killed her already? She's served her purpose.* "Drop to your knees, facedown, and throw down the spear."

"Fine." Otylia furrowed her brow but knelt before lowering her forehead to the stone and sliding the silver spear to me.

"A trade is a trade."

Chorna's northern thrill merged with mine as I pulled back the dagger and called his wind. We struck Darixa with our combined strength, launching her through the balcony on the hall's southern side. She screamed the whole way, but Otylia didn't move. Either she wasn't as weak as I'd believed, or Sabina had been waiting. I didn't care which. Victory was mine.

I lunged at her with the winds, the dagger flashing in my right hand and Grudzień pulsing in my left. Thunderstone to drain a goddess. Moonstone to control her mortals. Otylia had no defense without her spear, and the swirling gales stole the air she needed to speak the old tongue. She would die. I would have my freedom. And Krowik would be—

White light filled the dark hall. Blinding, it cast an aura over Otylia's furious expression. I didn't see the light spear until too late, and its shaft clanged against the dagger, throwing it from my grasp and sending me sprawling.

"Your illusions are getting better," I snapped as I caught myself midair and hovered in the hall's center. The spear she'd held before had disappeared in a puff of moonlight. *Always more lies.* Lightning cracked at my fingertips. The balconies connected me to the storm, the winds bursting through them and around us, but suffocation couldn't kill her. No, that would be too simple.

"Don't make me kill you, Wašek!" she pled, but no tears slipped from her eyes. Why would they? She'd killed me already.

I launched my lightning with Grudzień's shift. "Try."

The bolt struck before she could respond, burning her chest as the wave of black passed through her. Something changed in her gaze. It had held fear before, but now the anger and confidence faded to leave only the expression of a child waking from a nightmare.

So I struck again.

She was watching for the lightning this time. A magic shield shimmered between us, deflecting the strike before she threw out her arms and sent the shield crashing into me. I gritted my teeth, but *żityje* healed the ribs that cracked from the impact. So much of it rushed through me. But she was a goddess. I needed to kill her quickly before she drained me in an extended fight.

With a quick sweep of the winds, I pulled the dagger back to my free hand. This space was feeling cramped. My soul burned to fly with the storm. "Let's take this outside."

I burst up the stairs, the winds alerting me to her tailing close behind. Yes, she could fly, but the moon's pull was not the strength of the storm. All others were just intruders in my domain, and from above the tower, I watched as all within Huebia's walls burned. Frostmarked warriors and demons ravaged the people who were too afraid to fight back. Marzanna's forces were numerous, but it was Grudzień that had allowed her to control these lands.

Smoke curled into the heavy storm clouds, blocking sight beyond more than a few strides. Otylia sliced through them with her power illuminating the sky. No marks remained on her skin from my strikes, but they'd been merely distractions to allow me to retake the dagger.

I dove before she arrived. Her Moonstone-induced hesitation left her vulnerable as the winds buffeted her attempts to dodge, but that blasted spear met me again. Otylia was untrained with it, though, and barely deflected my attack by pure instinct. Grudzień sliced a gash into her stomach, just missing a fatal blow.

She bled nonetheless.

I licked the crimson liquor from my blade as she wheezed and gripped her side. Thunderstone and Moonstone weapons drew *żityje* from their victims, and the wound would heal slowly. Too slowly for her…

The Otylia I'd known my entire life would've raised her spear to fight back then, despite her wound. But my dagger sliced through the darkness without challenge. Whether it was Grudzień's push or her failed hopeless plea to 'save' me, the battle had sapped her will, and I was mere moments from victory. Until an eagle's screech tore at my ears.

Flames lit the sky. Bursting from the golden eagle's beak, they interrupted my attack, searing my skin and forcing me to spin away as my precious *żityje* slipped further.

"Stupid bird!" I snarled.

It landed upon Otylia's shoulder and whispered in her ear, the winds carrying the words to me, "You're not alone. We're here. All of us."

All of us?

My shock distracted me from the winds' warnings. Sharp pain struck my back, and I spun to find an arrow jutting from my spine. That was the least of my concerns. The winds were fighting my commands, and I froze as more figures emerged from the storm— Xobas with his curved blade, Ara with her bow, Narcyz and Andrij with spears and shields, Sabina with her nymph song joining the gales, Sosna curled around her huntress's leg, and a brown dog with familiar eyes. They were those I'd cared about once, but they meant nothing now.

The winds resisted my control as I fought to distance myself from the group. My wounds stitched themselves, but this changed everything. Mortals or not, they were another distraction on top of the disobedient winds.

"The winds hate you as they once did me," a voice said on the gales. "You changed that for me when you saved my daughter, but now you've lost your way."

Lightning snapped around me as Eryk's graying beard and long robes appeared. *Betrayer!* The płanetnik bore my Eclipsemark because *I* had spared him, and now he dared to face me? Otylia had turned him against me, just as she'd stolen Narcyz, Andrij, and even Xobas. When a god held great power, people worshiped, but they cursed when I found my own. Hypocrites!

"You don't need to do this," Xobas said, glancing toward the ground and swallowing. "Think what your mother would want for you."

Memories of her limp body struck me. Bidaês's fatal blow, me rushing to her side, and Kwiecień's power bursting forth to bring her back from Death's grip. Worry had covered her face when I'd told her of my demonic soul. A difficult thing for a mortal to understand. But she would be proud when she saw how strong I'd become, how I'd no longer allow brutal men like Father to take advantage of her.

I met Xobas's gaze, lip curling. "Don't you dare speak for her!"

"She'd hate to see you like this," the dog said in a familiar voice.

I stepped back on the winds. "Kuba?"

"Yeah, it's me," he replied, a whimper cutting off his words. "Guess there's a consequence for escaping Nawia the wrong way, but I don't regret jumping in front of that witch's ice. Never did. Never will."

Grudzień released another pulse that pushed them back.

Don't let them use our past. I winced, shaking off the sorrow that tried to grip my soul. *None of it matters.*

Kuba moved closer, unsteady on Eryk's gales. "You're my brother, Wacław. Brothers don't let each other do stupid things alone, but we also don't let each other do something we'll regret forever."

"Brothers don't betray each other either," I replied. "Yet you stand against me."

Narcyz shook his head. "Shut it! I've spent the last moon pounding the truth into your real brother's head. Don't make me do it to you too."

"You were supposed to let Mieczysław kill Mikołaj! Krowik's throne should be mine!"

"Mikołaj will become high chief. You'd never tell me to kill your brother. You've always cared too much about people you should hate."

Foreign thoughts pushed against my mind. Memories and feelings that threatened the rage in my soul. They sought to manipulate me, to take away my new power, but I wouldn't let them. "Enough!" I screamed, releasing my *żityje*.

Lightning burst from me. Otylia's allies scrambled back, but none could flee as I threw out my arms. The bolts split, arcing and chaining between them in a ring of pain. The mortals dropped as Eryk chased to catch them.

She's defenseless! I snarled and charged, stabbing at Otylia's chest for a final time.

Her light spear didn't stop me, and pleasure filled me as I plunged the dagger between her ribs. Ara's cry only amplified my glee. Even with Otylia's pain striking my own heart, I imbued it with my anger, using it to feed my demonic hunger.

Then she disappeared.

Like smoke, her body dissolved into moonlight as I crashed through where she'd been. *How? HOW?*

I yelled into the storm, surging my *żityje* into it and sending the winds mad. The hail whipped sideways and pelted my skin, but I'd numbed to the blizzard long ago.

"Your goddess is too afraid to actually fight?" I asked Sabina, who looked as surprised as me.

"I…"

I didn't give her time to finish. Spinning in a swirl of darkness, I threw the dagger, but a streak of silver deflected the blade and sliced toward me.

An unfamiliar emotion filled me—fear.

I readied for Otylia to slay me as I'd done to so many others. There was no surviving a god's weapon. But death never came.

Otylia's strike went wide of my body, and for a moment, I grinned at her foolishness. Then I saw Grudzień's darkness in her eyes. My arms were extended to steady me on the fighting winds. She wasn't aiming for me, and a blast shattered my vision as her spear plunged into the Moonblade.

A thousand visions struck me at once. They tore at my mind, my soul. And as I slipped from the sky, the last thing I saw was a wave of black swallowing my storm.

57

Otylia

I won't lose him. Not him…

VOICES CIRCLED ME, feeding on Wacław's fury and my own. They told stories of distant lands. Of conquest and intrigue. Life and death.

My moonlit illusion had tricked Wacław. His anger blinded him to the switch as my friends provided a needed distraction, and when I appeared again, striking at Grudzień was easy with his surprise.

Cracks of every color spread across the blade—darkness shredded by brilliant light. Whispers swirled in its glow, stealing reality's cold sting as I fell into a void.

Heat seared through the darkness. My breaths fell away as I struck a hard surface and dropped to my knees. I knew time's flow and the black sea at Oblivion's edge, but this was different, strange. Unlike Mokosz's visions or now my own, an alien force held this place stationary instead of rushing past. Then came the light.

It appeared in short bursts, exposing a vast plain of dead grasses. Distant at first, the bursts snapped like lightning that shattered the silence. I tried to steady myself. The flashes were drawing nearer. I had no intention of finding out why, but my legs refused to move.

"Go to Oblivion, you witch!" I cursed at Marzanna. The words came out as a mere whimper.

When the bolts were just strides away, they stopped and left me in the dying light of an eclipsed moon. Its red hue smothered the fields of brown like blood over a battlefield, and before me, it revealed a gaunt, frail woman whose long black hair was braided with twine and the bones of small animals. She furrowed her thick brows before sharply looking away.

"You pretend I'm a stranger," she said with disdain, her hands clutched her chest. "I see it in your eyes."

"Do I know you?" I asked.

"Have you ever not?"

I opened my mouth to reply but paused. Did I know her? Something about her face and her defensive, distrusting movements was familiar. Why?

"If you know me," I finally said, "then you know I hate questions like that."

"Do you hate them or fear their answers?" She glanced down at Dziewanna's bone amulet in her gloved hands. "You wish to know the truth of everything, but you aren't prepared for the responsibility that comes with it. You wish to isolate yourself so you can't lose another. Like Mother. Like the man we believed to be our father—not that he ever loved us. Like the boy who abandoned us and his father who wanted us dead."

"No..." I muttered, backing away as her face became clear. "You're *not* me!"

"See. Even now, you flee from what is before you, just like you flee Rod's gift. We isolate ourselves from the world so we cannot be wounded, but we'll never be safe. There's always more pain..."

I turned away, jaw clenched, but another bolt of light burst before me. A second woman emerged from it as my eyes watered from the brightness. Her cheeks were painted with what resembled demonic blood, forming jagged lines across her cheekbones and encircling her green eyes in a void. Unlike the first, she stood tall in a dress of a shadowy gray. Slits lined the bottom, and though I felt no wind, they swept around her like fog that smothered the ground.

I scowled at her and called for my spear. My power wouldn't answer. "What is this?"

The woman returned my spite. "You are pathetic. Cowering before Weles like a child and fleeing from the monster you've created."

"I couldn't save him! I didn't know!"

"Because you're too weak to harness your strength." She stepped toward me, summoning my spear into her own grasp. "Jaryło killed us, and Weles protected him! They entrapped us. They *used* us. And instead of sending this spear through our father's chest, you needed a demon's blood to survive." With a scoff, she held out the spear to me. "You enjoyed watching Jaryło suffer, and we can do the same to him again through this blood pact. We have the power of a goddess, of every ending in the Three Realms, and we can ruin those who've wronged us. Worshippers will come when they see our strength."

I met her gaze. It didn't waver, but before I could reply, the first figure whimpered behind me, "We can't."

"We *can*," the second hissed. "You would have us alone and afraid, but why hide when we can make our enemies suffer for what they've done?" She looked to me, holding out the spear again. "Marzanna is feared because she unleashed herself from Jaryło and sought the true power within her soul. How to use our hatred is our own choice, but rejecting it will leave us like *this* one—nothing but a coward."

"And you would have us dead," the first replied. "Everyone gone… fearing us. We cannot help them all, and revenge will only drive away the rest. Wašek is broken, but the real him will despise us if he sees the truth. Others will too."

I stumbled back as another flash struck the plain, a third woman appearing in its wake. *I need to get back to Wacław.* But how? These forms of me, or whatever they were, had me surrounded. Worse, they seemed to be expecting something from me.

"Get up!" the spiteful one shouted at the newest woman.

Sitting with her legs tucked to her chest, the third didn't reply. Her mangled hair draped over her tear-stained face as she cradled a black hellebore flower. She whispered in the old tongue, and I sensed an odd power radiating around her as she stared directly at me. Pain filled her sunken, dark eyes.

Memories of the moons after Mother's death flooded over me, striking my heart and squeezing until my knees crumbled. Those flowers had covered the ground the day after she'd passed. One had appeared beside me as I'd wept, and though I'd believed her spirit had placed it, it had been Wacław. Knowing that took none of its meaning from me now, years after I'd committed to keeping that hellebore alive with Dziewanna's power. Mother had left, but Wacław hadn't truly abandoned me. Tears stung my eyes. After all we'd faced, why had I abandoned him instead?

"That one never speaks," the second woman said.

I averted my gaze and paced through the tall grasses with my fingers brushing their tips. "She doesn't have to…" Her meaning was clear enough, and even with the memories passing, my heart ached. Loss's sting did not fade quickly.

"Don't consider her!" the second continued. "She allows childish sorrow to take control. Though Mother lives, trapped by Marzanna, she would rather weep than face the ice queen. Tears won't slay a goddess. Tears won't bring Wacław back to us."

Is she right?

"You feel no pain from our past?" I asked her, pushing down my emotions for now. But they boiled within me: fear, hatred, and sorrow alike making my stomach turn.

The shadowed woman shook her head.

"Then what do you feel?"

Her lip curled. "The thrill of vengeance. None dare betray me when they know I will make their existence torture."

I stepped to her with a deep breath, reflecting her own strong posture. Her ferocity was terrifying and wonderful at the same time. Yes, others feared her, but that was a signal of strength—one that would not be scorned if she were a man.

"Anger makes us strong," I whispered.

As I reached for the spear, the woman nodded and placed it in my grasp before disappearing into a mist. The first woman yelped. The crying woman's whispers ceased. I turned to each in turn, studying their reactions, but the first mumbled to herself and backed away with wide eyes. I followed with a hand extended.

"Fear keeps us safe."

The woman trembled as she placed the Bowmark necklace over my head. I offered a smile, but she vanished too, leaving only the third. I knelt alongside her with my silver spear in hand and Dziewanna's amulet cold against my collar. The woman simply clutched the hellebore.

"Sorrow reminds us to love."

Slowly, the woman held out the flower. "Find her," her quiet voice said. "Save him."

"I promise."

I reached for Mother's flower, and as my fingers graced its black petals, the final woman dissolved into nothing. With spear, amulet, and hellebore, each weighing on me, I took a long breath. My heart still throbbed. In my soul, though, I felt my purpose in each fragment of myself.

I'll coming Marzanna. I'll save Wašek. I'll rescue Mother. And you'll regret life itself when I find you.

58

Otylia

I know what I have to do.

REALITY RETURNED LIKE A PUNCH IN THE FACE. My head spun, and I struggled to grasp the moon's pull to keep me aloft as Grudzień's force exploded before me. Surely it had caused the vision, but no time had seemed to pass. Wacław tumbled away at what seemed a snail's speed.

Fight the fear.

I dove after him, ripping away my gloves before snatching his arm. Fury filled his gaze, but I held firm. Amid the wisps encircling us and the voices surging through our connection, the storm disappeared. There was no hail, no battle, no flames.

There was only his pain.

It washed over me. His memories of Jacek's beatings, Lubena's tears, Kuba's death, and his own heartbreak. We'd endured so much in the moons since the Drowning of Marzanna. His suffering, though, had begun far before. I searched deeper for its core. Beyond the loneliness and desire to prove himself, there was something greater. All demons were corrupted because of an unnatural action that had disrupted Destiny's call—whether it be a rusałka's suicide in the river, a zmora's abuse of her loved ones, or a poroniec's loss of their mother. Jaryło had claimed the blood moon corrupted Wacław, but not all born beneath the eclipse became demons.

Just those betrayed beneath it.

Our shared vision in the Lake of Reflection returned to me. Lubena's shriek had sent darkness swirling through the longhouse when Jacek commanded her child's exile. Only moments before, the high chief had promised to protect his son. A broken pact. A promise of unconditional love severed for political gain, for power. Jacek's death hadn't mended Wacław's soul as revenge had done for the rusałki and utopiecs because it wasn't death that had broken him.

It had been betrayal. And I'd only made it worse.

A flicker of light flashed in his eyes. Their usual bright blue breaking through the darkness before disappearing as quickly as it had come. My soul held the last fragment of his mortal one, and I sensed a fight within him at my touch. The demon was stronger, but I clung to that hope and called to him as we careened toward the fiery abyss below.

"I love you, Wašek, even when your darkness takes you from me. Even when I foolishly push you away in fear of what I've done. No matter how much the world breaks us, I will never abandon you again. I'll bear the burden I've given you until the Three Realms end and we fall to ash. Let me suffer for you as you have for me. Forever."

The fight grew within him, that glimmer of himself clawing at the demon's control. He warred with all his strength, but the demon fought my grasp.

Agony consumed my arm as he snarled and shot lightning into our joined grasps. My skin blackened and charred. Still I held on, desperate for an answer. My words had awoken his true soul, but a promise wasn't enough.

I opened my mind to the Threads of Life. Ours connected us and wrapped tightly around our bodies. Love of friends, of family, and of each other restricted us, bound us. Believing that to be weakness, Wacław's Thread was frayed and loose, but still his connections to Kuba, Xobas, and others pulsed with vibrant *żityje*. I'd thought the same as him before. But I understood now.

To love made us vulnerable—and stronger than we could ever be alone.

I grabbed hold of the Threads binding us. They wound around each other like the strands of a rope, straining but unbroken despite the pain between us. With all my strength, I held both him and the Threads as I unleashed all the *žityje* I held in my soul. A single whisper escaped my lips.

"*Živi.*" Live.

Our Threads ignited in a blinding glow, releasing a power so powerful it burned up my arms and coursed through my veins until it devoured me from the inside out. My body and mind were flames. Rage. Agony. Regret. They tore at my very being, but my drained soul fought back as I clung to my memories of the true Wašek. Of the boy who cared when no one else did. The one who'd protected me with no hope of victory. The one who'd endured frostbite and agony to purge Marzanna's Curse from me. The one who'd traversed both Jawia and Nawia to bring me home. I'd taken his soul to complete the Trials, but that boy still lived.

When I forced my eyes open, the world was darkness. Wacław no longer pulled away, but he writhed under what I assumed to be the same power I endured. Dark wisps curled around us. The winds hammered my ears amid the snow and lightning. Despite it all, the battle for Huebia seemed distant, as if moving in a parallel realm that lay trapped behind a veil. We were alone. But we bore the pain together.

"I'm here, Wašek!" I shouted through the gales. An emptiness filled me without *žityje's* power, but I willed myself to stay conscious, to fight on. "I won't leave you!"

The pain struck again. If he replied in that moment, I didn't hear. Time shifted oddly, *wrong*, and I couldn't tell whether we fell or rose. It didn't matter. Only freeing him from this corruption did. The pain, though…

I finally screamed as the power burned its way through me. My skin melted. My hair burst into flames. My bones snapped. Or none of it happened. The line between my mind and reality blurred, wisps of colors and pure darkness entrapping me in their visions as voices shouted all at once. I found Wacław's among them and clung to it. I listened to only his whisper amid the roar, weak as the demon fought to strangle it. I lent him my strength.

Light tore me into another realm, forcing me to close my eyes, but I hung onto that pure power. Far beyond anything I'd ever known, it cooled the pain and scattered the voices. They screeched and ran, leaving only Wacław's battered and beaten one. He wept. And I wept with him.

"I'm sorry," his soft voice cracked through the nothingness. "I'm so sorry…"

I just embraced him, pulling his head to my chest. "No, Wašek, I am. You gave me everything, but I ran."

"You were right to fear me. I… I fear myself."

"We have that in common." I sniffled, raising my gaze to the light above. "But you don't have to face the demon alone. Not anymore."

Before he could reply, the light vanished and agony returned. We plummeted through the storm as the demon attacked our souls. With our arms and Threads joined, though, we shared our strength silently between our falling souls. What pain was his or mine, I didn't know, but I didn't care. We would endure together. Or we would perish together.

The ground was near now. Crashing into it was a distant thought, my mind consumed with the torturous demonic attack, and I had no *žityje* to catch us anyway. It had all vanished in the ritual, more than I'd ever used at once. I didn't even know if it had worked. *It was worth the risk.*

I shut my eyes the moment before we struck earth, but something broke our fall. It was soft, light. My spinning mind struggled to comprehend what had happened, but we'd stopped nonetheless. Stone met my feet soon after.

Voices called out to me as I collapsed in a heap. Whether they were from End's power or someone living, I didn't know. Reality and vision were the same to me still, and only clinging to the stone with one hand and flesh with the other kept me grounded. Flesh?

I looked up at Wacław before me, my nails digging so hard into his forearm that black blood dripped from beneath my fingers. He didn't pull back. Instead, he gripped my arm with the same intensity, but I didn't recoil from the pain. It was the first sign of his return that I couldn't attribute to a vision. Pain meant this was real, that he was alive, and from the longing look in his eyes, that the boy I loved was in control again.

"Otylka?" he breathed, shaking against me.

Tears, blood, and sweat clung to us both as we embraced each other, but I laughed in relief. It didn't make sense. None of our time in this stupid land had. All I knew was that I had him back, and gods, I'd forgotten how alive being with him made me feel. "You have no idea how much I needed to hear that."

"I don't know what to say…"

So I kissed him. He didn't need to say anything. With my terror of losing him washed away, only the passion I had for him remained. I needed it in that moment. Through ash and blood, I needed him.

"The Frostmarked still rule the city," I said as we parted, barely. My nose brushed against his as I spoke. I never wanted to be further again. "We need to kill Minna and her scions to save the sacrificed poroniecs and free Vastroth."

A flicker of a smile crept over his face. "Always fighting."

I noticed it then, the change in his appearance. The darkness was gone from his eyes, replaced by the stunning blue I loved, but streaks of black, dead skin still covered his face and body beneath his tattered shirt. My heart sunk knowing he'd never truly be the same. What had I expected? The rusałki and utopiecs had kept their demonic forms after being saved, so why would he be any different? Beneath that stupid wide-brimmed hat and scarred skin, he was my Wašek. I clutched that thought.

His smile faded to sorrow as I met his gaze again. "What?" I asked.

"You…" He swallowed. "What did you do?"

"I don't know. I *felt* the demon's power enter me when it happened." Its harsh pain lingered.

"A pact," he whispered before raising his voice. "You took part of the demon's rage to forge a new promise to me. Why would you accept that pain?"

I shuddered beneath this new weight. Like claws raking through my mind, it wouldn't relent. "Because I had to save you. It was the only way."

"You don't deserve this," Wacław said, releasing me. "I feel the punishment you took for me."

But I wasn't listening to his plea. I stared down at my arm, where a mark burned across where his hand had been. No, not one mark but two.

"What... What is that?" he asked.

The symbols merged at the center of my forearm: my white downward arcing moon and Wacław's red eclipsed one joining. Their forms seemed to *belong* together. The Moonmark's dark diagonal streaks aligned with his silver ones, and my crescent filled the gap left by his eclipse.

What did it mean for a goddess to bear a demon's mark? For our marks to join?

The same symbol pulsed on Wacław's arm too, but he didn't seem to care. His gaze never left me. Already I scoffed at the foolish boy's return, but nothing could match the racing of my heart.

"I can't fix what I've done," he said, his heartache echoing in my chest. "But I'll do what I can to finish this."

"We both will. Are you okay?"

He groaned, trying to stand before stumbling into a house's wall with Grudzień hanging loosely in his grasp. "I'm fine, but the demon... *I* threw the dagger when you attacked. I don't know where it fell."

His movement tore me from my trance, and I surveyed the alley we'd landed in. Bloodstained snow covered everything. Luckily, no innocents had died from our fall. "I don't know."

A howl came from nearby. I spun, calling for my spear but coming up empty as Wacław gripped his Moonblade and drew on the winds. What came wasn't a wolf, though, and Kuba burst forth with his eyes wild and Sosna rushing behind.

"What happened?" he asked before curling into himself, watching Wacław warily. "That you or the demon?"

Sosna didn't wait for Wacław's answer before leaping onto him and licking his face. He smiled solemnly, wrapping the fox in his free arm. "It's me, Kuba. I'm a little surprised to see you as a dog, though."

"Jackal, actually!" Kuba exclaimed. "Don't really know what the difference is, but *some* of us seem to care a lot about that." He finished with a side-eye in my direction. "Nice sword. Narcyz is gonna be jealous."

More footsteps approached, and Sabina led the rest of our friends into the alley. I relaxed at the sight of her, unharmed. Even Ta peered from behind Amten, her eyes narrow, as Xobas huffed. "The time to talk with come later," the Simuk said. "First, we free this city."

Ara held the Thunderstone dagger out to Wacław, hilt first. "Looking for this?" she asked with one brow raised.

Cautiously, he took it. "I was. Thank you."

"You got the strength to fight?" Narcyz asked with his arms crossed. "Or were you too busy attacking us with your demonic lightning and fancy Moonblade?"

Wacław's head dropped. "I can fight, thanks to Otylia. Where's Minna? I'd be happy to send her to her goddess for a third time."

Anger burned within him as he mentioned Minna, and I silently asked him through our bond, *You still feel it, don't you? The demon's hunger.*

His eyes flicked to me, followed by a slow nod. *It's better, quieter, but yes, I don't think I'll ever escape it. Holding your hand silenced it, though.*

I feel it too.

The demon's pull was surely only a fragment of what Wacław had faced, but its dull demand for *żityje* ached within me. I feared what that meant. Had I taken part of his corruption?

Narcyz raised his brow. "What do you mean, a third time?"

"Marzanna has apparently brought Minna back from Nawia each time she's died," I replied, pushing away my worries for now, despite the lingering pain I doubted I'd ever escape. "Killing her again will sever the Frostmarked leadership here, and she's probably guarding the traitorous scions."

Ta ducked out from behind Amten, a wicked grin on her face as she scampered up to me. "I saw 'em at the base of the tower. They've got a bunch of them ice brain warriors blocking the clearing, but that's no problem for us, right?"

"For *you*." I gripped her shoulders. "I have no *żityje* left, but Wacław and my friends will fight with you."

"Why can't you share *żityje* like you would with a szeptucha?" Sabina asked. "Those marks…"

I swapped looks with Wacław. In truth, I had no idea what my *żivi* spell had done besides allowing me to endure his suffering like I'd promised. Too much was happening at once. "We can try, if you have enough to give."

He bowed. "For you, I do."

"Get up," I snapped, taking his hand. Touch might've not been necessary, but we didn't have time to test how our connection had changed. And I definitely didn't need him bowing to me. Not him.

End's visions pushed into me as our shared marks burned upon my arm. I saw all the events of the past weeks from his view. The demon's temptations. His slaughter at the tower and the city center. His killings of innocents in blind rage. His imprisonment and tortured memories, trying to escape the demon's control. They all came at once, and despite the thrill of *żityje* entering my soul, dread strangled me. One ritual could not undo the destruction Wacław had caused, nor would he forget. I knew him too well. Sorrow would drown him when this was over.

Only one thing gave me relief as he let go, the exchange finished—there had been no vision of the future when we'd touched.

Did that mean I'd prevented the horrors I'd seen before? I clung to the hope I had.

"Thank you," I whispered to him, retaking his hand before turning to our friends with my chin held high. They needed to see me strong. Even if my strength came from them.

"Let's free this city."

59

Wacław

What does this mean for me? What am I? Naw? Demon? Neither?

DARKNESS SWIRLED WITHIN ME, neither caged nor free. Otylia's ritual seemed to have quelled my demonic corruption, but it lingered like a scar. A reminder of what I'd done. An omen of what I was capable of.

The hunger all but disappeared with Otylia's hand in mine as we headed toward the city center—not that I needed another reason to hold her—and when she let go, I yearned to be with her again. There was a feeling of completion with her, as if my soul was fractured alone. The hunger returned in her absence too. I knew I'd never truly escape the need to consume *żityje*. The demon had been sedated, not slain.

What had it cost?

My heart twisted knowing Otylia had taken part of my burden in her plea. The demon had left its mark. Crimson and black stained her eye sockets, and her eyes themselves had shifted to pure white when she touched End's power. Many feared her already. What would they think of the goddess of endings now that she was tainted by a demon?

For a moment, I stared down at our shared mark now emblazoned on my arm. My mark would be another burden on her, and it was yet another bond between us we couldn't understand. Another way our relationship couldn't be simple.

Regret weighed heavy on my shoulders as we flew over the burning city, the damage evident without my storm. Surrendering to the demon's call had led to so many deaths. Though the others had claimed I wasn't the same as the monster they called the Płanetnik, they were wrong. I had allowed this to happen in my misery and pain, believing that anger could take it away and bring me what I'd always wanted. It couldn't. Hundreds died for me to learn that lesson, and nothing I did could ever make that right.

I tightened my grip on Grudzień's hilt as screams came from ahead. Otylia's attack had destroyed the Moonstone's emotional manipulation, sending a thin streak of every color diagonally across the sword's black blade like a beast's claw marks. It was the Alatyr shard of the final moon, of the year's end. And after the Płanetnik's pursuit of it, it didn't feel right in my grasp.

I missed Kwiecień. Even away from its moon, it had given me hope. Jaryło had stolen it. I would settle, though, for plunging Marzanna's own Moonblade into Minna's heart in retribution for how she and her goddess had used me. Then I would help Otylia free the poroniecs from their suffering.

I hope you feel your szeptucha's pain, Marzanna.

The clanging of metal and stone rang over the clearing at the Glasstone Tower's base. No longer fleeing in a Moonstone-induced panic, Vastrothie wielded crafting tools like weapons as they charged lines of Frostmarked—undead Frostmarked. I recognized the slashes and burns across the guards' bodies. They'd been the victims of my rampages, but Marzanna had brought them back to kill more, just without souls this time. My chest ached at that. I had to fix what I'd wrought.

Across the square, the Daughters of the Earth organized the assault from atop scattered rubble. The freed rusałki and utopiecs guarded their rear against strikes of zmory and other undead warriors, but they were badly outnumbered.

"They're trapped," I said, pointing to the growing ranks of attackers. Though the Daughters' szeptuchy raised walls of stone and spikes that impaled the demons and undead, the beasts lumbered on despite their wounds. They would reach the szeptuchy soon, and I sensed our allies' *żityje* dwindling.

Otylia spun toward Sabina. Her Moonmark was faintly visible beneath the nymph's collar—a worthy choice for her first szeptucha. I'd spent little time with Sabina in our escape, but it was obvious how much she'd helped Otylia when we'd been separated.

"Take Ta and Amten to help the Daughters," Otylia ordered.

The Mothermarked szeptucha who I assumed to be Ta objected, her head bandaged and a long coat like Kiin's draping over her thin frame, "But—"

"No," Otylia interrupted, nodding in my direction. "We can handle ourselves. I'm not alone anymore."

Sabina bowed her head and drifted to the young szeptucha. "Come along. The Daughters need us."

Ta muttered under her breath but flew away with Sabina and a large man clad in unusual armor that matched Otylia's own breastplate. Sabina could help others fly… I took a deep breath and tried to calm my mind. It would take time to get used to people channeling Otylia's power.

That could come later, though, because at the center of the semicircle of Frostmarked before the tower, Minna led seven szeptuchy who must've once been Mokosz's scions. They combined their strength to call the blizzard and send shards of ice piercing through the unarmored Vastrothie revolutionaries.

Bodies fell everywhere. The wounded couldn't escape as the demons closed in behind. Soon, the Daughters and their allies would be slaughtered, and I would be guilty of helping their killers.

So we charged. With Otylia at my side and both the winds and moon bringing our remaining friends, we descended as what had to be Jawia's oddest band of allies.

Kuba and Sosna yapped together when their paws met stone, but Otylia landed before them, raising a shield with her moon power. Shards of ice cracked against it moments later.

"Be careful!" she snapped. Even before her Ascension, she'd been terrifying when she wanted to be, but she radiated power now as her dark hair flared in the gales and her eyes flashed white. She confronted her enemies with more strength than any warrior.

"Take the flanks," I told the others. "I'll draw their attention."

I didn't wait for Xobas's objections, bounding forward with the winds at my back. The demon had been quelled, but the last moons had changed me. Its dangerous whispers had been right about one thing—hesitance wouldn't save anyone.

Ice shards pierced the storm from every direction. I gained satisfaction in knowing the scions considered me a more immediate threat than a *goddess*, but the attacks stressed my power. What the winds couldn't deflect they alerted me to, allowing me time to dodge and block the shards with Grudzień. Recent moons had granted me immense abilities beyond anything I'd dreamed of before. Xobas's lessons, though, kept me alive. Years of pounding instincts into my mind one bruise at a time.

Out of the corner of my eye, I saw Xobas, Narcyz, and Andrij arcing to the left with their shields locked together. Otylia must've taken the others to the right, and I hoped I'd given her enough *żityje* to protect them.

The scions' attention split between the groups. Minna, though, glared at me with her single remaining eye.

"You betray her again!" she hissed.

I winced in anticipation of my Frostmark's pain, but it never came. I raised my hand to call lightning to it, using another crucial portion of my *żityje*, and gasped at what I saw... or didn't see.

Marzanna's Frostmark was gone.

A shard pierced my sword-arm, and I snarled at the pain, pushing away my thoughts for now. "Marzanna has nothing but lies. She wanted me to become a monster, so I'll show her what that means!"

Lightning snapped from my hand. It should've hit any mortal, szeptucha or not, but Minna raised her arms unnaturally quick, creating a wall of ice that shattered when the bolt struck. Ice rained over her and sliced her skin. She smirked and, with a whisper in the old tongue, sent the jagged pieces straight at me. My whirlwind caught most, but too many slipped through. Valuable *żityje* slipped away to seal the wounds.

Xobas's group shouted as they fought the scion nearest to them. Another dropped to my right with an arrow protruding from her scalp, but three scions had Otylia pinned down, forced to use her moonshield to protect Ara and the others.

That left three for me. *Plenty to have fun.*

I launched into the air and over the endless array of shards. So close together, the scions were a serious threat. They took each other's hands as I drew the Thunderstone dagger and infused it with lightning. A ring of ice spears rose around them, forcing me away. Each chased me at great heights, and the hail twisted to strike from above. Like a thousand needles, they stabbed through my winds and impaled my limbs. But I refused to slow. The pain gave me strength, and I plunged it into the winds with a shout.

The blizzard scattered for a hundred strides. My whirlwind swirled within the clearing, shredding the shards and demolishing the szeptuchy's wall of ice. As it tumbled, I dropped into the gap. Channeling was powerful, but at close range, nothing beat a blade.

Minna barked at her scions, and one struck with a staff of ice. Futile. It shattered against Grudzień. Only the second's strike at my flank stopped the killing blow, but I blocked her staff and unleashed the lightning I'd stored in my dagger. It burst *through* her staff and charred her entire body. Her screams echoing through the storm's absence, I turned and swung Grudzień, its jagged edge slicing through the first's throat.

No thrill came with their deaths. The demon within remained silent, and instead, my stomach curled. That should've annoyed me, but I reveled in the return of my disgust. War. Death. Slaughter. They were horrific, not to be pursued. I killed only to protect.

Minna backed away, summoning twin ice daggers to her hands as her remaining scion gripped another staff. "Our queen doesn't need you anyway. She is infinitely more powerful than your false goddess, and the world will feel her presence!"

My patience was out. The whirlwind pulled constantly on my *žityje* and would drain me in minutes. *Time to end this.*

The staff-wielding szeptucha swung, but I threw out my arm, blasting her with the winds hard enough to launch her into the Glasstone Tower's wall. Despite the sounds of battle ringing around us, the *crack* of her skull against the stone pierced the noise. Another death. These scions-turned-szeptuchy had killed so many more.

"What does she do to you?" I asked Minna, dual-wielding Grudzień and Thunderstone dagger as I advanced. Lightning would take too much *žityje*. "Marzanna brings you back from Nawia, but there must be a cost."

Her lip curled as she crouched like a beast ready to hunt. I saw Bidaês's rage in her eyes. So familiar, it had possessed me only minutes before, an intoxicating draw that steals your mind. Never again would I let it take me, and my heart ached seeing its hold on others. If I couldn't even save myself, how could I save them?

"I have given her my soul," the witch replied. "And she has gifted me immortality."

Then she charged.

Minna was a wolf, rabid and hungry as she lashed out with her daggers. Spikes of ice rose at my feet, forcing me into her path, but I didn't want to flee. Magic was new. Melee was my home. I could match her here, and I blocked her first foray with ease.

Her ferocity kept her in the fight. Though I held my solid stance as Xobas had taught me so many times, combat wasn't a dance to her. It was brutal, raw. Her daggers found the chinks in my guard. When I blocked one high, the other went low with speed greater than even mine, and I had the winds pushing me with each stroke.

Marzanna had truly changed her. I'd faced szeptuchy before, but Yuliya had been mortal. Whatever Minna had become was something else, something that made the winds keep their distance. I was alone in this fight now. In battle, though, each movement focused on attack was one not dedicated to defense.

I switched from parrying to countering. Her dagger sliced at my neck, and instead of stepping back, I spun, ducking and stabbing at her leg.

My dagger found flesh. Her blood came red, but there was no reaction to her pain. She countered herself, driving a dagger into my back. A growl escaped my throat as I pushed away, her blade ripping muscle and tissue as it pulled free. The last of my safe *żityje* reserves came with it, but that was the difference between her and me. I healed. Her wound still bled. So I gave her another.

Her blade sliced my arm during the jab, but Grudzień had already plunged into her stomach, its Moonstone drawing upon her life force. *Why won't you fall?* She just stared at me with those crazed eyes and slashed across my torso. I stumbled back.

My mind searched for Otylia through the agony. *I need help. She doesn't feel pain.*

"We'll try!"

A shout echoed from nearby as Xobas led Narcyz and Andrij in an unruly charge, their scion lying dead behind them. Kuba and Sosna's teeth ripped into another, and Otylia stood over the final two with her silver spear coated in red. Her skin glowed with *żityje*, but it was different than after her Ascension. She'd been the light goddess of the moon then. Now, she was the goddess of the most brutal of endings.

My friends surrounded Minna like vultures to a fresh kill. They stabbed at her flanks, but the szeptucha's focus remained on me. Each rapid strike. Each slice that I desperately tried to parry, fighting the pain that dulled my reactions.

Kuba snarled when he saw my struggle. With a leap, his jackal jaws closed around Minna's arm, preventing her from attacking again. Only when I collapsed did she turn her attention from me.

Żityje streamed from the szeptucha as she chanted in the old tongue. Though surrounded, bleeding and grievously wounded, she fought on as if she were unharmed.

Shards streaked from her hands. I cried out to my friends, but the ice shot each direction faster than a shield could block. Screams rang around me. The people I loved suffering for my failure to finish Minna off. Memories flashed before me of Yuliya's ice shards killing Kuba just moons before, and I cursed myself for putting him in danger again.

Andrij dropped, breathing but bleeding heavily from his chest. Narcyz scowled at Minna as he scrambled to drag the Astiw away from danger. His own wounds stained his tunic. He didn't tend to them, instead ripping his sleeve before wrapping Andrij's chest. I'd never seen him so panicked.

The others bore marks from the shards too. None, though, backed down until Otylia stepped between them and Minna, pushing them back softly with her power.

Her eyes went white, and my heart stopped as hundreds of strands of light appeared. Twisting like string around and between each of us, they glowed brilliant colors. No one else reacted to them—if they could see them at all.

Only Minna moved, stabbing at Otylia as her legs dragged beneath her. But Otylia deflected the strike with her spear before dismissing it and taking hold of the strand wrapped around Minna.

Black, the szeptucha's strand stretched from her to beyond our sight. Otylia gripped the only part that glowed against Minna's chest, putting her dangerously close to the ice daggers. She showed no fear. And when Minna tried to slice her throat, Otylia whispered in the old tongue.

"*Sěti.*"

Light burst over us, so bright that the battle paused. Frostmarked and Vastrothie alike watched the act of a goddess. Bound to her, even I didn't understand what she'd said, and I stared in awe like the others as Minna's arm stopped. She and Otylia stood frozen in time. I didn't know whether to take advantage of the pause to kill Minna or wait for Otylia to work. My wounds made attacking impossible anyway, and I fought just to kneel as all of Huebia waited.

Otylka? I asked through our bond. *Are you okay?*

No reply came. Her spell's power hung in the air, but I felt her *žityje* fading. She'd started the fight with only half of what had remained in my soul—nothing by a goddess's standards. What happened if she ran out? What was she even doing? I didn't have to wait long for an answer.

Otylia's light vanished. Both she and Minna dropped, the color returning to her eyes as her body went limp. I cried out, but I was weak, too slow to reach Otylia before Ara, who cradled her head in her lap. Otylia's eyes met mine.

It wasn't her who spoke.

"No!" Minna screeched, gripping her head and writhing on the ground. All the Frostmarked watched their leader now. Few if any of them had ever heard Marzanna's voice, but they believed Minna spoke for her. "Nononono! It's lies. Lies! Lady Marzanna would never do such a thing. She has come to save us!"

"They aren't lies," Otylia's raspy voice replied. "They're memories."

Minna gripped an ice dagger in both hands, unable to stand as blood pooled around her. "If these are my memories, then I don't want them!"

Then she plunged the blade into her own head.

60

Otylia

Mother, I've found you.

MY SOUL WAS EMPTY. Not of *žityje* but of willpower. Each moment in the past moons had drained that strength from me, and I'd plunged so much of it into the demons I'd saved. Now, after trying to do the same to Minna, I had nothing left.

Nothing but the way to Mother.

Voices surrounded me as colors danced on End's wisps. To control my power required more energy than I had, and the chorus of noise just swallowed me deeper into my exhaustion, my unending agony. My friends' faces looked down at me with worry, their questions and care lost to me. I felt joy at seeing them safe. My other emotions, though, drifted with the wisps in the gusts of the eight winds.

"Otylka," Wacław's voice said through our bond. I was staring at him, I realized, and his face came into focus as I blinked. *"Otylka, you did it. She's dead."*

Dead? I tried to drop my head to the cold stone ground. Soft wool met it instead. *I wanted her to remember, not die.* I'd failed at that, but her memories had revealed more than I could've hoped.

Ara stroked my hair softly, as Mother had done when she would tell me stories of the gods and spirits. She must've caught me when

I fell, but I didn't remember it. I'd been too focused on restoring the memories Marzanna had stolen from Minna. Her Thread had shown how much of her life she'd forgotten, but it wasn't until I'd touched the living part that End showed me who she truly was. Not Minna—Vida.

"I knew her," I finally said aloud, pushing back the noise, but nothing could rid me of the voices in my head. Not completely.

"How?" Ara asked. Gods, it was good to see her again.

"Her name was Vida. She faced the szeptucha initiation with me, but Father claimed no god chose her, so she drowned." Her first death. Father had also said that unchosen initiates could be inhabited by something worse than Death, and that was enough to make me shudder. What had she become? And why would she choose to die again instead of remembering? "Vida's memories showed Marzanna bringing her to her palace. I know where it was, where Mother *is*."

Kuba cocked his head. "What do you mean?"

The taste of blood filled my mouth as I coughed. "Jaryło lied *again*. He needed an enemy powerful enough to convince Perun and Weles to back his claim on all of Jawia, so he helped Marzanna release a dark dragon called Czarnobóg. When Dziewanna found out before the equinox, Jaryło abandoned her at the palace. She's still there, guarded by Czarnobóg or whatever Marzanna meant by 'his brothers.' "

Wacław, scraped and bruised, crawled to me. He was drained, but his eyes shone like the summer sky. We probably looked like a mess after the demon's damage and the battle wounds we'd taken. In that moment, none of it mattered. Something finally made sense with him near.

"Czarnobóg's lies are powerful," he said, "but we have hope if we can find Dziewanna."

I raised my head. "You spoke to him?"

He nodded. "After Marzanna offered me Grudzień and protection for my lands in exchange for your death, Czarnobóg appeared to me. He called himself the first żmij. He said part of your divinity is in me, that I could use it to fight by his side and remake the Three Realms."

"Like how a part of your mortal soul is in me…"

"Probably, yes. It makes sense that the demon is silent when I'm with you, but I don't know what he meant by using your divinity."

So many questions…

Kuba approached, his head lowered like a dog who'd disobeyed its master. "Uh, sorry to interrupt, but we've got company."

"Stop right there!" Narcyz yelled from nearby. I groaned and rose with Ara's help as he jabbed his spear at the approaching crowd, keeping them away from Andrij, who lay wounded. "I swear to Perun, I'll kill you if you keep coming."

Ara rolled her eyes. "They don't even know who Perun is, you idiot."

"We want to thank her!" someone called from the crowd. "Please, let us see the Lady of Endings!"

Xobas glanced back at me. He held his weapons at the ready too, but unlike Narcyz, he could temper his emotions. "They don't *look* upset."

I took a deep breath and removed my arm from over Ara's shoulder. They'd likely seen her help me up, but I was supposed to be a goddess—the Earth Mother's granddaughter. *Just a few more minutes of strength.* Whether I had even that, I didn't know.

"I'm here," I said as loudly as I could muster.

An array of looks met me, from adoration to confusion to disgust. Splattered in blood, markings from Wacław's demonic soul, and a tattered, breastplate-covered dress that left more skin exposed than I would've liked, I probably looked like a demon. Maybe it was fine. My view of the world had changed significantly since I realized the gods were flawed… very flawed. They could see that I suffered too.

People recovered from their awe quickly, dropping to their knees before me with their heads to the stone. "Thank you!" they exclaimed. "You have brought our children home."

My breaths caught. "It worked?"

Then I saw them. Translucent, the children were among the crowd, their Threads connecting them to their families beside them. Mokosz had called them kłobuki—not demons but not living either. My power and freed them from the cave, and justice had allowed them a new chance.

I let myself smile through the pain clutching my body and soul. For Kiin and Yesike, for all the mothers who'd lost their children. This couldn't fix their broken hearts, but life as a spirit was better than the children spending eternity as poroniecs, cursing the Great Mother and all mothers like her. Rod had granted me the force of endings. Was this what he'd wanted? Was this the balance Mokosz had spoken of—restoring some life to those who'd lost theirs unnaturally?

Haggard footsteps approached from behind, and the crowd wavered as Wacław stopped beside me, Grudzień's gruesome blade at his side. "Dziewanna would be proud of you… I'm proud of you." Our connection revealed his regret, but even he managed a small smile. "I don't know what it really means to be a deity, but I'm pretty sure saving hundreds of children is as close as you can get."

"I didn't do it by myself," I replied, looking to our gathered friends and the Daughters scattered throughout the crowd.

He took my hand. "You're right, but without you, they would've never been free of their corruption. Marzanna would still rule Huebia, and the children would still be poroniecs. People need a leader."

"I'm no chieftess."

Ara huffed at my side. "Good. We don't need a chieftess. We need a goddess; *they* need a goddess."

"What happened to the Frostmarked?" Narcyz asked, finally lowering his spear. "There were demons and warriors and stuff. We can't just let them run free."

I didn't know, but as I scanned the crowd, I was surprised to see Frostmarked warriors among them. Their Threads bound them to kłobuki like everyone else. Mortals didn't see that, though, and they dragged the Frostmarked to my feet, one by one.

"Kill them!" the crowd cried. "Bury them alive as a gift to the Earth Mother! Sacrifice them to your demon if you have to."

The ruckus grew with each passing second, and Xobas gave me a worried glance. "It'll get worse. I've known you to act quickly before, so do it now."

"Enough!" I shouted at the top of my lungs.

Quickly, the roar turned to nothing more than murmurs. That one word had my throat aching already, but Xobas was right. This was my responsibility now. No matter the pain I carried, there was always another burden.

"Speak your case," I said to the captured warriors. Nearly fifty of them knelt before us, bloodied with their Frostmarks dulled on their exposed skin.

For a long while, none spoke. I forced myself to be patient, grinding my teeth as we waited. These men had served Marzanna and slaughtered innocents to feed blood to her altars and spread fear among the people. Unlike Wacław, no demon had compelled them to act. Could their words matter at all?

"We… We were afraid, goddess," one stammered, glancing up at me before returning his gaze to the ground.

"Afraid?" I asked. "Like these people were afraid when you invaded their homes, took their children and bled them beneath the tower?"

"We thought the Earth Mother betrayed us, that she'd taken our children because we rejected the easterners. We feared what she'd do next."

I furrowed my brow and crouched before the man. His brow was creased, his beard and long hair streaked with gray. "So you turned to Marzanna—the Winter Witch."

He nodded. "She promised us renewal if we took her mark, but when people started dying…"

"She'd kill our families if we objected!" another warrior added. "We had no choice."

"There's always a choice!" Narcyz snapped, stomping toward the man, who cowered beneath his glare.

"Narcyz…" Wacław muttered.

I raised a hand sharply. "No, Narcyz is right. They had a choice, but it was a blind one. Marzanna used Grudzień to push upon their fear and anger, to ignite their hatred of the outsiders and belief that the scions had slaughtered the children."

"You can't just let them go!" someone shouted from the crowd.

I met them with my glare. "So what *should* I do then? Slaughter more Vastrothie so Marzanna's halls can fill with the souls of the dead? Make them suffer for the pain they caused? What justice will mend their wrongs?"

No reply.

I paced along the line of warriors, studying each of their faces. *What am I going to do?* Most chiefs and kings would've executed them for their betrayal, but hadn't there been enough death? Was there no middle ground?

Wacław looked to Eryk, who floated in the sky, invisible to the mortals. *"It's worked once,"* he said through our bond. *"If we're going to fight Marzanna, we need every warrior we can get."*

Can we trust them?

"You can punish them with your mark if they disobey. Eryk and Narcyz are lucky I didn't discover their plan before they arrived."

You bear my mark too.

"And you bear mine. They are a symbol of allegiance. Give them a final choice to face Marzanna instead of serve her. Only punish those who remain loyal. What else do we have without mercy?"

Followed his gaze to Eryk. He had tried to kill us all in the Mangled Woods, but Marzanna had led him to believe she'd show him to his lost daughter. Wacław had seen his desperation and aided him in the search. Eryk had become our ally because of that, and without him, our friends couldn't have arrived to help me with Wacław.

I announced the decision to the crowd, dreading their disdain.

Red faced people made obscene gestures and shouted insults at the Frostmarked, but many quietly nodded. These men had been their neighbors once. They'd lost their children like so many others, and if they could serve to stop more from dying, then that was better than death. At least, that's what I hoped they believed. I had neither the will nor the strength to handle a riot.

With only a glare at the angriest members of the crowd, Xobas grabbed the first Frostmarked.

One-by-one, the warriors stood before me to choose. Each

bowed their head and confessed their crimes, and then each gritted their teeth through the pain as I placed my hand over their Frost-marks. Marzanna's power faded quickly to leave only my silver-white Moonmark behind. They bore their marks on their arms, exposed shoulders, or their faces, but never their necks. Such a place was re-served only for szeptuchy. Even Vida's mark, though, had been over her eye, and I shuddered to think what that meant. Was she even a szeptucha? Something worse?

Nearly all the warriors took my mark before one objected. The process had become almost automatic by then, the glow of my hand, the tug on my little remaining *żityje*, and the warrior's quiet ac-ceptance before the next approached. But this one was far from si-lent.

"You've killed us all!" he spat in my face, his hazel eyes boring into mine as he shook with rage. "The Horde spared us because we joined her ranks, but there's nothing stopping them now. We're all going to die!"

Wacław snarled, but I just opened myself to the Threads and took hold of the man's. The wisps faded. As did the crowd. Only his mem-ories filled my mind—his rage against the refugees, the attacks he'd planned with others on their food supplies, and his oath to his wife that he'd make the Earth Mother suffer for taking their newborn son. His only son.

I raised my gaze to the child's kłobuk spirit, watching amid the crowd with his and his father's Threads bound. There was another, though. A woman stood next to her kłobuk son with her hands cov-ering her mouth and tears wetting her eyes.

"I'm giving you a chance to stop her," I replied to the man. "I wasn't born beyond this realm like other gods. My entire life, I thought I was mortal until a few moons ago, and my tribe faces the Horde's threat your people do. I have a family, just like you. Either you can repent from the suffering you've caused and help me protect them, or you can find out how kindly Marzanna treats those who fail her."

His eyes widened. He stepped back, wobbling, and then burst into the crowd.

I cursed, and Wacław's worry joined with mine as the enraged people grabbed hold of the warrior. Xobas shouted for them to let him go, but it was no use. They wanted blood.

"This isn't the way," Wacław insisted. *"Execute him as you promised, but letting them tear him apart will only make things worse. It's not justice."*

Didn't you let them do the same just days ago? Spite filled my reply more than I'd wanted, and he backed away, face shadowed.

I leaped into the air with what remained of my *żityje*. The sun had nearly arrived, but the moon's pull was enough for me to hover over the crowd. The warrior lay bloodied against the stone, alive but barely moving as the enraged people kicked him over and over, only stopping when they noticed me.

"Justice will be done," I said, "but this is my ruling to carry out. Don't stain your hands with his blood in blind rage."

They backed away as the cold shaft of my silver spear met my hand. A circle formed around him, and I landed and offered to help the man up. He refused, staggering to his feet by himself, unable to look at me. Respect didn't matter. He would die nonetheless, and I would allow Wacław to take his heart. That would've made me sick moons before, but now it was necessary. Wacław's darkness was real. His power required *żityje*, and if that meant he took it from Marzanna's loyalists, so be it. The Frostmarked had been given a choice. Let them see the cost of serving the goddess of winter and death.

"For your loyalty to Marzanna, the Winter Witch, and for all the death you've caused," I announced, "I sentence you to death. May you find wisdom before returning from the realm of the dead."

The man offered no reply, so I struck quickly, sending my spear through his chest. End's wisps carried his soul's agony, and the crowd backed further as he dropped. I didn't. Instead, I stared down at the man who'd rejected mercy. His memories had shown his hatred, but had that been enough for him to die for?

I shook my head and turned away. "He's yours, Wacław."

"Are you sure?" he asked me silently. *"They'll think I'm a monster if they don't already."*

The Three Realms are dark. We'll need monsters to save them…

61

Wacław

I just want to leave forever. Why must we fight? Why do the gods war for nothing but spite, leaving us to fend for ourselves when their actions come due?

EXHAUSTION HUNG OVER ME HEAVIER than the heat of the summer sun. I couldn't forget what I'd done, who I'd killed. The demon had controlled me, yes, but it was a part of me—or more, I was a part of it. My mind in that time had been twisted by my own anger.

"We'll need monsters to save them."

Otylia's own words had admitted what I was, and she was right. Even with the demon quieted, I'd become something else. There was no returning to my old life. Eternity stretched before me like an unclimbable mountain, tearing me apart with each step, and I feared who I'd be when this ended... *if* this ended. Moons after leaving home, I barely recognized my own thoughts, let alone my appearance.

My scarred, shattered face stared back at me in one of the many mirrors within the Glasstone Tower. Black veins traced every curve of my cheek before cascading down my neck and chest like cracks in the frozen Krowik River. My skin was vaguely human at best, reddened in places and ghostly pale in others. Battle and travel had hardened my muscles and sunken my eyes. Otylia claimed they were the same blue she'd always loved, but all I saw were two black voids, engulfing all who dared to meet my gaze.

Nawie. Corrupted. Broken.

Other demons like me had regained their minds because of Otylia. Each I spoke to confirmed my struggles, the anger lurking deep inside them, asleep for now. And the hunger. It had dulled but never left. Ara had given me a vial of Zakir's creation, supposedly able to sedate that craving. I'd yet to try it.

Some part of me didn't want to forget the demon's pull. Remembering helped keep it at bay, ensuring it never rose again. Why pretend I would ever be whole? I'd tried for my entire life, and those years had been covered by Father's brutality.

Sleeping by Otylia's side was the only thing I looked forward to in the days after the Huebia Revolt. Even that gave me some fragment of completion. Nightmares haunted me when I closed my eyes, so I just held her, feeling her breaths rise and fall with mine.

Dreams cursed her too. Late in the night, she would burst awake at the moon's brightest, sweating and ranting about the things she'd seen. I hated End, as she called her force, and Rod for inflicting her with visions. She said she could control them when she was calm and centered. The demon upset that balance, stirring deep within her as it did to me. For that, I could only hate myself. The rest of her agony I blamed on Jaryło's blood oath—one I intended to make him regret.

Otylia was quiet about her visions, rarely offering clarity to the chaos she awoke with. I knew she saw me in them. No matter how hard she tried to hide it, the race of her heart and flick of her eyes away from me revealed the truth. I let her hold the secret. After all, she'd taken my burden when so many others would've plunged a blade through my head. She still threatened to do so daily, but I loved that sharp side of her. It reminded me I was one of the few that was blessed to see the real Otylka.

We never spoke about our argument that had started this all. We didn't need to. I'd lost my way, and Grudzień had ignited her fears—about both herself and me. Together, we'd face what came next as allies and lovers. The latter part would take some work, but nothing was easy anymore.

"You stare like an eligible girl before Noc Kupały," Otylia said with a laugh, throwing her silver fox pelt over her head. Fierce, a mix of light and dark. Just like her. "Come. Darixa awaits, and gods know Narcyz will impale you if you're late."

"He's too busy with Andrij." I eyed her in the mirror. "They'll probably be late themselves."

She raised her brow. "Please don't look at me like that. Not now."

I turned from the mirror and crossed the room to her. We'd commandeered the scions' old chambers for our group while we recovered, and from the plush beds to the elegant glass sculptures, ours was by far the most beautiful room I'd ever seen. Most couples would've thought it a dream.

We weren't most couples.

"I'm sorry," I said, taking her hands. End's power would prod at her, but she no longer winced when we touched, not when her existence had become a hundred cuts slashing at her mind. Though she'd been too reclusive to even kiss me since the battle, it was a step. Mending the pain I'd caused would take time. Ending Jaryło's pact would take a miracle.

"I know." She sighed, leaning her forehead against mine. She smelled of the sharp minerals Vastrothie women used as fragrance. Alluring, daring you to get too close and face her wrath. "I'm just too tired to consider romance right now, okay? It's not you."

I squeezed her hands. "We've literally been through Nawia and back, Otylka, and I made it so much worse when we returned. I can't blame you for anything."

"It'll get better, right?"

"Your sleepless nights or Jawia?"

"Any of it..." She raised her gaze to mine, and my heart ached from the pain in it. "Everyone expects me to lead, but I never asked for this, for power. I hate everyone relying on me." A frown crossed her face. "Stop smirking!"

That just made me smirk more, so she jabbed me in the stomach. "Denying you're a good goddess doesn't change it," I said with a much-needed laugh. "Everyone I know who wanted to lead did terrible things for the sake of power, me included. Not you."

"I killed that man in the city center and let you eat his heart."

"Yet you don't seek to be feared. Gods, you don't even seek to be worshiped, but that's exactly why we need you to unite these people: Vastroth, Krowik, Simuk, Zurgow, and Astiw. Our tribes and clans are divided. You're the only one who can make them put aside their differences to defeat the Horde while we figure out how to free Dziewanna and stop Marzanna."

I knelt before her, knowing she'd hate it. "People need someone to give them hope. You've done it for me, for the demons you've saved, and for the thousands of Vastrothie out there who'd feared for their lives under Marzanna's rule. Be the light they need in the darkness, like the moon."

She shook her head. "What about you? You negotiated with the clans. All the Sudiczki said was that I'd be your queen!"

Sudiczki? What did the goddesses of fate have to do with this? "I don't know what you're trying to say."

"I promise I'll tell you everything soon," she said, pacing. "Just know that during her Trial, Destiny told me more than she should have about our fates. Trust me?"

"I do."

"Thank you, Wašek." Taking my hands again and pulling me to my feet, she gave a wry smile. "You deserve to know the truth, but it's taken me longer than I hoped to figure it out for myself. What matters now, though, is what you will do if I'm the one bringing the tribes hope while we find Mother and face the Horde."

I cocked my head sarcastically. "If you're the moon, then someone needs to be the eclipse to make your enemies fear the night. I'll bleed Jaryło dry if it ends your agony and flay him if it doesn't. I'll slay the beasts guarding Dziewanna. Then I'll hunt Marzanna and Czarnobóg to the ends of the Three Realms."

Her eyes flicked from my eyes to my bare chest, scarred and blackened. "I never thought I'd hear something like that from you."

"You said it yourself. I've changed."

"But your heart hasn't."

"You're right." I stepped away, taking Grudzień from the table and holding its black blade into the rays from the colored glass above. The shattered streaks within the sword reflected the light in a rainbow around us. Light from darkness. "My heart belongs to you, and that's why I'll be your storm, your monster. Everyone knows what I've become, so use my power. Grant hope to the weary and strike terror into the hearts of the destroyers. Let Koschei the Deathless cower and flee to Marzanna and Czarnobóg, and then we'll see who they call the witch and the Half-Chief."

She drew near, our hearts racing through our bond. Darixa and the Vastrothie awaited, but I didn't care about the ceremony at that moment. Mokosz would name her the scion queen whether we were late or not. If only Otylia would be so irresponsible…

"We'll prove all of them wrong," she breathed, her eyes sharper than a Moonblade and her hips pressed against mine. "Weles, Jaryło, Marzanna, Czarnobóg, Jacek, Boz, all of them. We'll take the Alatyr shards and remake the Three Realms if we have to, but I swear upon Dziewanna's bow, I won't use your demon's fury for my own power."

"You won't need its fury, because you'll have mine."

Our lips met, but the kiss ended as quickly as it started. With a sweeping movement, she strode across the room, threw my embroidered Vastrothie robes at me, and pushed through the cloth covering the doorway. My breaths caught with her every step. Her glare over her shoulder set me in motion, though, and I followed, fixing my hair as I ran to catch up.

Narcyz beat us to the ceremony anyway. His mocking voice met me in the Hall of Scions, but it couldn't dull the feeling of my heart. A rare emotion in recent moons, yet one I needed more than anything. Joy. Despite all I'd done, Otylia still loved me, and I could take an eternity of Narcyz's insults as long as I knew I'd have her each day of those endless years. If only my regret were so bearable…

Otylia wasn't the only one this journey had brought me, though. As the Mothermarked szeptuchy conducted rituals to coronate Darixa as the scion queen, I had the honor of sitting by the loudest person in the room. Well, not a person.

"What they thinking, putting a nine-year-old in charge of a whole realm?" Kuba yapped far too loudly, forcing me to tap him on his jackal head. "C'mon! I mean, honestly, I would've just demanded dessert and a pointy stick at that age if you gave me—"

One glare from Otylia shut him up quicker than I'd ever seen. I couldn't blame him for being startled. Donning Vlatka in her golden eagle form on her shoulder, her silver fox pelt, a sleeveless white and gray Vastrothie coat over scorpion carapace armor, and trousers, Otylia didn't need End's force to portray herself as a leader going to war.

Her attire revealed clearly her scars and our shared marks—each a trial she'd conquered. Many would've considered them flaws. Even Weles's armband of wood and silver was a reminder of her father's attempts to control her, but she wasn't afraid to show the damage she'd taken. The woman I loved was still that untamable sorceress I'd known for years. Now, though, she no longer fled into the woods. She displayed each mark upon her skin like a warrior did his shield, proving to her enemies she'd faced far more frightening foes than them and lived.

She stood before the rebuilt altar of Mokosz with Darixa and the surviving Mothermarked szeptuchy. Her silver spear glinted in the sunlight streaming through the windows, and I had no doubt she considered sending it through Kuba's head. That familiar look of discomfort never left her face. She hated being the center of attention. She hated politics. Today was both.

Ildes, the eldest of the szeptuchy who'd apparently led the Daughters of the Earth in Sheresy, handed Otylia a craggy, irregular crown of copper and sandstone that looked incredibly uncomfortable.

The scions had never been crowned before. After the battle, though, Mokosz had broken her silence, declaring Darixa the sole ruler of the Dominion of Vastroth. No one dared to defy their 'Earth Mother' and 'Lady of Endings.' Otylia still wrinkled her nose whenever she heard that name. I agreed. It was too formal for her, but whispers of a new name for her had spread along with ever-changing legends of her granting demons second lives and slaying those with corrupted hearts.

Nemiza, they called her. Calamity. For destruction followed Otylia, but in her wake came renewal and an elongation of the Threads of Life. I hoped they were right.

"I see your worry for her," Xobas said quietly as Otylia placed the crown on Darixa's head. "That's good."

I swallowed, unable to look away from Otylia. "Really? I thought you'd say she's strong enough for me not to worry."

He chuckled. "Oh, she's stronger than any of us, but a leader's responsibility is to worry for their people. What Otylia fights for, she fights for hard, and the war to come will be bloody. It'll weigh heavy on her. Lessen that burden, Wacław, or she'll push until either she breaks or Marzanna does."

"I'll do my best."

"I know you will. The time ahead will be lonely and difficult for you both. Just never forget we're here for you, even if our lives will not span the centuries like your own."

I offered him a smile. "Thank you, Xobas. I don't know if I deserve you all, but I'm grateful. Returning to our lands will be a breath of fresh air. With Mikołaj and the Horde awaiting us, though, I'm glad to have friends by my side."

The ceremony soon came to an end, and the crowd bowed their heads as Darixa led the szeptuchy down the hall. Her Mothermark glowed a deep violet upon her forehead. When she passed, she looked my way, her mouth narrow and gaze unwavering. The disdain was deserved after I'd put her through Oblivion. Otylia believed she'd forgive me in time, but I wasn't so sure. Children remembered those who wronged them. All I could hope to do was spend each day mending the brokenness I'd caused. Luckily, I'd have an eternity to do exactly that, unless Marzanna or her Horde killed me first.

I tucked in behind the szeptuchy with Otylia and our friends. Their voices surrounded me as Otylia took my hand, calming my aching soul and at the same time amplifying my bond to her pain.

I'll fix this.

Mortals and immortals, szeptuchy and spirits, we'd endured so much together, and the path ahead lay mired in shadow. With them, though, I had hope. Even when we suffered. Even when we faced the darkness within the Three Realms and ourselves. Because we were together, we were strong.

War had come for our people. United we would face Koschei the Deathless and free Dziewanna from Marzanna's grip, or divided we would fall. I didn't know what lay ahead, but no matter what we faced, I would never fight alone again.

END OF BOOK 3

A Word From The Author

Each book I write teaches me a lesson. *The Daughters of the Earth* taught me many, as this stubborn story took more work than any book I've written before. From writing and then scrapping the first third of the book to juggling the addition of Narcyz and Ara as POV characters, it made me adapt in many new ways. I am grateful for that experience and for all of you for reading the book! The extended amount of work on this one just gets me more excited for book four, which will finally be bringing together many of the seeds I've planted so far. Thank you as always!

If you have enjoyed reading this story, please take the time to post an honest review on whatever retailer you purchased this book from. Every review helps new readers discover the series.

To receive your free copy of *The Rider in the Night*—the prequel novella to The Frostmarked Chronicles—other side-novellas attached to the series, and exclusive first looks at upcoming books, join my newsletter at www.Brendan-Noble.com.

-   Brendan

About the Author

Brendan Noble is a Polish and German-American author currently writing fantasy inspired by Slavic mythology: The Frostmarked Chronicles. Through these books and his "Slavic Saturday" post series on YouTube and his website, he hopes to bring the often-forgotten stories of eastern Europe into new light.

Shortly after beginning his writing career in 2019 with the publication of his debut novel, The Fractured Prism (Book 1 of The Prism Files), Brendan married his wife Andrea and moved to Rockford, Illinois from his hometown in Michigan. Since then, he has published six full-length novels, including four in The Prism Files and two in The Frostmarked Chronicles, along with a novella for the latter series.

Outside of writing, Brendan is a data analyst, soccer referee, and the president of Rockford FC (Rockford's semi-pro soccer club). His top interests include German, Polish, and American soccer/football, Formula 1, analyzing political elections across the world, playing extremely nerdy strategy video games, exploring with his wife, and reading.